PUFFIN BOOKS

Editor: Kaye Webb

BEVIS

Richard Jefferies was born on 6 November 1846 at Coate Farmhouse, just outside Swindon. By the farmhouse was Coate Reservoir where, as a boy, Dick made and sailed his own boat. You can still visit the reservoir – the New Sea – for it has been turned into a boating lake, and nearby you can visit the Jefferies Museum.

In his childhood it was very much wilder, and thick with kingfishers, snipe, redwing, great crested grebe. Once as a boy he saw an eagle flying high over it.

'Our Dick,' said his father 'is always poking about them hedges.' He learned to shoot when he was seven, and the Squire was so worried in case he shot his fat pheasants, that he often sent Haylock, the game-keeper, to give him what he called 'a bit of tongue-pie'.

Dick had a fine dog. Not a spaniel like Bevis's Pan, but a pointer called Juno. She was so well trained that she could pick a live fish out of the farmyard trough (where young Dick kept his catch) without doing it the slightest harm. And she could put it back.

But gradually Dick Jefferies discovered that he got far more pleasure from watching birds or hares than shooting them. He would aim, look keenly at a bird – then let the gun drop and simply stare.

He wrote the story of Bevis of Surbiton in Surrey, when he was very ill, partly made up from the real adventures of his boyhood. He died later at Goring in Sussex where you can see his grave. Nearby is the grave of another famous writer about the countryside, W. H. Hudson, who so loved the Bevis books that he insisted that when he died his gravestone should be exactly like that of Richard Jefferies.

This book is taken from *Bevis: the Story of a Boy.* The narrative has been slightly abridged, but retains all the original appeal of Richard Jefferies's first publication of a hundred years ago including the illustrations by E. H. Shepard.

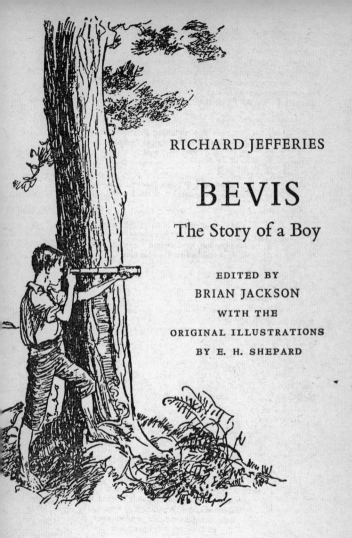

RICHARD JEFFERIES

BEVIS
The Story of a Boy

EDITED BY
BRIAN JACKSON
WITH THE
ORIGINAL ILLUSTRATIONS
BY E. H. SHEPARD

PUFFIN BOOKS

Puffin Books, Penguin Books Ltd, Harmondsworth, Middlesex, England
Penguin Books Inc., 7110 Ambassador Road, Baltimore, Maryland 21207, U.S.A.
Penguin Books Australia Ltd, Ringwood, Victoria, Australia
Penguin Books Canada Ltd, 41 Steelcase Road West, Markham, Ontario, Canada
Penguin Books (N.Z.) Ltd, 182–190 Wairau Road, Auckland 10, New Zealand

—

First published 1882
This abridged edition published in Puffin Books 1974
Reprinted 1976

—

Copyright © Brian Jackson, 1974
Illustrations copyright © E. H. Shepard, 1932

Made and printed in Great Britain by
Cox & Wyman Ltd,
London, Reading and Fakenham
Set in Intertype Lectura

BEVIS AND MARK FIGHT A BATTLE

Contents

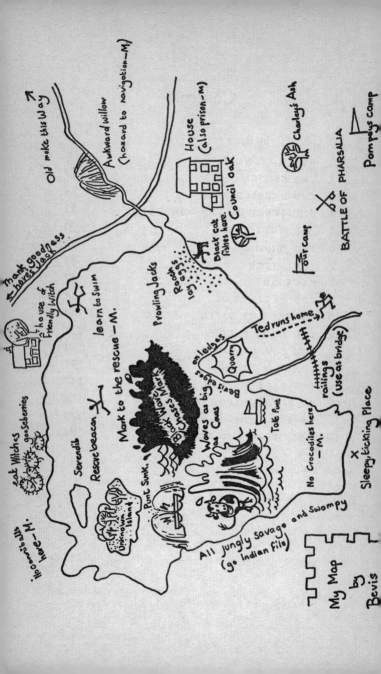

CHAPTER 1

Bevis at Work

ONE morning a large wooden case was brought to the farmhouse, and Bevis, impatient to see what was in it, ran for the hard chisel and the hammer, and would not consent to put off the work of undoing it for a moment. It must be done directly. The case was very broad and nearly square, but only a few inches deep, and was formed of thin boards. They placed it for him upon the floor, and, kneeling down, he tapped the chisel, driving the edge in under the lid, and so starting the nails. Twice he hit his fingers in his haste, once so hard that he dropped the hammer, but he picked it up again and went on as before, till he had loosened the lid all round.

After labouring like this, and bruising his finger, Bevis was disappointed to find that the case only contained a picture which might look very well, but was of no use to him. It was a fine engraving of 'An English Merry-making in the Olden Time', and was soon hoisted up and slung to the wall. Bevis claimed the case as his and began to meditate what he could do with it. It was dragged from the house into one of the sheds for him, and he fetched the hammer and his own special little hatchet, for his first idea was to split up the boards. Deal splits so easily, it is a pleasure to feel the fibres part, but upon consideration he thought it might do for the roof of a hut, if he could fix it on four stakes, one at each corner.

Away he went with his hatchet down to the withy-bed by the brook (where he intended to build the hut) to cut some stakes and get them ready. The brook made a sharp turn round the withy-bed, enclosing a tongue of ground which was called at home the 'Peninsula', because of its shape and being surrounded on three sides by water. This piece of land, which was not all withy, but partly open and partly copse, was Bevis's own territory, his own peculiar property, over which he was king.

He flew at once to attack a little fir, and struck it with the hatchet: the first blow cut through the bark and left a 'blaze' but the second did not produce anything like so much effect; the third, too, rebounded, though the tree shook to its top. Bevis hit it a fourth time, not at all pleased that the fir would not cut more easily, and then, fancying he saw something floating down the stream, dropped his hatchet and went to the edge to see.

It was a large fly struggling aimlessly, and as it was carried past a spot where the bank overhung and the grasses drooped into the water, a fish rose and took it, only leaving just the least circle of wavelet. Next came a dead dry twig, which a wood-pigeon had knocked off with his strong wings as he rose out of the willow-top where his nest was. The little piece of wood stayed a while in the hollow where the brook had worn away the bank, and under which was a deep hole; there the current lingered, then it moved quicker, till, reaching a place where the channel was narrower, it began to rush and rotate, and shot past a long green flag bent down, which ceaselessly fluttered in the swift water. Bevis took out his knife and began to cut a stick to make a toy boat, and then, throwing it down, wished he had a canoe to go floating along the stream and shooting over the bay; then he looked up the brook at the old pollard willow he once tried to chop down for that purpose.

The old pollard was hollow, large enough for him to stand inside on the soft, crumbling 'touchwood', and it seemed quite dead, though there were green rods on the top, yet it was so hard he could not do much with it, and wearied his arm to no purpose. Besides, since he had grown bigger he had thought it over, and considered that even if he burnt the tree down with fire, as he had half a mind to do, having read that that was the manner of the savages in wild countries, still he would have to stop up both ends with board, and he was afraid that he could not make it watertight.

And it was only the same reason that stayed his hand from barking an oak or a beech to make a canoe of the bark, remembering that if he got the bark off in one piece the ends would be open and it would not float properly. He knew how to bark a tree quite well, having helped the woodmen when the oaks were thrown, and he could have carried the short ladder out and so cut it high enough up the trunk (while the tree stood). But the open ends puzzled him; nor could he understand nor get anyone to explain to him how the wild men, if they used canoes like this, kept the water out at the end.

Once, too, he took the gouge and the largest chisel from the workshop, and the mallet with the beechwood head, and set to work to dig out a boat from a vast trunk of elm thrown long since, and lying outside the rick-yard, whither it had been drawn under the timber-carriage. Now, the bark had fallen off this piece of timber from decay, and the surface of the wood was scored and channelled by insects which had eaten their way along it. But though these little creatures had had no difficulty, Bevis with his gouge and his chisel and his mallet could make very little impression, and though he chipped out pieces very happily for half an hour, he had only formed a small hole. So that would not do; he left it, and the first shower filled the hole he had cut with water, and how the savages dug out their canoes with flint choppers he could not think, for he could not cut off a willow twig with the sharpest splinter he could find.

Of course, he knew perfectly well that boats are built of plank, but if you try to build one you do not find it so easy; the planks are not to be fitted together by just thinking you will do it. That was more difficult to him than gouging out the huge elm trunk; Bevis could hardly smooth two planks to come together tight at the edge or even to overlap, nor could he bend

them up at the end, and altogether it was a very cross-grained
piece of work this making a boat.

Pan, the spaniel, sat down on the hard, dry, beaten earth of
the workshop, and looked at Bevis puzzling over his plane and
his pencil, his foot-rule, and the paper on which he had
sketched his model; then up at Bevis's forehead, frowning over
the trouble of it; next Pan curled round and began to bite
himself for fleas, pushing up his nostril and snuffling and raging
over them. No. This would not do; Bevis could not wait long
enough: Bevis liked the sunshine and the grass under foot.
Crash fell the plank and bang went the hammer as he flung it
on the bench, and away they tore out into the field, the spaniel
rolling in the grass, the boy kicking up the tall dandelions,
catching the yellow disk under the toe of his boot and driving it
up into the air.

But though thrown aside like the hammer, still the idea
slumbered in his mind, and as Bevis stood by the brook, looking across at the old willow, and wishing he had a boat, all at
once he thought what a capital raft the picture packing-case
would make! The case was much larger than the picture which
came in it; it had not perhaps been originally intended for that
engraving. It was broad and flat: it had low sides; it would not
be water-tight, but perhaps he could make it – yes, it was just
the very thing. He would float down the brook on it; perhaps
he would cross the Longpond.

Like the wind he raced back home, up the meadow,
through the garden, past the cart-house to the shed where he
had left the case. He tilted it up against one of the uprights or
pillars of the shed, and then stooped to see if daylight was
visible anywhere between the planks. There were many streaks
of light, chinks which must be caulked, where they did not fit.
In the workshop there was a good heap of tow; he fetched it,
and immediately began to stuff it in the openings with his
pocket-knife. Some of the chinks were so wide, he filled them

up with chips of wood, with the tow round the chips, so as to wedge tightly.

The pocket-knife did not answer well. He got a chisel, but that cut the tow, and was also too thick; then he thought of an old table-knife he had seen lying on the garden wall, left there by the man who had been set to weed the path with it. This did much better, but it was tedious work, very tedious work; he was obliged to leave it twice – once to have a swing, and stretch himself; the second time to get a hunch of bread and butter.

Then on again, thrusting the tow in with the knife, till he had used it all, and still there were a few chinks open. He thought he would get some oakum by picking a bit of rope to pieces: there was no old rope about, so he took out his pocket-knife and stole into the wagon-house, where, first looking round to be sure that no one was about, he slashed at the end of a cart-line. The thick rope was very hard, and it was difficult to cut it; it was twisted so tight, and the rain and the sun had toughened it besides, while the surface was case-hardened by rubbing against the straw of the loads it had bound. He haggled it off at last, but when he tried to pick it to pieces he found the larger strands unwound tolerably well, but to divide them and part the fibres was so wearisome and so difficult that he did not know how to manage it. With a nail he hacked at it, and got quite red in the face, but the tough rope was not to be torn to fragments in a minute; he flung it down, then he recollected someone would see it, so he hurled it over the hedge into the lane.

He ran indoors to see if he could find anything that would do instead, and went up into the bench-room where there was another carpenter's bench (put up for amateur work), and hastily turned over everything; then he pulled out the drawer in his mamma's room, the drawer in which she kept odds and ends, and having upset everything, and mixed her treasures, he lighted on some rag which she kept always ready to bind round

14

the fingers that used to get cut so often. For a makeshift this, he thought, would do. He tore a long piece, left the drawer open, and ran to the shed with it. There was enough to fill the last chink he could see; so it was done. But it was a hundred and twenty yards to the brook, and though he could lift the case on one side at a time, he could not carry it.

He sat down on the stool (dragged out from the workshop) to think; why, of course he would fasten a rope to it, and so haul it along! Looking for a nail in the nail-box on the bench (for the rope must be tied to something), he saw a staple which would do much better than a nail, so he bored two holes with a gimlet, and drove the staple into the raft. There was a cord in the summer-house by the swing, which he used for a lasso – he had made a running noose, and could throw it over anything or anybody who would keep still – this he fetched, and put through the staple. With the cord over his shoulder he dragged the raft by main force out of the shed, across the hard, dry ground, through the gate, and into the field. It came very hard, but it did come, and he thought he should do it.

The grass close to the rails was not long, and the load slipped rather better on it, but farther out into the field it was longer, and the edge of the case began to catch against it, and when he came to the furrows it was as much as he could manage, first to get it down into the furrow, next to lift it up a little, else it would not move, and then to pull it up the slope. By stopping awhile and then hauling he moved it across three of the furrows, but now the cord quite hurt his shoulder, and had begun to fray his jacket. When he looked back he was about thirty yards from where he had started, not half-way to the gate-way, through which was another meadow, where the mowing grass was still higher.

Bevis sat down on the sward to rest, his face all hot with pulling, and almost thought he should never do it. There was a trail in the grass behind where the raft had passed like that left by a chain harrow. It wanted something to slip on; perhaps rollers would do like those that moved the great pieces of timber on to the saw-pit. As soon as he had got his breath again, Bevis went back to the shed, and searched round for some rollers. He could not find any wood ready that would do, but there was a heap of poles close by. He chose a large, round willow one, carried the stool down to it, got the end up on the stool, and worked away like a slave till he had sawn off three lengths.

These he took to the raft, put one under the front part, and arranged the other two a little way ahead. Next, having brought a stout stake from the shed, he began to lever the raft along, and was delighted at the ease with which it now moved. But this was only on the level ground and down the slope of the next furrow, so far it went very well, but there was a difficulty in getting it up the rise. As the grass grew longer, too, the rollers would not roll; and quite tired out with all his work, Bevis flung down his lever.

CHAPTER 2

The Launch

WHAT he wanted to do was to launch his raft before anyone saw or guessed what he was about, so that it might be a surprise to them and a triumph to him. Especially he was anxious to do it before Mark came; he might come across the fields any minute, or along the road, and Bevis wished to be afloat, so that Mark might admire his boat, and ask permission to step on board. Mark might appear directly; it was odd he had not heard his whistle before. Full of this thought away went Bevis back to the house, to ask Polly the dairymaid to help him; but she hunted him out with the mop, being particularly busy that day with the butter, and quite deaf to all his offers and promises. As he came out he looked up the field, and remembered that John was stopping the gaps, and was at work by himself that day; perhaps he would slip away and help him.

He raced up the meadow and found the labourer, with his thick white leather gloves and billhook, putting thorn bushes in the gaps, which no one had made so much as Bevis himself.

'Come and help me,' said Bevis. Now John was willing enough to leave his work and help Bevis do anything – for anything is sweeter than the work you ought to do – besides which he knew he could get Bevis to bring him out a huge mug of ale for it.

But he grinned and said nothing, and simply pointed through the hedge. Bevis looked, and there was the Bailiff with his back against the great oak, under which he once went to sleep. The Bailiff was older now, much older, and though he was so stout and big he did not do much work with his hands. He stood there, leaning his back against the oak, with his hazel staff in his hand, watching the stone-pickers, who were gathering up the bits of broken earthenware and rubbish from among the cowslips out of the way of the scythe; watching, too, the plough yonder in the arable field beyond; and with his eyes now and then on John. While those grey eyes were about, work, you may be sure, was not slack. So Bevis pouted, and picked up a stone, and threw it at the Bailiff, taking good care, however, not to hit him. The stone fell in the hedge behind the Bailiff, and made him start, as he could not think what creature it could be, for rabbits and weasels and other animals and birds move as silently as possible, and this made a sharp tap.

Bevis returned slowly down the meadow, and as he came near the house, having now given up hope of getting the raft to the brook, he caught sight of a cart-horse outside the stable. He ran and found the carter's lad, who had been sent home with the horse; the horse had been hauling small pieces of timber out of the mowing-grass with a chain, and the lad was just going to take off the harness.

'Stop,' said Bevis, 'stop directly, and hitch the chain on my raft.'

The boy hesitated; he dared not disobey the carter, and he had been in trouble for pleasing Bevis before.

'This instant,' said Bevis, stamping his foot; 'I'm your master.'

'No; that you beant,' said the boy slowly, very particular as to facts; 'your feyther be my master.'

'You do it this minute,' said Bevis, hot in the face, 'or I'll *kill* you; but if you'll do it I'll give you – sixpence.'

The boy still hesitated, but he grinned; then he looked round, then he turned the horse's head – unwilling, for the animal thought he was going to the manger – and did as Bevis told him. Behind the strong cart-horse the raft was nothing, it left a trail all across the grass right down to the brook; Bevis led the way to the drinking-place, where the ground sloped to the water. The boy once embarked in the business, worked with a will – highly delighted himself with the idea – and he and Bevis together pushed the raft into the stream.

'Now you hold the rope,' said Bevis, 'while I get in,' and he put one foot on the raft.

Just then there came a whistle, first a long low call, then a quaver, then two short calls repeated.

'That's Mark,' said Bevis, and in he hastened. 'Push me off,' for one edge of the raft touched the sandy shore.

'Holloa!' shouted Mark, racing down the meadow from the gate-way; 'stop a minute! let me – '

'Push,' said Bevis.

The boy shoved the raft off; it floated very well, but the moment it was free of the ground and Bevis's weight had to be entirely supported, the water squirted in around the edges.

'You'll be drownded,' said the carter's boy.

'Pooh!' said Bevis.

'I shall jump in,' said Mark, making as if he were about to leap.

'If you do I'll hit you,' said Bevis, doubling his fists; 'I say – '

For the water rushed in rapidly, and was already half an inch deep. When he caulked his vessel, he stopped all the seams of the bottom but he had overlooked the chinks round the edges, between the narrow planks that formed the gunwales or sides, and the bottom to which they were fastened.

Bevis moved towards the driest side of the raft, but directly he stepped there and depressed it with his weight the water rushed after him, and he was deeper than ever in it. It came even over his boots.

'Let I get in,' said the boy; 'mine be water-tights.'

'Pull me back,' said Bevis.

Mark seized the rope, and he and the boy gave such a tug that Bevis, thrown off his balance, must have fallen into the brook had he not jumped ashore and escaped with one foot wet through to the ankle.

'Yaa – you!' they heard a rough voice growling, like a dog muttering a bark in his throat, and instantly the carter's lad felt a grip on the back of his neck. It was the Bailiff who marched him up the meadow, holding the boy by the neck with one hand and leading the cart-horse with the other. Bevis and Mark were too full of the raft even to notice that their assistant had been hauled off.

First they pulled till they had got it ashore; then they tilted it up to let the water run out; then they examined the chinks where it had come in.

'Here's my handkerchief,' said Mark; 'put that in.'

The handkerchief, a very dirty one, was torn into shreds and forced into the chinks. It was not enough, so Bevis tore up his; still there were holes. Bevis roamed up and down the grass in his excitement, gazing round for something to stop these leaks.

'I know,' said he suddenly, 'moss will do. Come on.'

He made for a part of the meadow much overshadowed by trees, where the moss threatened to overcome the grass altogether, so well did it flourish in the coolness and moisture, for the dew never dried there even at noonday. The Bailiff had torn it up by the harrow, but it was no good, it would grow. Bevis always got moss from here to put in his tin can for the worms when he went fishing. Mark was close behind him, and together they soon had a quantity of moss. After they had filled the chinks as they thought, they tried the boat again, Bevis insisting on his right to get in first as it was his property. But it still leaked, so they drew it out once more and again caulked the seams. To make it quite tight Bevis determined to put some clay as well, to line the chinks with it like putty. So they had to go home to the garden, get the trowel out of the summer-house where Bevis kept such things, and then dig up a few lumps of clay out of the mound.

There was only one place where there was any clay accessible, they knew the spot well – was there anything they did not know? Working up the lumps of clay with their hands and the water so as to soften and render it plastic, they carefully lined the chinks, and found when they launched the raft that this time it floated well and did not admit a single drop. For the third time, Bevis stepped on board, balancing himself with a pole he had brought down from the garden, for he had found before that it was difficult to stand upright on a small raft. Mark pushed him off; Bevis kept one end of the pole touching the bottom, and so managed very well. He guided the raft out of the drinking-place, which was like a little pond beside the brook, and into the stream.

There the current took it, and all he had to do was to keep it from grounding on the shallows, where the flags were rising out of the mud, or striking against the steep banks where the cowslips overhung the water. With his feet somewhat apart to stand the firmer, his brow frowning (with resolution), and the pole tight in his hands – all grimed with clay – Bevis floated slowly down the stream. The sun shone hot and bright, and he had of course left his hat on the sward where it had fallen off as he stooped to the caulking: the wind blew and lifted his hair: his feet were wet. But he never noticed the heat, nor the wind, nor his wet feet, nor his clayey hands. He had done it – he was quite lost in his raft.

Round the bend the brook floated him gently, past the willow where the wood-pigeon built (he was afraid to come near his nest while they were about), past the thick hawthorn bushes white with may-bloom, under which the blackbirds love to stay in the hottest days in the cool shadow by the water. Where there were streaks of white sand sifted by the stream from the mud, he could see the bottom: under the high bank there was a swirl as if the water wrestled with something under the surface: a water-rat, which had watched him coming from a tiny terrace, dived with a sound like a stone dropped quietly in: the stalks of flags grazed the bottom of the raft, he could hear them as it drew on: a jack struck and rushed wildly up and

down till he found a way to slip by; the raft gave a heave and
shot swiftly forward where there had once been a bay and was
still a fall of two inches or so: a bush projected so much that he
could with difficulty hold the boughs aside and prevent the
thorns from scratching his face: a snag scraped the bottom of
the boat and the jerk nearly overthrew him – he did not mind
that, he feared lest the old stump had started a' seam, but
fortunately it had not done so.

Then there was a straight course, a broad and open reach, at
which he shouted with delight. The wind came behind and
pushed his back like a sail, and the little silvery ripples ran
before him, and dashed against the shore, destroying themselves and their shadows under them at the same time. The raft
floated without piloting here, steadily on. Bevis lifted his pole
and waved his hand in triumph.

From the gate-way the carter's lad watched him; he had got
away from the angry Bailiff. From the garden ha-ha, near the
rhubarb patch, Polly the dairymaid watched him, gesticulating
every now and then with her arms, for she had been sent to call
him to dinner. Mark, wild with envy and admiration and desire
to share the voyage, walked on the bank, begging to come in,
for Bevis to get out or let him join him, threatening to leap
aboard from the high bank where the current drifted the raft
right under him, pulling off his shoes and stockings to wade in
and seize the craft by main force; then, changing his mind,
shouting to Bevis to mind a boulder in the brook, and pointing
to the place.

The raft swept with steady, easy motion down the straight
broad reach; Bevis did not need his pole, he stood without its
help, all aglow with joy.

The raft came to another bend, and Bevis with his pole
guided it round, and then, looking up, stamped his foot with
vexation, for there was an ancient, hollow willow right in front,
so bowed down that its head obstructed the fair way of the
stream. He had quite hoped to get down to the Peninsula, and

to circumnavigate it, and even shoot the cataract of the dam below, and go under the arch of the bridge, and away yet farther. He was not fifty yards from the Peninsula, and Mark had run there to meet him; but here was this awkward tree, and before he could make up his mind what to do, bump the raft struck the willow, then it swung slowly round and one side grounded on bank, and he was at a standstill.

He hit the willow with his pole, but that was of no use, and called to Mark. Bevis pushed the willow with his pole, Mark pulled at a branch, and together they could shake it, but they could not move it out of the way; the stream was blocked as if a boom had been fastened across it. The voyage was over.

While they consulted, Polly came down, having failed to make them hear from the garden, and after she had shaken them each by the shoulder brought them to reason. Though she would have failed in that too had not the willow been there, not for dinner or anything would Bevis have abandoned his adventure, so bent was he always on the business he had in hand.

But the willow was obstinate, they could not get past it, so reluctantly he agreed to go home. First Polly had to fetch his hat, which was two hundred yards away on the grass by the drinking-place; then Mark had to put his shoes and stockings on, and take one off again because there was a fragment of stone in it. Next, Bevis had to step into the raft again – a difficult thing to do from the tree – in order to get the cord fastened to the staple to tie it up, not that there was the least risk of the raft floating away, still these things as you know, ought to be done quite properly.

After he had tied the cord or painter to a branch of the willow as firmly as possible, at last he consented to come. But then catching sight of the carter's lad, he had first to give him his sixpence, and also to tell him that if he dared go near the raft, even to look at it, he would be put into the brook. Besides which he had to wash his hands, and by the time Mark and he

reached the table the rest had finished. The people looked at them rather blackly, but they did not mind or notice in the least, for their minds were full of projects to remove the willow, about which they whispered to each other.

Pan raced beside them after dinner to the ha-ha wall, down which they jumped one after the other into the meadow. The spaniel hesitated on the brink, not that he feared the leap, which he had so often taken, but reflection checked him. He watched them a little way as they ran for the brook, then turned and walked very slowly back to the house; for he knew that now dinner was over, if he waited till he was remembered, a plateful would come out for him.

CHAPTER 3

The Mississippi

THEY found the raft as they had left it, except that petals of the may-bloom, shaken from the hawthorn bushes by the breeze, as they came floating down the stream had lodged against the vessel like a white line on the water. Already, too, the roach, which love a broad shadow to play about its edge, had come underneath, but when they felt the shaking of the bank from the footsteps turned aside, and let the current drift them down. Bevis fetched his hatchet from the Peninsula and began to hack at the willow; Mark, not without some difficulty, got leave to climb into the raft, and sit in the centre. The chips flew, some fell on the grass, some splashed into the brook; Bevis made a broad notch just as he had seen the men do it; and though his arm was slender, the fire behind it drove the edge of steel into the wood. The willow shook, and its branches, which touched the water, ruffled the surface.

But though the trunk was hollow it was a long way through, and when Bevis began to tire he had only cut in about three inches. They must tow the raft back to the drinking-place. Bevis untied the cord with which the raft was fastened to the willow, and stepped on board.

'Don't pull too quick,' he said to Mark, giving him the cord; 'or perhaps I shall run aground.'

'But you floated down,' said Mark. 'Let me get in, and you tow; it's my turn.'

'Your turn?' shouted Bevis, standing up as straight as a bolt. 'This is *my* raft.'

'But you always have everything, and you floated down, and I have not; you have everything, and – '

'You are a great story,' said Bevis, stamping so that the raft
shook and the ripples rushed from under it. 'I don't have everything, and you have more than half; and I gave you my engine
and that box of gun-caps yesterday: and I hate you, and you
are a big story.'

Out he scrambled, and seizing Mark by the shoulders, thrust
him towards the raft with such force that it was with difficulty
Mark saved himself from falling into the brook. He clung to the
willow – the bark gave way under his fingers – but as he slipped
he slung himself over the raft and dropped on it.

'Take the pole,' said Bevis, still very angry, and looking black
as thunder. 'Take the pole, and steer so as not to run in the
mud, and not to hit against the bank. Now then,' and putting
the cord over his shoulder, off he started.

Mark had as much as ever he could do to keep the raft from
striking one side or the other.

'Please don't go so fast,' he said.

Bevis went slower, and towed steadily in silence. After they
had passed the hawthorn under the may-bloom, Mark said
'Bevis,' but Bevis did not answer.

'Bevis,' repeated Mark, 'I have had enough now; stop, and
you get in.'

'I shall not,' said Bevis. 'You are a great story.'

In another minute Mark spoke again:

'Let me get out and tow you now.' Bevis did not reply. 'I say
– I say – I say, Bevis.'

No use. Bevis towed him the whole way, till the raft touched
the shallow shore of the drinking-place. Then Mark got out and
helped him drag the vessel well up on the ground, so that it
should not float away.

'Now,' said Bevis, after it was quite done. 'Will you be a
story any more?'

'No,' said Mark, 'I will not be a story again.'

So they walked back side by side to the willow tree; Mark,
who was really in the right, feeling in the wrong. At the tree

Bevis picked up the auger, and told him to bore the hole. Mark began, but suddenly stopped.

'What's the good of boring the hole when we have not got any gunpowder?' said he.

'No more we have,' said Bevis. 'This is very stupid, and they will not let me have any, though I have got some money, and I have a great mind to buy some and hide it. Just as if we did not know how to use powder, and as if we did not know how to shoot! Oh, I know! We will go and cut a bough of alder – there's ever so many alders by the Longpond – and burn it and make charcoal; it makes the best charcoal, you know, and they always use it for gunpowder, and then we can get some saltpetre. Let me see – '

'The Bailiff had some saltpetre the other day,' said Mark.

'So he did: it is in the dairy. Oh yes, and I know where some sulphur is. It is in the garden-house, where the tools are, in the orchard; it's what they use to smother the bees with – '

'That's on brown paper,' said Mark; 'that won't do.'

'No, it's not. You have to melt it to put it on paper, and dip the paper in. This is in a piece, it is like a short bar, and we will pound it up and mix them all together and make capital gunpowder.'

'Hurrah!' cried Mark, throwing down the auger. 'Let's go and cut the alder. Come on!'

'Stop,' said Bevis. 'Lean on me, and walk slow. Don't you know you have caught a dreadful fever, from being in the swamps by the river, and you can hardly walk, and you are very thin and weak? Lean on my arm and hang your head.'

Mark hung his head, turning his rosy cheeks down to the buttercups, and dragged his sturdy fever-stricken limbs along with an effort.

'Humph!' said a gruff voice.

'It's the Indians!' cried Bevis, startled, for they were so absorbed they had not heard the Bailiff come up behind them. They quite jumped, as if about to be scalped.

'What be you doing to that tree?' said the Bailiff.

'Find out,' said Bevis. 'It's not your tree: and why don't you say when you're coming?'

'I saw you from the hedge,' said the Bailiff. 'I was telling John where to cut the bushes for the new harrow.' That caused the rustling in the forest. 'You'll never chop he down.'

'That we shall, if we want to.'

'No, you won't – he stops your ship.'

'It isn't a ship: it's a raft.'

'Well, you can't get by.'

'That we can.'

'I thinks you be stopped,' said the Bailiff, having now looked at the tree more carefully. 'He be main thick' – with a certain sympathy for stolid, inanimate obstruction.

'I tell you, people like us are never stopped by anything,' said Bevis. 'We go through forests, and we float down rivers, and we shoot tigers, and move the biggest trees ever seen – don't we, Mark?'

'Yes, that we do: nothing is anything to us.'

'Of course not,' said Bevis. 'And if we can't chop it down or blow it up, as we mean to, then we dig round it. Oh, Mark, I say! I got! Let's dig a canal round it.'

'How silly we were never to think of that!' said Mark. 'A canal is the very thing – from here to the creek.'

He meant where the stream curved to enclose the Peninsula: the proposed canal would make the voyage shorter.

'Cut some sticks – quick!' said Bevis. 'We must plug out our canal – that is what they always do first, whether it is a canal, or a railway, or a drain, or anything. And I must draw a plan. I must get my pocket-book and pencil. Come on, Mark, and get the spade while I get my pencil.'

Off they ran. The Bailiff leaned on his hazel staff, one hand against the willow, and looked down into the water, as calmly as the sun itself reflected there. When he had looked awhile he shook his head and grunted: then he stumped away; and after a dozen yards or so, glanced back, grunted, and shook his head again. It could not be done. The tree was thick, the earth hard – no such thing; his sympathy, in a dull unspoken way, was with the immovable.

Mark went to work with the spade, throwing the turf he dug up into the brook; while Bevis, lying at full length on the grass, drew his plan of the canal. He drew two curving lines parallel, and half an inch apart, to represent the bend of the brook, and then two as straight as he could manage, across, so as to shorten the distance, and avoid the obstruction. The rootlets of the grass held tight, when Mark tried to lift the spadeful he had dug, so that he could not tear them off.

He had to chop them at the side with his spade first, and then there was a root of the willow in the way; a very obstinate stout root, for which the little hatchet had to be brought to cut it. Under the softer turf the ground was very hard, as it had long been dry, so that by the time Bevis had drawn his plan and stuck in little sticks to show the course the canal was to take, Mark had only cleared about a foot square, and four or five inches deep, just at the edge of the bank, where he could thrust it into the stream.

'Let us have another float down,' said Mark. 'Let me float down, and I will drag you all the way up this time.'

'All right,' said Bevis.

So they launched the raft, and Mark got in and floated down, and Bevis walked on the bank, giving him directions how to pilot the vessel, which as before was brought up by the willow leaning over the water. Just as they were preparing to tow it back again, and Bevis was climbing out on the willow to get into the raft, they heard a splashing down the brook.

'What's that?' said Mark. 'Is it Indians?'

'No, it's an alligator. At least, I don't know. Perhaps it's a canoe full of Indians. Give me the pole quick. There now, take the hatchet. Look out!'

The splashing increased; then there was a 'Yowp!' and Pan,

the spaniel, suddenly appeared out of the flags by the osier-bed. He raced across the ground there, and jumped into the brook again, and immediately a moorcock, which he had been hunting, scuttled along the water, beating with his wings, and scrambling with his long legs hanging down, using both air and water to fly from his enemy. As he came near he saw Bevis on the willow, and rose out of the brook over the bank. Bevis hit at him with his pole, but missed, and Mark hurled the hatchet in vain. The moorcock flew straight across the meadow to another withy-bed, and then disappeared. It was only by threats that they stopped the spaniel from following.

Pan having got his plateful by patiently waiting about the doorway, after he had licked his chops, and turned up the whites of his eyes, to see if he could persuade them to give him any more, walked into the rick-yard, and choosing a favourite spot upon some warm straw – for straw becomes quite hot under sunshine – lay down and took a nap. When he awoke, having settled matters with the fleas, he strolled back to the ha-ha wall, and, seeing Bevis and Mark still busy by the brook, went down to know what they were doing. But first going to a place he well knew to lap he scented the moorcock, and gave chase.

'Come here,' said Bevis; and, seizing the spaniel by the skin of his neck, he dragged him in the raft, stepped in quickly after, and held Pan while Mark hauled at the tow-line. But when Bevis had to take the pole to guide the raft from striking the bank Pan jumped out in a moment, preferring to swim rather than to ride in comfort, nor could any persuasions or threats get him on again. He barked along the shore, while Mark hauled and Bevis steered the craft.

Having beached her at the drinking-place on the shelving strand, they thought they had better go up the river a little way, and see if there were any traces of Indians; and, following the windings of the stream, they soon came to the hatch. Above the hatch the water was smooth, as it usually is where it is deep and approaching the edge, and Bevis's quick eye caught sight of a tiny ripple there near one bank, so tiny that it hardly extended across the brook, and disappeared after the third wavelet.

'Keep Pan there!' he said. 'Hit him – hit him harder than that; he doesn't mind.'

Mark punched the spaniel, who crouched; but, nevertheless, his body crept, as it were, towards the hatch, where Bevis was climbing over. Bevis took hold of the top rail, put his foot on the rail below, all green and slippery with weeds where the water splashed, like the rocks where the sea comes, then his other foot farther along, and so got over with the deep water in front, and the roar of the fall under, and the bubbles rushing down the stream. The bank was very steep, but here was a notch to put the foot in, and a stout hawthorn stem – the thorns of which had long since been broken off for the purpose – gave him something to hold to and by which to lift himself up.

Then he walked stealthily along the bank – it overhung the dark deep water, and seemed about to slip in under him. There was a plantation of trees on that side, and on the other a hawthorn hedge, so that it was a quiet and sheltered spot. As he came to the place where he had seen the ripple, he looked closer, and in among a bunch of rushes, with the green stalks standing up all round it, he saw a moorhen's nest. It was made of rushes, twined round like a wreath, or perhaps more like a large green turban, and there were three or four young moorhens in it. The old bird had slipped away as he came near, and diving under the surface rose ten yards off under a projecting bush.

Bevis dropped on his knee to take one of the young birds, but in an instant they rolled out of the nest, with their necks thrust out in front, and fell splash in the water, where they swam across, one with a piece of shell clinging to its back, and another piece of shell was washed from it by the water. Pan was by his side in a minute; he had heard the splash, and seen the young moorhens, and with a whine, as Mark kicked him — unable to hold him any longer — he rushed across.

'They are such pretty dear little things,' said Bevis, in an ecstasy of sentiment, calling to Mark. 'Lie down!' banging Pan with a dead branch which he hastily snatched up. The spaniel's back sounded hollow as the wood rebounded, and broke on his ribs. 'Such dear little things! I would not have them hurt for anything.'

Bang again on Pan's back, who gave up the attempt, knowing from sore experience that Bevis was not to be trifled with. But by the time Mark had got there the little moorhens had hidden in the grasses beside the stream, though one swam out for a minute, and then concealed itself again.

The moorhens did not appear again, so they went back and sat on the top of the steep bank, their legs dangling over the edge above the bubbling water.

A broad cool shadow from the trees had fallen over the hatch, for the afternoon had gone on, and the sun was declining behind them over the western hills. A broad cool shadow, whose edges were far away, so that they were in the midst of it. The thrushes sang in the ashes, for they knew that the quiet evening, with the dew they love, was near. A bullfinch came to the hawthorn hedge just above the hatch, looked in and out once or twice, and then stepped inside the spray near his nest. A yellow-hammer called from the top of a tree, and another answered him across the field. Afar in the mowing-grass the crake lifted his voice, for he talks more as the sun sinks.

The swirling water went round and round under the fall, with lines of white bubbles rising, and quivering masses of yellowish foam ledged on the red rootlets under the bank and against the flags. The swirling water, ceaselessly beaten by the descending stream coming on it with a long-continued blow, returned to be driven away again. A steady roar of the fall, and a rippling sound above it of bursting bubbles and crossing wavelets of the hastening stream, notched and furrowed over stones, frowning in eager haste. The rushing and the coolness, and the song of the brook and the birds, and the sense of the sun sinking, stilled even Bevis and Mark a little while. They sat and listened, and said nothing; the delicious brook filled their ears with music.

'I am hungry,' said Mark. 'What ought we to have to eat; what is right on the Mississippi? I don't believe they have tea. There is Polly shouting for us.'

'No,' said Bevis thoughtfully; 'I don't think they do. How stupid of her to stand there shouting and waving her handkerchief, as if we could not find our way straight across the trackless prairie. I know — we will have some honey! Don't you know? Of course the hunters find lots of wild honey in the hollow trees. We will have some honey; there's a big jar full.'

So they got over the hatch, and went home, leaving their tools scattered hither and thither beside the Mississippi. They climbed up the ha-ha wall, putting the toes of their boots where the flat stones of which it was built, without mortar, were farthest apart, and so made steps while they could hold to the wiry grass-tufts on the top.

'Where's your hat?' said Polly to Bevis.

'I don't know,' said Bevis. 'I suppose it's in the brook. It doesn't matter.'

CHAPTER 4

Discovery of the New Sea

NEXT morning Bevis went out into the meadow to try and find a plant, whose leaves, or one of them, always pointed to the north, like a green compass lying on the ground. There was one in the prairies by which the hunters directed themselves across those oceans of grass without a landmark as the mariners at sea. Why should there not be one in the meadows here – in these prairies – by which to guide himself from forest to forest, from hedge to hedge, where there was no path? If there was a path it was not proper to follow it, nor ought you to know your way; you ought to find it by sign.

He had 'blazed' ever so many boughs of the hedges with the hatchet, or his knife if he had not got the hatchet with him, to realize his route through the woods. When he found a nest begun or finished, and waiting for the egg, he used to cut a 'blaze' – that is, to peel off the bark – or make a notch, or cut a bough off about three yards from the place, so that he might easily return to it, though hidden with foliage. No doubt the grass had a secret of this kind, and could tell him which was the way, and which was the north and south if he searched long enough.

So the raft being an old story now, as he had had it a day, Bevis went out into the field, looking very carefully down into the grass. Just by the path there were many plantains, but their long narrow leaves did not point in any particular direction, no two plants had their leaves parallel. The blue scabious had no leaves to speak of, nor had the red knapweed, nor the yellow rattle, nor the white moon-daisies, nor golden buttercups, nor red sorrel. There were stalks and flowers, but the plants of the mowing-grass, in which he had no business to be walking, had very little leaf. He tried to see if the flowers turned more one way than the other, or bowed their heads to the north, as men seem to do, taking that pole as their guide, but none did so. They leaned in any direction, as the wind had left them, or as the sun happened to be when they burst their green bonds and came forth to the light.

The wind came past as he looked and stroked everything the way it went, shaking white pollen from the bluish tops of the tall grasses. The wind went on and left him and the grasses to themselves. 'How should I know which was the north or the south of the west from these?' Bevis asked himself, without framing any words to his question. There was no knowing. Then he walked to the hedge to see if the moss grew more on one side of the elms than the other, or if the bark was thicker and rougher.

After he had looked at twenty trees he could not see much difference; those in the hedge had the moss thickest on the eastern side (he knew which was east very well himself, and wanted to see if the moss knew), and those in the land just through it had the moss thickest on their western side, which was clearly because of the shadow. The trees were really in a double row, running north and south, and the coolest shadow was in between them, and so the moss grew there most. Nor were the boughs any longer or bigger any side more than the other, it varied as the tree was closely surrounded with other trees, for each repelled its neighbour. None of the trees, nor the moss, nor grasses cared anything at all about north or south.

Bevis sat down in the mowing-grass, though he knew the Bailiff would have been angry at such a hole being made in it; and when he was sitting on the ground it rose as high as his head. He could see nothing but the sky, and while he sat there looking up he saw that the clouds all drifted one way, towards his house. Presently a starling came past, also flying straight for the house, and after a while another. Next three bees went over as straight as a line, all going one after another that way. The bees went because they had gathered as much honey as they could carry, and were hastening home without looking to the right or to the left. The starlings went because they had young in their nests in a hole of the roof by the chimney, and they had found some food for their fledglings. So now he could find his way home across the pathless prairie by going the same way as the clouds, the bees, and the starlings.

But when he had reached home he recollected that he ought to know the latitude, and that there were Arabs or some other people in Africa who found out the latitude of the place they were in by gazing at the sun through a tube. Bevis considered a little, and then went to the rick-yard, where there was a large elder bush, and cut a straight branch between the knots with his knife. He peeled it, and then forced out the pith, and thus made a tube. Next he took a thin board, and scratched a circle on it with the point of the compasses, and divided it into degrees. Round the tube he bent a piece of wire, and put the ends through a gimlet-hole in the centre of the board. The ends were opened apart, so as to fasten the tube to the board, allowing it to rotate round the circle. Two gimlet holes were bored at the top corners of the board, and string passed through so that the instrument could be attached to a tree or post.

He was tying it to one of the young walnut trees as an upright against which to work his astrolabe, when Mark arrived, and everything had to be explained to him. After they had glanced through the tube, and decided that the raft was at least ten degrees distant, it was clearly of no use to go to it today, as they could not reach it under a week's travel. The best thing, Mark thought, would be to continue their expedition in some other direction.

'Let's go round the Longpond,' said Bevis; 'we have never been quite round it.'

'So we will,' said Mark. 'But we shall not be back to dinner.'

'As if travellers ever thought of dinner! Of course we shall take our provisions with us.'

'Let's go and get our spears,' said Mark.

'Let's take Pan,' said Bevis.

'Where is your old compass?' said Mark.

'Oh, I know – and I must make a map; wait a minute. We ought to have a medicine-chest; the savages will worry us for physic: and very likely we shall have dreadful fevers.'

'So we shall, of course; but perhaps there are wonderful plants to cure us, and we know them and the savages don't – there's sorrel.'

'Of course, and we can nibble some hawthorn leaf.'

'Or a stalk of wheat.'

'Or some watercress.'

'Or some nuts.'

'No, certainly not; they're not ripe,' said Bevis, 'and unripe fruit is very dangerous in tropical countries.'

'We ought to keep a diary,' said Mark. 'When we go to sleep who shall watch first, you or I?'

'We'll light a fire,' said Bevis. 'That will frighten the lions; they will glare at us, but they can't stand fire – you hit them on the head with a burning stick.'

So they went in, and loaded their pockets with huge double slices of bread-and-butter done up in paper, apples, and the leg of a roast duck from the pantry. Then came the compass, an old one in a brass case; Mark broke his nails opening the case, which was tarnished, and the card at once swung round to the north, pointing to the elms across the road from the window of the sitting-room. Bevis took the bow and three arrows, made of the young wands of hazel which grow straight, and Mark was armed with a spear, a long ash rod with sharpened end, which they thrust in the kitchen fire a few minutes to harden in the proper manner.

Besides which, there was Bevis's pocket-book for the diary, and a large sheet of brown paper for the map; you see travellers have not always everything at command, but must make use of what they have. Pan raced before them up the footpath; the gate that led to the Longpond was locked, and too high to be climbed easily, but they knew a gap, and crept through on hands and knees.

'Take care there are no cobras or rattlesnakes among those dead leaves,' said Mark, when they were half-way through, and quite over-arched and hidden under brambles.

'Stick your spear into them,' said Bevis, who was first, and Mark, putting his spear past him, stirred up the heap of leaves.

'All right,' said he. 'But look at that bough – is it a bough or a snake?'

There was an oak branch in the ditch, crooked and grey with lichen, half concealed by rushes; its curving shape and singular hue gave it some resemblance to a serpent. But when he stabbed at it with his spear it did not move; and they crept through without hurt. As they stood up in the field the other side they had an anxious consultation as to what piece of water it was they were going to discover; whether it was a lake in Central Africa, or one in America.

'I'm tired of lakes,' said Mark. 'They have found out such a lot of lakes, and the canoes are always upset, and there is such a lot of mud. Let's have a new sea altogether.'

'So we will,' said Bevis. 'That's capital – we will find a new sea where no one has ever been before. Look!' – for they had now advanced to where the gleam of the sunshine on the mere was visible through the hedge – 'look! there it is, is it not wonderful?'

'Yes,' said Mark, 'write it down in the diary; here's my pencil. Be quick; put "Found a new sea" – be quick – there, come on – let's run – hurrah!'

They dashed open the gate, and ran down to the beach. It was a rough descent over large stones, but they reached the edge in a minute, and as they came there was a splashing in several places along the shore. Something was striving to escape, alarmed at their approach. Mark fell on his knees, and put his hand where two or three stones, half in and half out of water, formed a recess, and feeling about drew out two roach, one of which slipped from his fingers; the other he held. Bevis rushed at another splashing; but he was not quick enough, for it was difficult to scramble over the stones, and the fish swam away just as he got there. Mark's fish was covered with tiny slippery specks. The roach had come up to leave their eggs under the stones. When they had looked at the fish they put it back in the water, and with a kind of shake it dived down and made off. As they watched it swim out they now saw that three or four yards from the shore there were crowds upon crowds of fish travelling to and fro, following the line of the land.

A black cat came down the bank some way off, and they saw her swiftly dart her paw into the water, and snatch out a fish. The scales shone silver white, and reflected the sunshine into their eyes like polished metal as the fish quivered and leaped under the claw. They walked along the shore, climbing over stones, but the crowds of roach were everywhere; till presently they came to a place where the stones ceased, and there was a shallow bank of sand shelving into the water and forming a point.

There the fish turned round and went back. Thousands kept coming up and returning, and while the stayed here watching, gazing into the clear water, which was still and illuminated to the bottom by the sunlight, they saw two great fish come side by side up from the depths beyond and move slowly, very slowly, just over the sand. They were two huge tench, five or six pounds a-piece, roaming idly away from the muddy holes they lie in. But they do not stay in such holes always, and once now and then you may see them like this as in a glass tank. The pair did not go far; they floated slowly rather than swam, first a few yards one way and then a few yards the other. Bevis and Mark were breathless with eagerness.

'Go and fetch my fishing-rod,' whispered Bevis, unable to speak loud; he was so excited.

'No, you go,' said Mark; 'I'll stay and watch them.'

'I shan't,' said Bevis sharply, 'you ought to go.'

'I shan't,' said Mark.

Just then the tench, having surveyed the bottom there, turned and faded away into the darker deep water.

'There,' said Bevis, 'if you had run quick!'

'I won't fetch everything,' said Mark.

'Then you're no use,' said Bevis. 'Suppose I was shooting an elephant, and you did not hand me another gun quick, or another arrow; and suppose – '

'But *I* might be shooting the elephant,' interrupted Mark, 'and you could hand me the gun.'

'Impossible,' said Bevis; 'I never heard anything so absurd. Of course it's the captain who always does everything; and if there was only one biscuit left, of course you would let me eat it, and lie down and die under a tree, so that I might go on and reach the settlement.'

'I *hate* dying under a tree,' said Mark, 'and you always want everything.'

Bevis said nothing, but marched on very upright and very angry, and Mark followed, putting his feet into the marks Bevis left as he strode over the yielding sand. Neither spoke a word. The shore trended in again after the point, and the indentation was full of weeds, whose broad brownish leaves floated on the surface. Pan worked about and sniffed among the willow bushes on their left, which, when the lake was full, were in the water, but now that it had shrunk under the summer heat were several yards from the edge.

Bevis, leading the way, came to a place where the strand, till then so low and shelving, suddenly became steep, where a slight rise of the ground was cut as it were through by the water, which had worn a cliff eight or ten feet above his head. The water came to the bottom of the cliff, and there did not

41

seem any way past it except by going away from the edge into the field, and so round it. Mark at once went round, hastening as fast as he could to get in front, and he came down to the water on the other side of the cliff in half a minute, looked at Bevis, and then went on with Pan.

Bevis, with a frown on his forehead, stood looking at the cliff, having determined that he would not go round, and yet he could not get past because the water, which was dark and deep, going straight down, came to the bank, which rose from it like a wall. First he took out his pocket-knife and thought he would cut steps in the sand, and he did cut one large enough to put his toe in; but then he recollected that he should have nothing to hold to. He had half a mind to go back home and get some big nails and drive into the hard sand to catch hold of, only by that time Mark would be so far ahead he could not overtake him and would boast that he had explored the new sea first. Already he was fifty yards in front, and walking as fast as he could. How he wished he had his raft, and then that he could swim! He would have jumped into the water and swum round the cliff in a minute.

He saw Mark climbing over some railings that went down to the water to divide the fields. He looked up again at the cliff, and almost felt inclined to leave it and run round and overtake Mark. When he looked down again Mark was out of sight, hidden by hawthorn bushes and the branches of trees. Bevis was exceedingly angry, and he walked up and down and gazed round in his rage. But as he turned once more to the cliff, suddenly Pan appeared at an opening in the furze and bramble about half-way up. The bushes grew at the side, and the spaniel, finding Bevis did not follow Mark, had come back and was waiting for him. Bevis, without thinking, pushed into the furze, and immediately he saw him coming, Pan, eager to go forward again, ran along the face of the cliff about four feet from the top. He seemed to run on nothing, and Bevis was curious to see how he had got by.

The bushes becoming thicker, Bevis had at last to go on hands and knees under them, and found a hollow space, where there was a great rabbit-bury, big enough at the mouth for Pan to creep in. When he stood on the sand thrown out from it he could see how Pan had done it; there was a narrow ledge, not above four inches wide, on the face of the cliff. It was only just wide enough for a footing, and the cliff fell sheer down to the water; but Bevis, seeing that he could touch the top of the cliff, and so steady himself, never hesitated a moment.

He stepped on the ledge, right foot first, the other close behind it, and held lightly to the grass at the edge of the field above, only lightly lest he should pull it out by the roots. Then he put his right foot forward again, and drew his left up to it, and so along, keeping the right first (he could not walk properly, the ledge being so narrow), he worked himself along. It was quite easy, though it seemed a long way down to the water (it always looked very much farther down than it does up), and as he glanced down he saw a perch rise from the depths, and it occurred to him in the moment what a capital place it would be for perch-fishing.

He could see all over that part of the lake, and noticed two moorhens feeding in the weeds on the other side, when puff! the wind came over the field, and reminded him, as he involuntarily grasped the grass tighter, that he must not stay in such a place where he might lose his balance. So he went on, and a dragon-fly flew past out a little way over the water and then back to the field, but Bevis was not to be tempted to watch his antics: he kept steadily on, a foot at a time, till he reached a willow on the other side, and had a bough to hold. Then he shouted, and Pan, who was already far ahead, stopped and looked back at the well-known sound of triumph.

Running down the easy slope, Bevis quickly reached the railings and climbed over. On the other side a meadow came down to the edge, and he raced through the grass and was already half-way to the next rails when someone called 'Bevis!' and

there was Mark coming out from behind an oak in the field.
Bevis stopped, half-pleased, half-angry.

'I waited for you,' said Mark.

'I came across the cliff,' said Bevis.

'I saw you,' said Mark.

'But you ran away from me,' said Bevis.

'But I am not running now.'

'It is very wrong when we are on an expedition,' said Bevis.
'People must do as the captain tells them.'

'I won't do it again,' said Mark.

'You ought to be punished,' said Bevis, 'you ought to be put
on half-rations. Are you quite sure you will never do it
again?'

'Never.'

'Well then, this once you are pardoned. Now, mind in future,
as you are lieutenant, you set a good example. There's a
summer snipe'.

Out flew a little bird from the shore, startled as Pan came
near, with a piping whistle, and, describing a semicircle, returned to the hard mud fifty yards farther on. It was a summer
snipe, and when they approached, after getting over the next
railings, it flew out again over the water, and making another
half-circle passed back to where they had first seen it. Here the
strand was hard mud, dried by the sun, and broken up into
innumerable holes by the hoofs of cattle and horses which had
come down to drink from the pasture, and had to go through
the mud into which they sank when it was soft. Three or four
yards from the edge there was a narrow strip of weeds, showing that a bank followed the line of the shore there. It was so
unpleasant walking over this hard mud, that they went up into
the field, which rose high, so that from the top they had a view
of the lake.

They gazed across the broad water over the gleaming ripples
far away, for the light wind did not raise them by the shore,
and traced the edge of the willows and the weeds.

'The savages are in hiding,' said Bevis, after a pause. 'Perhaps they're having a feast. This would be a good place to begin the map as we can see so far. Let's sit down.'

'Let's get behind a tree, then,' said Mark; 'else if we stay still long perhaps we shall be seen.'

So they went a little farther to an ash, and sat down by it. Bevis spread out his sheet of brown paper.

'Give me an apple,' said Mark, 'while you draw.' Bevis did so, and then, lying on the ground at full length, began to trace out the course of the shore.

'There ought to be names,' said Mark. 'What shall we call this?'

'It is the Gulf,' said Bevis; 'Fir Tree Gulf,' as he noticed the tops of the fir trees. 'And that island on the left side there is Serendib.'

'Where Sinbad went?'

'Yes; and that one by it is the Unknown Island, and a magician lives there in a long white robe, and he has a serpent a hundred feet long coiled up in a cave under a bramble bush, and the most wonderful things in the world.'

'Let's go there,' said Mark.

'So we will,' said Bevis, 'directly we have got a ship.'

'Write the names down,' said Mark. 'Put them on the map before we forget them.'

Bevis wrote them on the map, and then they started again upon their journey. They followed the path and crossed the head of the gulf.

A slow stream entered the lake there, and they went down to the shore, where it opened to the larger water. Under a great willow, whose tops rose as high as the firs, and an alder or two, it was so cool and pleasant, that Mark, as he played with the water with his spear, pushing it this way and that, and raising bubbles, and a splashing as a whip sings in the air, thought he should like to dabble in it. He sat down on a root and took off his shoes and stockings, while Bevis, going a little way up the

N

Mississippi
River

The Arms

Our
House

W

Fir
Tree
Gulf

The
Forest

The
Nile

The
Shallows

Trees
here

Trees
here

Sweet
River

Falls

stream, flung a dead stick into it, and then walked beside it as it floated gently down. But he walked much faster than the stick floated, there was so little current.

'Mark,' said he, suddenly stopping, and taking up some of the water in the hollow of his hand, 'Mark!'

'Yes. What is it?'

'This is fresh water. Isn't it lucky?'

'Why?'

'Why, you silly, of course we should have died of thirst. *That's* the sea' (pointing out). 'That will save our lives.'

'So it will,' said Mark, putting one foot into the water and then the other. Then looking back, as he stood half up his ankles, 'We can call here for fresh water when we have our ship – when we go to the Unknown Island.'

'So we can,' said Bevis. 'We must save a barrel and fill it. But I wonder what river this is,' and he walked back again beside it.

Mark walked farther out till it was over his ankles, and then till it was half as deep as his knee. He jumped up both feet together, and splashed as he came down, and shouted. Bevis shouted to him from the river. Next they both shouted together and a dove flew out of the firs and went off.

'What river is this?' Bevis called presently.

'Oh!' cried Mark suddenly; and Bevis glancing round saw him stumble, and, in his endeavour to save himself, plunge his spear into the water, as if it had been the ground, to steady himself; but the spear, though long, touched nothing up to his hand. He bent over. Bevis held his breath, thinking he must topple and fall headlong; but somehow he just saved himself, swung round and immediately he could, ran out upon the shore. Bevis rushed back.

'What was it?' he asked.

'It's a hole,' said Mark, whose cheeks had turned white, and now became red, as the blood came back. 'An awful deep hole – the spear won't touch the bottom.'

As he waded out at first on shelving sand he laughed, and shouted, and jumped, and suddenly, as he stepped, his foot went over the edge of the deep hole; his spear, as he tried to save himself with it, touched nothing, so that it was only by good fortune that he recovered his balance.

Mark was much frightened, and sat down on the root to put on his shoes and stockings. Bevis took the spear, and going to the edge, and leaning over and feeling the bottom with it, he could find the hole, where the spear slipped and touched nothing, about two yards out.

'It is a horrid place,' he said. 'How should I have got you out? I wish we could swim.'

'So do I,' said Mark. 'And they will never let us go out in a boat by ourselves – I mean in a ship to the Unknown Island – till we can.'

'No; that they won't,' said Bevis. 'We must begin to swim directly. My papa will show me, and I will show you. But how should I have got you out if you had fallen? Let me see; there's a gate up there.'

'It is so heavy,' said Mark. 'You could not drag it down, and fling it in quick enough. If we had the raft up here.'

'Ah, yes. There is a pole loose there – that would have done.' He pointed to some railings that crossed the stream. The rails were nailed, but there was a pole at the side, only thrust into the bushes. 'I could have pulled that out and held it to you.'

Mark had now got his shoes on, and they started again, looking for a bridge to cross the stream, and continue their journey round the New Sea. As they could not see any they determined to cross by the railings, which they did without much trouble, holding to the top bar, and putting their feet on the second, which was about three inches over the water. The stream ran deep and slow; it was dark, because it was in shadow, for the trees hung over from each side. Bevis, who was first, stopped in the middle and looked up it. There was a thick hedge and trees each side, and a great deal of fern on the

48

banks. It was straight for a good way, so that they could see some distance till the boughs hid the rest.

'I should like to go up there,' said Mark. 'Some day, if we can get a boat under these rails, let us go up it.'

'So we will,' said Bevis. 'It is proper to explore a river. But what river is this?'

'Is it the Congo?' said Mark.

'Oh! no. The Congo is not near this sea at all. Perhaps it's the Amazon.'

'It can't be the Mississippi,' said Mark. 'That's a long way off now. I know – see, it runs slow, and it's not clear, and we don't know where it comes from. It's the Nile.'

'So it is,' said Bevis. 'It is the Nile, and some day we will go up to the source.'

They travelled on some way and found the ground almost level and so thick with sedges and grass that they walked in a forest of green up to their waists. There was no shadow, and after a while they wearied of stepping through the sedges, sinking a little at every step. Beyond the swamp was the gulf they had gone round, and across it the yellow sand-quarry facing them. It looked a very long way off.

CHAPTER 5

'We Must Go On'

'We shall never get round,' said Mark, 'just see what a way we have come, and we are not half up one side of the sea yet.'

'I wonder how far it is back to the quarry,' said Bevis. 'These sedges are so tiresome.'

'We shall never get round,' said Mark, 'and I am getting hungry, and Pan is tired of the rushes too.'

Pan, with his red tongue lolling out at one side of his mouth, looked up, showed his white tusks and wagged his tail at the mention of his name. He had ceased to quest about for some time; he had been walking just at their heels in the path they made.

'We *must* go on,' said Bevis, 'we *can't* go back; it is not proper. Travellers like us never go back. I wish there were no more sedges. Come on.'

He marched on again. But now they were tired, this spurt soon died away, and they stopped again.

'It is as hot as Central Africa,' said Mark, fanning himself with his hat.

'I am not sure that we are not in Central Africa,' said Bevis. 'There are hundreds of miles of reeds in Africa, and as we have crossed the Nile very likely that's where we are.'

They went on again a little way.

'Why, this is a wood!' said Mark, looking round. Ash-stoles and poles surrounded them on every side.

'So it is,' said Bevis. 'No, it's a jungle.'

They walked forward and came to an open space, round about a broad spreading oak.

'I shall sit down here,' said Bevis.

But as they were about to sit down, Pan, who had woken up when he scented rabbits, suddenly disappeared in a hollow.

'What's that,' said Mark. He went to see, and heard a sound of lapping.

'Water!' shouted Mark, and Bevis came to him. Deep down in a narrow channel there was the merest trickle of shallow water, but running, and clear as crystal. It came from chalk, and it was limpid.

Pan could drink, but they could not. His hollow tongue lapped it up like a spoon; but it was too shallow to scoop up in the palm of the hand, and they had no tube of 'gix', or reed, or oat straw, or buttercup stalk to suck through. They sprang into the channel itself, alighting on a place the water did not cover, but with the stream under their feet they could not drink. Nothing but a sparrow could have done so.

Presently Bevis stooped, and with his hands scratched away the silt which formed the bottom, a fine silt of powdered chalk, almost like quicksand, till he had made a bowl-like cavity. The stream soon filled it, but then the water was thick, being disturbed, and they had to wait till it had settled. Then they lapped too, very carefully, with the hollow palm, taking care that the water which ran through their fingers should fall below, and not above the bowl, or the weight of the drops would disturb it again. With perseverance they satisfied their thirst; then they returned to the oak, and took out their provisions; they could eat now.

'This is a jolly jungle,' said Mark, with his mouth full.

'That's a banyan,' said Bevis, pointing with the knuckle-end of the drum-stick he was gnawing at the oak over them. 'It's about eleven thousand years old.'

Then Mark took the drum-stick, and had his turn at it. When it was polished, Pan had it: he cracked it across with his teeth, just as the hyenas did in the cave days, for the animals never learnt to split bones, as the earliest men did. Pan cracked it very disconsolately: his heart was with the fleshpots.

Boom!

They started. It seemed to come from an immense distance. A pheasant crowed as he heard it in the jungle close by them, and a second farther away.

'What can it be?' whispered Mark. 'Is there anything here?' – glancing around.

'There may be some genii,' said Bevis quietly. 'Very likely there are some genii: they are everywhere. But I do not know what that was. Listen!'

They listened: the wood was still; so still, they could hear a moth or a chafer entangled in the leaves of the oak overhead, and trying to get out. Looking up there, the sky was blue and clear, and the sunlight fell brightly on the open space by the streamlet. There was nothing but the hum. The long, long summer days seem gradually to dispose the mind to expect something unusual.

Bevis and Mark listened, but heard nothing, except the entangled chafer, the midsummer hum, and, presently, Pan snuffling, as he buried his nostrils in his hair to bite a flea. They laughed at him, for his eyes were staring, and his flexible nostrils turned up as if his face was not alive but stuffed. The boom did not come again, so they finished their dinner.

'I feel jolly lazy,' said Mark. 'You ought to put the things down on the map.'

'So I did,' said Bevis, and he got out his brown paper, and Mark held it while he worked.

'Write that there is a deep hole there,' said Mark, 'and awful crocodiles: that's it. Now Africa – you want a very long stroke there; write reeds and bamboos.'

'No, not bamboos, papyrus,' said Bevis. 'Bamboos grow in India, where we are now. There's some,' pointing to a tall wild parsnip, or 'gix' on the verge of the streamlet.

'I'm so lazy,' said Mark. 'I shall go to sleep.'

'No you won't,' said Bevis. 'I ought to go to sleep, and you ought to watch. Get your spear and now take my bow.'

Mark took the bow sullenly.

'You ought to stand up, and walk up and down.'

'I can't,' said Mark very short.

'Very well; then go farther away, where you can see more round you. There, sit down there.' Mark sat down at the edge of the shadow of the oak. 'Don't you see you can look into the channel; if there are any savages they are sure to creep up the channel. Do you see?'

'Yes, I see,' said Mark.

'And mind nothing comes behind that woodbine,' pointing to a mass of woodbine which hung from some ash-poles, and stretched like a curtain across the view there. 'That's a very likely place for a tiger; and keep your eye sharp on those nut-tree bushes across the brook – most likely you'll see the barrel of a matchlock pushed through there.'

'I ought to have a matchlock,' said Mark.

'So you did; but we had to start with what we had, and it is all the more glory to us if we get through. Now mind you keep awake.'

'Yes,' said Mark.

Bevis, having given his orders settled himself very comfortably on the moss at the foot of the oak, tilted his hat aside to shelter him still more, and, with a spray of ash in his hand to ward off the flies, began to forget. In a minute up he started.

'Mark!'

'Yes;' still sulky.

'There's another oak – no it's a banyan – up farther; behind you.'

'I know.'

'Well, if you hear any rustle there, it's a python.'

'Very well.'

'And those dead leaves and sticks in the hole there by the stump of that old tree?'

'I see.'

'There's a cobra there.'

'All right.'

'And if a shadow comes over suddenly.'

'What's that, then?' said Mark.

'That's the roc from Sinbad's Island.'

'I say, Bevis,' as Bevis settled himself down again. 'Bevis, don't go to sleep.'

'Pooh!'

'But it's not nice.'

'Rubbish.'

'Bevis.'

'Don't talk silly.'

In a minute Bevis was fast asleep. He always slept quickly, and the heat and the exertion made him forget himself still quicker.

CHAPTER 6

The Jungle

MARK was alone. He felt without going nearer that Bevis was asleep, and dared not wake him lest he should be called a coward. He moved a little way so as to have the oak more at his back, and to get a clearer view on all sides. Then he looked up at the sky, and whistled very low. Pan, who was half asleep too, got up slowly, and came to him; but finding that there was nothing to eat, and disliking to be stroked and patted on such a hot day, he went back to his old place, the barest spot he could find, mere dry ground.

Mark sat, bow and arrow ready in his hand, the arrow on the string, with the spear beside him, and his pocket-knife with the big blade open, and looked into the jungle. It was still and silent. The chafer had got loose, and there was nothing but the hum overhead. He kept the strictest watch, scarce allowing himself to blink his eyes. Now he looked steadily into the brushwood he could see some distance, his glance found a way through between the boughs, till presently after he had searched out these crevices, he could command a circle of view.

Like so many slender webs his lines of sight thus drawn through mere chinks of foliage radiated from a central spot, and at the end of each he seemed as if he could feel if anything moved as much as he could see it. Each of these webs strained at his weary mind, and even in the shade the strong glare of the summer noon pressed heavily on his eyelids. Had anything moved, a bird or a moth, or had the leaves rustled, it would have relieved him. This expectation was a continual effort. His eyes closed, he opened them, frowned and blinked; then he reclined on one arm as an easier position. His eyes closed, the shrill midsummer hum sounded low and distant, then loud; suddenly it ceased – he was asleep.

The sunburnt woodbine, the oaks dotted with coppery leaves where the second shoot appeared, the ash-poles rising from the hollow stoles and whose pale sprays touching above formed a green surface, hazel with white nuts, stiff, ragged thistles on the stream bank, burrs, with brown-tipped hooks, the hard dry ground, all silent, fixed, held in the light.

The sun slipped through the sky like a yacht under the shore where the light wind coming over a bank just fills the sails, but leaves the surface smooth. Through the smooth blue the sun slipped silently, and no white fleck of foam cloud marked his speed. But in the deep narrow channel of the streamlet there was a change – the tiny trickle of water was no longer illumined by the vertical beams, a slight slant left it to run in shadow.

Burr! came a humble-bee whose drone was now put out as he went down among the grass and leaves, now rose again as he travelled. Burr! The faintest breath of air moved without rustling the topmost leaves of the oaks. The humble-bee went on, and disappeared behind the stoles.

A little flicker of movement happened among the woodbine, not to be seen of itself, but as a something interrupting the light like a larger mote crossing the beam. The leaves of the woodbine in one place were drawn together and coated with a white web, and a tiny bird came to take away the destroyer. Then mounting to a branch of ash sang, 'Sip, sip – chip, chip!'

Again the upper leaves of the oak moved and jostling together caused a slight sound. Coo! coo! there was a dove beyond the hazel bushes across the stream. The shadow was more aslant and rose up the stalks of the rushes in the channel. Over the green surface of the ash sprays above, the breeze drew and rippled it like water. A jay came into the farther oak and scolded a distant mate.

Presently Pan awoke, nabbed another flea, looked round and shook his ears, from which some of the hair was worn by continual rubbing against the bushes under which he had crept for so many years. He felt thirsty, and remembering the stream, went towards it, passing very lightly by Bevis, so closely as to almost brush his hat. The slight pad, pad of his paws on the moss and earth conveyed a sense of something moving near him to Bevis's mind. Bevis instantly sat up, so quickly, that the spaniel, half alarmed, ran some yards.

Directly Bevis sat up he saw that Mark had fallen asleep. He thought for a moment, and then took a piece of string from his pocket. Stepping quietly up to Mark he made a slip-knot in the string, lifted Mark's arm and put his hand through the loop above the wrist, then he jerked it tight. Mark scrambled up in terror – it might have been the python:

'Oh! I say!'

Before he could finish, Bevis had dragged him two or three steps towards an ash-pole, when Mark, thoroughly awake, jerked his arm free, though the string hung to it.

'How dare you?' said Bevis, snatching at the string, but Mark pushed him back. 'How dare you? you're a prisoner.'

'I'm not,' said Mark very angrily.

'Yes, you are; you were asleep.'

'I don't care.'

'I will tie you up.'

'You shan't.'

'If you sleep at your post, you have to be tied to a tree, you know you have, and be left there to starve.'

'I won't.'

'You must, or till the tigers have you. Do you hear? stand still!'

Bevis tried to secure him, Mark pushed him in turn.

'You're a wretch.'

'I hate you!'

'I'll kill you!'

57

'I'll shoot you!'

Mark darted aside and took his spear; Bevis had his bow in an instant and began to draw it. Mark, knowing that Bevis would shoot his hardest, ran for the second oak. Bevis in his haste pulled hard, but let the arrow slip before he could take aim. It glanced upon a bough and shot up nearly straight into the air, gleaming as it went – a streak of light – in the sunshine. Mark stopped by the oak, and before Bevis could fetch another arrow poised his spear and threw it. The spear flew directly at the enemy, but in his haste Mark forgot to throw high enough, he hurled it point-blank, and the hardened point struck the earth and chipped up crumbling pieces of dry ground; then it slid like a serpent some way through the thin grasses.

Utterly heedless of the spear, which in his rage he never saw, Bevis picked up an arrow from the place where he had slept, fitted the notch to the string and looked for Mark, who had hidden behind the other oak. Guessing that he was there, Bevis ran towards it, when Mark shouted to him:

'Stop! I say, it's not fair; I have nothing, and you'll be a coward.'

Bevis paused, and saw the spear lying on the ground.

'Come and take your spear,' he said directly; 'I won't shoot.' He put his bow on the ground. Mark ran out, and had his spear in a moment. Bevis stooped to lift his bow, but suddenly in his turn cried:

'Stop! Don't throw; I want to say something.'

Mark, who had poised his spear, put it down again on the grass.

'We ought not to fight now,' said Bevis. 'You know we are exploring; people never fight then, else the savages kill those who are left; they wait till they get home, and then fight.'

'So they do,' said Mark; 'but I shall not be left tied to a tree.'

'Very well, not this time. Now we must shake hands.'

They shook hands, and Pan, seeing that there was now no

58

danger of a chance knock from a flying stick, came forth from
the bush where he had taken shelter.

'But you want everything your own way,' said Mark sulk-
ily.

'Of course I do,' said Bevis, glaring at him, 'I'm captain.'

'But you do when you are not captain.'

'You are a big story.'

'I'm not.'

'You are.'

'I'm not.'

'People are not to contradict me,' said Bevis, looking very
defiant indeed, and standing bolt upright. 'I say I am captain.'

Mark did not reply, but picked up his hat, which had fallen
off. Without another word each gathered up his things, then
came the question which way to go? Bevis would not consult
his companion; his companion would not speak first. Bevis shut
his lips very tight, pressing his teeth together; he determined
to continue on and try to get round the New Sea. He was not
sure, but fancied they should do so by keeping somewhat to the
right. He walked to the channel of the stream, sprang across it,
and pushing his way through the hazel bushes, went in that
direction; Mark followed silently, holding his arm up to stop
the boughs, which as Bevis parted them swung back sharply.

After the hazel bushes there was fairly clear walking between the ash-poles and a path, very little used, if at all, and
green, but still a path – a trodden line – and Bevis went along
it, as it seemed to lead in the direction he wished. By the side of
the path he presently found a structure of ash sticks, and
stopped to look at it. At each end four sticks were driven into
the ground, two and two, the tops crossing each other so as to
make a small V. Longer sticks were laid in these V's, and others
across at each end.

'It's a little house,' said Mark, forgetting the quarrel. 'Here's
some of the straw on the ground; they thatch it in winter and
crawl under.' (It was about three feet high.)

'I don't know,' said Bevis.'

'I'm sure it is,' said Mark. 'They are little men, the savages who live here, they're pigmies, you know.'

'So they are,' said Bevis, quite convinced, and likewise forgetting his temper. 'Of course they are, and that's why the path is so narrow. But I believe it's not a house, I mean not a house to live in. It's a place to worship at, where they have a fetish.'

'I think it's a house,' said Mark.

'Then where's the fireplace?' asked Bevis decidedly.

'No more there is a fireplace,' said Mark thoughtfully. 'It's a fetish-place.'

Bevis went on again, leaving the framework behind. Across those bars the barley was thrown in autumn for the pheasants, which feed by darting up and down a single ear at a time; but by keeping the barley off the ground there is less waste. They knew this very well.

'Bevis,' said Mark presently.

'Yes.'

'Let's leave this path.'

'Why?'

'Most likely we shall meet some savages – or perhaps a herd of wild beasts, they rush along these paths in the jungle and crush over everything – perhaps elephants.'

'So they do,' said Bevis, and hastily stepped out of the path into the wood again. They went under more ash-poles where the pigeon's nests were numerous; they counted five all in sight at once, and only a few yards apart, for they could not see far through the boughs. Some of the birds were sitting, others were not. Mark put up his spear and pushed one off her nest. There was a continual fluttering all round them as the pigeons came down to, or left their places. Never had they seen so many nests – they walked about under them for a long time, doing nothing but look up at them and talk about them.

'I know,' said Bevis, 'I know – these savages here think the pigeon's sacred, and don't kill them — that's why there are so many.'

Not much looking where they were going, they came out into a space where the poles had been cut in the winter, and the stoles bore only young shoots a few feet high. There was a single wagon track, the ruts overhung with grasses and bordered with rushes, and at the end of it, where it turned, they saw a cock pheasant. They tried to go through between the stoles, but the thistles were too thick and the brambles and briers too many; they could flourish here till the ash poles grew tall and kept away the sun. So they followed the wagon track, which led them again under the tall poles.

To avoid the savages they kept a very sharp look-out, and paused if they saw anything. There was a huge brown crooked monster lying asleep in one place, they could not determine whether an elephant or some unknown beast, till, creeping nearer from stole to bush and bush to stole, they found it to be a thrown oak, from which the bark had been stripped, and the exposed sap had dried brown in the sun.

'When shall we come to the New Sea again?' said Mark presently, as they were moving more slowly through the thicker growth.

'I cannot think,' said Bevis. 'If we get lost in this jungle, we may walk and walk and never come to anything except banyan trees, and cobras, and tigers, and savages.'

'Are you sure we have been going straight?'

'How do I know?'

'Did you follow the sun?' asked Mark.

'No, indeed, I did not; if you walk towards the sun you will go round and round, because the sun moves.'

'I forgot. Oh! I know, where's the compass?'

'How stupid!' said Bevis. 'Of course it was in my pocket all the time.'

He took it out, and as he lifted the brazen lid the white card swung to and fro with the vibration of his hand.

'Rest your hand against a pole,' said Mark. This support steadied Bevis's hand, and the card gently came to a standstill. The north, with the three feathers point straight at him.

'Now, which way was the sea?' said Mark, trying to think of the direction in which they had last seen it. 'It was that side,' he said, holding out his right hand; he faced Bevis.

'Yes, it was,' said Bevis. 'It was on the right hand, now that would be east, [to Mark], 'so if we go east we might be right.'

He started with the compass in his hand, keeping his eye on it, but then he could not see the stoles or bushes, and walked against them, and the card swung so he could not make a course.

'What a bother it is,' he said, stopping, 'the card won't keep still. Let me see!' He thought a minute, and as he paused the three feathers settled again. 'There's an oak,' he said. 'The oak is just east. Come on.' He went to the oak, and then stopped again.

'I see,' said Mark, watching the card till it stopped. 'The elder bush is east now.'

They went to the elder bush and waited: there was a great thistle east next, and afterwards a bough which had fallen. Thus they worked a bee-line, very slow but almost quite true. The ash-poles rattled now as the breeze freshened and knocked them together.

'What a lot of leaves,' said Bevis presently; 'I never saw such a lot.'

'And they are so deep,' said Mark. They had walked on dead leaves for some little while before they noticed them, being so eagerly engaged with the compass. Now they looked the ground was covered with brown beech leaves, so deep, that although their feet sank into them, they could not feel the firm ground, but walked on a yielding substance. A thousand woodcock might have thrown them over their heads and hidden easily had it been their time of year. The compass led them straight over the leaves, till in a minute or two they saw that

they were in a narrow deep coombe. It became narrower and
with steeper sides till they approached the end, when the chalk
showed not white but dull as it crumbled, the flakes hanging at
the roots of minute plants.

'I don't like these leaves,' said Mark. 'There may be a cobra,
and you can't see him; you may step on him without knowing.'

Hastily he and Bevis scrambled a few feet up the chalky side;
the danger was so obvious they rushed to escape it before
discussing. When they had got over this alarm, they found the
compass still told them to go on, which they could not do
without scaling the coombe. They got up a good way without
much trouble, holding to hazel boughs, for the hazel grows on
the steepest chalk cliffs, but then the chalk was bare of all but
brambles, whose creepers came down towards them; why do
bramble creepers, like water, always come down hill? Under
these the chalk was all crumbled, and gave way under foot, so
that if they put one foot up higher it slipped with their weight,
and returned them to the same level.

Two rabbits rushed away, and were lost beneath the brambles. Without conscious thinking they walked aslant, and so gained a few feet every ten yards, and then came to a spot where the crust of the top hung over, and from it the roots of beech trees came curving down into the hollow space in search of earth. To one of these they clung by turns, some of the loose chalky clods fell on them, but they hauled themselves up over the projecting edge. Bevis went first, and took all the weapons from Mark; Pan went a long way round.

At the summit there was a beautiful beech tree, with an immense round trunk rising straight up, and they sat down on the moss, which always grows at the foot of the beech, to rest after the struggle up. As they sat down they turned round facing the cliff, and both shouted at once:

'The New Sea!'

CHAPTER 7

The Witch

THE blue water had lost its glitter, for they were now between it and the sun, and the freshening breeze, as it swept over, darkened the surface. They were too far to see the waves, but that they were rising was evident since the water no longer reflected the sky like a mirror. The sky was cloudless, but the water seemed in shadow, rough and hard. It was full half a mile or more down to where the wood touched the shore of the New Sea and shut out their view, so that they could not tell how far it extended. Serendib and the Unknown Island were opposite, and they could see the sea all round them from the height where they sat.

'We left the sea behind us,' said Mark. 'The compass took us right away from it.'

'We began wrong somehow,' said Bevis. In fact they had walked in a long curve, so that when they thought the New Sea was on Mark's right, it was really on his left hand. 'I must put down on the map that people must go west, not east, or they will never get round.'

'It must be thousands of miles round,' said Mark; 'thousands and thousands.'

'So it is,' said Bevis, 'and only to think nobody ever saw it before you and me.'

'What a long way we can see,' said Mark, pointing to where the horizon and the blue wooded plain below, beyond the sea, became hazy together. 'What country is that?'

'I do not know; no one has ever been there.'

'Which way is England?' asked Mark.

'How can I tell when I don't know where we are?'

The ash sprays touching each other formed a green surface beneath them, extending to the right and left – a green surface into which every now and then a wood-pigeon plunged, closing his wings as the sea-birds dive into the sea. They sat in the shadow of the great beech, and the wind, coming up over the wood, blew cool against their faces. The swallows had left the sky, to go down and glide over the rising waves below.

'Come on,' said Bevis, incapable of rest unless he was dreaming. 'If we keep along the top of the hill we shall know where we are going and perhaps see a way round presently.'

They followed the edge of the low cliff as nearly as they could, walking under the beeches where it was cool and shady, and the wind blew through. Twice they saw squirrels, but they were too quick, and Bevis could not get a shot with his bow.

'We ought to take home something,' said Mark. 'Something wonderful. There ought to be some pieces of gold about, or a butterfly, as big as a plate. Can't you see something?'

'There's a dragon-fly,' said Bevis. 'If we can't catch him, we can say we saw one made of emerald, and here's a feather.'

He picked up a pheasant's feather. The dragon-fly refused to be caught, he rushed up into the air nearly perpendicularly; and seeing another squirrel some way ahead, they left the dragon-fly and crept from beech trunk to beech trunk towards him.

'It's a red squirrel,' whispered Mark. 'That's a different sort.' In summer the squirrels are thought to have redder fur than in winter. Mark stopped now, and Bevis went on by himself; but the squirrel saw Pan, who had run along and came out beyond him. Bevis shot as the squirrel rushed up a tree, and his arrow struck the bark, quivered a moment, and stuck there.

'The savages will see someone has been hunting,' said Mark. 'They are sure to see that arrow.'

In a few minutes they came to some hazel bushes, and pushing through these there was a lane under them in a hollow ten feet deep. They scrambled down and followed it, and came to a boulder-stone, on which some specks sparkled in the sunshine, so that they had no doubt it was silver ore. Round a curve of the lane they emerged on the brow of a green hill, very steep; they had left the wood behind them. The trees from here hid the New Sea, and in front, not far off, rose the Downs.

'What are those mountains?' asked Mark.

'The Himalayas, of course,' said Bevis. 'Let's go to them.'

They went along the brow. It was delicious walking there, for the sun was now much lower, and the breeze cool, and beneath them were meadows, and a brook winding through. But suddenly they came to a deep coombe – a nullah.

'Look!' said Mark, pointing to a chimney just under them. The square top, blackened by soot, stood in the midst of apple trees, on whose boughs the young green apples showed. The thatch of the cottage was concealed by the trees.

'A hut!' said Bevis.

'Savages!' said Mark. 'I know, I'll pitch a stone down the chimney, and you get your bow ready, and shoot them as they rush out.'

'Capital!' said Bevis. Mark picked up a flint, and 'chucked' it – it fell very near the chimney; they heard it strike the thatch and roll down. Mark got another, and most likely, having found the range, would have dropped it into the chimney this time, when Bevis stopped him.

'It may be a witch,' he said. 'Don't you know what John told us? If you pitch a stone down a witch's chimney it goes off bang! and the stone shoots up into the air like a cannon-ball.'

'I remember,' said Mark. 'But John is a dreadful story. I don't believe it.'

'No, no more do I. Still we ought to be careful. Let's creep down and look first.'

They got down the hillside with difficulty, it was so steep and slippery – the grass being dried by the sun. At the bottom there was a streamlet running along deep in a gully, a little pool of the clearest water to dip from, and a green sparred wicket-gate in a hawthorn hedge about the garden. Peering cautiously through the gate they saw an old woman sitting under the porch beside the open door, with a black teapot on the window-ledge, close by, and a blue teacup, (in which she was soaking a piece of bread), in one hand.

'It's a witch,' whispered Mark. 'There's a black cat by the wallflowers – that's a certain sign.'

'And two sticks with crutch-handles,' said Bevis. 'But just look there.' He pointed to some gooseberry bushes loaded with the swelling fruit, than which there is nothing so pleasant on a warm, thirsty day. They looked at the gooseberries, and thirsted for them; then they looked at the witch.

'Let's run in and pick some, and run out quick,' whispered Mark.

'You stupid; she'd turn us into anything in a minute.'

'Well – shoot her first,' said Mark. 'Take steady aim; John says if you draw their blood they can't do anything. Don't you remember, they stuck the last one with a prong.'

'Horrid cruel,' said Bevis.

'So it was,' said Mark; 'but when you want goose-berries.'

'I wish we had some moly,' said Bevis; 'you know, the plant Ulysses had. Mind before we start next time we must find some. Who knows what fearful magic people we might meet?'

'It was stupid not to think of it,' said Mark. 'Do you know, I believe she's a mummy.'

'Why?'

'She hasn't moved; and I can't see her draw her breath.'

'No more she does. This is a terrible place.'

'Can we get away without her seeing?'

'I believe she knows we're here now, and very likely all we have been saying.'

'Did she make that curious thunder we heard?'

'No; a witch isn't strong enough; it wants an enchanter to do that.'

'But she knows who did it?'

'Of course she does. There, she's moved her arm; she's alive. Aren't those splendid gooseberries?'

'I'll go in,' said Bevis; 'you hold the gate open, so that I can run out.'

'So I will; don't go very near.'

Bevis fitted an arrow to the string, and went up the garden path. But as he came near, and saw how peaceful the old lady looked, he removed the arrow from the string again. She took off her spectacles as he came up; he stopped about ten yards from her.

'Mrs Old Woman, are you a witch?'

'No, I bean't a witch,' said the old lady; 'I wishes I was; I'd soon charm a crock o' gold.'

'Then, if you are not a witch, will you let us have some gooseberries? here's sixpence.'

'You med have some if you wants 'em; I shan't take yer money.'

'What country is this?' said Bevis, going closer as Mark came up beside him

'This be Calais.'

'Granny, don't you know who they be?' said a girl, coming round the corner of the cottage. She was about seventeen, and very pretty with the bloom which comes on sweet faces at that age. Though they were but boys they were tall, and both handsome; so she had put a rose in her bosom. 'They be Measter Bevis and Measter Mark. You know, as lives at Longcot.'

'Aw, to be sure.' The old lady got up and curtsyed. 'You'll come in, won't 'ee?'

They went in and sat down on chairs on the stone floor. The girl brought them a plate of the gooseberries and a jug of spring water. Bevis had not eaten two before he was up and

looking at an old gun in the corner; the barrel was rusty, the brass guard tarnished, the ramrod gone, still it was a gun.

'Will it go off?' he said.

'Feyther used to make un,' said the girl.

Next he found a big black book, and lifted up the covers, and saw a rude engraving of a plant.

'Is that a magic book?' said he.

'I dunno,' she replied. 'Mebbie. Granny used to read un.'

It was an old herbal.

'Can't you read?' said Bevis.

The girl blushed and turned away.

'A' be a lazy wench,' said the old woman. 'A' can't read a mossel.'

'I bean't lazy.'

'You be.'

Bevis, quite indifferent to that question, was peering into every nook and corner, but found nothing more.

'Let's go,' said he directly.

Mark would not stir till he had finished the gooseberries.

'Tell me the way round the – the – ' he was going to say 'sea', but recollected that they would not be able to understand how he and Mark were on an expedition, nor would he say pond – 'round the water', he said.

'The Longpond?' said the girl. 'You can't go round there's the marsh – not unless you goes back to Wood Lane and nigh handy your place.'

'Which way did 'ee come?' asked the old woman.

'They come through the wood,' said the girl. 'I seen um; and they had the spannul.'

She was stroking Pan, who loved her, as she had fed him with a bone. She knew the enormity of taking a strange dog through a wood in the breeding-season.

'How be um going to get whoam?' said the old woman.

'We're going to walk, of course,' said Bevis.

'It's four miles.'

'Pooh! We've come thousands. Come on, Mark; we'll get round somehow.'

But the girl convinced him after a time that it was not possible, because of the marsh and the brook, and showed him too how the shadows of the elms were lengthening in the meadow outside the garden at the foot of the hill. Bevis reluctantly decided that they must abandon the expedition for that day, and return home. The girl offered to show them the way into the road. She led them by a narrow path beside the streamlet in the gully, and then along the steep side of the hill, where there were three or four more cottages, all built on the slope, steep as it was. The path in front of the doors had a kind of breastwork, that folk might not inadvertently tumble over and roll – if not quite sober – into the gully, beneath. Yet there were small gardens behind, which almost stood up on end, the vegetables appearing over the roofs.

Upon the breastwork or mound they had planted a few flowers, all yellow, or yellow-tinged, marigolds, sunflowers, wallflowers, a stray tulip, the gaudiest they knew.

Six or eight children were about. One sat crying in the midst of the path, so unconscious under the wrong he had endured as not to see them, and they had to step right over his red head. Some stared at them with unchecked rudeness; one or two curtsied or tugged at the forelocks. The happiest of all was sitting on the breastwork (of dry earth) eating a small turnip from which he had cut the dirt and rind with a rusty table-knife. As they passed he grinned and pushed the turnip in their faces, as much as to say. 'Have a bite.' Two or three women looked out after they had gone by, and then some one cried, 'Baa!' making a noise like a sheep, at which the girl who led them flushed up, and walked very quickly, with scorn and rage and hatred flashing in her eye. It was a taunt. Her father was in jail for lamb-stealing. Her name was Aholibah, and they taunted her by dwelling on the last syllable.

The path went to the top of the hill, and round under a red

barn, and now they could see the village, of which these detached cottages were an outpost, scattered over the slope, and on the plain on the other side of the coombe, a quarter of a mile distant.

'There's the windmill,' said the girl, pointing to the tower-like building. 'You go tow-ward he. He be on the road. Then you turn to the right till you comes to the handing-post. Then you go to the left, and that's take 'ee straight whoam.'

'Thank you,' said Bevis. 'I know now; it's not far to Big Jack's house. Please have this sixpence,' and he gave her the coin, which he had unconsciously held in his hand ever since he had taken it out to pay for the gooseberries. It was all he had; he could not keep his money.

She took it, but her eyes were on him, and not on the money; she would have liked to have kissed him. She watched them till she saw they had got into the straight road, and then went back, but not past the cottages.

They found the road very long, very long and dull, and dusty and empty, except that there was a young labourer – a huge fellow – lying across a flint heap asleep, his mouth open and the flies thick on his forehead. Bevis pulled a spray from the hedge and laid it gently across his face. Except for the sleeping labourer, the road was vacant, and every step they took they went slower and slower. There were no lions here, or monstrous pythons, or anything magic.

'We shall never get home,' said Mark.

'I don't believe we ever shall,' said Bevis; 'I hate this road.'

While they yawned and kicked at stray flints, or pelted the sparrows on the hedge, a dog-cart came swiftly up behind them. It ran swift and smooth and even-balanced, the slender shafts bending slightly like the spars of a yacht.

It was drawn by a beautiful chestnut mare, too powerful by far for many, which struck out with her fore feet as if measuring space and carrying the car of a god in the sky, throwing her feet as if there were no road but elastic air beneath them. The man was very tall and broad and sat upright – a wonderful thing in a countryman. His head was broad like himself, his eyes blue, and he had a long thick yellowy beard. The reins were strained taut like a yacht's cordage, but the mare was in the hollow of his strong hand.

They did not hear the hoofs till he was close, for they were on a flint heap, searching for the best to throw.

'It's Jack,' said Mark.

Jack looked them very hard in the face, but it did not seem to dawn upon him who they were till he had gone past a hundred yards, then he pulled up and beckoned. He said nothing, but tapped the seat beside him. Bevis climbed up in front, Mark knelt on the seat behind – so as to look in the direction they were going. They drove two miles and Jack said nothing, then he spoke:

'Where have you been?'

'To Calais.'

'Bad – bad,' said Jack. 'Don't go there again.' At the turnpike it took him three minutes to find enough to pay the toll. He had a divine mare, his harness, his cart were each perfect. Yet for all his broad shoulders he could barely muster up a groat. He pulled up presently when there were but two fields between them and the house at Longcot; he wanted to go down the lane, and they alighted to walk across the fields. After they had got down and were just turning to mount the gate, and the mare obeying the reins had likewise half turned, Jack said:

'Hum!'

'Yes,' said Mark from the top bar.

'How are they all at home?' i.e. at Mark's.

'Quite well,' said Mark.

'All?' said Jack again.

'Frances bruised her arm – '

'Much?' anxiously.

'You can't see it – her skin's like a plum,' said Mark; 'if you just pinch it it shows.'

74

'Hum!' and Jack was gone.

Late in the evening they tried hard to catch the donkey, that Mark might ride home. It was not far, but now the day was over he was very tired, so too was Bevis. Tired as they were, they chased the donkey up and down – six times as far as it was to Mark's house – but in vain, the moke knew them of old, and was not to be charmed or cowed. He showed them his heels, and they failed. So Mark stopped and slept with Bevis, as he had done so many times before. As they lay awake in the bed-room, looking out of the window opposite at a star, half awake and half asleep, suddenly Bevis started up on his arm.

'Let's have a war,' he said.

'That would be first-rate,' said Mark, 'and have a great battle.'

'An awful battle,' said Bevis, 'the biggest and most awful ever known.'

'Like Waterloo?'

'Pooh!'

'Agincourt?'

'Pooh!'

'Mal – Mal,' said Mark, trying to think of Malplaquet.

'Oh! more than anything,' said Bevis; 'somebody will have to write a history about it.'

'Shall we wear armour?'

'That would be bow and arrow time. Bows and arrows don't make any banging.'

'No more they do. It wants lots of banging and smoke – else it's nothing.'

'No; only chopping and sticking.'

'And smashing and yelling.'

'No – and that's nothing.'

'Only if we have rifles,' said Mark thoughtfully; 'you see, people don't see one another; they are so far off, and nobody stands on a bridge and keeps back all the enemy all by him-self.'

'And nobody has a triumph afterwards with elephants and chariots, and paints his face vermilion.'

'Let's have bow and arrow time,' said Mark; 'it's much nicer – and you sell the prisoners for slaves and get heaps of money, and do just as you like, and plough up the cities that don't please you.'

'Much nicer,' said Bevis; 'you very often kill all the lot and there's nothing silly. I shall be King Richard and have a battle-axe – no, let's be the Normans.'

'Wouldn't King Arthur do?'

'No; he was killed, that would be stupid. I've a great mind to be Charlemagne.'

'Then I shall be Roland.'

'No; you must be a traitor.'

'But I want to fight your side,' said Mark.

'How many are there we can get to make the war?'

They consulted, and soon reckoned up fourteen or fifteen.

'It will be jolly awful,' said Mark; 'there will be heaps of slain.'

'Let's have Troy,' said Bevis.

'That's too slow,' said Mark; 'it lasted ten years.'

'Alexander the Great – let's see; whom did he fight?'

'I don't know; people nobody ever heard of – nobody particular, Indians and Persians and all that sort.'

'I know,' said Bevis; 'of course! I know. Of course I shall be Julius Caesar!'

'And I shall be Mark Antony.'

'And we will fight Pompey.'

'But who shall be Pompey?' said Mark.

'Pooh! there's Bill, and Wat, and Ted; anybody will do for Pompey.'

CHAPTER 8

Savages

WHEN Bevis's papa found that they could not be kept from roaming, and were bent on boating on the Longpond, which was a very different matter from the shallow brook, where they were never far from shore, and out of which they could scramble, he determined to teach Bevis and his friend to swim. They had begged very hard to be allowed to have one of the boats in order to circumnavigate the New Sea, which it was so difficult to walk round; and he promised them if they would really try to swim, that they should have the boat as a reward.

The very first morning they took a leaping-pole with them, a slender ash sapling, rather more than twice their own height, which they picked out from a number in the rick-yard, intending to jump to and fro the brook on the way. But before they had got half-way to the brook they altered their minds, becoming eager for the water, and raced to the bathing-place. The pole was now to be an oar, and they were to swim, supported by an oar, like shipwrecked people.

Soon as he had had a plunge or two, Bevis put one arm over the pole and struck out with the other, thinking that he should be able in that way to have a long swim. Directly his weight pressed on the pole it went under, and did not support him in the least. He put it next beneath his chest, with both arms over it, but immediately he pushed off down it went again. Mark took it and got astride, when the pole let his feet touch bottom.

'It's no use,' he said. 'What's the good of people falling overboard with spars and oars? What stories they must tell.'

'I can't make it out,' said Bevis; and he tried again, but it was no good, the pole was an encumbrance instead of a support, for it insisted upon slipping through the water lengthways, and would not move just as he wished. In a rage he gave it a push, and sent it ashore, and turned to swimming to the rail. They did not know it, but the governor, still anxious about them, had gone round a long distance, so as to have a peep at them from the hedge on the other side of Fir-Tree Gulf by the Nile. He could tell by the post and rails that they did not go out of their depth, and went away without letting them suspect his presence.

When they got out, they had a run in the sunshine, which dried them much better than towels. The field sloped gently to the right, and their usual run was on the slope beside a nut-tree hedge towards a group of elms. All the way there and back the sward was short and soft, almost like that of the Downs, which they could see, and dotted with bird's-foot lotus, over whose yellow flowers they raced. But this morning, after they had returned from the elms with an enormous mushroom they had found there, they ran to the old quarry, and along the edge above. The perpendicular sandcliff fell to an enclosed pool beneath, in which, on going to the very edge, they could see themselves reflected. Some hurdles and flakes – a stronger kind of hurdle – had been placed here that cattle might not wander over, but the cart-horses, who rub against everything, had rubbed against them and dislodged two or three. These had rolled down, and the rest hung half over.

While they stood still looking down over the broad waters of their New Sea, the sun burned their shoulders, making the skin red. Away they ran back to dress, and taking a short path across a place where the turf had partly grown over a shallow excavation pricked their feet with thistles, and had to limp the rest of the way to their clothes. Now, there were no thistles on their proper race-course down to the elms and back.

As they returned home they remembered the brook, and

went down to it to jump with the leaping-pole. But the soft ooze at the bottom let the pole sink in, and Bevis, who of course must take the first leap, was very near being hung up in the middle of the brook. Under his weight, as he sprang off, the pole sank deep into the ooze, and had it been a stiffer mud the pole would have stopped upright, when he must have stayed on it over the water, or have been jerked off among the flags. As it was it did let him get over, but he did not land on the firm bank, only reaching the mud at the side, where he scrambled up by grasping the stout stalk of a willow-herb. In future he felt with the butt of the pole till he found a firm spot, where it was sandy, or where the matted roots of grasses and flags had bound the mud hard. Then he flew over well up on the grass.

Mark took his turn, and as he put the butt in the water a streak of mud came up where a small jack-fish had shot away. So they went on down the bank leaping alternately, one carrying the towels while the other flew over and back.

'Here's the raft!' shouted Mark, who was ahead, looking out for a good place.

'Is it?' said Bevis, running along the other side. They had so completely forgotten it, that it came upon them like something new. Bevis took a leap and came over, and they set to work at once to launch it. The raft slipped gradually down the shelving shore of the drinking-place, and they thrust it into the stream. Bevis put his foot on board, but immediately withdrew it, for the water rushed through twenty leaks spurting up along the joins. Left on the sand in the sun's rays the wood of the raft shrank a little, opening the planking, while the clay they had daubed on to caulk the crevices had cracked, and the moss had dried up and was ready to crumble. The water came through everywhere, and the raft was half-full even when left to itself without any pressure.

'We ought to have thatched it,' said Mark. 'We ought to have made a roof over it. Let's stop the leaks.'

'Oh, come on,' said Bevis, 'don't let's bother. Rafts are no good, no more than poles or oars when you fall overboard. We shall have a ship soon.'

The raft was an old story, and he did not care about it. He went on with the leaping-pole, but Mark stayed a minute and hauled the raft on shore as far as his strength would permit. He got about a quarter of it on the ground, so that it could not float away, and then ran after Bevis.

They went into the Peninsula, and looked at all the fir trees, to see if any would do for the mast for the blue-boat they were to have. As it had no name, they called it the blue boat to distinguish it from the punt. Mark thought an ash-pole would do for the mast, as ash-poles were so straight and could be easily shaved to the right size; but Bevis would not hear of it, for masts were never made of ash, but always of pine, and they must have their ship proper. He selected a tree presently, a young fir, straight as an arrow, and started Mark for the axe, but before he had gone ten yards Mark came back, saying that the tree would be of no use unless they liked to wait till next year, because it would be green, and the mast ought to be made of seasoned wood.

'So it ought,' said Bevis. 'What a lot of trouble it is to make a ship.'

But as they sat on the railing across the isthmus swinging their legs, Mark remembered that there were some fir-poles which had been cut a long time since behind the great wood-pile, between it and the walnut trees, out of sight. Without a word away they ran, chose one of these and carried it into the shed where Bevis usually worked. They had got the dead bark off and were shaving away when it was dinner-time, which they thought a bore, but which wise old Pan, who was never chained now, considered the main object of life.

Next morning as they went through the meadow, where the dew still lingered in the shade, on the way to the bathing-place, taking Pan with them this time, they hung about the path picking clover-heads and sucking the petals, pulling them out and putting the lesser ends in their lips, looking at the white and pink bramble flowers, noting where the young nuts began to show, pulling down the woodbine, and doing everything but hasten on to their work of swimming. They stopped at the gate by the New Sea, over whose smooth surface slight breaths of mist were curling, and stood kicking the ground and the stones as flighty horses paw.

'We ought to be something,' said Mark discontentedly.

'Of course we ought,' said Bevis. 'Things are very stupid unless you are something.'

'Lions and tigers,' said Mark, growling, and showing his teeth.

'Pooh!'

'Shipwrecked people on an island.'

'Fiddle! They have plenty to do and are always happy, and we are not.'

'No; very unhappy. Let's try escaping – prisoners running away.'

'Hum! Hateful!'

'Everything's hateful.'

'So it is.'

'This is a very stupid sea.'

'There's nothing in it.'

'Nothing anywhere.'

'Let's be hermits.'

'There's always only one hermit.'

'Well, you live that side' (pointing across), 'and I'll live this.'

'Hermits eat pulse and drink water.'

'What's pulse?'

'I suppose it's barley-water.'

'Horrid.'

'Awful.'

'You say what we shall be then.'

'Pan, you old donk,' said Bevis, rolling Pan over with his

foot. Lazy Pan lay on his back, and let Bevis bend his ribs with his foot.

'Caw, caw!' a crow went over the down to the shore, where he hoped to find a mussel surprised by the dawn in shallow water.

Bang! 'Hoi! Hoi! Yah!' The discharge was half a mile away, but the crow altered his mind, and flew over the water as near the surface as he could without touching. Why do birds always cross the water in that way?

'That's Tom,' said Mark. Tom was the bird-keeper. He shot first, and shouted after. He potted a hare in the corn with bits of flint, a button, three tin-tacks, and a horse-stub, which scraped the old barrel inside, but slew the game. That was for himself. Then he shouted his loudest to do his duty – for other people. The sparrows had flown out of the corn at the noise of the gun, and settled on the hedge; when Tom shouted they were frightened from the hedge, and went back into the wheat. From which learn this, shoot first and shout after.

'Shall we say that was a gun at sea?' continued Mark.

'They are always heard at night,' said Bevis. 'Pitch black, you know.'

'Everything is somehow else,' said Mark.

Pan closed his idle old eyes, and grunted with delight as Bevis rubbed his ribs with his foot. Bevis put his hands in his pockets and sighed deeply. The sun looked down on these sons of care, and all the morning beamed.

'Savages!' shouted Mark, kicking the gate to with a slam that startled Pan up. 'Savages, of course!'

'Why?'

'They swim, donk: don't they? They're always in water, and they have catamarans and ride the waves and dance on the shore, and blow shells – '

'Trumpets?'

'Yes.'

'Canoes?'

'Yes.'

'No clothes?'

'No.'

'All jolly?'

'Everything.'

'Hurrah!'

Away they ran towards the bathing-place to be savages, but Mark stopped suddenly, and asked what sort they were? They decided that they were the South Sea sort, and raced on again, Pan keeping pace with a kind of shamble; he was too idle to run properly. They dashed into the water, each with a wood pigeon's feather (which they had found under the sycamore-trees above the quarry) stuck in his hair. At the first dive the feathers floated away. Upon the other side of the rails there was a large aspen-tree whose lowest bough reached out over the water, which was shallow there.

Though they made such a splashing, when Bevis looked over

the railings a moment, he saw some little roach moving to and fro under the bough. The wavelets from his splashing rolled on to the sandy shore, rippling under the aspen. As he looked, a fly fell on its back out of the tree, and struggled in vain to get up. Bevis climbed over the rails, picked an aspen leaf, and put it under the fly, which was thus on a raft, and tossed up and down as Mark dived, was floated slowly by the undulations to the strand. As he got over the rails a kingfisher shot out from the mouth of the Nile opposite, and crossed aslant the gulf, whistling as he flew.

'Look!' said Mark. 'Don't you know that's a sign. Savages read signs, and those birds mean that there are heaps of fish.'

'Yes, but we ought to have a proper language.'

'Kalabala-blong!' said Mark.

'Hududu-blow-fluz!' replied Bevis.

'Ikiklikah,' and Mark disappeared.

'Noklikah,' said Bevis, giving him a shove under as he came up to breathe.

'That's not fair,' said Mark, scrambling up.

More splashing and shouting, and the rocks resounded. The echo of their voices returned from the quarry and the high bank under the firs.

As they went homewards they walked round to the little sheltered bay where the boats were kept, to look at the blue boat and measure for the mast. It was beside the punt, half drawn up on the sand, and fastened to a willow root. She was an ill-built craft with a straight gunwale, so that when afloat she seemed lower at stem and stern than abeam, as if she would thrust her nose into a wave instead of riding it. The planks were thick and heavy and looked as if they had not been bent enough to form the true buoyant curve.

The blue paint had scaled and faded, the rowlocks were mended with a piece cut from an old rake-handle, there was a small pool of bilge-water in the stern-sheets from the last shower, full of dead insects, and yellow willow leaves. A clumsy vessel put together years ago in some by-water of the far distant Thames above Oxford, and not good enough even for that unknown creek. She had drifted somehow into this landlocked pond and remained unused, hauled on the strand beneath the willows; she could carry five or six, and if they bumped her well on the stones it mattered little to so stout a frame.

Still she was a boat, with keel and curve, and like lovers they saw no defect. Bevis looked at the hole in the seat or thwart, where the mast would have to be stepped, and measured it (not having a rule with him) by cutting a twig just to the length of the diameter. Mark examined the rudder and found that the lines were rotten, having hung dangling over the stern in the water for so long. Next they stepped her length, stepping on the sand outside, to decide on the height of the mast, and where the ropes were to be fastened, for they meant to have some standing rigging.

At home afterwards in the shed, while Bevis shaved the fir-pole for the mast, Mark was set to carve the leaping-pole, for the South Sea savages have everything carved. He could hardly cut the hard dried bark of the ash, which had shrunk on and become like wood. He made a spiral notch round it, and then searched till he found his old spear, which had to be ornamented and altered into a bone harpoon. A bone from the kitchen was sawn off while in the vice, and then half through two inches from the largest end. Tapping a broad chisel gently, Mark split the bone down to the sawn part, and then gradually filed it sharp. He also filed three barbs to it, and then fitted the staff of the spear into the hollow end. While he was engraving lines and rings on the spear with his pocket-knife, the dinner interrupted his work.

Bevis, wearying of the mast, got some flints, and hammered them to split off flakes for arrowheads, but though he bruised his fingers, he could not chip the splinters into shape. The fracture always ran too far, or not far enough. John Young, the labourer, came by as he was doing this sitting on the stool in the shed, and watched him.

'I see a man do that once,' said John.

'How did he do it? Tell me: what's the trick?' said Bevis, impatient to know.

'Aw, I dunno; I see him at it. A' had a gate-hinge snopping um.'

The iron hinge of a gate, if removed from the post, forms a fairly good hammer, the handle of iron as well as the head.

'Where was it? what did he do it for?'

'Aw, up in the downs. Course he did it to sell um.'

Bevis battered his flints till he was tired; then he took up the last and hurled it away in a rage with all his might. The flint whirled over and over and hummed along the ground till it struck a small sarsen or boulder by the wood-pile, put there as a spurstone to force the careless carters to drive straight. Then it flew into splinters with the jerk of the stoppage.

'Here's a sharp 'un,' said John Young, picking up a flake, 'and here's another.'

Altogether there were three pointed flakes which Bevis thought would do. Mark had to bring some reeds next day from the place where they grew, half a mile below his house in a by water of the brook. They were green, but Bevis could not wait to dry them. He cut them off a little above the knot or joint, split the part above, and put the flint flake in, and bound it round and round with horsehair from the carter's store in the stable. But when they were finished, they were not shot off, lest they should break; they were carried indoors into the room upstairs where there was a bench, and which they made their armoury.

They made four or five darts next of deal shaved to the thickness of a thin walking-stick, and not quite so long. One end was split in four – once down and across that – and two pieces of cardboard doubled up thrust in, answering the purpose of feathering. There was a slight notch two-thirds up the shaft, and the way was to twist a piece of twine round it there crossed over a knot so as just to hold, the other end of the twine firmly coiled about the wrist, so that in throwing the string was taut and the point of the dart between the fingers. Hurling it, the string imparted a second force, and the dart, twirling like an arrow, flew fifty or sixty yards.

Slings they made with a square of leather from the sides of old shoes, a small hole cut out in the centre that the stone might not slip, but these they could never do much with, except hurl pebbles from the rick-yard, rattling up into the boughs of the oak, on the other side of the field. The real arrows to shoot with – not the reed arrows to look at – were tipped with iron nails filed to a sharp point. They had much trouble in feathering them; they had plenty of goose feathers (saved from the Christmas plucking), but to glue them properly was not easy.

CHAPTER 9

The Catamaran

WITH all their efforts, they could not make a blow-tube, such as is used by savages. Bevis thought and thought, and Mark helped him, and Pan grabbed his fleas, all together in the round blue summer-house; and they ate a thousand strawberries, and a basketful of red currants, ripe, from the wall close by, and two young summer apples, far from ready, and yet they could not do it. The tube ought to be at least as long as the savage, using it, was tall. They could easily find sticks that were just the thickness, and straight, but the difficulty was to bore them through. No gimlet or auger was long enough; nor could they do it with a bar of iron, red-hot, at the end: they could not keep it true, but always burned too much one side or the other.

Perhaps it might be managed by inserting a short piece of tin tubing, and making a little fire in it, and gradually pushing it down as the fire burnt. Only, as Bevis pointed out, the fire would not live in such a narrow place without any draught. A short tube was easily made out of elder, but not nearly long enough. The tinker, coming round to mend the pots, put it into their heads to set him to make a tin blow-pipe, five feet in length; which he promised to do, and sent it in a day or two. But as he had no sheet of tin broad enough to roll the tube in one piece, he had made four short pipes and soldered them together. Nothing would go straight through it because the joints were not quite perfect: inside there was a roughness which caught the dart and obstructed the puff, for a good blow-tube must be as smooth and well bored as a gun-barrel.

When they came to look over their weapons, they found they had not got any throw-sticks, nor a boomerang. Throw-sticks were soon made by cutting some with a good thick knob; and a boomerang was made out of a curved branch of ash, which they planed down smooth one side, and cut to a slight arch on the other.

'This is a capital boomerang,' said Bevis. 'Now we shall be able to knock a rabbit over without any noise, or frightening the rest, and it will come back and we can kill three or four running.'

'Yes, and one of the mallards,' said Mark. 'Don't you know? – they are always too far for an arrow, and besides, the arrow would be lost if it did not hit. Now we shall have them. But which way ought we to throw it – the hollow first, or the bend first?'

'Let's try,' said Bevis, and ran with boomerang from the shed into the field.

Whiz! Away it went, bend first, and rose against the wind till the impetus ceased, when it hung for a moment on the air, and slid to the right, falling near the summer-house. Next time it turned to the left, and fell in the hedge; another time it hit the hay-rick: nothing could make it go straight. Mark tried his hardest, and used it both ways, but in vain – the boomerang rose against the wind, and, so far, acted properly, but directly the force with which it was thrown was exhausted, it did as it liked, and swept round to the left or the right, and never once returned to their feet.

'A boomerang is a stupid thing,' said Bevis, 'I shall chop it up. I hate it.'

'No; put it upstairs,' said Mark, taking it from him. So the boomerang was added to the collection in the bench-room. A crossbow was the next thing, and they made the stock from a stout elder branch, because when the pith was taken out, it left a groove for the bolt to slide up. The bow was a thick brier, and the bolt flew thirty or forty yards, but it did not answer, and they could hit nothing with it. A crossbow requires delicate adjustment, and, to act well, must be made almost as accurately as a rifle.

They shot a hundred times at the sparrows on the roof, who were no sooner driven off than they came back like flies, but never hit one; so the crossbow was hung up with the boomerang. Bevis, from much practice, could shoot far better than that with his bow and arrow. He stuck up an apple on a stick, and after six or seven trials hit it at twenty yards. He could always hit a tree. Mark was afraid to throw his bone-headed harpoon at a tree, lest the head should break off; but he had another, without a bone head, to cast; and he too could generally hit a tree.

'Now we are quite savages,' said Bevis, one evening, as they sat up in the bench room, and the sun went down red and fiery, opposite the little window, filling the room with a red glow and gleaming on their faces. It put a touch of colour on the pears, which were growing large, just outside the window, as if they were ripe towards the sunset. The boomerang on the wall was lit up with the light; so was a parcel of canvas on the floor, which they had bought at Latten town, for the sails of their ship.

There was an oyster barrel under the bench, which was to contain the fresh water for their voyage, and there had been much discussion as to how they were to put a new head to it.

'We ought to see ourselves on the shore with spears and things when we are sailing round,' said Mark.

'So as not to be able to land for fear.'

'Poisoned arrows,' said Mark. 'I say, how stupid! we have not got any poison.'

'No more we have. We must get a lot of poison.'

'Curious plants nobody knows anything about but us.'

'Nobody ever heard of them.'

'And dip our arrows and spears in the juice.'

'No one ever gets well after being shot with them.'

'If the wind blows hard ashore and there are no harbours it will be awful with the savages all along waiting for us.'

'We shall see them dancing and shouting with bows and throw-sticks, and yelling.'

'That's you and me.'

'Of course. And very likely if the wind is very hard we shall have to let down the sails, and fling out an anchor and stay till the gale goes down.'

'The anchor may drag.'

'Then we shall crash on the rocks.'

'And swim ashore.'

'You can't. There's the breakers and the savages behind them. I shall stop on the wreck, and the sun will go down.'

'Red like that,' pointing out of window.

'And it will blow harder still.'

'Black as pitch.'

'Horrible.'

'No help.'

'Fire a gun.'

'Pooh!'

'Make a raft.'

'The clouds are sure to break, or something.'

'I say,' said Bevis, 'won't all these things' – pointing to the weapons – 'do first-rate for our war?'

'Capital. There will be arrows sticking up everywhere all over the battle-field.'

'Broken lances and horses without riders.'

'Dints in the ground.'

'Knights with their backs against trees and heaps of soldiers chopping at them.'

'Flashing swords! the ground will shake when we charge.'

'Trumpets!'

'Groans!'

'Grass all red!'

'Blood-red sun like that!' The disk growing larger as it

neared the horizon shone vast through some distant elms.

'Flocks of crows.'

'Heaps of white bones.'

'And we will take the shovels and make a tumulus by the shore.'

The red glow on the wall dimmed slowly, the colour left the pear, and the song of a thrush came from the orchard.

'I want to make some magic,' said Bevis, after a pause. 'The thing is to make a wand.'

'Genii are best,' said Mark. 'They do anything you tell them.'

'There ought to be a black book telling you how to do it somewhere,' said Bevis; 'but I've looked through the bookcase and there's nothing.'

'Are you sure you have quite looked through!'

'I'll try again,' said Bevis. 'There's a lot of books, but never anything that you want.'

'I know,' said Mark suddenly. 'There's the bugle in the old cupboard – that will do for the war.'

'So it will; I forgot it.'

'And a flag.'

'No; we must have eagles on a stick.'

Knock! They jumped; Polly had hit the ceiling underneath with the handle of a broom.

'Supper.'

When they went to bathe next morning, Bevis took with him his bow and arrows, intending to shoot a pike. As they walked beside the shore they often saw jack basking in the sun at the surface of the water, and only a few yards distant. He had fastened a long thin string one end to the arrow and the other to the bow, so that he might draw the arrow back to him with the fish on as the savages do. Mark brought his bone-headed harpoon to try and spear something, and between them they also carried a plank, which was to be used as catamaran.

A paddle they had made was tied to it for convenience, that

their hands might not be too full. Mark went first with one end
of the plank on his shoulder, and Bevis followed with the other
on his, and as they had to hold it on edge it rather cut them.
Coming near some weeds where they had had seen a jack the
day before, they put the catamaran down, and Bevis crept
quietly forward. The jack was not there, but motioning to Mark
to stand still, Bevis went on to where the first railings stretched
out into the water.

There he saw a jack about two pounds weight basking within
an inch of the surface, and aslant to him. He lifted his bow
before he went near, shook out the string that it might slip
easily like the coil of a harpoon, fitted the arrow, and holding it
almost up, stole closer. He knew if he pulled the bow in the
usual manner the sudden motion of his arms would send the
jack away in an instant. With the bow already in position, he
got within six yards of the fish, which, quite still, did not seem
to see anything, but to sleep with eyes wide open in the sun.
The shaft flew, and like another arrow the jack darted aslant
into deep water.

Bevis drew back his arrow with the string, not altogether
disappointed, for it had struck the water very near if not
exactly at the place the fish had occupied. But he thought the
string impeded the shaft, and took it off for another trial. Mark
would not stay behind; he insisted upon seeing the shooting, so
leaving the catamaran on the grass, they moved gently along
the shore. After a while they found another jack, this time
much larger, and not less than four pounds weight, stationary,
in a tiny bay, or curve of the land. He was lying parallel to the
shore, but deeper than the first, perhaps six inches beneath
the surface. Mark stood where he could see the dark line of the
fish, while Bevis, with the bow lifted and an arrow half-drawn,
took one, two, three, and almost another step forward.

Aiming steadily at the jack's broad side, just behind the
front fins, where the fish was widest, Bevis grasped his bow
firm to keep it from the least wavering (for it is the left hand

that shoots), drew his arrow, and let go. So swift was the shaft, unimpeded, and drawn too this time almost to the head, in traversing the short distance between, that the jack, quick as he was, could not of himself have escaped. Bevis saw the arrow enter the water, and, as it seemed to him, strike the fish. It did indeed strike the image of the fish, but the real jack slipped beneath it.

Bevis looked and looked, he was so certain he had hit it, and so he had hit the mark he aimed at, which was the refraction, but the fish was unhurt. It was explained to him afterwards that the fish appears higher in the water than it actually is, and that to have hit it he should have aimed two inches underneath, and he proved the truth of it by trying to touch things in the water with a long stick. The arrow glanced after going two feet or so deep, and performed a curve in the water exactly opposite to that it would have traced in the air. In the air it would have curved over, in the water it curved under, and came up to the surface not very far out; the water checked it so. Bevis fastened the string again to another arrow, and shot it out over the first, so that it caught and held it, and he drew them both back.

They fetched the catamaran, and went on till they came to the point where there was a wall of stones rudely put together to shield the land from the full shock of the waves.

They marched on, and presently launched the catamaran. It would only support one at a time astride and half in the water, but it was a capital thing. Sitting on it, Bevis paddled along the shore nearly to the rocky wall and back, but he did not forget his promise, and was not out of his depth; he could see the stones at the bottom all the time. Mark tried to stand on the plank, but one edge would go down and pitch him off. He next tried to lie on it on his back, and succeeded so long as he let his legs dangle over each side, and so balanced it. Then they stood away, and swam to it as if it had been the last plank of a wreck.

'Look!' said Mark, after they had done this several times. He was holding the plank at arm's length with his limbs floating. 'Look!'

'I see. What is it?'

'This is the way. We ought to have held the jumping-pole like this. This is the way to hold an oar and swim.'

'So it is,' said Bevis, 'of course, that's it; we'll have the punt, and try with a scull.'

Held at arm's length, almost anything will keep a swimmer afloat; but if he puts it under his arms or chest, it takes a good-sized spar. Splashing about, presently the plank, forgotten for the moment, slipped away, and, impelled by the waves they made, floated into deep water.

'I'm sure I could swim to it,' said Bevis, and he was inclined to try.

'We promised not,' said Mark.

'You stupe – I know that; but if there's a plank, that's not dangerous then.' 'Stupe' was their word for stupid. He waded out till the water was over his shoulders, and tried to lift him.

'Don't – don't,' said Mark. Bevis began to lean his chest on the water.

'If you're captain,' cried Mark, 'you ought not to.'

'No more I ought,' said Bevis, coming back. 'Get my bow.'

'What for?'

'Go and get my bow.'

'I shan't, if you say it like that.'

'You shall. Am I not captain?'

Mark was caught by his own argument, and went out on the sward for the bow.

'Tie the arrow on with the string,' shouted Bevis. Mark did it, and brought it in, keeping it above the surface. Bevis climbed on the railings, half out of water, so that he could steady himself with his knees against the rail.

'Now, give me the bow,' he said. He took good aim and the

nail, filed to a sharp point, was driven deep into the soft deal of the plank. With the string he hauled the catamaran gently back, but it would not come straight; it slipped sideways (like the boomerang in the air) and came ashore under the aspen bough.

When they came out they bathed again in the air and the sunshine; they rolled on the sward, and ran. Bevis, as he ran and shouted, shot off an arrow, with all his might to see how far it would go. It went up, up, and curving over, struck a bough at the top of one of the elms, and stopped there by the rooks' nests. Mark shouted and danced on the bird's-root lotus, and darted his spear heedless of the bone head. It went up into the hazel boughs of the hedge among the young nuts, and he could not get it till dressed, for the thistles.

After they had dressed they took the catamaran to the quarry to leave it there (somewhat out of sight lest anyone should take it for firewood), so as to save the labour of carrying it to and fro. There was a savage of another tribe in the quarry, and they crept on all fours, taking great pains that he should not see them. It was the old man who was supposed to look after the boats, and generally to watch the water. Had they not been so occupied they would have heard the thump, thump of the sculls as he rowed, or rather moved the punt up to where the narrow mound separated the New Sea from the quarry.

He was at work scooping out some sand, and filling sacks with the best, with which cargo he would presently voyage home, and retail it to the dairymaids and at the roadside inns to eke out that spirit of juniper-berries needful to those who have dwelt long by marshy places. They need not have troubled to conceal themselves from this stranger savage. He would not have seen them if they had stood close by him. A narrow life narrows the sweep of the eye. Miserable being, he could see no farther than one of the mussels of the lake, which travel in a groove. His groove led to the sanded inn-kitchen, and his shell was shut to all else. But they crept like skirmishers, dragging the catamaran laboriously behind them, using every undulation of the ground to hide themselves, till they had got it into the hollow, where they left it beside a heap of stones. Then they had to crawl out again, and for thirty yards along the turf, till they could stand up unseen.

'Let's get the poison,' said Mark, as they were going home.

So they searched for the poison-plants. The woody nightshade they knew very well, having been warned long ago against the berries. It was now only in flower, and it would be some time before there were any berries; but after thinking it over they decided to gather a bundle of stalks, and soak them for the deadly juice. There were stems of arum in the ditches, tipped with green berries. These they thought would do, but shrank from touching. The green looked unpleasant and slimy.

Next they hunted for mandragora, of which John Young had given them an account. It grew in waste places, and by the tombs in the churchyard, and shrieked while you pulled it up. This they could not find. Mark said perhaps it wanted an enchanter to discover it, but he gathered a quantity of the dark green milfoil from the grass beside the hedge and paths, and crammed his pockets with it. Some of the lads had told him that it was a deadly poison. It is the reverse – thus reputation varies – for it was used to cure medieval sword-cuts. They passed the water-parsnip, unaware of its pernicious qualities, looking for noisome hemlock.

'There's another kind of nightshade,' said Bevis, 'because I read about it in that old book indoors, and it's much stronger than this. We must have some of it.'

They looked a long time, but could not find it; and, full of their direful object, did not heed sounds of laughter on the other side of the hedge they were searching, till they got through a gap and jumped into the midst of a group of haymakers resting for lunch. The old men had got a little way apart by themselves, for they wanted to eat like Pan. All the women were together in a 'gaggle', a semicircle of them sitting round a young girl who lounged on a heap of mown grass, with a huge labourer lying full length at her feet. She had a piece of honeysuckle in her hand, and he had a black wooden 'bottle' near him.

There was a courting going on between these two, and all the other women, married and single, collected round them, to aid in the business with jokes and innuendoes.

Bevis and Mark instantly recognized in the girl the one who at 'Calais' had shown them the road home, and in the man at her feet the fellow who was asleep on the flint-heap.

Her large eyes, like black cherries – for black eyes and black cherries have a faint tint of red behind them – were immediately bent full on Bevis as she rose and curtsyed to him. Her dress at the throat had become unhooked, and showed the line to which the sun had browned her, and where the sweet clear whiteness of the untouched skin began. The soft roundness of the swelling plum as it ripens filled her common print, torn by briars, with graceful contours. In the shadow of the oak her large black eyes shone larger, loving and untaught.

Bevis did not speak. He and Mark were a little taken aback, having jumped through the gap so suddenly from savagery into haymaking. They hastened through a gateway into another field.

'How do you keep a-staring arter they!' said the huge young labourer to the girl. 'Yen you seen he afore! It's onely our young measter.'

'I knows,' said the girl, sitting down as Bevis and Mark disappeared through the gateway. 'He put a bough on you to keep the flies off while you were sleeping.'

'Did a'? Then why didn't you ax 'un for a quart?'

She had slipped along the fields by the road that day, and had seen Bevis put the bough over her lover's face as he slept on the flint-heap – where she left him. The grateful labourer's immediate idea was to ask Bevis for some beer.

Behind the hedge Bevis and Mark continued their search for deadly poison. They took some 'gix', but were not certain that it was the true hemlock.

'There's a sort of sorrel that's poison,' said Mark.

'And heaps of roots,' said Bevis.

They were now near home, and went in to extract the essence from the plants they had. The nightshade yielded very little juice from its woody bines, or stalks; the 'gix' not much more: the milfoil, well bruised and squeezed gave most. They found three small phials: the nightshade and 'gix' only filled a quarter of the phials used for them, Mark had a phial three parts full of milfoil. These they arranged in a row on the bench in the bench-room under the crossbow and boomerang, for future use in war. They did not dip their arrows or harpoon in yet, lest they should poison any fish or animal they might kill, and so render it unfit for food.

CHAPTER 10

Making Sails

THE same evening, having got a great plateful of cherries, they went to work in the bench-room to cut out the sails from the parcel of canvas. There had been cherries in town weeks before, but these were the first considered ripe in the country, which is generally later. With a cherry in his mouth, Bevis spread the canvas out upon the floor, and marked it with his pencil. The rig was to be fore and aft, a mainsail and jib; the mast and gaff, or as they called it, the yard, were already finished. It took forty cherries to get it cut out properly, then they threw the other pieces aside, and placed the sails on the floor in the position they would be when fixed.

'You are sure they're not too big,' said Mark, 'if a white squall comes?'

'There are no white squalls now,' said Bevis on his knees, thoughtfully sucking a cherry-stone. 'It's cyclones now. The sails are just the right size, and of course we can take in a reef. You cut off – let me see – twenty bits of string, a foot – no, fifteen inches long: it's for the reefs.'

Mark began to measure off the string from a quantity of the largest make, which they had bought for the purpose.

'There's the block,' he said. 'How are you going to manage about the pulley to haul up the mainsail?'

'The block's a bore,' mused Bevis, rolling his cherry-stone about. 'I don't think we could make one – '

'Buy one.'

'Pooh! There's nothing in Latten; why you can't buy anything.' Mark was silent, he knew it was true. 'If we make a slit

in the mast and put a little wheel in off a window-blind or
something – '

'That would do first-rate.'

'No it wouldn't; it would weaken the mast, stupe, and the
first cyclone would snap it.'

'So it would. Then we should drift ashore and get eaten.'

'Most likely.'

'Well, bore a hole and put the cord through that; that would
not weaken it much.'

'No; but I know! A curtain-ring! Don't you see, you fasten
the curtain-ring – it's brass – to the mast, and put the rope
through, and it runs easy – brass is smooth.'

'Of course. Who's that?'

Some small stones came rattling in at the open window, and
two voices shouted:

'I say! Holloa!'

Bevis and Mark went to the window and saw two of their
friends, Bill and Wat, on the garden path below.

'When's the war going to begin?' asked Wat.

'Tell us about the war,' said Bill.

'The war's not ready,' said Bevis.

'Well, how long is it going to be ?'

'Make haste.'

'Everybody's ready.'

'Lots of them. Do you think you shall want any more?'

'I know six,' said the third voice, and Tim came round the
corner, having waited to steal a strawberry, 'and one's a whop-
per.'

'Let's begin.'

'Now then.'

'Oh! don't make such a noise,' said Bevis. The sails and the
savages had rather put the war aside, but Mark had talked of it
to others, and the idea spread in a minute; everybody jumped
at it, and all the cry was War!

'Make me lieutenant,' said Andrew, appearing from the orchard.

'I want to carry the flag.'

'Come down and tell us.'

'How are we to tell you if you keep talking?' said Mark; Bevis put his head out of window by the pears, and they were quiet.

'I tell you the war's not ready,' he said; 'and you're as bad as rebels – I mean you're a mutiny to come here before you're sent for, and you ought to be shot' – ('Executed', whispered Mark behind him), 'executed, of course.'

'How are we to know when it's ready?'

'You'll be summoned,' said Bevis. 'There will be a muster-roll and a trumpet blown, and you'll have to march a thousand miles.'

'All right.'

'And the swords have to be made, and the eagles, besides the map of the roads and the grub' – ('Provisions,' said Mark) – 'provisions, of course, and all the rest, and how do you think a war is to be got ready in a minute, you stupes!' in a tone of great indignation.

They grumbled: they wanted a big battle on the spot.

'If you bother me much,' said Bevis, 'while I'm getting the fleet ready, there shan't be a war at all.'

'Are you getting a fleet?'

'Here are the sails,' said Mark, holding up some canvas.

'Well, you won't be long?'

'You'll let us know?'

'Shall we tell anybody else?'

'Lots,' said Bevis; 'tell lots. We're going to have the biggest armies ever seen.'

'Thousands,' said Mark. 'Millions!'

'Millions!' said Bevis.

'Hurrah!' they shouted.

'Here,' said Bevis, throwing the remainder of the cherries out like a shower among them.

'Are you coming to quoits?'

'Oh! no,' said Mark, 'we have so much to do; now go away.' The soldiery moved off through the garden, snatching lawlessly at any fruit they saw.

'Mark,' said Bevis on his knees again, 'these sails will have to be hemmed, you know.'

'So they will.'

'We can't do it. You must take them home to Frances, and make her stitch them; roll them up and go directly.'

'I don't want to go home,' said Mark. 'And perhaps she won't stitch them.'

'I'm sure she will; she will do anything for me.'

'So she will,' said Mark rather sullenly. 'Everybody does everything for you.'

Bevis had rolled up the sails, quite indifferent as to what people did for him, and put them into Mark's unwilling hands.

'Now you can have the donkey, and mind and come back before breakfast.'

'I can't catch him,' said Mark.

'No; no more can I – stop. John Young's sure to be in the stable: he can.'

'Ah,' said Mark, brightening up a little, 'that moke is a beast.'

John Young, having stipulated for a 'pot', went to catch the donkey; they sat down in the shed to wait for him, but as he did not come for some time they went after him. They met him in the next field leading the donkey with a halter, and red as fire from running. They took the halter and sent John away for the 'pot'. There was a wicked thought in their hearts, and they wanted witnesses away. So soon as John had gone, Mark looked at Bevis, and Bevis looked at Mark. Mark growled, Bevis stamped his feet.

'Beast!' said Mark.

'Wretch!' said Bevis.

'You – you – you, Thing,' said Mark; they ground their teeth, and glared at the animal. They led him all fearful to a tree, a little tree but stout enough; it was an ash, and it grew somewhat away from the hedge. They tied him firmly to the tree, and then they scourged this miserable citizen.

All the times they had run in vain to catch him; all the times they had had to walk when they might have ridden one behind the other on his back; all his refusals to be tempted; all the wrongs they had endured at his heels boiled in their breasts. They broke their sticks upon his back, they cut new ones, and smashed them too, they hurled the fragments at him, and then got some more.

Mark fetched a pole to knock him the harder as it was heavy; Bevis crushed into the hedge, and brought out a dead log to hurl at him, – the same Bevis who put an aspen leaf carefully under the fly to save it from drowning. The sky was blue, and the evening beautiful, but no one came to help the donkey.

When they were tired, they sat down and rested, and after they were cooler, and had recovered from the fatigue, they loosed him – quite cowed this time and docile, and Mark, with the parcel of sails, got on his back. After all this onslaught there did not seem any difference in him except that his coat had been well dusted. This immunity aggravated them; they could not hurt him.

'Put him in the stable all night,' said Bevis, 'and don't give him anything to eat.'

'And no water,' said Mark, as he rode off. 'So I will.'

And so he did. But the donkey had cropped all day, and was full, and just before John Young caught him had had a draught, rather unusual for him and equal to an omen, at the drinking-place by the raft. The donkey slept, and beat them.

After Mark had gone Bevis returned to the bench-room, and fastened a brass curtain-ring to the mast, which they had carried up there. When he had finished, noticing the three phials of poison, he thought he would go and see if he could find out any more fatal plants. There was an ancient encyclopaedia in the book-case, in which he had read many curious things, such as would not be considered practical enough for modern publication, which must be dry or nothing. Among the rest was a page of chemical signs and those used by the alchemists, some of which he had copied off for magic. Pulling out the volumes, which were piled haphazard, like bricks shot out of a cart, there was one that had all the alphabets employed in the different languages, Coptic, Gothic, Ethiopic, Syriac, and so on. The Arabic took his fancy as the most mysterious – the sweeping curves, the quivering lines, the blots where the reed pen thickened, there was no knowing what such writing might not mean.

Bevis copied the alphabet, and then he made a roll of a broad sheet of yellowish paper torn from the end of one of the large volumes, a fly-leaf, and wrote the letters upon it in such a manner as their shape and flowing contour arranged themselves. With these he mingled the alchemic signs for fire and air and water, and so by the time the dusk crept into the parlour and filled it with shadow he had completed a manuscript. This he rolled up and tied with string, intending to bury it in the sand of the quarry, so that when they sailed round in the ship they might land and discover it.

Mark returned to breakfast, and said that Frances had promised to hem the sails, and thought it would not take long. Bevis showed him the roll.

'It looks magic,' said Mark. 'What does it mean?'

'I don't know,' said Bevis. 'That is what we shall have to find out when we discover it. Besides the magic is never in the writing; it is what you see when you read it – it's like looking in a looking-glass, and seeing people moving about a thousand miles away.'

'I know,' said Mark. 'We can put it in a sand-martin's hole, then it won't get wet if it rains.'

They started for the bathing-place, and carefully deposited the roll in a sand-martin's hole some way up the face of the quarry, covering it with sand. To know the spot again, they counted and found it was the third burrow to the right, if you stood by the stone-heap and looked straight towards the first sycamore tree. Having taken the bearings, they dragged the catamaran down to the water, and had a swim. When they came out, and were running about on the high ground by the sycamores, they caught sight of a dog-cart slowly crossing the field a long way off, and immediately hid behind a tree to reconnoitre the new savage, themselves unseen.

'It's Jack,' said Bevis; 'I'm sure it is.' It was Jack, and he was going at a walking pace, because the track across the field was rough, and he did not care to get to the gateway before the man sent to open it had arrived there. His object was to look at some grass to rent for his sheep.

'Yes, it's Jack,' said Mark, very slowly and doubtfully. Bevis looked at him.

'Well, suppose it is; he won't hurt us. We can easily shoot him if he comes here.'

'But the letter,' said Mark.

'What letter?'

Mark had started for his clothes, which were in a heap on the sward; he seized his coat, and drew a note much frayed from one of the pockets. He looked at it, heaved a deep sigh, and ran with all his might to intercept Jack. Bevis watched him tearing across the field and laughed; then he sat down on the grass to wait for him.

Mark, out of breath and with thistles in his feet, would never have overtaken the dog-cart had not Jack seen him coming and stopped. He could not speak, but handed up the note in silence, more like Cupid than messengers generally. He panted so that he could not run away directly, as he had intended.

'You rascal,' said Jack, flicking at him with his whip. 'How long have you had this in your pocket?'

Mark tried to run away, he could only trot; Jack turned his mare's head, as if half-inclined to drive after him.

'If you come,' said Mark, shaking his fist, 'we'll shoot you and stick a spear into you. Aha! you're afraid! aha!'

Jack was too eager to read his note to take vengeance. Mark walked away jeering at him. The reins hung down, and the mare cropped as the master read. Mark laughed to think he had got off so easily, for the letter had been in his pocket a week, though he had faithfully promised to deliver it the same day – for a shilling. Had he not been sent home with the sails it might have remained another week, till the envelope was fretted through.

Frances asked if he had given it to Jack. Mark started, 'Ah,' said she, 'you have forgotten it.'

'Of course I have,' said Mark. 'It's so long ago.'

'Then you did really?'

'How stupid you are,' said Mark; and Frances could not press him further, lest she should seem to anxious about Jack. So the young dog escaped, but he did not dare delay longer, and had not Jack happened to cross the field meant to have ridden up to his house on the donkey. When Jack had read the note he looked at the retreating figure of Cupid and opened his lips, but caught his breath as it were and did not say it. He put his whip aside as he drove on, lest he should unjustly punish the mare.

Mark strolled leisurely back to the bathing-place, but when he got there Bevis was not to be seen. He looked round at the water, the quarry, the sycamore trees. He ran down to the water's edge with his heart beating and a wild terror causing a whirling sensation in his eyes, for the thought in the instant came to him that Bevis had gone out of his depth. He tried to shout 'Bevis!' but he was choked; he raised his hands; as he looked across the water he suddenly saw something white moving among the fir trees at the head of the gulf.

He knew it was Bevis, but he was so overcome he sat down

on the sward to watch, he could not stand up. The something white was stealthily passing from tree to tree like an Indian. Mark looked round, and saw his own harpoon on the grass, but at once missed the bow and arrows. His terror had suspended his observation, else he would have noticed this before.

Bevis, when Mark ran with the letter to Jack, had sat down on the sward to wait for him, and by and by, while still, and looking out over the water, his quiet eye became conscious of a slight movement opposite at the mouth of the Nile. There was a ripple, and from the high ground where he sat he could see the reflection of the trees in the water there undulate, though their own boughs shut off the light air from the surface. He got up, took his bow and arrows, and went into the firs. The dead dry needles or leaves on the ground felt rough to his naked feet, and he had to take care not to step on the hard cones. A few small bramble bushes forced him to go aside, so that it took him some little time to get near the Nile.

Then he had to always keep a tree trunk in front of him, and to step slowly that his head might not be seen before he could see what it was himself. He stooped as the ripples on the other side of the brook became visible; then gradually lifting his head, sheltered by a large alder, he traced the ripples back to the shore under the bank, and saw a moor-cock feeding by the roots of a willow. Bevis waited till the cock turned his back, then he stole another step forward to the alder.

It was about ten yards to the willow which hung over the water, but he could not get any nearer, for there was no more cover beyond the alder – the true savage is never content unless he is close to his game. Bevis grasped his bow firm in his left hand, drew the arrow quick but steadily – not with a jerk – and as the sharp point covered the bird, loosed it. There was a splash and a fluttering and he knew instantly that he had hit. 'Mark! Mark!' he shouted, and ran down the bank, heedless of the jagged stones. Mark heard, and came racing through the firs.

'Here's where the arrow went in.'

'Feel how warm he is.'

'Let's eat him.'

'All right. Make a fire.'

Thus the savages gloated over their prey. They went back up the bank and through the firs to the sward.

'Where shall we make the fire?' said Mark. 'In the quarry?'

'That old stupe may come for sand.'

'So he may. Let's make it here.'

'Everybody would see.'

'By the hedge towards the elms then.'

'No. I know, in the hollow.'

'Of course, nobody would come there.'

'Pick up some sticks.'

'I shall dress – there are brambles.'

'Come and help me.'

So they dressed, and then found that Mark had broken a nail, and Bevis had cut his foot with the sharp edge of a fossil shell projecting from one of the stones. But that was a trifle; they could think of nothing but the bird. While they were gathering armfuls of dead sticks from among the trees, they remembered that John Young, who always paunched the rabbits and hares and got everything ready for the kitchen, said coots and moorhens must be skinned, they could not be plucked because of the 'dowl'.

Dowl is the fluff, the tiny featherets no fingers can remove. So after they had carried the wood they had collected to the round hollow in the field beyond the sycamore trees, they took out their knives, and haggled the skin off. They built their fire very skilfully; they had made so many in the Peninsula (for there is nothing so pleasant as making a fire out of doors) that they had learnt exactly how to do it. Two short sticks were stuck in the ground and a third across to them, like a triangle. Against this frame a number of the smallest and driest sticks were leaned, so that they made a tiny hut. Outside these there was a second layer of longer sticks; all standing, or rather leaning against the first.

If a stick is placed across, lying horizontally, supposing it catches fire, it just burns through the middle and that is all, the ends go out. If it is stood nearly upright, the flame draws up it; it is certain to catch; it burns longer and leaves a good ember. They arranged the rest of their bundles ready to be thrown on when wanted, and then put some paper, a handful of dry grass, and a quantity of the least and driest twigs, like those used in birds'-nests, inside the little hut. Then having completed the pile they remembered they had no matches.

'It's very lucky,' said Bevis. 'If we had we should have to throw them away. Matches are not proper.'

'Two pieces of wood,' said Mark. 'I know; you rub them together till they catch fire, and one piece must be hard and the other soft.'

'Yes,' said Bevis, and taking out his knife he cut off the end of one of the larger dead branches they had collected, and made a smooth side to it. Mark had some difficulty in finding a soft piece to rub on it, for those which touched soft crumbled when rubbed on the hard surface Bevis had prepared. A bit of willow seemed best, and Bevis seized it first, rubbed it to and fro till his arm ached and his face glowed. Mark, lying on the grass, watched to see the slight tongue of flame shoot up, but it did not come.

Bevis stopped, tired, and putting his hand on the smooth surface found it quite warm, so that they had no doubt they could do it in time. Mark tried next, and then Bevis again, and Mark followed him; but though the wood became warm it would not burst into flame, as it ought to have done.

CHAPTER 11

The Mast Fitted

'This is very stupid,' said Bevis, throwing himself back at full length on the grass, and crossing his arms over his face to shield his eyes from the sun.

'They ought not to tell us such stupid things,' said Mark. 'We might rub all day.'

'I know,' said Bevis, sitting up again. 'It's a drill; it's done with a drill. Give me my bow — there, don't you know how Jonas made the hole in Tom's gun?'

Jonas the blacksmith, a clever fellow in his way, drilled out a broken nipple in the bird's keeper's muzzle-loading gun, working the drill with a bow. Bevis and Mark, always on the watch everywhere, saw him do it.

They cut a notch or hole in the hard surface of the thicker bough, and shaped another piece of wood to a dull point to fit in it. Bevis took this, placed it against the string of his bow, and twisted the string round it. Then he put the point of the stick in the hole; Mark held the bough firm on the ground, but immediately he began to work the bow backwards and forwards, rotating the drill alternate ways, he found that the other end against which he pressed with his chest would quickly fray a hole in his jacket. They had to stop and cut another piece of wood with a hole to take the top of the drill, and Bevis now pressed on this with his left hand (finding that it did not need the weight of his chest), and worked the bow with his right.

The drill revolved swiftly, it was really very near the savages' fire-drill; but the expected flame did not come. The wood was not dry enough, or the point of friction was not accurately adjusted; the wood became quite hot, but did not ignite.

Bevis flung down the bow without a word, heaving a deep sigh of rage.

'Flint and steel,' said Mark presently.

'Hum!'

'There's a flint in the gateway,' continued Mark. 'I saw it just now; and you can knock it against the end of your knife – '

'You stupe; there's no tinder.'

'No more there is.'

'I hate it – it's horrid,' said Bevis. 'What's the use of trying to do things when everything can't be done?'

He sat on his heels as he knelt, and looked round scowling. There was the water – no fire to be obtained from thence; there was the broad field – no fire there; there was the sun overhead.

'Go home directly, and get a burning-glass – unscrew the telescope.'

'Is it proper?' said Mark, not much liking the journey.

'It's not matches,' said Bevis sententiously.

Mark knew it was of no use, he had to go, and he went, taking off his jacket before he started, as he meant to run a good part of the way. It was not really far, but as his mind was at the hollow all the while the time seemed twice as long. After he had gone Bevis soon found that the sunshine was too warm to sit in, though while they had been so busy and working their hardest they had never noticed it. Directly the current of occupation was interrupted the sun became unbearable. Bevis went to the shadow of the sycamores, taking the skinned bird with him, lest a wandering beast of prey – some weasel or jackal – should pounce on it.

Far out over the water he saw the Unknown Island, and remembered that when they sailed there in the ship there was no knowing what monsters or what enchantments they might encounter. So he walked out from the trees into the field to look for some moly to take with them, and resist Circe.

He found three button mushrooms, and put them in his

pocket. Wandering on among the buttercup stalks and bunches of grass, like a butterfly drawn hither and thither by every speck of colour, he came to a little white flower on a slender stem a few inches high, which he gathered for moly. Putting the precious flower – good against sorcery – in his breast-pocket for safety, he rose from his knees, and saw Mark coming by the sycamores.

Mark was hot and tired with running, yet he had snatched time enough to bring four cherries for Bevis. He had the burning-glass – a lens unscrewed from the telescope, and sitting on the grass they focused the sun's rays on a piece of paper. The lens was powerful and the summer sun bright, so that in a few seconds there was a tiny black speck, then the faintest whiff of bluish smoke, then a leap of flame, and soon another, till the paper burned, and their fire was lit. As the little hut blazed up they put some more boughs on, and the dead leaves attached to them sent up a thin column of smoke.

'The savages will see that,' said Mark, 'and come swarming down from the hills.'

'We ought to have made the fire in a hole,' said Bevis, 'and put turf on it.'

'What ever shall we do?' said Mark. 'They'll be here in a minute.'

'Fetish,' said Bevis. 'I know, cut that stick sharp at the end, tie a handful of grass on it – be quick – and run down towards the elms and stick it up. Then they'll think we're doing fetish, and won't come any nearer.'

'First-rate,' said Mark, and off he went with the stick, and thrust it into the sward with a wisp of grass tied to the top. Bevis piled on the branches, and when he came back there was a large fire. Then the difficulty was how to cook the bird? If they put it on the ashes, it would burn and be spoiled; if they hung it up, they could not make it twist round and round, and they had no iron pot to boil it; or earthenware pot to drop red-hot stones in, and so heat the water without destroying the vessel. The only thing they could do was to stick it on a stick, and hold it to the fire till it was roasted, one side at a time.

'The harpoon will do,' said Bevis. 'Spit him on it.'

'No,' said Mark; 'the bone will burn and get spoiled – spit him on your arrow.'

'The nail will burn out and spoil my arrow, and I've lost one in the elms. Go and cut a long stick.'

'You ought to go and do it,' said Mark; 'I've done everything this morning.'

'So you have; I'll go,' said Bevis, and away he went to the nut-tree hedge. He soon brought back a straight hazel-rod to which he cut a point, the bird was spitted, and they held it by turns at the fire, sitting on the sward.

It was very warm in the round, bowl-like hollow, the fire at the bottom and the sun overhead, but they were too busy to heed it. Mark crept on hands and knees up the side of the hollow while Bevis was cooking, and cautiously peered over the edge to see if any savages were near. There was none in sight; the fetish kept them at a distance.

'We must remember to take the burning-glass with us when we go on our voyage,' said Bevis.

'Perhaps the sun won't shine.'

'No. Mind you tell me we will take some matches too; and if the sun shines use the glass, and if he doesn't, strike a match.'

'We shall want a camp-fire when we go to war,' said Mark.

'Of course we shall.'

'Everybody keeps on about the war,' said Mark. 'They're always at me.'

'I found these buttons,' said Bevis; 'I had forgotten them.'

He put the little mushrooms, stems upwards, on some embers which had fallen from the main fire. The branches as they burned became white directly, coated over with a film of ash, so that except just in the centre they did not look red, though glowing with heat under the white layer. Even the flames were but just visible in the brilliant sunshine, and were paler in colour than those of the hearth. Now and then the thin column of grey smoke, rising straight up out of the hollow, was puffed aside at its summit by the light air wandering over the field. As the butterflies came over the edge of the hollow into the heated atmosphere, they fluttered up high to escape it.

'I'm sure it's done,' said Mark, drawing the stick away from the fire. The bird was brown and burnt in one place, so they determined to eat it and not spoil it by over-roasting. When Bevis began to carve it with his pocket-knife he found one leg quite raw, the wings were burnt, but there was a part of the breast and the other leg fairly well cooked. These they ate, little pieces at a time, slowly, and in silence, for it was proper to like it. But they did not pick the bones clean.

'No salt,' said Mark, putting down the piece he had in his hand.

'No bread,' said Bevis, flinging the leg away.

'We don't do it right somehow,' said Mark. 'It takes such a long time to learn to be savages.'

'Years,' said Bevis, picking a mushroom from the embers. It burnt his fingers and he had to wait till it was cooler. The mushrooms were better, their cups held some of the juice as they cooked, retaining the sweet flavour. They were so small, they were but a bite each.

'I am thirsty,' said Mark. Bevis was the same, so they went down towards the water. Mark began to run down the slope, when Bevis suddenly remembered.

'Stop,' he cried: 'you can't drink there.'

'Why not?'

'Why of course it's the New Sea. We must go round to the Nile; it's fresh water there.'

So they ran through the firs to the Nile, and lapped from the brook. On the way home a little boy stepped out from the trees on the bank where it was hight, and he could look down at them.

'I say!' he had been waiting for them – 'say!'

'Well!' growled Mark.

'Bevis,' said the boy. Bevis looked up, he could not demean himself to answer such a mite. The boy looked round to see that he was sure of his retreat through the trees to the gap in the hedge he could crawl through, but they would find it difficult. Besides, they would have to run up the bank, which was thick with brambles. He got his courage together and shouted in his shrill little voice.

'I say, Ted says he shan't play if you don't have war soon.'

Mark picked up a dead branch and hurled it at the mite; the mite dodged it, and it broke against a tree, then he ran for his life, but they did not follow. Bevis said nothing till they reached the blue summer-house at home and sat down. Then he yawned.

'War is a bother,' he said, putting his hand in his pockets, and leaning back in an attitude of weary despair at having to do something. If the rest would not have played, he would have egged them on with furious energy till they did. As they were eager he did not care.

'Oh, well!' said Mark, nodding his head up and down as he spoke, as much as to indicate that he did not care personally; but still, 'Oh, well! all I know is, if you don't go to war Ted will have one all to himself, and have a battle with somebody else. I believe he sent Charlie.' Charlie was the mite.

'Did he say he would have a war all to himself?' said Bevis, sitting upright.

'I don't know,' said Mark, nodding his head. 'They say lots of things.'

'What do they say?'

'Oh, heaps; perhaps you don't know how to make war, and perhaps – '

'I'll have the biggest war,' said Bevis, getting up, 'that was ever known, and Ted's quite stupid. Mind, he doesn't have any more cherries, that's certain. I hate him – awfully! Let's make the swords.'

'All right,' said Mark, jumping up, delighted that the war was going to begin. He was as eager as the others, only he did not dare say so. Most of the afternoon they were cutting sticks for swords, and measuring them so as to have all the same length.

Next morning the governor went with them to bathe, as he wanted to see how they were getting on with their swimming. They had the punt, and the governor stopped it about twenty yards from the shore, to which they had to swim. Bevis dived first, and with some blowing and spluttering and splashing managed to get to where he could bottom with his feet. He could have gone farther than that, but it was a new feeling to know that he was out of his depth, and it made him swim too fast and splash. Mark having seen that Bevis could do it, and knowing he could swim as far as Bevis could, did it much better.

The governor was satisfied and said they could now have the blue boat, but on two conditions, first, that they still kept their promise not to go out of their depth, and secondly, that they were to try and see every day how far they could swim along the shore.

If they would practise along the shore in their depth till they could swim from the rocky point to the rails, about seventy yards, he would give them each a present, and they could then go out of their depth. He was obliged to be careful about the depth till they could swim a good way, because he could not be always with them, and fresh water is not so buoyant as the sea, so that young swimmers soon tire.

The same day they carried the mast up, and fitted it in the hole in the thwart. The mast was a little too large, but that was soon remedied. The bowsprit was lashed to the ring to which the painter was fastened, and at its inner end to the seat and mast. Next the gaff was tried, and drew up and down fairly well through the curtain-ring. But one thing they had overlooked — the sheets, or ropes for the jib, must work through something,

and they had not provided any staples. Besides this there was the rudder to be fitted with a tiller instead of the ropes. Somehow they did not like ropes; it did not look like a ship. This instinct was right, for ropes are not of much use when sailing; you have no power on the rudder as with a tiller.

After fitting the mast and bowsprit they unshipped them, and carried them home for safety till the sails were ready. Bevis wanted Mark to go and ask Frances to be quick, but Mark was afraid to return just yet, as Frances would now know from Jack that he had forgotten the letter. Every now and then bundles of sticks for swords, and longer ones for spears and darts, and rods for arrows, were brought in by the soldiery. All these were taken upstairs into the bench-room, or armoury, because they did not like their things looked at or touched, and there was a lock and key to that room. Bevis always kept the key in his pocket now.

They could not fit a head to the oyster barrel for the fresh water on the voyage, but found a large round tin canister with a tight lid, and which would go inside the oyster barrel. The tin canister would hold water, and could be put in the barrel, so as to look proper. More sticks kept coming, and knobbed clubs, till the armoury was crowded with the shafts of weapons. Now that Bevis had consented to go to war, all the rest were eager to serve him, so that he easily got a messenger to take a note (as Mark was afraid to go) to Frances to be quick with the stitching.

In the evening Bevis tore another broad folio page or fly leaf from one of the big books in the parlour, and took it out into the summer house, where they kept an old chair – the back gone – which did very well for a table. Cutting his pencil, Bevis took his hat off and threw it on the seat which ran round inside; then kneeling down, as the table was so low, he proceeded to draw his map of the coming campaign.

CHAPTER 12

The Council of War

'I say!'

'Battleaxes – '

'St George is right – '

'Hold your tongue.'

'Pikes twenty feet long.'

'Marching two and two.'

'Do stop.'

'I shall be general.'

'That you won't.'

'Romans had shields.'

'Battleaxes are best.'

'Knobs with spikes.'

'I say – I say!'

'You're a donkey!'

'They had flags – '

'And drums.'

'I've got a flute.'

'I – '

'You!'

'Yes, *me.*'

'Hi!' 'Tom.' 'If you hit me, I'll hit you.' 'Now.' 'Don't.' 'Be quiet.' 'Go on.' 'Let's begin.' 'I will' – buzz – buzz – buzz – !

Phil, Tom, Ted, Jim, Frank, Walter, Bill, 'Charl', Val, Bob, Cecil, Sam, Fred, George, Harry, Michael, Jack, Andrew, Luke, and half a dozen more were talking all together, shouting across each other, occasionally fighting, wrestling, and rolling over on the sward under an oak. There were two up in the tree, bellowing their views from above, and little Charlie ('Charl') was astride of a bough which he had got hold of, swinging up and down, and yelling like the rest. Some stood by the edge of the water, for the oak was within a few yards of the New Sea, and alternately made ducks and drakes, and turned to contradict their friends.

On higher ground beyond, a herd of cows grazed in perfect peace, while the swallows threaded a maze in and out between them, but just above the grass. The New Sea was calm and smooth as glass, the sun shone in a cloudless sky, so that the shadow of the oak was pleasant; but the swallows had come down from the upper air, and Bevis, as he stood a little apart listening in an abstracted manner to the uproar, watched them swiftly gliding in and out. He had convened a council of all those who wanted to join the war in the fields, because it seemed best to keep the matter secret, which could not be done if they came to the house, else perhaps the battle would be interfered with. This oak was chosen as it was known to everyone.

It grew alone in the meadow, and far from any path, so that they could talk as they liked. They had hardly met ten minutes when the confusion led to frequent blows and pushes, and the shouting was so great that no one could catch more than disjointed sentences. Mark now came running with the map in his hand; it had been forgotten, and he had been sent to fetch it. As he came near, and they saw him, there was a partial lull.

'What an awful row you have been making,' he said, 'I heard it all across the field. Why don't you choose sides?'

'Who's to choose?' said Ted, as if he did not know that he should be one of the leaders. He was the tallest and biggest of them all, a head and shoulders above Bevis.

'You, of course,' came in chorus.

'And you needn't look as if you didn't want to,' shouted somebody, at which there was a laugh.

'Now, Bevis, Bevis! Sides.' They crowded round, and pulled Bevis into the circle.

'Best two out of three,' said Mark. 'Here's a penny.'

'Lend me one,' said Ted.

Phil handed him the coin.

'You'll never get it back,' cried one of the crowd. Ted was rather known for borrowing on the score of his superior strength.

'Bevis, you're dreaming,' as Bevis stood quiet and motionless, still in his far-away mood. 'Toss.'

Bevis tossed, the penny spun, and he caught it on the back of his hand; Mark nudged him.

'Cry.'

'Head,' said Ted. Mark nudged again; but it was a head. Mark stamped his foot.

'Tail,' and it was a tail; Ted won the toss.

'I told you how to do it,' whispered Mark to Bevis in a fierce whisper, 'and you didn't.'

'Choose,' shouted everybody. Ted beckoned to Val, who came and stood behind him. He was the next biggest, very easy tempered and a favourite, as he would give away anything.

'Choose,' shouted everybody again. It was Bevis's turn, and of course he took Mark. So far it was all understood, but it was now Ted's turn, and no one knew whom he would select. He looked round and called Phil, a stout, short, slow-speaking boy, who had more pocket-money, and was more inclined to books than most of them.

'Who shall I have?' said Bevis aside to Mark.

'Have Bill,' said Mark. 'He's strong.'

Bill was called, and came over. Ted took another – rank and file – and then Bevis, who was waking up, suddenly called 'Cecil'.

'You stupe,' said Mark. 'He can't fight.'

Cecil, a shy, slender lad, came and stood behind his leader.

'You'll lose everybody,' said Mark. 'Ted will have all the big ones. There, he's got Tim. Have Fred; I saw him knock George over once.'

Fred came, and the choosing continued, each trying to get the best soldiers, till none were left but little Charlie, who was an odd one.

'He's no good,' said Ted; 'you can put him in your pocket.'

'I hate you,' said Charlie; 'after all the times I've run with messages for you. Bevis, let me come your side.'

'Take him,' said Ted; 'but mind, you'll have one more if you do, and I shall get someone else.'

'Then he'll get a bigger one,' said Mark. 'Don't have him; he'll only be in the way.'

Charlie began to walk off with his head hanging.

'Cry-baby,' shouted the soldiery. 'Pipe your eye.'

'Come here,' said Bevis; Charlie ran back delighted.

'Well, you have done it,' said Mark in a rage. 'Now Ted will have another twice as big. What's the use of my trying when you are so stupid! I never did see. We shall be whopped anyhow.'

Quite heedless of these reproaches, Bevis asked Ted who were to be his lieutenants.

'I shall have Val and Phil,' said Ted.

'And I shall have Mark and Cecil,' said Bevis. 'Let us count. How many are there on each side? Mark, write down all ours. Haven't you a pocket-book? Well, do it on the back of the map. Ted, you had better do the same.'

'Phil,' said Ted, who was not much of a student, 'you put down the names.'

Phil, a reader in a slow way, did as he was bidden. There were fifteen on Bevis's side, and fourteen on Ted's, who was to choose another to make it even.

'There's the muster-roll,' said Mark, holding up the map.

'But how shall we know one another?' said George.

'Who's friend, and who's enemies,' said Fred.

'Else we shall all hit one another anyhow,' said another.

'Stick feathers in our hats.'

124

'Ribbons round our arms would be best,' said Cecil. 'Hats may be knocked off.'

'Ribbons will do first-rate,' said Bevis. 'I'll have blue; Ted, you have red. You can buy heaps of ribbon for nothing.'

'Phil,' said Ted, 'have you got any money?'

'Half a crown.'

'Lend us, then.'

'No, I shan't,' said Phil: 'I'll buy the ribbons myself.'

'Let's have a skirmish now,' said Bill. 'Come on, Val,' and he began to whirl his hands about.

'Stop that,' said Bevis. 'Ted, there's a truce, and if you let your fellows fight it's breaking it. Catch hold of Bill – Mark, Cecil, hold him.'

Bill was seized, and hustled round behind the oak, and kept there till he promised to be quiet.

'But when are we going to begin?' asked Jack.

'Be quick,' said Luke.

'War! war!' shouted half a dozen, kicking up their heels.

'Hold your noise,' said Ted, cuffing one of his followers. 'Can't you see we're getting on as fast as we can. Bevis, where are we going to fight?'

'In the Plain,' said Bevis. 'That's the best place.'

'Plenty of room for a big battle,' said Ted. 'Oh, you've got it on the map, I see.'

The Plain was the great pasture beside the New Sea, where Bevis and Mark bathed and ran about in the sunshine. It was some seventy or eighty acres in extent, a splendid battle-field.

'We're not going to march,' said Mark, taking something on himself as lieutenant.

'We're not going to march,' said Bevis. 'But I did not tell you to say so; I mean we are not going to march the thousand miles, Ted; we will suppose that.'

'All right,' said Ted.

'But we're going to have camps,' continued Bevis. 'You're

going to have your camp just outside the hedge towards the hills, because you live that side, and you will come that way. Here' – he showed Ted a circle drawn on the map to represent a camp – 'that's yours; and this is ours on this side, towards our house, as we shall come that way.'

'The armies will encamp in sight of each other,' said Phil. 'That's quite proper. Go on, Bevis. Shall we send our scouts?'

'We shall light fires and have proper camps,' said Bevis.

'And bring our great-coats and cloaks, and a hamper of grub,' interrupted Mark, anxious to show that he knew all about it.

Bevis frowned, but went on. 'And I shall send one of my soldiers to be with you, and you will send one of yours to be with me – '

'Whatever for?' said Ted. 'That's a curious thing.'

'Well, it's to know when to begin. When we are all there, we'll hoist up a flag – a handkerchief will do on a stick – and you will hoist up yours, and then when the war is to begin, you will send back my soldier, and I will send back yours, and they will cross each other as they are running, and when your soldier reaches you, and mine reaches me – '

'I see,' said Ted, 'I see. Then we are to march out so as to begin quite fair.'

'That's it,' said Bevis. 'So as to begin at the same minute, and not one before the other. I have got it already, and you need not have sent people to worry me to make haste about the war.'

'Well, how was I to know if you never said anything?' said Ted.

'And who are we to be?' said Val. 'Saxons and Normans, or Crusaders, or King Arthur – '

'We're all to be Romans,' said Bevis.

'Then it will be the Civil War,' said Phil, who had read most history.

'Of course it will,' said Bevis, 'and I am to be Julius Caesar, and Ted is to be Pompey.'

'I won't be Pompey,' said Ted; 'Pompey was beat.'

'You must,' said Bevis.

'I shan't.'

'But you *must.*'

'I won't be beaten.'

'I shall beat you easily.'

'That you won't,' very warmly.

'Indeed I shall,' said Bevis quite composedly, 'as I am Caesar I shall beat you very easily.'

'Of course we shall,' added Mark.

'You won't; I've got the biggest soldiers, and I shall drive you anyhow.'

'No, you won't.'

'I've got Val and Phil and Tim, and I mean to have Ike, so now –'

'There, I told you,' said Mark to Bevis. 'He's got all the biggest, and Ike is a huge big donk of a fellow.'

'It's no use,' said Bevis, not in the least ruffled; 'I shall beat you.'

'Not you,' said Ted, hot and red in the face. 'Why, I'll pitch you in the water first.'

'Take you all your time,' said Bevis, shutting his lips tighter and beginning to look a little dangerous.

'Shut up,' said Val.

'Stop,' said Phil and Bill and George, pressing in.

'Hush,' said Cecil. 'It's a truce.'

'Well, I won't be Pompey,' said Ted sullenly.

'Then we must have somebody who will,' said Bevis sharply, 'and choose again.'

'I wouldn't mind,' said someone in the crowd.

'Nor I,' said another.

'If I was general I wouldn't mind being Pompey. Let me, Bevis.'

'Who's that,' said Ted. 'If anyone says that I'll smash him.' When he found he could so easily be superseded he surrendered. 'Well, I'll be Pompey,' he said, 'but mind I shan't be beat.'

'Pompey ought to win if he can,' said Val; 'that's only fair.'

'What's the use of fighting if we are to be beat?' said Phil.

'Of course,' said Bevis, 'how very stupid you all are! Of course, Ted is to win if he can; he's only to be called Pompey to make it proper. I know I shall beat him, but he's to beat us if he can.'

'I'm only to be called Pompey, mind,' said Ted; 'mind that. We are to win if we can.'

'Of course;' and so this delicate point was settled after very nearly leading to an immediate battle.

'Hurrah for Pompey!' shouted George, throwing up his hat.

'Hurrah for Caesar!' said Bill, hurling up his. This was the signal for a general shouting and uproar. They had been quiet ten minutes, and were obliged to let off their suppressed energy. There was a wild capering round the oak.

'Ted Pompey,' said Charlie, little and impudent, 'what fun it will be to see you run away!' For which he had his ears pulled till he squealed.

'Now,' shouted Mark. 'Let's get it all done. Come on.' The noise subsided somewhat, and they gathered round as Ted and Bevis began to talk again.

'Caesar,' said Phil to Bevis, 'if you're Caesar and Ted's Pompey, who are we? We ought to have names too.'

'I'm Mark Anthony,' said Mark, standing bolt upright.

'Very well,' said Bevis. 'Phil, you can be – let me see, Varro.'

'All right, I'm Varro,' said Phil; 'and who's Val? Oh, I know' – running names over in his mind – 'he's Crassus. Val Crassus, do you hear?'

'Capital,' said Crassus. 'I'm ready.'

'Then there's Cecil,' said Mark; 'who's he?'

'Cecil!' said Phil. 'Cecil – Cis – Cis – Scipio, of course.'

'First-rate,' said Mark. 'Scipio Cecil, that's your name.'

'Write it down on the roll,' said Bevis. The names were duly registered; Pompey's lieutenants as Val Crassus and Phil Varro, and Caesar's as Mark Antony and Scipio Cecil. After which there was a great flinging of stones into the water and more shouting.

'Let's see,' said Ted. 'If there's fifteen each side, there will be five soldiers to each, five for captains, and five for lieutenants.'

'Cohorts,' said Phil. 'A cohort each, hurrah!'

'Do be quiet,' said Ted. 'How can we go on when you make such a row? Caesar Bevis, are all the swords ready?'

'No,' said Bevis. 'We must fix the lengths, and have them all the same.'

They got a stick, and after much discussion cut it to a certain length as a standard; Mark took charge of it, and all the swords were to be cut off by it, and none to be any thicker. There were to be cross-pieces nailed or fastened on, but the ends were to be blunt and not sharp.

'No sticking,' said Ted. 'Only knocking.'

'Only knocking and slashing,' said Bevis. 'Stabbing won't do, and arrows won't do, nor spears.'

'Why not?' said Mark, who had been looking forward to darting his javelin at Ted Pompey.

'Because eyes will get poked out,' said Bevis, 'and there would be a row. If anybody got stuck and killed, there would be an awful row.'

'So there would,' said Mark. 'How stupid! Just as if people could not kill one another without so much fuss!'

'And no hitting at faces,' said Bevis, 'else if somebody's marked there will be a bother.'

'No,' said Ted. 'Mind, no slashing faces. Knock swords together.'

'Knock swords together,' said Bevis. 'Make rattling and shout.'

'Shout,' said Mark, bellowing his loudest.

'How shall we know when we're killed?' said Cecil.

'Well, you *are* a stupe,' said Val. 'Really you are.' They all laughed at Cecil.

'But I don't know,' said Ted Pompey. 'You just think, how shall we know who's beat? Cecil's not so silly.'

'No more he is,' said Mark. 'Bevis, how is it to be managed?'

'Those who run away are beaten,' said Charlie. 'You'll see Ted run fast enough.' Away he scampered himself to escape punishment.

'Of course,' said Bevis. 'One way will be if people run away. Oh! I know, if the camp is taken.'

'Or if the captain is taken prisoner,' said Phil; 'and tied up with a cord.'

'Yes,' continued Bevis. 'If the captain is taken prisoner, and if the eagles are captured –'

'Eagles,' said Ted Pompey.

'Standards,' said Phil. 'That's right: are we to have proper eagles, Caesar Bevis?'

'Yes,' said Bevis. 'Three brass rings round sticks will do. Two eagles each, don't you see, Ted, like flags, only eagles, that's proper.'

'Who keeps the ground wins the victory,' said Cecil.

'Right,' said Ted. 'I shall soon tie up Bevis – we must bring cords.'

'You must catch him first,' said Mark.

'Captains must be guarded,' said Val. 'Strong guards round them and awful fighting there,' licking his lips at the thought of it.

'Captain Caesar Bevis,' said Tim, who had not spoken before, but had listened very carefully. 'Is there to be any punching?'

'Hum!' Bevis hesitated, and looked at Ted.

'I think so,' said Ted, who had long arms and hard fists.

'If there's punching,' cried Charlie from the oak, into which he had climbed for safety; 'if there's punching, only the big blokes can play.'

'No punching,' said Mark eagerly, not that he feared, being stout and sturdy, but seizing at anything to neutralize Ted's big soldiers.

'No punching,' shouted a dozen at once; 'only pushing.'

'Very well,' said Bevis, 'no punching, and no tripping – pushing and wrestling quite fair.'

'Wrestling,' said Ted directly. 'That will do.'

'Stupid,' said Mark to Bevis; then louder, 'Only nice wrestling, no "scrumpshing".'

'No "scrumpshing",' shouted everybody.

Ted stamped his foot, but it was of no use. Everybody was for fair and pleasant fighting.

'Never mind,' said Ted. 'We'll shove you out of the field.'

'Yah! Yah!' said Charlie, making faces at him.

'If anyone does what's agreed shan't be done,' said Mark, still anxious to stop Ted's design; 'that will lose the battle, even if it's won.'

'It ought to be all fair,' said Val, who was very big, but straightforward.

'If anything's done unfair, that counts against whoever does it,' said Cecil.

'No sneaking business,' shouted everybody. 'No sneaking and hitting behind.'

'Certainly not,' said Bevis. 'All quite fair.'

'Somebody must watch Ted, then,' said Charlie from the oak.

Ted picked up a piece of dead stick and threw it at him. He dodged it like a squirrel.

'If you say such things,' said Bevis, very angry, 'you shan't fight. Do you hear?'

'Yes,' said Charlie, penitent. 'I won't any more. But it's true,' he whispered to Fred under him.

'Everything's ready now, isn't it?' said Ted.

'Yes, I think so,' said Bevis.

'You haven't fixed the day,' said Val.

'No, more I have.'

'Let's have it today,' said Fred.

They caught it up and clamoured to have the battle at once.

'The swords are not ready,' said Mark.

'Are the eagles ready?' asked Phil.

'Two are,' said Mark.

'The other two shall be made this afternoon,' said Bevis. 'Phil, will you go into Latten for the blue ribbon for us; here's three shillings.'

'Yes,' said Phil, 'I'll get both at once – blue and red, and bring you the blue.'

'Tomorrow, then,' said Fred. 'Let's fight tomorrow.'

But they found that three of them were going out tomorrow. So, after some more discussion, the battle was fixed for the day after, and it was to begin in the evening, as some of them could not come before. The camps were to be made as soon after six o'clock as possible, and this agreed to, the council broke up, though it was understood that if anything else occurred to any one, or the captains wished to make any alterations, they were to send dispatches by special messengers to each other. The swords and eagles for Ted's party were to be fetched the evening before, and smuggled out of the window when it was dark, that no one might see them.

'Hurrah!'

So they parted, and the oak was left in silence, with the grass all trampled under it. The cattle fed down towards the water and the swallows wound in and out around them.

CHAPTER 13

The War Begins

As they were walking home Mark reproached Bevis with his folly in letting Ted, who was so tall himself, choose almost all the big soldiers.

'It's no use to hit you, or pinch you, or frown at you, or anything,' grumbled Mark; 'you don't take any more notice than a tree. Now Pompey will beat us hollow.'

'If you say any more,' said Bevis, 'I will hit you; and it is you who are the donk. I did not want the big ones. I like lightning-quick people, and I've got Cecil, who is as quick as anything – '

'What's the use of dreaming like a tree when you ought to have your eyes open; and if you're like that in the battle – '

'I tell you the knights were not the biggest; they very often fought huge people and monsters. And don't you remember how Ulysses served the giant with one eye?'

'I should like to bore a hole through Ted like that,' said Mark. 'He's a brute, and Phil's as cunning as ever he can be, and you've been and lost the battle.'

'I tell you I've got Cecil, who is as quick as lightning, and all the sharp ones, and if you say any more I won't speak to you again, and I'll have some one else for lieutenant.'

Mark nodded his head, and growled to himself, but he did not dare go farther. They worked all the afternoon in the bench-room, cutting off the swords to the same length, and fastening on the cross-pieces. They did not talk, Mark was sulky, and Bevis on his dignity. In the evening Phil came with the ribbons.

Next morning, while they were making two more eagles for

Pompey, Val Crassus came to say he thought they ought to have telescopes, as officers had field-glasses; but Bevis said they were not invented in the time of their war. The day was very warm, still, and cloudless, and, after they had fixed the three brass rings on each long rod for standards, Bevis brought the old grey book of ballads out of the parlour into the orchard. Though he had used it so often he could not find his favourite place quickly, because the pages were not only frayed but some were broader than others, and would not run through the fingers, but adhered together.

When he had found 'Kyng Estmere', he and Mark lay down on the grass under the shadow of a damson tree, and chanted the verses, reading them first, and then singing them. Presently they came to where:

> 'Kyng Estmere threwe the harpe asyde,
>   And swith he drew his brand;
> And Estmere he, and Adler yonge,
>   Right stiffe in stour can stand.
>
> 'And aye their swords soe sore can byte,
>   Through help of gramaryè,
> That soone they have slayne the Kempery men,
>   Or frost them forth to flee.'

These they repeated twenty times, for their minds were full of battle; and Bevis said after they had done the war they would study gramaryè or magic. Just afterwards Cecil came to ask if they ought not to have bugles, as the Romans had trumpets, and Bevis had a bugle somewhere. Bevis thought it was proper, but it was of no use, for nobody could blow the bugle but the old Bailiff, and he could only get one long note from it, so dreadful that you had to put your hands to your ears if you stood near. Cecil also said that in his garden at home there was a bay tree, and ought they not to have wreaths for the victors? Bevis said that was capital, and Cecil went home with orders from Caesar to get his sisters to make some wreaths of bay for their triumph when they had won the battle.

Soon after sunset that evening the Bailiff looked in, and said there was some sheet lightning in the north, and he was going to call back some of the men to put tarpaulins over two or three loaded wagons, as he thought, after so much dry, hot weather, there would be a great storm. The lightning increased very much, and after it grew dusk the flashes lit up the sky. Before sunset the sky had seemed quite cloudless, but now every flash showed innumerable narrow bands of clouds, very thin, behind which the electricity played to and fro.

While Bevis and Mark were watching it, Bevis's governor came out, and looking up said it would not rain and there was no danger; it was a sky-storm, and the lightning was at least a mile high. But the lightning became very fierce and almost incessant, sometimes crooked like a scimitar of flame, sometimes jagged, sometimes zigzag; and now and then vast acres of violet light, which flooded the ground and showed every tree and leaf and flower, all still and motionless; and after which, though lesser flashes were going on, it seemed for a moment quite dark, so much was the eye overpowered.

Bevis and Mark went up into the bench-room, where it was very close and sultry, and sat by the open window with the swords for Pompey bound up in two bundles, and the standards, but they were half afraid no one would come for them. Their shadows were perpetually cast upon the white wall opposite as the flashes came and went. The crossbow and lance, the boomerang and knobbed clubs were visible, and all the tools on the bench. Now and then, when the violet flashes came, the lightning seemed to linger in the room, to fill it with a blaze and stop there a moment. In the darkness that followed one of these they heard a voice call 'Bevis' underneath the window, and saw Phil and Val Crassus, who had come for the swords. Mark lowered the bundles out of the window by a cord, but when they had got them they still stood there.

'Why don't you go?' said Mark.

'Lightning,' said Val. 'It's awful.' It really was very powerful.

The pears on the wall, and everything however minute stood out more distinctly defined than in daytime.

'It's a mile high,' said Bevis. 'It won't hurt you.'

'Ted wouldn't come,' said Phil. 'He's gone to bed, and covered his head. You don't know how it looks out in the fields, all by yourself; it's all very well for you indoors.'

'I'll come with you,' said Bevis directly; up he jumped and went down to them, followed by Mark.

'Why wouldn't Ted come?' said Mark.

'He's afraid,' said Phil, 'and so was I till Val said he would come with me. Will lightning come to brass?' The flashes were reflected from the brass rings on the standards.

'I tell you it won't hurt,' said Bevis, quite sure, because his governor had said so. But when they had walked up the field and were quite away from the house and the trees which partly obstructed the view, he was amazed at the spectacle, for all the meadow was lit up; and in the sky the streamers of flame rose in and out and over each other, till you could not tell which flash was which in the confusion of lightning. Bevis became silent and fell into one of his dream states, when, as Mark said, he was like a tree. He was lost – something seemed to take him out of himself. He walked on, and they went with him, till he came to the gate opening on the shore of the New Sea.

'Oh, look!' they all said at once.

All the broad, still water, smooth as glass, shone and gleamed, reflecting back the bright light above; and far away they saw the wood (where Bevis and Mark once wandered) as plain as at noontide.

'I can't go home tonight,' said Phil. Val Crassus said he could sleep at his house, which was much nearer; but he, too, hesitated to start.

'It *is* awful,' said Mark.

'It's nothing,' said Bevis. 'I like it.' The continuous crackling of the thunder just then deepened, and a boom came rolling down the level water from the wooded hill. Bevis frowned, and held his lips tight together. He was startled, but he would not show it.

'I'll go with you,' he said; and though Mark pointed out that they would have to come back by themselves, he insisted. They went with Pompey's lieutenants till Val's house, lit up by lightning, was in sight; then they returned. As they came into the garden, Bevis said the battle ought to be that night, because it would read so well in the history afterwards. The lightning continued far into the night, and still flashed when sleep overcame them.

Next morning Bevis sprang up and ran to the window, afraid it might be wet; but the sun was shining and wind was blowing tremendously, so that all the willows by the brook looked grey as their leaves were turned, and the great elms by the orchard bowed to the gusts.

'It's dry,' shouted Bevis, dancing.

'Hurrah!' said Mark, and they sang.

> 'Kyng Estmere threwe his harpe asyde,
> And swith he drew his brand.'

This was the day of the great battle, and they were impatient for the evening.

About dinner-time there came a special messenger from Pompey with a letter, which was in Pompey's name, but Phil's handwriting. 'Ted Pompey to Caesar Bevis. Please tell me who you are going to send to be with me in my camp, and let him come to the stile in Barn Copse at half past five, and I will send Tim to be with you till the white handkerchiefs are up. And tell me if the lieutenants are to carry the eagles, or some one else.'

Bevis wrote back: 'Caesar to Pompey greeting' – this style he copied from his books – 'Caesar will send Charlie to be with you, as he can run quick, though he is little. The lieutenants are not to carry the eagles, but a soldier for them. And Caesar wishes you health.'

Then in the afternoon Mark had to go and tell Cecil and others, who were to send on the message to the rest of their party, to meet Bevis at the gate by the New Sea at half past five, and to mind and not be one moment later. While Mark was gone, Bevis roamed about the garden and orchard, and back again to the stable and sheds, and then into the rick-yard, which was strewn with twigs and branches torn off from the elms that creaked as the gale struck them; then indoors, and from room to room. He could not rest anywhere, he was so impatient.

At last he picked up the little book of the Odyssey, with its broken binding and frayed margin, from the chair where he had last left it; and taking it up into the bench-room, opened it at the twenty-second book, where his favourite hero wreaked his vengeance on the suitors. With his own bow in his right hand, and the book in his left, Bevis read, marching up and down the room, stamping and shouting aloud as he came to the passages he liked best:

'Swift as the word the parting arrow sings,
And bears thy fate, Antinous, on its wings!

* * * *

'For fate who fear'd amidst a feastful band?
And fate to numbers, by a single hand?

* * * *

'Two hundred oxen every prince shall pay:
The waste of years refunded in a day.
Till then thy wrath is just – Ulysses burn'd
With high disdain, and sternly thus return'd.

* * * *

'Soon as his store of flying fates was spent,
Against the wall he set the bow unbent;
And now his shoulders bear the massy shield,
And now his hands two beamy javelins wield.'

Bevis had dropped his bow and seized one of Mark's spears, not hearing, as he stamped and shouted, Mark coming up the stairs. Mark snatched up one of the swords, and as Bevis turned they rattled their weapons together, and shouted in their fierce joy. When satisfied they stopped, and Mark said he had come by the New Sea, and the waves were the biggest he had ever seen there, the wind was so furious.

They had their tea, or rather they sat at table, and rushed off as soon as possible; who cared for eating when war was about to begin! Seizing an opportunity, as the coast was clear, Mark ran up the field with the eagles, which, having long handles, were difficult to hide. Cecil and Bill took the greatcoat, and a railway-rug, which Bevis meant to represent his general's cloak. He followed with the basket of provisions on his shoulder, and was just thinking how lucky they were to get off without any inquiries, when he found they had forgotten the matches to light the camp-fire. He came back, took a box, and was going out again when he met Polly the dairymaid.

'What are you doing now?' she said. 'Don't spoil that basket with your tricks – we use it. What's in it?' putting her hand on the lid.

'Only bread-and-butter and ham, and summer apples. It's a picnic.'

'A picnic. What's that ribbon for?' Bevis wore the blue ribbon round his arm.

'Oh! that's nothing.'

'I've half a mind to tell – I don't believe you're up to anything good.'

'Pooh! don't be a donk,' said Bevis. 'I'll give you a long piece of the ribbon when I come back.'

Off he went, having bribed Scylla, but he met Charybdis in the gateway, where he came plump on the Bailiff!

'What's up now?' he gruffly inquired.

'Picnic.'

'Mind you don't go bathing; the waves be as big as cows.'

'Bathing,' said Bevis, with intense contempt. 'We don't bathe in the evening. Here, you — ' donk, he was going to say, but forbore; he gave the Bailiff a summer apple, and went on. The Bailiff bit the apple, muttered to himself about 'mischief', and walked towards the rick-yard. In a minute Mark came to meet Bevis.

'You did him?' he said.

'Yes,' said Bevis, 'and Polly too.'

'Hurrah!' shouted Mark. 'They're all there but one, and he's coming in five minutes.'

Bevis found his army assembled by the gate leading to the New Sea. Each soldier wore a blue ribbon round the left arm for distinction; Tim, who had been sent by Pompey to be with them till all was ready, wore a red one.

'Two and two,' said Caesar Bevis, taking his sword and instantly assuming a general's authoritative tone. He marshalled them in double file, one eagle in front, one half-way down, where his second lieutenant, Scipio Cecil, stood; the basket carried in the rear as baggage. Caesar and Mark Antony stood in front side by side.

'March,' said Bevis, starting, and they followed him.

The route was beside the shore, and so soon as they left the shelter of the trees the wind seemed to hit them a furious blow, which pushed them out of order for a moment. The farther they went the harder the wind blew, and flecks of brown foam like yeast came up and caught against them. Rolling in the same direction as they were marching, the waves at each undulation increased in size, and when they came to the bluff Bevis walked slowly a minute, to look at the dark hollows and the ridges from whose crests the foam was driven.

But here leaving the shore he led the army, with their brazen eagles gleaming in the sun, up the slope of the meadow where the solitary oak stood, and so beside the hedgerow till they reached the higher ground. The Plain, the chosen battlefield, was on the other side of the hedge, and it had been arranged that the camps should be pitched just without the actual campaigning-ground. On this elevated place the gale came along with even greater fury; and Mark Antony said that they would never be able to light a camp-fire that side, they must get through and into shelter.

'I shall do as I said,' shouted Bevis, scarcely audible, for the wind blew the words down his throat. But he kept on till he found a hawthorn bush, with brambles about the base, a detached thicket two or three yards from the hedge, and near which there was a gap. He stopped, and ordered the standard-bearer behind him to pitch the eagle there. The army halted, the eagles were pitched by thrusting the other end of the rods into the sward, the cloaks, coats, and rug thrown together in a heap, and the soldiers set to work to gather sticks for the fire. Of these they found plenty in the hedge, and piled them up in the shelter of the detached thicket.

Bevis, Mark Antony, and Scipio Cecil went through the gap to reconnoitre the enemy. They immediately saw the smoke of his camp-fire rising on the other side of the Plain, close to a gateway. The smoke only rose a little above the hedge there – the fire was on the other side – and was then blown away by the wind. None of Pompey's forces were visible.

'Ted, I mean Pompey, was here first,' said Mark Antony. 'He'll be ready before us.'

'Be quick with the fire,' shouted Caesar.

'Look,' said Scipio Cecil. 'There's the punt.'

Behind the stony promontory at the quarry they could see the punt from the high ground where they stood; it was partly drawn ashore just inside Fir-Tree Gulf, so that the projecting point protected it like a breakwater. The old man (the watcher) had started for the quarry to get a load of sand as usual, never thinking, as how should he think? that the gale was so furious. But he found himself driven along anyhow, and unable to row back; all he could do was to steer and struggle into the gulf, and so behind the Point, where he beached his unwieldy vessel.

141

Too much shaken to dig sand that day, and knowing that he could not row back, he hid his spade and the oars, and made for home on foot. But the journey by land was more dangerous than that by sea, for he insensibly wandered into the high-road, and came to an anchor in the first inn, where, relating his adventures on the deep with the assistance of ardent liquor, he remained.

Bevis, who had gone to light the fire with the matches in his pocket, now returned through the gap, and asked if anything had been seen of Pompey's men. As he spoke a Pompeian appeared, and mounting the spars of the distant gate displayed a standard, to which was attached a white handkerchief, which fluttered in the breeze.

'They're ready,' said Mark Antony. 'Come on. Which way shall we march? Which way are you going?'

The smoke of Caesar's fire rose over the hedge, and swept down by the gale trailed along the ground towards Pompey's. Bevis hastened back to the camp, and tied his handkerchief to the top of an eagle, Mark followed. 'Which way are you going?' he repeated. 'Where shall we meet then? What are you going to do?'

'I don't know,' said Caesar, angrily pushing him. 'Get away.'

'There,' growled Mark Antony to Scipio, 'he doesn't know what he's going to do, and Phil is as cunning as — '

The standard-bearer sent by Caesar pushed by him, got through the gap, and held up the white flag, waving it to attract more attention. In half a minute, Pompey's flag was hauled down, and directly afterwards some one climbed over the gate and set out running towards them. It was Charlie.

'Run, Tim,' said Caesar Bevis; 'we're ready.'

Tim dashed through the gap, and set off with all his might.

'Two and two,' shouted Caesar. 'Stand still, will you?' as they moved towards the opening. 'Take down that flag.'

The eagle-bearer resumed his place behind him. Caesar signing to the legions to remain where they were, went forward and stood on the mound. He watched the runners and saw them pass each other nearly about the middle of the great field, for though little, Charlie was swift of foot, and full of the energy which is more effective than size.

'Let's go.'

'Now then.'

'Start.'

The legions were impatient and stamped their feet, but Caesar would not move. In a minute or two Charlie reached him, red and panting with running.

'Now,' shouted Bevis, 'march!' and he leaped into the field; Charlie came next, for he would not wait to take his place in the ranks. The legions rushed through anyhow, eager to begin the fray.

'Two and two,' shouted Caesar, who would have no disorder.

'Two and two,' repeated his first lieutenant, Mark Antony.

'Two and two,' said Scipio Cecil, punching his men into place.

On they went, with Caesar leading, straight across the windswept plain for Pompey's camp. The black swifts flew about them, but just clearing the grass, and passing so close as seem almost under foot. There were hundreds of them, they come down from the upper air and congregate in a great gale; they glided over the field in endless turns and windings. Steadily marching, the army had now advanced a third part of the way across the field.

'Where's Pompey?' said Scipio Cecil.

'Where shall we meet and fight?' said Mark Antony.

'Silence,' shouted Bevis, 'or I'll degrade you from your rank, and you shan't be officers.'

They were silent, but everyone was looking for Pompey and thinking just the same. There was the gate in full view now,

and the smoke of Pompey's camp, but none of the enemy was visible. Bevis was thinking and trying to make out whether Pompey was waiting by his camp, or whether he had gone round behind the hedge, and if so, which way – to the right towards the quarry, or to the left towards the copse – but he could not decide, having nothing to guide him.

But though uncertain in his own mind, he was general enough not to let the army suppose him in doubt. He strode on in silence, but keeping the sharpest watch, till they came to the wagon-track, crossing the field from left to right. It had worn a gully or hollow way leading down to the right to the hazel hedge, where there was a gate. They came to the edge of the hollow way, where there were three thick hawthorn bushes and two small ash trees.

'Halt!' said Caesar Bevis, as the bushes partly concealed them from view. 'Stay here. Let no one move.'

Bevis himself went round the trees and looked again, but he could see nothing: Pompey and his army were nowhere in sight. He could not tell what to do, and returned slowly, thinking, when looking down the hollow way an idea struck him.

'Scipio, take your men' – ('Cohort,' said Antony) – 'take your cohort, jump into the road, and go down to the gate there. Keep out of sight – stoop: slip through the gate, and go up inside the hedge, dart round the corner and seize Ted's camp. Quick! And mind, if they're all there, of course you're not to fight, but come back. Now – quick.'

Scipio Cecil jumped into the hollow way followed by his five soldiers, and stooping so as to be hidden by the bank, ran towards the gate in the hazel hedge. They watched him till the cohort had got through the gate.

'Now what shall we do?' said Mark Antony.

'How can I tell what to do when Pompey isn't anywhere?' said Bevis, in a rage.

'Put me up a tree,' said Charlie, 'perhaps I could see.'

'You've no business to speak,' said Bevis; but he used the

idea and told two of them to 'bunt' (shove) Charlie up one of the ash trees till he could grasp a branch. Then Charlie, agile as a squirrel, was up in a minute.

'There's no one in their camp,' he shouted down. 'Cecil's rushing on it. Pompey, oh! I can see him.'

'Where?'

'There by the copse,' pointing to the left and partly behind them.

'Which way is he going?' asked Bevis.

'That way,' – to the left.

'Our camp,' said Mark.

'That's it,' said Bevis. 'Come down, quick. Turn to the left, (to the army). 'No, stop. Charlie, how many are there with Pompey?'

'Six, ten – oh, I can't count: I believe it's all. I can't see any anywhere else.'

'Quick!' shouted Bevis, turning his legions to the left. 'Quick march! Run!'

CHAPTER 14

The Battle of Pharsalia

THEY left Charlie to get down how he could, and started at a sharp pace to meet and intercept Pompey. Now, if Pompey had continued his course behind the hedge all the way, he must have got to Caesar's camp first, as Caesar could not crush through the hedge. But when Pompey came to the gate, from which the wagon tracks issued into the field, he saw that he could make a short cut thence to the gap by Caesar's camp, instead of marching round the irregular curve of the hedge. Caesar, though running fast to meet him, was at that moment passing a depression in the ground, and was out of sight. Pompey seized so favourable an opportunity, came through the gate, and ordering 'Quick march!' ran towards the gap. When Caesar came up out of the depression he saw Pompey's whole army running with their backs almost turned away from him towards the gap by the camp. They seemed to flee, and Caesar's legions beholding their enemies' backs, raised a shout. Pompey heard, and looking round, saw Caesar charging towards his rear. He halted and faced about, and at the same time saw that his own camp was in Caesar's possession; for there was an eagle at the gate there, and his baggage was being pitched over. Nothing daunted, Pompey ordered his soldiers to advance, and pushed them with his own hands into line, placing Crassus and Varro, one at either end.

As he came running, Caesar saw that the whole of Pompey's army was before them, while he had but two-thirds of his, and regretted now that he had so hastily detached Scipio's cohort. But waving his sword, he ran at the head of his men, keeping them in column. They were but a hundred yards apart, when

Pompey faced about, and so short a distance was rapidly traversed.

Caesar's sword was the first to descend with a crash upon an enemy's weapon, but Antony was hardly a second later, and before they could lift to strike again, the legion behind, with a shout, pushed them by its impetus right through Pompey's line.

When Caesar Bevis stopped running, and looked round, there was a break in the enemy's army, which was divided into two parts. Bevis instantly made at the part on his left (where Phil Varro commanded), instinctively, to crush this half with all his soldiers. But as they did not know what his object was, for he had not time even to give an order, only four or five followed him. The rest paused and faced Val Crassus; and these Ted Pompey and six or seven of his men at once attacked.

Bevis met Phil Varro, and crossed swords with him. Clatter! crash! snap! thump! bang! They slashed and warded: Bevis's shoulder was stung with a sharp blow. He struck back, and his sword sliding down Varro's, broke the cross-piece, and rapped his fingers smartly. Before Varro could hit again, two others, fighting, stumbled across and interrupted the combat.

'Keep together! Keep together!' shouted Phil Varro. 'Ted – Pompey, Pompey! Keep together!'

Slash! swish! crash! thump! 'Hit him! Now then! He's down! Hurrah!' Crash! Crack – a sword split and flew in splinters.

'Follow Bevis!' shouted Mark. 'Stick to Bevis! Fred! Bill! Quick!' He had privately arranged with these two, Fred and Bill, who were the biggest on their side, that all three should keep close to Bevis and form a guard. Mark was very shrewd, and he guessed that Ted Pompey, being so much stronger and well-supported with stout soldiers, would make every effort to seize Caesar, who was slightly built, and bind him prisoner. He did not tell Bevis that he had arranged this, for Bevis was a stickler for his imperial authority, and if Mark had told him, would be quite likely to countermand it.

Whirling his sword with terrible fury, Caesar Bevis had cut his way through all between. Slight as he was, the intense energy within him carried him through the ranks. He struck a sword from one; overthrew another rushing against him; sent a third on his knees, and reaching Phil, hit him on the arm so heavy a blow that, for a moment, he could not use his weapon, but gave way and got behind his men.

'Hurrah!' shouted Mark. 'Follow Bevis! Stick to Bevis!'

'Here I am,' said Bill, the young giant, hitting at Varro.

'So am I,' said Fred, the other giant, and slashing Varro on the side. Varro turned aside to defend himself, when Mark Antony rushed at and overturned him thump on the sward.

'Hurrah! Down they go!' Such a tremendous shout arose in another direction, that Caesar Bevis, Mark, and the rest, turned fresh from their own victory to see their companions thrashed.

'Over with them!'

Ted Pompey, Val Crassus, and the other half of the divided line had attacked the remainder of the legion, which paused, and did not follow Caesar. Separated from Bevis, they fought well, and struggled hard to regain him; and, while they could keep their assailants at sword's length, maintained the battle. But Varro's shout, 'Keep together! Keep together! Pompey! Keep together!' reminded Ted of what Phil Varro had taught him, and, signing to Crassus and his men to do the same, he crossed his arms, held his head low, and, with Crassus and the rest, charged, like bulls with eyes closed, disregarding the savage chops and blows he received. The manoeuvre was perfect successful; their weight sent them right over Caesar's men, who rolled on the ground in all directions.

'There!' said Mark, 'what did I tell you?'

'Come on!' shouted Caesar Bevis, and he ran to assist the fallen. He fell on Crassus, who chanced to be nearest, with such violence that Val gave way, when Bevis left him to attack

Ted. Ted Pompey, nothing loth, lifted his sword and stepped to meet him.

'Bill! Fred!' shouted Mark; and these three, hustling before Caesar Bevis, charged under Pompey's sword, for he could not hit three ways at once; and, thump, he measured his length on the grass.

'Cords! Ropes!' shouted Mark. 'Bill – the rope. Hold him down, Fred! Oh! You awful stupe! Oh!'

He stood stock-still, mouth agape; for Bevis, pushing Fred aside as he was going to kneel on Ted as men kneel on a fallen horse's head, seized Ted by the arm and helped him up.

'Three to one's not fair,' he said. 'Ted, get your sword and fight *Me*.'

Ted looked round for his sword, which had rolled a yard or two. At the same moment Varro, having got on his feet again, rushed and struck Caesar a sharp blow on his left arm. He turned, Varro struck again, but Fred guarded it off on his sword. Three soldiers, with Varro, surrounded Fred and Bevis, and, for the moment, they could do nothing but fence off the blows. Ted Pompey having found his sword, ran to aid Varro, when Mark hit him: he turned to strike at Mark, but a body of soldiers, with George and Tim at their head, rushed by, fighting with others, and bore Mark and Ted before them bodily. In a second all was confusion. On both sides the leaders were separated from their troops, the battle spread out, covering forty yards or more, and twenty individual combats raged at once. All the green declivity was covered with scattered parties, and no one knew which had the better.

'Keep together! Keep together!' shouted Varro, as he struck and rushed to and fro. 'I tell you, keep together! Ted! Ted! Pompey! Keep together!'

Swish! slash! clatter! thump! Hurrah! 'He's down!' 'Quick!' 'You've got it!' 'Take that!' Slash! But the slain rose again and renewed the fight.

Shrewd Mark Antony having knocked his man over, paused

on the higher part of the slope where he chanced to be, and looked down on the battle. He noted Phil Varro go up to Pompey and urge something. Pompey seemed to yield, and shouted, 'A tail! a tail! Crassus! George! Tim! A tail!'

Mark dashed down the slope to Bevis, who was fighting on the level ground. He hastened to save the battle for a 'tail' is a terrible thing. The leader, who must be the biggest, gets in front, the next biggest behind him, a third behind, and so on to the last, forming a tail, which is in fact a column, and so long as it keeps formation will bore a hole through a crowd. Before he could get to Caesar, for so many struck at him in passing that it took him some time to pass fifty yards, the tail was made — Pompey in front, next Val Crassus, then Varro, then Ike (a big fellow, but who had as yet done nothing, and was no good except for the weight of his body), then George, then Tim, and two more. Eight of them in a mighty line, which began to descend the slope.

'Look!' said Mark Anthony at last, touching Caesar Bevis, 'look there! It's a tail!'

'It doesn't matter,' said Bevis, looking up.

'Doesn't matter! Why, they'll *hunt* us!'

And Pompey did hunt them, downright hunt them along. Before Fred and Bill could come at Mark's call, before they could shake themselves free of their immediate opponents, Pompey came thundering down, and swept everything before him.

'Out of the way!' cried Mark. 'Bevis, out of the way! Oh! Now!' He wrung his hands and stamped.

Bevis stood and received the charge which Pompey led straight at him. Pompey, with his head down and arms crossed to defend it, ran with all his might. Bevis, never stirring, lifted his sword. There was a part of Pompey's bare head which his arms did not cover. It was a temptation, but he remembered the agreement, and he struck with all his strength on Pompey's left arm. So hard was the blow that the tough sword snapped,

151

and Pompey groaned with pain, but in the same instant Caesar felt as if an oak or a mountain had fallen on him. He was hurled to the ground with stunning force, and the column passed over him, one stepping on his foot.

There he lay for half a minute, dazed, and they might easily have taken him prisoner, but they could not stop their rush till they had gone twenty or thirty yards. By that time, Mark, Fred, and Bill had dragged Bevis up, and put a sword which they snatched from a soldier into his hand. He limped, and looked pale and wild for a minute, but his blood was up, and he wanted to renew the fight. They would not let him, they pulled him along.

'It's no use,' said Mark; 'you can't. We must get to the trees. Here, lean on me. Run. Sycamores! Sycamores!' he shouted.

'Sycamores! trees!' shouted Fred and Bill to their scattered followers. They urged Caesar to run, he limped, but kept pace with them somehow. Pompey had turned by now, and went through a small body of Caesar's men, who had rushed towards him when they saw he was down, just as if they had been straws. Still they checked the column a little, as floating beams check heavy waves, and so gave Caesar time to get more ahead.

'Sycamores!' Mark continued to shout as he ran, and the broken legions easily understood they were to rally there. At that moment the battle was indeed lost. Pompey ranged triumphant. Leading his irresistible and victorious column with shouting, he chased the flying Caesar.

Little Charlie, left in the ash-tree, could not get down, but saw the whole of the encounter. The lowest bough was too high to drop from, the trunk too large to clasp and slide down. He was imprisoned, and helpless, with the war in sight. He chafed and raged and shouted, till the tears of vexation rolled down his cheeks. Full of fiery spirit, it was torture to him to see the battle in which he could not take part. For awhile, watching the first shock, he forgot everything else in the interest of the fight; but presently, when the combatants separated, and were strewn as it were over the slope, he saw how easily at that juncture any united body could have swept the field, and remembered Scipio Cecil. Why did not Cecil come?

He looked that way, and from his elevation could see Cecil standing on the gate by Pompey's camp. Having sacked the camp, put the fire out, and thrown all the coats over the gate into a heap in the field, Scipio did not know what next he ought to do, and wondered that no orders had reached him from Caesar. He got up on the highest bar except one of the gate, but could see no one, the undulations of the ground completely concealing the site of the conflict. He did not know what to do; he waited a while and looked again. Once he fancied he heard shouting, but the gale was so strong he could not be certain.

Charlie in the ash-tree now seeing Pompey form the tail, or column, worked himself into a state of frenzy. He yelled, he screamed to Scipio to come, till he was hoarse, and gasped with the straining of his throat; but the howling of the tremendous wind through the trees by the gate, prevented Scipio from hearing a word. Had he known Charlie was in the tree he might have guessed there was something wrong from his frantic gestures, but he did not, and as there were so many scattered trees in the field, there was nothing to make him look at that one in particular. Charlie waved his handkerchief – all in vain.

He could see the crisis, but could not convey a knowledge of it to the idle cohort. He looked again at the battle. Caesar was down and trampled under foot. He threw up his arms, and almost lost his balance in his excitement. The next minute Caesar was up and he and his lieutenant were flying from Pompey. The column chased them, and the whole scene – the flight and the pursuit – passed within a short distance, half a stone's throw of the ash tree.

Quite wild, and lost to everything but his anger, Charlie the next second was out on a bough, clinging to it like a cat. He crawled out some way, till the bough bent a little with his weight. His design was to get out till it bowed towards the ground, and so lowered him – a perilous feat! He got half a yard further, and then swung under it, out and out, till the branch gave a good way. He tried again, and looked down; the ground was still far below. He heard a shout, it stimulated him. He worked out farther, till the branch cracked loudly; it would break, but would not bend much farther. His feet hung down now; he only held by his hands. Crack! Another shout! He looked down wildly, and in that instant saw a little white knob – a button mushroom in the grass. He left hold, and dropped. The little mushroom saved him, for it guided him, steadied his drop; his feet struck it and smashed it, and his knees giving under him, down he came.

But he was not hurt, his feet, as he hung from the bowed branch, were much nearer the earth than it had looked to him from his original perch, and he alighted naturally. The shock dazed him at first, as Bevis had been confused a few minutes previously. In a minute he was all right, and running with all his speed towards Scipio.

As Caesar ran, with the shout of victorious Pompey close behind, he said, 'If we could charge the column sideways we could break it – '

'If,' snorted Mark, with the contempt of desperation; 'If – of course!'

Caesar was right, but he had not got the means just then. Next minute they reached the first sycamore, not ten yards in front of Pompey. As they turned to face the enemy, with their backs to the great tree, Pompey lowered his head, crossed his arms, and the column charged. Nothing could stop that on-slaught, which must have crushed them, but Bevis, quick as thought, pushed Mark and Fred one way and Bill the other, stepping after the latter. Ted Pompey, with his eyes shut, and all the force of his men thrusting behind, crashed against the tree.

Down he went recoiling, and two or three more behind him.

Thwack! thwack! The four defenders hammered their enemies before they could recover the shock.

'Quick!' cried Mark; 'tie him – prisoner – quick,' pulling a cord from his pocket, and putting his foot on Ted, who was lying in a heap.

Before any one could help Mark the heap heaved itself up, and Val Crassus and Phil Varro hauled their half-stunned leader back out of reach.

Crash! clatter! bang! thwack!

'Backs to trees! Stand with backs to trees!' shouted Bevis, hitting out furiously. 'We shall win! Here, Bill!'

They planted themselves, these four, Bevis, Mark, Fred, and Bill, with their backs to the great trunk of the sycamore, standing a foot or two in front of it for room to swing their swords, and a little way apart for the same reason. The sycamore formed a bulwark so that none could attack them in rear.

The column, as it recoiled, widened out, and came on again in a semicircle, surrounding them.

'Give in!' shouted Val. 'We're ten to one!' (that was not numerically correct). 'Give in! You'll all be prisoners in a minute!'

'That we shan't,' said Bill, fetching him a sideway slash.

'If we could only get Scipio up,' said Mark. 'Where is he! Can't we get him?'

'I forgot him,' said Bevis. 'There, take that,' as he warded a cut and returned it. 'I forgot him. Look out Fred, that's it. Hurrah! Mark!' as Mark made a successful cut. 'How stupid.' In the heat and constant changes of the combat they had totally forgotten Cecil and his cohort.

'Why, we've been fighting two to three,' said Bill, 'and they haven't done us yet.'

'But we mean to,' said Tim, and Bill shrank involuntarily under an unexpected knock.

'Some more of you – there,' shouted Ted Pompey, as he came to himself, and saw a number of soldiers in the rear

155

watching the combat. 'You' – in a rage – 'you go round behind and worry them there; and some of you get up in the tree and hit down.

'Oh! botheration!' said Mark, as he heard the last order.

'We *must* get Cecil somehow,' said Bevis.

'Now then,' yelled Ted Pompey, stamping in terrible fury, 'do as I tell you; go round the tree, and "bunt" somebody up into it!'

Like knights with their backs to the tree, the four received them. The swords crossed and rattled, and for two or three minutes nothing else was heard; they were too busy to shout. The eight of the column would have succeeded better had not so many of the others pressed in to get a safe knock at Bevis, hitting from behind the bigger ones so as to be themselves in safety. These impeded Val and Phil and the first line.

One and all struck at Bevis. The dust flew from his coat, his shoulders smarted, his arms were sore, his left arm, which he used as a guard like a shield, almost numb with knocks.

His face grew pale with anger. He frowned and set his lips tight together, his eyes gleamed. The hail of blows descended on him, and though his wrist began to weary, he could not repay one-tenth of that they gave him.

'Give in! give in!' shouted Val, who was in front of him, and he put his left hand on Bevis's shoulder. With a twist of his wrist Bevis hit his right hand so sharp a knock that the sword flew out of it, and for second Val was daunted.

'Give in! give in!' shouted Phil, pushing to Val's assistance. 'You're done! It's no good. You can't help it. Hurrah!'

Two soldiers appeared in the fork of the tree above. Though so huge the trunk was short, and they began to strike down on Mark, who was forced to stand out so far from the tree that he was in great danger of being seized, and would have been, had they not been so bent on Bevis.

Bevis breathed hard and panted. So thick came the hail that he could do nothing. If he lifted his sword it was beaten down, if he struck, ten knocks came for one. He received his punishment in silence. Tim had the cord to bind him ready: they made a noose to throw over his head.

'Stick to Bevis,' shouted Mark. 'Bevis – Bevis – stick to Bevis – Fred – ah!' a smart knock made him grind his teeth, and four or five assailants rushing in separated him from Caesar.

Bevis was beaten on his knee. He crouched, his left side against the tree with his left hand against it, hitting wild and savage, and still keeping a short clear space with his sword.

'Stop!' cried Val, himself desisting. 'That's enough. Stop! stop! Don't hit him! He's done. We've got him! Now, Phil.'

Phil and Tim rushed in with the noose: Bevis sprang up, drove his head into Phil and sent him whirling with Tim under. Bevis made good use of the moment's breathing time he thus obtained, punishing three of his hardest thrashers.

'Keep together,' shouted Phil as he got up on his knees. 'If Ted would only do as I said. Hurrah!'

They had hammered Bevis by sheer dint of knocks down on his knees again. Fred and Bill in vain tried to get to him; they were attacked front and rear; Mark quite beside himself with rage, pushed, wrestled, and struck, but they encompassed him like bees. Bevis could hit no more; he warded as well as he could, he could not return.

'Shame! shame!' cried Val, pulling two back, one with each hand. 'Don't hit him! He's down!'

'Why doesn't he give in, then?' said Phil, black as thunder.

Ted Pompey, who had watched this scene for a moment without moving, smiled grimly as he saw Bevis could not hit.

'Now,' said he, 'Phil, Tim, George – Val's too soft. Come on – keep close – in we go and have him. Hurrah! Hang it! I say!'

'Whoop!'

CHAPTER 15

Scipio's Charge

SCIPIO's cohort rushed them clean away from the sycamore. In a mass, Scipio Cecil and his men (fetched by Charlie) with half or more of Caesar's scattered soldiers, who rallied at once to Cecil's compact party, rushed them right away. Cecil forced his men to be quiet as they ran; they saw the point, and there was not a sound till in close order they fell on Pompey. Pompey, Val, Phil, and the whole attacking party were swept away like leaves before the wind. Had they seen Scipio coming, or heard him, or in the least expected him, it would not have been so. But thus suddenly burst on from the rear, they were helpless, and carried away by the torrent.

In a second Bevis, Mark, Fred, and Bill found themselves free. Bevis stood up and breathed again. They came to him. 'Are you hurt?' said Mark.

'Not a bit,' said Bevis, laughing as he shook himself together. 'Look there!'

Whirled round and round by the irresistible pressure of the crowd, Pompey and his lieutenants were hurried away, shouting and yelling but unable even to strike, so closely were they hemmed in.

'They've got my eagle,' said Mark in a fury. His standard-bearer had been overthrown while he defended himself at the tree, and the eagle taken from him.

'Phil's down,' said Fred. 'So's Tim! And Ike! Hurrah!'

'Look at little Charlie hitting!' said Bill.

'Shout for Charlie,' said Bevis. 'Capital!'

'My eagle,' said Mark.

'Quick,' said Bevis suddenly. 'Mark — quick; you and Fred,

and Bill, and these' – three or four soldiers who came up now
things looked better – 'run quick, Mark, and get in the hollow,
you know where we cooked the bird, they're going that way.
See, Ted's beginning to fight again, and you will be behind him.
Make an ambush, don't you see? Seize him as he goes by.
Quick! I'm tired, I'll follow in a minute.'

Off ran Mark, Fred, Bill, and the rest, and making a little
circuit, got into the bowl-like hollow. The crowd with Scipo
Cecil was still thrusting Pompey and his men before them, but
Ted had worked himself free by main force, and he and Val
Crassus, side by side, were fighting as they were forced backwards. Step by step they went backwards, but disputing every
inch, straight back for the hollow where Mark and his party
were crouching. In half a minute, Ted would certainly be
taken.

'Victory!' shouted Bevis, in an ecstasy of delight. He had
been leaning against the sycamore: he stood up and stepped
just in front of it to see better, shading his eyes (for his hat had
gone long since) with his left hand, the point of his sword
touching the ground. He was alone; he rejoiced in the triumph
of his men. The gale blew his hair back and brushed his cheek.
His colour rose; a light shone in his eyes.

'We've won!' he shouted. Just then the hurricane smote the
tree, and as there was less noise near him, he heard a bough
crack above. He looked up, thinking it might fall; it did not,
but when he looked back Ted was gone.

'He's down!' said Bevis. 'They've got him.'

He could see Mark Antony, who had risen out of the hollow;
thus caught between two forces, Scipio pushing in front, the
Pompeians broke and scattered to the right in a straggling line.

'Hurrah! But where's Ted? Hurrah!'

Bevis was so absorbed in the spectacle that, though the fight
was only a short distance from him, the impulse to join it did
not move him. He was lost in the sight.

'They're running!'

'I've got you!'

Ted Pompey pounced on him from behind the sycamore tree; Bevis involuntarily started forward, just escaping his clutch, struck, parried, and struck again.

Pompey, while driven backwards step by step by Scipio, had suddenly caught sight of Bevis standing alone by the sycamore. He slipped from Scipio, and ran round just as Bevis looked up at the cracking bough, and Mark sprang out of the hollow. Scipio's soldiers shouted, seeing Pompey as they thought running away. Mark for a moment could not understand what had become of him, the next he was occupied in driving the Pompeians as they yielded ground. Pompey running swiftly got round behind the tree and darted on Caesar, whose strategy had left him alone, intending to grasp him and seize him by main force.

Caesar Bevis slipped from him by the breadth of half an inch.

Pompey hit hard, twice, thrice; crash, clatter. His arm was strong, and the sword fell heavy; rattle, crash. He hit his hardest, fearing help would come to Bevis. Swish! slash!

Twack! He felt a sharp blow on his shoulder. Bevis kept him off, saw an opportunity, and cut him. With swords he was more than Ted's match. He and Mark had so often practised they had both become crafty at fencing. The harder Ted hit, over-balancing himself to put force into the blow, and the less able to recover himself quickly, the easier Bevis warded, and every three knocks gave Ted a rap. Ted danced round him, trying to get an advantage; he swung his sword to and fro in front of him horizontally. Bevis retired to avoid it past the sycamore. Finding this answer, Ted swung it all the more furiously, and Bevis retreated, watching his chance, and they passed several trees on to the narrow breadth of level short sward between the trees and the quarry.

Ted's chest heaved with the fury of his blows; Bevis could not ward them, at least not so as to be able to strike afterwards. But suddenly, as Ted swung it still fiercer, Bevis resolutely received the sword full on his left arm – thud, and stopped it. Before Ted could recover himself Bevis hit his wrist, and his sword dropped from it on the ground.

Ted instantly rushed in and grappled with him. He seized him, and by sheer strength whirled him round and round, so that Bevis's feet but just touched the sward. He squeezed him, and tried to get him across his hip, to throw him; but Bevis had his collar, and he could not do it. Bevis got his feet the next instant, and worked Ted, who breathed hard, back.

The quarry was very near, they were hardly three yards from the edge of the cliff; the sward beneath their feet was short when the sheep had fed it close to the verge, and yellow with lotus flowers. Yonder far below were the waves, but they saw nothing but themselves.

The second's pause, as Bevis forced Ted back two steps, then another, then a fourth, as they glared at each other, was over. Ted burst on him again. He lifted Bevis, but could not for all his efforts throw him. He got his feet again.

'You punched me!' hissed Ted between his teeth.

'I didn't.'

'You did.' Ted hit him with doubled fist. Bevis instantly hit back. They struck without much parrying. At this, as at swords, Bevis's quick eye and hand served him in good stead. He kept Ted back; it was at wrestling Ted's strength was superior. Ted got a straight-out blow on the chin; his teeth rattled.

He hurled himself bodily on Bevis; Bevis stepped back and avoided the direct hug, and the cliff yawned under him. Into Ted's mind there flashed a picture, something he had seen when two men were fighting in the road. Without a thought, it was done in the millionth of a second, he tripped Bevis. Bevis staggered, swung round, half saved himself, clutched at Ted's arm, and put his foot back over the cliff on to nothing.

Ted did but see his face, and Bevis was gone. As he fell he disappeared; the hedge hid him. Crash!

T–F

Ted's face became of a leaden pallor, his heart stopped beating; an uncontrollable horror seized upon him. Some inarticulate sound came from between his teeth. He turned and fled down the slope into the firs, through the fields, like the wind, for his home under the hills. He fled from his own act. How many have done that who could have faced the world! Bevis, he knew, was dead. As he ran he muttered to himself, constantly repeating it, 'His bones are all smashed; I heard them. His bones are all smashed.' He never stopped till he reached his home. He rushed upstairs, locked his door, and got into bed with all his things on.

Bevis was not dead, nor even injured. He had scarcely fallen ten feet before he was brought up by a flake, which is a stronger kind of hurdle. It was one of those originally placed along the edge of the precipice to keep cattle from falling over. It had become loose, and a horse rubbing against it sent it over weeks before. The face of the cliff there had been cut into a groove four or five feet wide years ago by the sand-seekers. This groove went straight down to a deep pool of water, which had filled up the ancient digging for the stone of the lower stratum. As the flake tumbled it presently lodged aslant the cutting, and it was in that position when Bevis fell on it.

His weight drove it down several feet farther, when the lower part caught in a ledge at that side of the groove, and it stopped with a jerk. The jerk cracked one bar of the flake, which was made much like a very slender gate, and it was this sound which Ted in his agony of mind mistook for the smashing bones.

Bevis when he struck the flake instinctively clutched it, and it was well that he did so, or he would have rolled over into the pool. For the moment when he felt his foot go into space he lost conscious awareness. He really was conscious, but he had no control, or will, or knowledge at the time, or memory afterwards. That moment passed completely out of his life, till the jerk of the flake brought him to himself. He saw the pool underneath as through the bars of a grating, and clasped the flake still firmer.

In that position, lying on it, he remained for a minute, getting his breath, and recognizing where he was. Then he rose up a little, and shouted 'Mark!' The gale took his voice out over the New Sea, whose waves were rolling past not more than twenty yards from the base of the cliff.

'Mark!' No one answered. He sat upon the flake still holding it, and began to try to think what he should do if Mark did not come.

His first thought was to climb up somehow, but when he looked he saw that the sand was as straight as a wall. Steps might be cut in the soft sand, and he put his hand in his pocket for his knife, when he reflected that steps for the feet would be of no use unless he had something to hold on to as well. Then he looked down, inclined for the moment to drop into the water, which would check his fall, and bring him up without injury, only the sides of the pool were as steep as the cliff itself, so that anyone swimming in it could not climb up to get out.

He recollected the frog which he and Mark put in the stone trough, to see how it swam, and how it went round and round, and could not escape. So he should be if he fell into the pool. He could only swim round and round until his strength failed him. If the flake broke, or tipped, or slipped again, that was what would happen.

Bevis sat still, and tried to think; and while he did so he looked out over the New Sea. The sun was now lower, and all the waves were touched with purple, as if the crests had been sprinkled with wine. The wind blew even harder, as the sun got near the horizon, and fine particles of sand were every now and then carried over his head from the edge of the precipice.

What would Ulysses have done? He had a way of getting out of everything; but try how he would, Bevis could not think of any plan, especially as he feared to move much, lest the insecure platform under him should give way. He could see his reflection in the pool beneath, as if it were waiting for him to come in reality.

While he sat quite still, pondering, he thought he heard a rumbling sound, and supposed it to be the noise of tramping feet, as the legions battled above. He shouted again, 'Mark! Mark!' and immediately wished he had not done so, lest it should be a party fetched by Pompey to seize him; for if he was captured the battle would be lost. He did not know that Pompey had fled, and feared that his shout would guide his pursuers, forgetting in his excitement that if he could not get up to them, neither could they get down to him. He kept still looking up, thinking that in a minute he should see faces above.

But none appeared, and suddenly there was another rumbling noise, and directly afterwards a sound like scampering, and then a splash underneath him. He looked, and some sand was still rolling down, sprinkling the pool. 'A rabbit,' thought Bevis. 'It was a rabbit and a weasel. I see – of course! Yes; if it was a rabbit then there's a ledge, and if there's a ledge I can get along.'

Cautiously he craned his head over the edge of the flake, carefully keeping his weight as well back as he could. There was a ledge about two feet lower than the flake, very narrow, not more than three or four inches there; but having seen so many of these ledges in the quarry before, he had no doubt it widened. As that was the extreme end, it would be narrowest there. He thought he could get his foot on it, but the difficulty was what to hold to.

It was of no use, putting his foot on a mere strip like that unless there was something for his hand to grasp. Bevis saw a sandmartin pass at that moment, and it occurred to him that if he could find a martin's hole to put his hand in, that would steady him. He felt round the edge of the groove, when, as he extended himself to do so, the flake tipped a little, he drew back hastily. His chest thumped with sudden terror, and he sat still to recover himself. A humble-bee went by round the edge of the groove, and presently a second, buzzing close to him, and seeing these two he remembered that one had passed before, making three humble-bees.

'There must be thistles,' said Bevis to himself, knowing that humble-bees are fond of thistle-flowers, and that there were quantities of thistles in the quarry. 'If I can catch hold of some thistles, perhaps I can do it.' He wanted to feel round the perpendicular edge again, but feared that the flake would tip. In half a minute he got his pocket-knife, opened the largest blade, and worked it into the sand farthest from the edge – in the corner – so as to hold the flake there like a nail.

Then with the utmost caution, and feeling every inch of his way, he put his hand round the edge, and moving it about presently felt a thistle. Would it hold? that was the next thing; or should he pull it up if he held to it? How could he hold it tight, the prickles would hurt so. He knew that thistles generally have deep roots and are hard to pull up, so he thought it would be firm, and besides, if there was most likely several, and three or four would be stronger.

Taking out his handkerchief, he put his hand in it, and twisted it round his wrist to make a rough glove, then he knelt up close to the sand wall, and steadied himself before he started. The flake creaked under these movements, and he hesitated. Should he do it, or should he wait till Mark missed him and searched? But the battle – the battle might be lost by then, and Mark and all his soldiers driven from the field, and Pompey would triumph, and fetch long ladders, and take him prisoner.

Bevis frowned till a groove ran up the centre of his forehead, then he moved towards the verge of the flake, and slowly put his foot over till he felt the narrow ledge, at the same time searching about with his hand for the thistle. Now he had his foot on the ledge, and his hand on the stem of the thistle; it was very stout, which reassured him, but the prickles came through the handkerchief. A moment's pause, and he sprang round and stood upright on the ledge.

His spring broke the blade of the knife, and the flake upset and crashed down splash into the pool.

The prickles of the thistle dug deep into his hand, causing exquisite pain.

He clung to the thistle, biting his lips, till he had got his other foot on. One glance showed him his position.

The moment he had his balance he let go of the thistle, and ran along the ledge, which widened to about nine inches or a foot, tending downwards. Running kept him from falling, just as a bicycle remains upright while in motion.

In four yards he leapt down from the ledge to a much broader one, ran along that six or seven yards, still descending, sprang from it down on a wide platform, thence six or eight feet on to an immense heap of loose sand, into which he sank above his knees, struggled, slipping as he went down its yielding side, and landed on his hands and knees on the sward below, while still the wavelets raised by the fall of the flake were breaking in successive circles against the sides of the pool.

He was up in a moment, and stamped his feet alternately to shake the sand off; then he pulled out some of the worst of the thistle points stuck in his hand, and kicked his heels up and danced with delight.

Without looking back he ran up on the narrow bank between the excavation and the New Sea, as the nearest place to look round from. The punt was just there inside the headland. He saw that the waves, though much diminished in force by the point, had gradually worked it nearly off the shore. He could see nothing of the battle, but remembering a place where the ascent of the quarry was easy, and where he and Mark had often run up the slope, which was thinly grown with grass, he started there, ran up, and was just going to get out on the field when he recollected that he was alone, and had no sword, so that if Pompey had got a party of his soldiers, and was looking for him, they could easily take him prisoner. He determined to reconnoitre first, and seeing a little bramble bush and a thick growth of nettles, peered out from beside this cover. It was well that he did so.

Val Crassus, with a strong body of Pompeians, was coming from the sycamores direct towards him. They were not twenty yards distant when Bevis saw them, and instantly crouched on hands and knees under the brambles. He heard the tramp of their feet, and then their voices.

'Where can he be?'

'Are you sure you looked all through the firs?'

'Quite sure.'

'Well, if he isn't in the firs, nor behind the sycamores, nor anywhere else, he *must* be in the quarry,' said Crassus.

'So I think.'

'I'm sure.'

'Ted's got him down somewhere.'

'Perhaps he's hiding from Ted.'

'Can you see him now in the quarry?'

They crowded on the edge, looking over Bevis into the excavated hollow beneath. Now Bevis had not noticed when he crouched that he had put his hand almost on the mouth of a wasp's nest, but suddenly feeling something tickle the back of his hand, he moved it, and instantly a wasp, which had been crawling over it, stung him. He pressed his teeth together, and shut his eyes in the endeavour to repress the exclamation which rose; he succeeded, but could not help a low sound in his chest. But they were so busy crowding round and talking they did not hear it.

'I can't see him.'

'He's not there.'

'He may be hidden behind the stone-heaps. There's a lot of nettles down there,' said Crassus.

'Yes,' said another, and struck the nettles by Bevis, cutting down three or four with his sword.

'Anyhow,' said Crassus, 'we're sure to have him, he can't get away; and Mark's a mile off by this time.'

'Look sharp then; let's go down and hunt round the stone-heaps.'

'There's the old oak,' said someone; 'It's hollow; perhaps he's in that.'

'Let's look in the oak as we go round to get down, and then behind the stones. Are there any caves?'

'I don't know,' said Crassus. 'Very likely. We'll see. March.'

They moved along to the left; Bevis opened his eyes, and saw the sting and its sheath left sticking in his hand. He drew it out, waited a moment, and then peered out again from the brambles. Crassus and the cohort were going towards the old hollow oak, which stood not far from the quarry on low ground by the shore of the New Sea, so that their backs were towards him. Bevis stood out for a second to try and see Mark. There was not a sign of him, the field was quite deserted, and he remembered that Crassus had said Mark was a mile away. 'The battle's lost,' said Bevis to himself. 'Mark has fled, and Pompey's after him, and they'll have me in a minute.'

He darted down the slope into the hollow, which concealed him for the time, and gave him a chance to think. 'If I go out on the Plain they'll see me,' he said to himself; 'if I run to the firs I must cross the open first; if I hide behind the stones, they're coming to look. What shall I do? The New Sea's that side, and I can't. Oh!'

He was over the bank and on the shore in a moment. The jutting point was rather higher than the rest of the ground there, and hid him for a minute. He put his left knee on the punt, and pushed hard with his right foot. The heavy punt, already loosened by the waves, yielded, moved, slid off the sand, and floated. He drew his other knee on, crept down on the bottom of the punt, and covered himself with two sacks, which were intended to hold sand. He was, too, partly under the seat, which was broad. The impetus of his push off and the wind and waves carried the punt out, and it was already fifteen or twenty yards from the land when Crassus and his men appeared.

They had found the oak empty, and were returning along the shore to search the quarry. The wind brought their voices out over the water.

'Mind, he'll fight if he's there.'

'Pooh! we're ten to one.'

'Well, he hits hard.'

'And he can run. We shall have to catch him when we find him; he can run like a hare.'

'Look!'

'The punt's loose.'

'So it is.'

'Serves the old rascal right. Hope it will sink.'

'It's sure to sink in those big waves,' said Crassus. 'Come on,' and down he went into the quarry, where they looked behind the stone-heaps and every place they could think of, in vain.

CHAPTER 16

Bevis in the Storm

In the punt Bevis remained quite still under the sacks while Crassus searched the quarry for him, then looked up in the sycamores, and afterwards went to the hazel hedge. Bevis, peeping out from under the broad seat, saw him go there, and knew that he could not see over the New Sea from the lower ground, but as others might at any moment come on the hill, he considered it best to keep on the bottom of the boat. The punt at first floated slowly, and was sheltered by the jutting point, but still the flow of the water carried it out, and in a little time the wind pushed it more strongly as it got farther from shore. Presently it began to roll with the waves, and Bevis soon found some of the inconveniences of a flat-bottomed vessel.

The old punt always leaked, and the puntsman being too idle to bale till compelled, the space between the real and the false bottom was full of water. As she began to roll this water went with a sound like 'swish' from side to side, and Bevis saw it appear between the edge of the boards and the side. When she had drifted quite out of the gulf and met the full force of the waves every time they lifted her, this bilge-water rushed out over the floor. Bevis was obliged to change his position, else he would soon have been wet through. He doubled up the two sacks and sat on them, reclining his arms on the seat so as to be as low down and as much concealed as possible.

This precaution was really needless, for both the armies were scattered, the one pursuing and the other pursued, in places where they could not see him, and even had they moved by the shore they would never have thought of looking for him where he was. He could not know this, and so sat on the sacks. The punt was now in the centre of the storm, and the waves seemed immense to Bevis. Between them the surface was dark, their tops were crested with foam, which the wind blew off against him, so that he had to look in the direction he was going (and not back) to escape the constant shower of scud in his face.

The punt being so cumbrous and heavy did not rise buoyantly as the waves went under, but hung on them, so that the crests of the larger waves frequently broke over the gunwale and poured a flood of water on board. There were crevices too in her sides, which in ordinary times were not noticed, as she was never loaded deep enough to bring them down to the water-line. But now the waves rising above these found out the chinks, and rushed through in narrow streams.

The increase of the water in the punt again forced Bevis to move, and he sat up on the seat with his feet on the sacks. The water was quite three inches above the false bottom, and rushed from side to side with a great splash, of course helping to heel her over. Bevis did not like this at all; he ceased singing, and looked about him.

It seemed a mile (it was not so far) back to the quarry, such a waste of raging waves and foam! On either side the shore was a long, long way; he could not swim a tenth as far. He recognized on his left the sedges where he and Mark had wandered, and found that he was rapidly coming near the two islands. He began to grow anxious, thinking that the boat would not keep afloat very much longer. The shore in front beyond the island was a great way, and from what he knew of it he believed it was encumbered far out with weeds through which, if the punt foundered, he could not swim, so that his hope was that she would strike either the Unknown Island or Serendib.

Both were now near, and he tried to discover whether the current and wind would throw him on them. A long white streak parallel to the course of the storm marked the surface of the water, rising and falling with the waves like a ribbon, and this seemed to pass close by Serendib. The punt being nearly on the streak he hoped he should get there. If he only had something to row with! The Old Man of the Sea had hidden the sculls, and had not troubled to bring the movable seat with him, as he did not want it. The movable seat would have made a good paddle. As for the stretcher it was fixed nailed to the floor.

He could do nothing paddling with his hand; in calm weather he might, but not in such a storm of wind. If he only had something to paddle with he could have worked the punt into the lines so as to strike on Serendib. As it was he could do nothing; if he had only had his hat he could have baled out some of the water, which continued to rise higher.

Drifting as the waves chose he saw that Serendib was a low, flat island. The Unknown Island rose into a steep sand bluff at that end which faced him. Against this bluff the waves broke with tremendous fury, sending the spray up to the bushes on the top. Bevis watched to see where the punt would ground, or whether it would miss both islands and drift through the narrow channel between them.

He still thought it might hit Serendib, when it once more rotated, and that brought it in such a position that the waves must make it crash against the low steep cliff of the Unknown Island. Bevis set his teeth, and prepared to dig his nails into the sand, when just as the punt was within three waves of the shore, it seemed to pause. This was the reflux – the under-tow, the water recoiling from the bank – so that the boat for half a moment was suspended or held between the two forces.

Before he had time to think what was best to do the punt partly swung round, and the rush of the current, setting between the islands, carried it along close beside the shore. The bluff now sloped, and the waves rushed up among the bushes and trees. Bevis watched, saw a chance, and in an instant stepped on the seat, and leaped with all his might. It was a long way, but he was a good jumper, and his feet landed on the ground. He would even then have fallen back into the water had he not grasped a branch of alder.

For a moment he hung over the waves, the next he drew himself up, and was safe. He stepped back from the edge, and instinctively put his left arm round the alder trunk, as if clinging to a friend. Leaning against the tree he saw the punt, pushed out by the impetus from his spring, swing round and drift rapidly between the islands. It went some distance, and then began to settle, and slowly sank.

Bevis remained holding the tree till he had recovered himself, then he moved farther into the island, and went a little way up the bluff, whence he saw that the sun had set. He soon forgot his alarm, and as that subsided began to enjoy his position. 'What a pity Mark was not with me!' he said to himself. 'I am so sorry. Only think, I'm really shipwrecked. It's splendid!' He kicked up his heels, and a startled blackbird flew out of a bramble bush and across the water.

Bevis watched him fly aslant the gale till he lost sight of him in the trees on shore. Looking that way – north-west – his quick eyes found out a curious thing. On that side of the island there was a broad band of weeds stretching towards the shore, and widening the farther it extended.

Watching the green undulations he looked farther and saw that at some distance from the island there were banks covered with sedges, and the channel between the weeds (showing deeper water) wound in among these. Next he went up on the top of the cliff, and found a young oak tree growing on the summit, to which he held while thus exposed to the full strength of the wind, and every now and then the spray flew up and sprinkled him.

Shading his eyes with his hand (for the wind seemed to hurt them) he looked towards the quarry, which appeared yellow at this distance. He saw a group of people, as he supposed Pompey's victorious army, passing by the sycamores.

'It's no use, Ted,' he said to himself, 'you can't find me, and you can't win. I've done you.'

The group was really Mark and the rest searching for him. After a while they went over the hill, and Bevis could not see them.

Bevis came down from the cliff, and thought he would see how large the island was, so he went all round it, as near the edge as he could. It was covered with wood, and there were the thickest masses of bramble he had ever seen. He had to find a way round these, so that it took him some time to get along. Some firs too obstructed his path, and he found one very tall spruce. At last he reached the other extremity, where the ground was low, and only just above the water, which was nearly smooth there, being sheltered by the projecting irregularities of the shore.

Returning he had in one place to climb over quantities of stones, for the bank just there was steeper, and presently compelled him to go more inland. The island seemed very large, in shape narrow and long, but so thickly overgrown with bushes and trees that he could not see across it. The surface was uneven, for he went down into a hollow which seemed beneath the level of the water, and afterwards came to a steep bank, on rounding which he was close to the place from which he started.

Not having had anything to eat since dinner (for they shirked their tea), and having gone through all these labours, Bevis began to feel hungry, but there was nothing to eat on his island, for the berries were not yet ripe. First he whistled, then he wished Mark would come, then he walked up to the cliff and climbed into the oak on the summit.

'Mark is sure to come,' he said to himself. Just then he saw the full moon, which had risen above the distant hills, and shining over the battle-field touched the raging waves with tarnished silver.

He looked at the great round shield on which the heraldic

174

markings were dimmed by its own gleam. He almost fancied he could see it move, so rapidly did it sweep upwards. It was clear and bright as if wind-swept, as if the hurricane had brushed it. Bevis watched it a little while, and then he thought of Mark. The possibility that Mark would not know where he was never entered his mind, nor did it occur to him that perhaps even Mark would hesitate to venture out in such a tempest of wind: so strong was his faith in his companion.

The wind blew so hard up in the tree, he presently got down, and descended the slope till the ridge sheltered him. He sat on the rough grass, put his hands in his pockets, and whistled again to assure himself that he liked it. But he was hungry, and the time seemed very slow, and he could not quite suppress an inward feeling that shipwreck when one was quite alone was not altogether so splendid. It was so dull.

'Kaack! kaack!' like an immensely exaggerated and prolonged 'quack' without the 'qu'; a harsh shriek resounding over the water even above the gale.

'A heron,' thought Bevis. 'If only I had a gun, or my bow now.' He took a stone, and peered out over the water on the side the cry came from, which was where the weeds were. The surface was dim and shadowy in that direction, and he could not see the heron. He returned and sat down on the grass. He could not think of anything to do, till at last he resolved to build a hut of branches, as shipwrecked people did. But when he came to pull at the alder branches, those of any size were too tough; the aspen were too high up; and the firs too small.

'Stupid,' he said to himself. 'This *is* stupid.' Once more he returned to the foot of the slope, and sat down on the grass.

Before him there were the shadowy trees and bushes, and behind he could hear the boom of the waves, yet it never occurred to him how weird the place was. All he wanted was to be at something.

'Why ever doesn't Mark come?' he repeated to himself. Just

then he chanced to put his hand in his jacket pocket, and instantly jumped up delighted. 'Matches!' He took out the box, which he had used to light the camp-fire, and immediately set about gathering materials for a fire. 'The proper thing to do,' he thought. 'The very thing!'

He soon began to make a pile of dead wood, when he stopped and, lifting the bundle in his arms, carried it up the slope, nearly to the top of the cliff, where he put it down behind a bramble bush. He thought that if he made the fire on the height it would be a guide to Mark, but down in the hollow no one could see it. To get together enough sticks took some time; for the moon though full and bright only gave light where the beams fell direct. In the shadow he could hardly see at all.

Having arranged the pile, and put all the larger sticks on one side, ready to throw on presently, he put some dry leaves and grass underneath, as he had no straw or papers, struck a match and held it to them. Some of the leaves smouldered, one crackled, and the dry grass lit a little, but only just where it was in contact with the flame of the match. The same thing happened with ten matches, one after the other. The flame would not spread. Bevis on his knees thought a good while, and then he set to work and gathered some more leaves, dry grass, and some thin chips of dry bark. Then he took out the sliding drawer of the match-box, and placed it under these, as the deal of which it was made would burn like paper. The outer case he was careful to preserve, because they were safety matches, and lit only on the prepared surface.

In and around the little drawer he arranged half a dozen matches, and then lit them, putting the rest in his pocket. The flame caught the deal, which was as thin as a wafer, then the bark and tiny twigs, then the dry grass and larger sticks. It crept up through the pile, crackling and hissing. In three minutes, it had hold of the boughs, curling its lambent point round them, as a cow licks up the grass with her tongue. The bramble bush sheltered it from the gale, but let enough wind through to cause a draught.

Up sprang the flames, and the bonfire began to cast out heat, and red light flickering on the trees. Bevis threw on more branches, the fire flared up and gleamed afar on the wet green carpet of undulating weeds. He hauled up a fallen pole, the sparks rose as he hurled it on.

'Hurrah!' shouted Bevis, dancing and singing:

> 'Kyng Estmere threwe his harpe asyde,
> And swith he drew his brand;
> And Estmere he, and Adler yonge,
> Right stiffe in stour can stand!'

'Adler will be here in a minute.' He meant Mark.

CHAPTER 17

Mark is Put in Prison

BUT Adler was himself in trouble. After they had waited some time in the camp, thinking that Bevis would be certain to return there sooner or later, finding that he did not come, the whole party, with Mark at their head, searched and researched the battle-field and most of the adjacent meadows, not overlooking the copse. Mark next ran home, hoping that Bevis for some reason or other might have gone there, and asked himself whether he had offended him in any way, and was that why he had left the fight? But he could not recollect that he had done anything.

Bevis, of course, was not at home, and Mark returned to the battle-field, every minute now adding to his anxiety. It was so unlike Bevis that he felt sure something must be wrong.

'Perhaps he's drowned,' said Val.

'Drowned,' repeated Mark, with intense contempt; 'why he can swim fifty yards.'

Fifty yards is not far, but it would be far enough to save life on many occasions. Val was silenced; still Mark, to be certain, went along the shore, and even some way up the Nile. By now the others had left, one at a time, and only Val, Cecil, and Charlie remained.

The four hunted again, then they walked slowly across the field, trying to think. Mark picked up Bevis's hat, which had fallen off in the battle; but to find Bevis's hat was nothing, for he had a knack of leaving it behind him.

'Perhaps he's gone to your place,' said Charlie, meaning Mark's home.

Mark shook his head. 'But I wish you would go and see,' he said; he dared not face Frances.

'So I will,' said Charlie, always ready to do his best, and off he went.

Charlie's idea gave rise to another, that Bevis might be gone to Jack's home in the Downs, and Val offered to go and inquire, though it was a long, long walk.

He set out, Cecil went with him, and Mark, left to himself, walked slowly home, hoping once more Bevis might have returned. As he came in with Bevis's hat in his hand, the servants pounced upon him. Bevis was missed, there had been a great outcry, and all the people were inquiring for him. Several had come to the kitchen to gossip about it. The uproar would not have been so great so soon but it had got out that there had been a battle.

'You said it was a picnic,' said Polly, shaking Mark.

'You told I so,' said the Bailiff, seizing his collar.

'Let me go,' shouted Mark, punching.

'Well, what have you done with him? Where is he?'

Mark could not tell, and between them, four or five to one, they hustled him into the cellar.

'You must go to jail.' said the Bailiff grimly. 'Bide there a bit.'

'How can you find Bevis without me?' shouted Mark, who had just admitted he did not know where Bevis was. But the Bailiff pushed him stumbling down the three stone steps, and he heard the bolt grate in the staple. Thus the general who had just won a great battle was thrust ignominiously into a cellar.

Mark kicked and banged the door, but it was of solid oak, without so much as a panel to weaken it, and though it resounded it did not even shake. He yelled till he was hoarse, and hit the door till his fists became numbed. Then suddenly he sat down quite quiet on the stone steps, and the tears came into his eyes. He did not care for the cellar, it was about Bevis — Bevis was lost somewhere and wanted him, and he *must* go to Bevis.

Dashing the tears away, up he jumped, and looked round to see if he could find anything to burst the door open. There was but one window, deep set in the thick wall, with an iron upright bar inside. The glass was yellowish-green, in small panes, and covered with cobwebs, so that the light was very dim. He could see the barrels large and small, and as his eyes became accustomed to the semi-darkness some meat – a joint – and vegetables on a shelf, placed there for coolness. Out came his pocket-knife, and he attacked the joint savagely, slashing off slices anyhow, for he (like Bevis) was hungry, and so angry he did not care what he did.

As he ate he still looked round and round the cellar and peered into the corners, but saw nothing, though something moved in the shadow on the floor – no doubt a resident toad. Mark knew the cellar perfectly, and he had often seen tools in it, as a hammer, used in tapping the barrels, but though he tried hard he could not find it. It must have been taken away for some purpose. He stamped on the floor, and heard a rustle as a startled mouse rushed into its hole.

The light just then seemed to increase, and turning towards the window he saw the full round moon. As it crossed the narrow window the shadow of the iron bar fell on the opposite wall, then moved aside, and in a very few minutes the moon began to disappear as she swept up into the sky. He watched the bright shield for awhile, then as he looked down he thought of the iron bar, and out came his knife again.

The bar was not let into the stonework, the window recess inside was encased with wood, and the bar, flattened at each end, was fastened with three screws. Mark endeavoured to unscrew these, he quickly broke the point of his knife, and soon had nothing but a stump left. The stump answered better than the complete blade, and he presently got the screws out. He then worked the bar to and fro with such violence that he wrenched the top screws clean away from the wood there. But just as he lifted the bar to smash all the panes and get out, he saw that the frame was far too narrow for him to pass through.

Inside the recess was wide enough, but it was not half so broad where the glass was. The bar was really unnecessary; no one could have got in or out, and perhaps that was why it had been so insecurely fastened, as the workmen could hardly have helped seeing it was needless.

Mark hurled the bar to the other end of the cellar, where it knocked some plaster off the wall, then fell on an earthenware vessel used to keep vegetables in, and cracked it. He stamped up and down the cellar, and in his bitter and desperate anger had half a mind to set all the taps running for spite.

'Let me out,' he yelled, thumping the door with all his might. 'Let me out; you've no business to put me in here. If the governor was at home, I know he wouldn't, and you're beasts — you're *beasts*.'

He was right in so far that the governor would not have locked him in the cellar; but the governor was out that evening, and Bevis's mamma, so soon as she found he was missing, had had the horse put in the dog-cart, and went to fetch him. So Mark fell into the hands of the merciless. No one even heard him howling and bawling and kicking the heart of oak, and when he had exhausted himself he sat down again on a wooden frame made to support a cask. Presently he went to the door once more, and shouted through the keyhole, 'Tell me if you have found Bevis!'

There was no answer. He waited, and then sat down on the frame, and asked himself if he could get up through the roof. By standing on the top of the largest cask he thought he could touch the rafters, but no more, and he had no tool to cut his way through with. 'I know,' he said suddenly, 'I'll smash the lock.' He searched for the iron bar, and found it in the earthenware vessel.

He hit the lock a tremendous bang, then stopped, and began to examine it more carefully. His eyes were now used to the dim light, and he could see almost as well as by day, and he found that the great bolt of the lock quite three inches thick, shot into an open staple driven into the door-post, a staple much like those used to fasten chains to.

In a minute he had the end of the iron bar inside the staple. The staple was strong, and driven deep into the oaken post, but he had a great leverage on it. The bar bent, but the staple came slowly, then easier, and presently fell on the stones. The door immediately swung open towards him.

Mark dashed out with the bar in his hand, fully determined to knock anyone down who got in his way, but they were all in the road, and he reached the meadow. He dropped the bar, and ran for the battle-field. Going through the gate that opened on the New Sea, something pushed through beside him against his ankles. It would have startled him, but he saw directly it was Pan. The spaniel had followed him: it may be with some intelligence that he was looking for his master.

'Pan! Pan!' said Mark, stooping to stroke him, and delighted to get some sympathy at last. 'Come on.'

Together they raced to the battle-field.

Then from the high ground Mark saw the beacon on the island, and instantly knew it was Bevis. He never doubted it for a moment. He looked at the beacon, and saw the flames shoot up, sink, and rise again; then he ran back as fast as he could to the head of the water, where the boats were moored in the sandy corner. Fetching the sculls from the tumbling shed where they were kept, he pushed off in the blue boat which they were fitting up for sailing, never dreaming that the first voyage in it would be like this. Pan jumped in with him.

In his haste, not looking where he was going, he rowed into the weeds, and was some time getting out, for the stalks clung to the blade of the scull as if an invisible creature in the water were holding it. Soon after he got free he reached the waves, and in five minutes, coming out into the open channel, the boat began to dance up and down. With wind and waves and oar he drove along at a rapid pace, past the oak where the council had been held, past the jutting point, and into the broad waters, where he could see the beacon, if he glanced over his shoulder.

The boat now pitched furiously, as it seemed to him rising almost straight up, and dipping as if she would dive into the deep. But she always rose again, and after her came the wave she had surmounted rolling with a hiss and bubble eager to overtake him. The crest blew off like a shower in his face, and just as the following roller seemed about to break into the stern-sheets it sank. Still the wave always came after him, row as hard as he would, like vengeance, black, dire, and sleepless.

Lit up by the full moon, the raging waters rushed and foamed and gleamed around him. Though he afterwards saw tempests on the ocean, the waves never seemed so high and so threatening as they did that night, alone in the little boat. The storms, indeed, on inland waters are full of dangers, perhaps more so than the long heaving billows of the sea, for the waves seemed to have scarcely any interval between, racing, quick, short and steep, one after the other.

This great black wave – for it looked always the same – chased him eagerly, overhanging the stern. Pan sat there on the bottom, as it looked, under the wave. Mark rowed his hardest, trying to get away from it. Hissing, foaming, with the rush and roar of the wind, the wave ran after. When he ventured to look round he was close to the islands, so quickly had he travelled.

Bevis was standing on the summit of the cliff with a long stick burning at the end in his hand. He held it out straight like the arm of a signal, then waved it a little, but kept it pointing in the same direction. He was shouting his loudest, to direct Mark, who could not hear a sound, but easily guessed that he meant him to bear the way he pointed. Mark pulled a few strokes and looked again, and saw the white spray rushing up

the cliff, though he could not hear the noise of the surge.

Bevis was frantically waving the burning brand; Mark understood now, and pulled his left scull hardest. The next minute the current setting between the islands seized the boat, and he was carried by as if on a mountain torrent. Everything seemed to whirl past, and he saw the black wave that had followed him dashed to sparkling fragments against the cliff.

He was taken beyond the island before he could stay the boat, then he edged away out of the rush behind the land, where the water was much smoother, and was able presently to row back to it in the shelter. Bevis came out from the trees to meet him, and taking hold of the stem of the boat drew it ashore. Mark stepped out, and Pan, jumping on Bevis, barked round him.

Bevis told him how it had all happened, and danced with delight when he heard how Mark had won the battle, for he insisted that Mark had done it. They went to the beacon fire, and then Mark, now his first joy was over, began to grumble because Bevis had been really shipwrecked and he had not. He wished he had smashed his boat against the cliff now. Bevis said they could have another great shipwreck soon. Mark wanted to stop all night on the island, but Bevis was hungry.

'And besides,' said he, 'there's the governor; he will be awfully frightened about us, and he ought to know.'

'So he did,' said Mark. 'Very well; but mind, there is to be a jolly shipwreck.'

Scamps as they were, they both disliked to give pain to those who loved them. It was the knowledge that the governor would never have put him in the cellar that stopped Mark from the spiteful trick of turning on the taps. Bevis was exceedingly angry about Mark having been locked up. He stamped his foot, and said the Bailiff should know.

They got into the boat, and each took a scull, but when they were afloat they paused, for it occurred to both at once that they could not row back in the teeth of the storm.

'We shall have to stop on the island now,' said Mark, not at all sorry. Bevis, however, remembered the floating breakwater of weeds and the winding channel on that side, and told Mark about it. So they rowed between the weeds, and so much were the waves weakened that the boat barely rocked. Now the boat was steady, Pan sat in front, and peered over the stem like a figure-head. Presently they came to the sand or mudbanks where the water was quite smooth, and here the heron rose up.

'We ought to have a gun,' said Bevis; 'it's a shame we haven't got a gun.'

'Just as if we didn't know how to shoot,' said Mark indignantly.

'Just as if,' echoed Bevis; 'but we will have one, somehow.'

The boat as he spoke grounded on a shallow; they got her off, but she soon grounded again, and it took them quite three-quarters of an hour to find the channel, so much did it turn and wind. At last they were stopped by thick masses of weeds, and a great bunch of the reed-mace, often called bulrushes, and decided to land on the sandbank. They hauled the boat so far up on the shore that she could not possibly get loose, and then walked to the mainland.

There the bushes and bramble thickets again gave them much trouble, but they contrived to get through into the wildest-looking field they had ever seen. It was covered with hawthorn trees, bunches of thistles, bramble bushes, rushes, and numbers of green ant-hills, almost as high as their knees. Skirting this, as they wound in and out of the ant-hills, they startled some peewits, which rose with their curious whistle, and two or three white tails, which they knew to be rabbits, disappeared round the thistles.

It took them some time to cross this field; the next was barley, very short; the next wheat, and then clover; and at last they reached the head of the water, and got into the meadows. Thence it was only a short way home, and they could see the house illuminated by the moonlight.

PART TWO

BEVIS AND MARK ON
THE UNKNOWN ISLAND

Contents

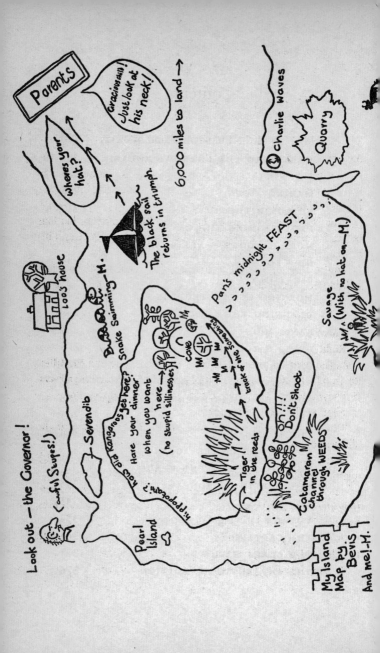

CHAPTER 1

Voyage to the Unknown Island

AFTER breakfast they got afloat, and when away from the trees the boat began to sail fast, and every now and then the bubbles rushed from under the bow. Mark sat on the ballast, or rather reclined, and Bevis steered.

'This is the best sail we've had,' said Mark, putting his legs out as far as he could, leaning his back against the seat and his head against the mast. 'It's jolly.'

'You're steering too much to the right – that way,' he cried, holding out his right arm.

'Is that better?'

'More over.'

'There.'

'Right.'

As the boat fell off a little from the wind, obeying the tiller, Bevis, now the foresail was out of his line of sight, could see the Unknown Island. They were closer than they had thought.

'Shall we land on Serendib?'

'Oh! no – on your island,' said Mark. 'Steer as close to the cliff as you can.'

Bevis did so, and the boat approached the low sandy cliff against which the waves had once beat with such fury. The wavelets now washed sideways past it with a gentle splashing; they were not large enough to make the boat dance, and if they had liked they could have gone up and touched it.

'It looks very deep under it,' said Mark, as Bevis steered into the channel, keeping two or three yards from shore.

'Ready,' he said; 'get ready to furl the mainsail.'

Mark partly unfastened the halyard, and held it in his hand. Almost directly they had passed the cliff they were in the lee of the island, which kept off the wind. The boat moved, carried on by its impetus through the still water, but the sails did not draw. In a minute Bevis told Mark to let the mainsail down, and as it dropped Mark hauled the sail in or the folds would have fallen in the water. At the same moment Bevis altered the course, and ran her ashore some way below where he had leaped off the punt, and where it was low and shelving. Mark was out with the painter the instant she touched, and tugged her up on the strand. Bevis came forward and let down the foresail; then he got out.

'Captain,' said Mark, 'may I go round the island?'

'Yes,' said the captain, and Mark stepped among the bushes to explore. Bevis went a little way and sat down under a beech. The hull of the boat was hidden by the undergrowth, but he could see the slender mast and some of the rigging over the boughs. The sunshine touched the top of the smooth mast, which seemed to shine above the green leaves. There was the vessel; his comrade was exploring the unknown depths of the wood; they were far from the old world and the known countries.

Yet they were only half mariners, and were obliged to wait for a fair wind. If it changed while they were on the island they would have to row back. He was no longer satisfied; he went down to the boat, stepped on board, and hoisted the sails. The trees and the island itself so kept off the wind that it was perfectly calm, and the sails did not even flutter. He stepped on shore, and went a few yards where he could look back and get a good view of the vessel, trying to think what it could be they did not do, or what it could be that was wrong.

He looked at her all over, from the top of the mast to the tiller, and he could not discover anything. Bevis walked up and down, he worked himself quite into a fidget. He went into the wood a little way, half inclined to go after Mark as he felt so restless. All at once he took out his pocket-book and pencil and sat down on the ground just where he was, and drew a sailing-boat such as he had seen. Then he went back to the shore, and sketched their boat on the other leaf. His idea was to compare the sailing-boats he had seen with theirs.

When he had finished his outline-drawing he saw directly that there were several differences. The mast in the boat sketched from memory was much higher than the mast in the other. Both sails, too, were larger than those he had had made. The bowsprit projected farther, but the foresail was not so much less in proportion as the mainsail. The foresail looked almost large enough, but the mainsail in the boat was not only smaller, it was not of the same shape.

'It must be made bigger,' Bevis thought. 'The mainsail must be made ever so much larger, and it must reach to where I sit. That's the mistake – you can see it in a minute. Mark! Mark!' He shouted and whistled.

Mark came presently running. 'I've been all round,' he said panting, 'and I've – '

'This is it,' said Bevis, holding up his pocket-book.

'I've seen a huge jack – a regular shark. I believe it was a shark – and three young wild ducks, and some more of those parrots up in the trees.'

'The mainsail – '

'There's lot of things you know are there, and you can't find,' said Mark; 'there's a tiger, I believe, in the bushes and reeds at the other end. If I had had my spear I should have gone and looked, and there's boa-constrictors, and a hippopotamus was here last night, and heaps of jolly things, and I've found a place to make a cave. Come and see' (pulling Bevis).

'I'll come,' said Bevis, 'in a minute. But just look, I've found out what was wrong – '

'And how to tack?'

'Yes.'

'Then let's do it, and tack and get shipwrecked, and live here.'

'But we must sail properly first,' said Bevis. 'I shan't do anything till we can sail properly: now this is it. Look.'

He showed Mark the two sketches, and how their mainsail did not reach back far enough towards the stern.

'Bigger sails will go faster, and smash the ship splendidly against the rocks,' said Mark. 'There'll be a crash and a grinding, and the decks will blow up, and there'll be an awful yell as everybody is gulped up but you and me.'

'While we're doing it, we'll make another bowsprit, too – longer,' said Bevis.

'Why didn't we think of it before?' said Mark. 'How stupid! Now you look at it, you can see it in a minute. And we had to sail half round the world to find it.'

'That's just it,' said Bevis. 'You sail forty thousand miles to find a thing, and when you get there you can see you left it at home.'

'We have been stupes,' said Mark. 'Let's do it directly. I'll shave the new mast, and you take the sails. And now come and see the place for the cave.'

Bevis went with him, and Mark took him to the bank or bluff inside the island which Bevis had passed when he explored it the evening of the battle. The sandy bank rose steeply for some ten or fifteen feet, and then it was covered with brambles and fern. There was a space at the foot clear of bushes and trees, and only overgrown with rough grasses. Beyond this there were great bramble thickets, and the trees began again about fifty yards away, encircling the open space. The spot was almost in the centre of the island, but rather nearer the side where there was a channel through the weeds than the other.

'The sand's soft and hard,' said Mark. 'I tried it with my knife; you can cut it, but it won't crumble.'

'We should not have to prop the roof,' said Bevis.

'No, and it's as dry as chips; it's the most splendid place for a cave that ever was.'

'So it is,' said Bevis. 'Nobody could see us.'

He looked round. The high bank shut them in behind, the trees in front and each side. 'Besides, there's nobody to look. It's capital.'

'Will you do it?' said Mark.

'Of course I will – directly we can sail properly.'

'Hurrah!' shouted Mark, hitting up his heels, having caught that trick from Bevis. 'Let's go home and begin the sails. Come on.'

'But I know one thing,' said Bevis, as they returned to the boat; 'if we're going to have a cave, we must have a gun.'

'That's just what I say. Can't we borrow one? I know, you put up Frances to make Jack lend us his rifle. She's fond of you – she hates me.'

Frances was Mark's elder sister. And their good friend Jack – who farmed close by – was rather fond of her.

'I'll try,' said Bevis. 'How ought you to get a girl to do anything?'

'Stare at her,' said Mark. 'That's what Jack does, like a donk at a thistle when he can't eat any more.'

'Does Frances like the staring?'

'She pretends she doesn't, but she does. You stare at her, and act stupid!'

'Is Jack stupid?'

'When he's at our house,' said Mark. 'He's as stupid as an owl. Now she kisses you, and you just whisper and squeeze her hand, and say it's very tiny. You don't know how conceited she is abuot her hand – can't you see – she's always got it somewhere where you can see it; and she sticks her foot out so' (Mark put one foot out); 'and don't you move an inch, but stick close to her, and get her into a corner or in the arbour. Mind, though, if you don't keep on telling her how pretty she is, she'll box your ears. That's why she hates me –'

'Because you don't tell her she's pretty. But she is pretty.'

'But I'm not going to be always telling her so – I don't see that she's anything very beautiful either – you and I should look nice if we were all the afternoon doing our hair, and if we walked like that and stuck our noses up in the air; and kept grinning, and smacked ourselves with powder, and scent, and all such beastly stuff. Now Jack's rifle – '

'We could make it shoot,' said Bevis, 'if we had it all to ourselves, and put bullets through apples stuck up on a stick, or smash an egg – '

'And knock over the parrots up in the trees.'

'I *will* have a gun,' said Bevis, kicking a stone with all his might. 'Are you sure Frances could get Jack – '

'Frances get Jack to do it! Why, I've seen him kiss her foot.'

They got on board laughing and set the sails, but as the island kept the wind off, Mark had to row till they were beyond the cliff. Then the sails filled and away they went.

'See! we're getting to places where people live again,' said Mark presently 'I say, shall we try the anchor?'

'Yes. Let down the mainsail first.'

Mark let it down, and then put the anchor over. It sank rapidly drawing the cable after it. The cable tightened, and the boat brought up and swung with her stem to the wind. Mark found that they did not want all the cable; he hauled it in till there was only about ten feet out; so that, allowing for the angle, the water was not much more than five or six feet deep. They were off the muddy shore, lined with weeds. Rude as the anchor was, it answered perfectly. In a minute or two they hauled it up, set the mainsail, and sailed almost to the harbour, having to row the last few yards because the trees kept much of the breeze off. They unshipped the mast, and carried it and the sails home.

In the evening Mark set to work to shave another and somewhat longer pole for the new mast, and Bevis took the sails and some more canvas to Frances. He was not long gone, and when he returned said that Frances had promised to do the work immediately.

'Did you do the cat and mouse?' said Mark. 'Did you stare?'

'I stared,' said Bevis, 'but there were some visitors there –'

'Stupes?'

'Stupes, so I couldn't get on very well. She asked me what I was looking at, and if she wasn't all right –'

'She meant her flounces; she thinks of nothing but her flounces.'

'But I began about the rifle, and she said perhaps, but she really had no influence with Jack.'

'Oh!' said Mark with a snort. 'Another buster.'

'And she couldn't think why you didn't come home. She had forgiven you a long time, and you were always unkind to her, and she was always forgiving you.'

'Busters,' said Mark. 'She's on telling stories from morning to night.'

'I don't see why you should be afraid of her; she can't hurt you.'

'Not hurt me! Why, if you've done anything, it's nigglenaggle, niggle-naggle, and she'll play you every nasty trick, and set the Old Moke on to look cross; and then when Jack comes, it's "Mark, dear, Mark," and wouldn't you think she was a sweet darling who loved her brother!'

Mark tore off a shaving.

'One thing though,' he added. 'Won't she serve Jack out when he's got her and obliged to have her. As if I didn't know why she wants me to come home. All she wants is to send some letters to him.'

'Postman. I see,' said Bevis.

'But I'll go,' said Mark. 'I'll go and fetch the sails tomorrow. I should like to see the jolly Old Moke; and don't you see? If I take the letters she'll be pleased and get the rifle for us.'

It was exceedingly disrespectful of Mark to speak of his governor as the Old Moke; his actual behaviour was very different from his speech, for in truth he was most attached to his father. The following afternoon Mark walked over and got the sails, and as he had guessed, Frances gave him a note for

Jack which he had to deliver that evening. They surprised the donkey; Mark mounted and rode off.

Bevis went on with the mast and the new gaff and bowsprit, and when Mark got back about sunset he had the new mast and rigging fitted up in the shed to see how it looked. The first time they made a mast it took them a long while, but now, having learned exactly how to do it, the second had soon been prepared. The top rose above the beam of the shed, and the mainsail stretched out under the eave.

'Hoist the peak up higher,' said the governor. Being so busy they had not heard him come. 'Hoist it up well, Mark.'

Mark gave another pull at the halyard, and drew the peak, or point of the gaff, up till it stood at a sharp angle.

'The more peak you can get,' said the governor, 'the more leverage the wind has, and the better she will answer the rudder.'

He was almost as interested in their sailing as they were themselves, and had watched them from the bank of the New Sea concealed behind the trees. But he considered it best that they should teach themselves, and find out little by little where they were wrong.

From the shore the governor had watched them vainly striving to tack, and could but just refrain from pointing out the reason. When he saw them fitting up the enlarged sails and the new mast, he exulted almost as much as they did themselves. 'They will do it,' he said to himself, 'they will do it this time.'

Then to Bevis, 'Pull the mainsail back as far as you can, and don't let it hollow out, not hollow and loose. Keep it taut. It ought to be as flat as a board. There – ' He turned away abruptly, fearing he had told them too much.

'As flat as a board,' repeated Bevis. 'So I will. But we thought it was best hollow, didn't we?' There was still enough light left to see to step the mast, so they carried the sails and rigging up to the boat, and fitted them the same evening.

CHAPTER 2

The Pinta

IN the morning the wind blew south, coming down the length
of the New Sea. Though it was light and steady it brought
larger waves than they had yet sailed in, because they had so
far to roll. Still they were not half so high as the day of the
battle, and came rolling slowly, with only a curl of foam now
and then. The sails were set, and as they drifted rather than
sailed out of the sheltered harbour, the boat began to rise and
fall, to their intense delight.

'Now it's proper sea,' said Mark.

'Keep ready,' said Bevis. 'She's going. We shall be across in
two minutes.'

He hauled the mainsheet taut, and kept it as the governor
had told him, as flat as a board. Smack! The bow hit a wave,
and threw handfuls of water over Mark, who knelt on the ballast forward, ready to work the foresheets. He shouted with
joy, 'It's sea, it's real sea!'

Smack! smack! His jacket was streaked and splotched with
spray; he pushed his wet hair off his eyes. Sish! sish! with a
bubbling hiss the boat bent over, and cut into the waves like a
knife. So much more canvas drove her into the breeze, and as
she went athwart the waves every third one rose over the
windward bow like a fountain, up the spray flew, straight up,
and then horizontally on Mark's cheek. There were wide dark
patches on the sails where they were already wet.

Bevis felt the tiller press his hand like the reins with a strong
fresh horse. It vibrated as the water parted from the rudder
behind. The least movement of the tiller changed her course.
Instead of having to hold the tiller in such a manner as to keep

the boat's head up to the wind, he had now rather to keep her off; she wanted to fly in the face of the breeze, and he had to moderate such ardour. The broad mainsail taut, and flat as a board, strove to drive the bow up to windward.

'Look behind,' said Mark. 'Just see.'

There was a wake of opening bubbles and foam, and the waves for a moment were smoothed by their swift progress. Opposite the harbour the New Sea was wide, and it had always seemed a long way across, but they had hardly looked at the sails and the wake, and listened to the hissing and splashing, than it was time to tack.

'Ready,' said Bevis. 'Let go.'

Mark let go, and the foresail bulged out and fluttered, offering no resistance to the wind. Bevis pushed the tiller over, and the mainsail having its own way at last drove the head of the boat into the wind, half round, three-quarters; now they faced it, and the boat pitched. The mainsail shivered; its edge faced the wind.

'Pull,' said Bevis the next moment.

Mark pulled the foresheet tight to the other side. It drew directly, and like a lever brought her head round, completing the turn. The mainsail flew across. Bevis hauled the sheet tight. She rolled, heaved, and sprang forward.

'Hurrah! We've done it! Hurrah!'

They shouted and kicked the boat. Wish! the spray flew, soaking Mark's jacket the other side, filling his pocket with water, and even coming back as far as Bevis's feet. Sish! sish! The wind puffed, and the rigging sang; the mast leaned; she showed her blue side; involuntarily they moved as near to windward as they could.

Wish! The lee gunwale slipped along, but just above the surface of the water, skimming like a swallow. Smack! Such a soaker. The foresail was wet; the bowsprit dipped twice. Swish! The mainsail was dotted with spray. Smack! Mark bent his head, and received it on his hat.

'Ready!' shouted the captain.

The foresheet slipped out of Mark's hand, and flapped, and hit him like a whip till he caught the rope. The mainsail forced her up to the wind; the foresail tightened again, levered her round. She rolled, heaved, and sprang forward.

Next time they did it better, and without a word being spoken. Mark had learned the exact moment to tighten the sheet, and she came round quicker than ever. In four tacks they were opposite the bluff, the seventh brought them to the council oak. As the wind blew directly down the New Sea each tack was just the same.

Bevis began to see that much depended upon the moment he chose for coming about, and then it did not always answer to go right across. If he waited till they were within a few yards of the shore the wind sometimes fell, the boat immediately lost way, or impetus, and though she came round it was slowly, and before she began to sail again they had made a little leeway. He found it best to tack when they were sailing full speed, because when he threw her head up to windward she actually ran some yards direct against the wind, and gained so much. Besides what they had gained coming aslant across the water, at the end of the tacks she shot up into the eye of the wind, and made additional headway like that. So that by watching the breeze, and seizing the favourable opportunity, he made much more than he would have done by merely travelling as far as possible.

His workmanship grew better as they advanced. He seemed to feel all through the boat from the rudder to mast, from the sheet in his hand to the bowsprit. The touch, the feeling of his hand, seemed to penetrate beyond the contact of the tiller, to feel through wood and rope as if they were a part of himself like his arm. He responded to the wind as quickly as the sail. If it fell, he let her off easier, to keep the pace up; if it blew, he kept her closer, to gain every inch with the increased impetus. He watched the mainsail, hauled taut like a board, lest it should shiver. He watched the foresail, lest he should keep too close, and it should cease to draw. He stroked, and soothed, and caressed, and coaxed her to put her best foot foremost.

As they advanced the New Sea became narrower, till just before they came opposite the battle-field the channel was but a hundred yards or so wide. In these straits the waves came with greater force and quicker; they were no higher, but followed more quickly, and the wind blew harder, as if also confined. It was tack, tack, tack. No sooner were the sheets hauled, and they had begun to forge ahead, than they had to come about. Flap, flutter, pitch, heave, on again. Smack! smack! The spray flew over. Mark buttoned his jacket to his throat, and jammed his hat down hard on his head.

The rope, or sheet, twisted once round Bevis's hand, cut into his skin, and made a red weal. He could not give it a turn round the cleat because there was no time. The mainsail pulled with almost all its force against his hand. Just as they had got the speed up, and a shower of spray was flying over Mark, round she had to come. Pitch, pitch, roll, heave forward, smack! splash! bubble! smack!

Each tack only gained a few yards, so that they crossed and recrossed nearly twenty times before they began to get through the strait. The sails were wet now, and drew the better; they worked in silence, but without a word, each had the same thought.

'It will do now,' said Mark.

'Once more,' said Bevis.

'Now,' said Mark, as they had come round.

'Yes!'

From the westward shore Bevis kept her close to the wind, and as the water opened out, he steered for Fir-Tree Gulf. He calculated that he should just clear the stony promontory. Against the rock wall the waves dashed and rose up high above it; the spray was carried over the bank and into the quarry. The sandbank or islet in front was concealed, the water running over it, but its site was marked by boiling surge.

The waves broke over it, and then met other waves thrown back from the wall; charging each other, they sprang up in pointed tips, which parted and fell. Over the grassy bank above rolled brown froth, which was then lifted and blown away. This was one of those places where the wind always seems to blow with greater force. In a gale from the south-west it was difficult to walk along the bank, and even now with only a light breeze the waves ran at the stony point as if they were mad. Bevis steered between Scylla and Charybdis, keeping a little nearer the sunken islet this time, the waves roared and broke on each side of them, froth caught against the sails, the boat shook as the reflux swept back and met the oncoming current; the rocky wall seemed to fly by, and in an instant they were past and in the gulf.

Hauling into the wind, the boat shot out from the receding shore, and as they approached the firs they were already half across to the Nile. Returning, they had now a broad and splendid sea to sail in, and this tack took them up so far that next time they were outside the gulf. It was really sailing now, long tacks, or 'legs', edging aslant up into the wind, and leaving the quarry far behind.

'It's splendid,' said Mark. 'Let me steer now.'

Bevis agreed, and Mark crept aft on hands and knees, anxious not to disturb the trim of the boat; Bevis went forward and took his place in the same manner, buttoning his jacket and turning up his collar.

Mark steered quite as well. Bevis had learned how to work the boat, to coax her, from the boat and the sails themselves. Mark had learned from Bevis, and much quicker. Mark steered and handled the sheet, and brought her round as handily as if he had been at it all the time.

These lengthened zigzags soon carried them far up the broad water, and the farther they went the smaller the waves became, having so much the less distance to come, till presently they were but big ripples, and the boat ceased to dance. As the waves did not now oppose her progress so much, there was but little spray, and she slipped through faster. The motive power, the wind, was the same; the opposing force, the waves, less. The speed increased, and they soon approached Bevis's island, having worked the whole distance up against the wind. They agreed to land, and Mark brought her to the spot where they had got out before. Bevis doused the mainsail, leaped out, and tugged her well aground. After Mark had stepped ashore they careened the boat and baled out the water.

There was no tree or root sufficiently near to fasten the painter to, so they took out the anchor, carried it some way inland, and forced one of the flukes into the ground. The boat was quite safe and far enough aground not to drift off, but it was not proper to leave a ship without mooring her. Mark wanted to go and look at the place he thought so well adapted for a cave, so they walked through between the bushes, when he suddenly remembered that the vessel in which they had just accomplished so successful a voyage had not got a name.

'The ship ought to have a name,' he said. 'Blue boat sounds stupid.'

'So she ought,' said Bevis. 'Why didn't we think of it before? There's *Arethusa, Agamemnon, Sandusky, Orient* – '

'*Swallow, Viking, St George* – but that won't do,' said Mark. 'Those are ships that sail now and some have steam; what were old ships – '

'*Argo*,' said Bevis. 'I wonder what was the name of Ulysses' ship – '

'I know,' said Mark, '*Pinta* – that's it. One of Columbus's ships, you know. He was the first to go over there, and we're the first on the New Sea.'

'So we are; it shall be *Pinta*, I'll paint it, and the island ought to have a name too.'

'Of course. Let's see: Tahiti?' said Mark.

'Loo-choo?'

'Celebes?'

'Carribbees?'

'Cyclades? But those are a lot of islands, aren't they?'

'Formosa is a good name,' said Bevis. 'It sounds right. But I don't know where it is – it's somewhere.'

'Don't matter – call it New Formosa.'

'Capital,' said Bevis. 'The very thing; there's New Zealand and New Guinea. Right. It's New Formosa.'

'Or the Land of Magic.'

'New Formosa or the Magic Land,' said Bevis. 'I'll write it down on the map we made when we get home.'

'Here's the place,' said Mark. 'This is where the cave ought to be,' pointing at a spot where the sandy cliff rose nearly perpendicular; 'and then we ought to have a hut over it.'

'Poles stuck in and leaning down and thatched.'

'Yes, and a palisade of thick stakes stuck in, in front of the door.'

'So that no one could take us by surprise at night.'

'And far enough off for us to have our fire inside.'

'Twist bushes in between the stakes.'

'Quite impassable to naked savages.'

'How high?'

'Seven feet.'

'Or very nearly.'

'We could make a bed, and sleep all night.'

'Wouldn't it be splendid to stop here altogether?'

'First-rate; no stupid silliness.'

'No bother.'

'Have your dinner when you like.'

'Nobody to bother where you've been to.'

'Let's live here.'

'All right. Only we must have a gun to shoot birds and things to eat,' said Bevis. 'It's no use unless we have a gun; it's not proper, nor anything.'

'No more it is,' said Mark; 'we *must* have a gun. Go and stare at Frances.'

'But it takes such a time, and then you know how slow Jack is. It would take him three months to make up his mind to lend us the rifle.'

'So it would,' said Mark.

'I know,' said Bevis, suddenly kicking up his heels, then standing on one foot and spinning round – 'I know!'

'What is it? Quick! Tell me!'

'Make one,' said Bevis.

'Make one?'

'A matchlock,' said Bevis. 'Make a matchlock. And a matchlock is quite proper, and just what they used to have – '

'But the barrel?'

'Buy an iron tube,' said Bevis. 'They have lots at Latten, at the ironmonger's; buy an iron pipe, and stop one end – '

'I see,' said Mark. 'Hurrah!' and up went his heels, and there was a wild capering for half a minute.

'The bother is to make the breech,' said Bevis. 'It ought to screw but we can't do that.'

'Ask the blacksmith,' said Mark; 'we need not let him know what it's for.'

'If he doesn't know we'll find out somehow,' said Bevis. 'Come on, let's do it directly. Why didn't we think of it before?'

They returned towards the boat.

'Just won't it be splendid,' said Mark. 'First, we'll get everything ready, and then get shipwrecked proper, and be as jolly as anything.'

'Matchlocks are capital guns,' said Bevis; 'they're slow to shoot with, you know, but they kill better than rifles. They have long barrels, and you put them on a rest to take steady aim, and we'll have an iron ramrod too, so as not to have the bother of making a place to put the rod in the stock, and to ram down bullets to shoot the tigers or savages.'

'Jolly!'

'The stock must be curved,' said Bevis; 'not like the guns, broad and flat, but just curved, and there must be a thing to hold the match: and just remind me to buy a spring to keep the hammer up, so that it shall not fall till we pull the trigger – it's just opposite to other guns, don't you see? The spring is to keep the match up, and you pull against the spring. And there's a pan and a cover to it – a bit of tin would do capital – and you push it open with your thumb. I've seen lots of matchlocks in glass cases, all inlaid gold and silver.'

'We don't want that.'

'No, all we want is the shooting. The match is the bother –'

'Would tar-cord do?'

'We'll try; first let's make the breech. Take up the anchor.'

Mark picked up the anchor, and put it on board. They launched the *Pinta*, and set sail homewards, Mark steering. As they were running right before the wind, the ship went at a great pace.

'That's the Mozambique,' said Bevis, as they passed through the strait where they had had to make so many tacks before.

'Land ho!' said Mark, as they approached the harbour. 'We've had a capital sail.'

'First-rate,' said Bevis. 'But let's make the matchlock.'

Now that he had succeeded in tacking he was eager to go on to the next thing, especially the matchlock gun. The hope of shooting made him three times as ready to carry out Mark's plan of the cave on the island. After furling the sails, and leaving everything shipshape, they ran home and changed their jackets, which were soaked.

CHAPTER 3

Making a Gun

TALKING upstairs about the barrel of the gun, they began to think it would be an awkward thing to bring home: people would look at them walking through the town with an iron pipe, and when they had got it home, other people might ask what it was for. Presently Mark remembered that John Young went to Latten that day with the horse and cart to fetch things; now if they bought the tube, Young could call for it, and bring it in the cart and leave it at his cottage. Downstairs they ran, and up to the stables.

'John!' said Bevis.

'Eez – eez,' replied the man, looking under the horse's neck and meaning 'Yes, yes.'

'Fetch something for us,' said Mark.

'Pint?' said John laconically.

'Two,' said Bevis.

'Ar-right,' ['all right'] said John, his little brown eyes twinkling. 'Ar-right, you.' For a quart of ale there were few things he would not have done: for a gallon his soul would not have had a moment's consideration, if it had stood in the way.

They explained to him what they wanted him to do.

'Have you got a grate in your house?' said Bevis.

'A yarth,' said John, meaning an open hearth. 'Burns wood.'

'Can you make a hot fire – very hot – on it?'

'Rayther. Bellers.' By using the bellows.

'What could we have for an anvil?'

'Be you going a blacksmithing?'

'Yes – what will do for an anvil?'

'Iron quarter,' said John. 'There's an ould iron in the shed.

208

Shall I take he whoam?' An iron quarter is a square iron weight weighing 28 lb.: it would make a useful anvil. It was agreed that he should do so, and they saw him put the old iron weight, rusty and long disused, up in the cart.

'If you wants anybody to blow the bellers,' said he, 'there's our Loo – she'll blow for yer. Be you going to ride?'

'No,' said Bevis; 'we'll go across the fields.'

Away they went by the meadows footpath, a shorter route to the little town, and reached it before John and his cart. At the ironmonger's they examined a number of pipes, iron and brass tube. The brass looked best, and tempted them, but on turning it round they fancied the join showed, and was not perfect, and of course that would not do. Nor did it look so strong as the iron, so they chose the iron, and brought five feet of stout tube – the best in the shop – with a bore of ⅝ths; and afterwards a brass rod, which was to form the ramrod. Brass would not cause a spark in the barrel.

John called for these in due course, and left them at his cottage. The old rogue had his quart, and the promise of a shilling, if the hearth answered for the blacksmithing. In the evening, Mark, well primed as to what he was to ask, casually looked in at the blacksmith's down the hamlet. The blacksmith was not in the least surprised; they were both old frequenters; he was only surprised one or both had not been before.

Mark pulled some of the tools about, lifted the sledge, which stood upright, and had left its mark on the iron 'scale' which lay on the ground an inch deep. Mark lifted the sledge, put it down, twisted up the vice, and untwisted it, while Jonas, the smith, stood blowing the bellows with his left hand, and patting the fire on the forge with his little spud of a shovel.

'Find anything you want,' he said presently.

'I'll take this,' said Mark. 'There's sixpence.' He had chosen a bit of iron rod, short, and thicker than their ramrod. Bevis had told him what to look for.

'All right, sir – anything else?'

'Well,' said Mark, moving towards the door, 'I don't know' –
then stopping with an admirable assumption of indifference,
'Suppose you had to stop up one end of a pipe, how should you
do it?'

'Make it white-hot,' said the smith. 'Bring it to me.'

'Will white-hot shut tight?'

'Quite tight – it runs together when hit. Bring it to me. I say,
where's the punt?' grinning. His white teeth gleamed between
his open lips – a row of ivory set in a grimy face.

'The punt's at the bottom,' said Mark, with a louring coun-
tenance.

'Nice boys,' said the smith. 'You're very nice boys. If you was
mine – ' He took up a slender ash-plant that was lying on the
bench, and made it ply and whistle in the air.

Mark tossed his chin, kicked the door open, and walked off.

'I say! – I say!' shouted the smith. 'Bring it to me.'

'Keep yourself to yourself,' said Mark loftily. Boys indeed!

The smith swore, and it sounded in his broad chest like the
noise of the draught up the furnace. He was angry with himself
– he thought he had lost half a crown, at least, by just swishing
the stick up and down. If you want half a crown, you must
control your feelings.

Mark told Bevis what the smith had said, and they went to
work, and the same evening filed off the end of the rod Mark
had bought. Bevis's plan was to file this till it almost fitted the
tube, but not quite. Then he meant to make the tube red-hot –
almost white – and insert the little block. He knew that heat
would cause the tube to slightly enlarge, so that the block
being cold could be driven in; then as the tube cooled it would
shrink in and hold it tight, so that none of the gas of the powder
could escape.

The block was to be driven in nearly half an inch below the
rim; the rim was to be next made quite white-hot, and in that
state hammered over till it met in the centre, and overlapped a
little. Again made white hot, the overlapping (like the paper of

210

a paper tube doubled in) was to be hammered and solidly welded together. The breech would then be firmly closed, and there would not be the slightest chance of its blowing out. This was his own idea, and he explained it to Mark.

They had now to decide how long the barrel should be: they had bought rather more tube than they wanted. Five, or even four feet would be so long, the gun would be inconvenient to handle, though with a rest, and very heavy.

Finally, they fixed on forty inches, which would be long but not too long; with a barrel of three feet four inches they ought, they considered, to be able to kill at a great distance. Adding the stock, say fifteen inches, the total length would be four feet seven.

Next morning, taking their tools and a portable vice in a flag-basket, as they often did to the boat, they made a detour and went to John Young's cottage. On the doorstep there sat a little girl without shoes or stockings; her ragged frock was open at her neck. At first, she looked about twelve years old, as the original impression of age is derived from height and size. In a minute or two she grew older, and was not less than fourteen. The rest of the family were in the fields at work, Loo had been left to wait upon them. Already she had a huge fire burning on the hearth, which was of brick; the floor too was brick. With the door wide open they could hardly stand the heat till the flames had fallen. Bevis did not want so much flame; embers are best to make iron hot. Taking off their jackets they set to work, put the tube in the fire, arranged the anvil, screwed the vice to the deal table, which, though quite clean, was varnished with grease that had sunk into the wood, selected the hammer which they thought would suit, and told Loo to fetch them her father's hedging-gloves.

These are made of thick leather, and Mark thought he could hold the tube better with them, as it would be warm from one end to the other. The little block of iron, to form the breech, was filed smooth, so as to just *not* fit the tube. When the tube was nearly white-hot, Mark put on the leather gloves, seized and placed the colder end on the anvil, standing the tube with the glowing end upwards.

Bevis took the iron block, or breech-piece, with his pincers, inserted it in the white-hot tube, and drove it down with a smart tap. Some scale fell off and dropped on Mark's shirt-sleeve, burning little holes through to his skin. He drew his breath between his teeth – so sudden and keen was the pain of the sparks – but did not flinch. Bevis hastily threw his jacket over Mark's arms, and then gave the block three more taps, till it was flush with the top of the tube.

By now the tube was cooling, the whiteness superseded by a red, which gradually became dull. Mark put the tube again in the fire, and Loo was sent to find a piece of sacking to protect his arm from the sparks. His face was not safe, but he had sloped his hat over it, and held his head down. There were specks on his hat where the scale or sparks had burnt it. Loo returned with a sack, when Bevis, who had been thinking, discovered a way by which Mark might escape the sparks.

He pulled the table along till the vice fixed to it projected over the anvil. Next time Mark was to stand the tube upright just the same, but to put it in the vice, and tighten the vice quickly, so that he need not hold it. Bevis had a short punch to drive the black or breech-piece deeper into the tube. Loo, blowing at the embers, with her scorched face close to the fire, declared that the tube was ready. Mark drew it out and in two seconds it was fixed in the vice, but with the colder end in contact with the anvil underneath. Bevis put his punch on the block and tapped it sharply till he had forced it half an inch beneath the rim.

He now adjusted it for the next heating himself, for he did not wish all the end of the tube to be so hot; he wanted the end itself almost white-hot, but not the rest. While it was heating they went out of doors to cool themselves, leaving Loo to blow steadily at the embers. She watched their every motion as intent as a cat a mouse; she ran with her naked brown feet to fetch and carry; she smiled when Mark put on the leather gloves, for she would have held it with her hands, though it had been much hotter.

She would have put her arm on the anvil to receive a blow from the hammer; she would have gone down the well in the bucket if they had asked her. Her mind was full of this wonderful work – what could they be making? But her heart and soul was filled with these great big boys with their sparkling eyes and their wilful, imperious ways. How many times she had watched them from afar! To have them so near was almost too great a joy; she was like a slave under their feet; they regarded her less than the bellows in her hands.

Directly the tube was white-hot at the extremity, she called them. Mark set the tube up; Bevis carefully hammered the rim over, folding it down on the breech-lock. Another heating, and he hammered the yielding metal still closer together, welding the folds. A third heating, and he finished it, deftly levelling the projections. The breech was complete, and it was much better done than they had hoped. As it cooled the tube shrank on the block; the closed end of the tube shrank too, and the breech-piece was incorporated into the tube itself.

Loo, seeing them begin to put their tools in the flag-basket, asked, with tears in her eyes, if they were not going to do any more? They had been there nearly three hours, for each heating took some time, but it had not seemed ten minutes to her. Bevis handed the barrel to her, and told her to take great care of it; they would come for it at night. It was necessary to smuggle it up into the armoury at home, and that could not be done by day. She took it. Had he given it in charge of a file of soldiers it could not have been safer; she would watch it as a bird does her nest.

Just then John came in, partly for his luncheon, partly out of curiosity to see how they were getting on. 'Picters you be!' said John.

Pictures they were — black and grimy, not so much from the iron as the sticks and logs, half burnt, which they had handled; they were, in fact, streaked and smudged with charcoal. Loo instantly ran for a bowl of water for them to wash, and held the towel ready. She watched them down the hill, and wished they had kicked her or pulled her hair. Other boys did; why did not they touch her? They might have done so. Next time she thought she would put her naked foot so that they would step on it; then if she cried out perhaps they would stroke her.

In the afternoon they took two spades up to the boat. The wind had fallen as usual, but they rowed to New Formosa. The *Pinta* being deep in the water and heavy with ballast, moved slowly, and it was a long row. Mark cut two sticks, and these were driven into the face of the sand cliff, to show the outline of the proposed cave. It was to be five feet square, and as deep as they could dig it.

They cleared away the loose sand and earth at the foot in a few minutes, and began the excavation. The sand at the outside was soft and crumbled, but an inch deep it became harder, and the work was not anything like so easy as they had supposed. After pecking with the spades for a whole hour, each had only cut out a shallow hole.

'This is no good,' said Mark; 'we shall never do it like this.'

'Pickaxes,' said Bevis.

'Yes; and hatchets,' said Mark. 'We could chop this sand best.'

'So we could,' said Bevis. 'There are some old hatchets in the shed; we'll sharpen them; they'll do.'

They worked on another half-hour, and then desisted, and cutting some more sticks stuck them in the ground in a semi-circle before the cliff, to mark where the palisade was to be fixed. The New Sea was still calm, and they had to row through the Mozambique all the way to the harbour.

In the evening they ground two old hatchets, which, being much worn and chipped, had been thrown aside, and then searched among the quantities of stored and seasoned wood and poles for a piece to make the stock of the matchlock. There was beech, oak, elm, ash, fir – all sorts of wood lying about in the shed and workshop. Finally, they selected a curved piece of ash, hard and well seasoned. The curve was nearly what was wanted, and being natural it would be much stronger. This was carried up into the armoury to be shaved and planed into shape.

At night they went for the barrel. Loo brought it, and Bevis, as he thought, accidentally stepped on her naked foot, crushing it between his heel and the stones at the door. Loo cried out.

'Oh, dear!' said he, 'I am so sorry. Here – here's sixpence, and I'll send you some pears.'

She put the sixpence in her mouth and bit it, and said nothing. She indented the silver with her teeth, disappointed because he had not stroked her, while she stood and watched them away.

They smuggled the barrel up into the armoury, which was now kept more carefully locked than ever, and they even put it where no one could see it through the keyhole. In the morning, as there was a breeze from the westward, they put the hatchets on board the *Pinta*, and sailed away for New Formosa. The wind was partly favourable, and they reached the island in three tacks. The hatchets answered much better, cutting out the sand well, so that there soon began to be two holes in the cliff.

They worked a little way apart, each drilling a hole straight in, and intending to cut away the intervening wall afterwards, else they could not both work at once. By dinner-time there was a heap of excavated sand and two large holes. The afternoon and evening they spent at work on the gun. Mark shaved at the stock; Bevis filed a touch-hole to the barrel; he would have liked to have drilled the touch-hole, but that he could not do without borrowing the blacksmith's tools, and they did not want him to know what they were about.

For four days they worked with their digging at the cave in the morning, and making the matchlock all the rest of the day.

CHAPTER 4

Building the Hut

POWDER was easily got from Latten; they bought a pound of loose powder at three-halfpence the ounce. This is like black dust, and far from pure, for if a little be flashed off on paper or white wood it leaves a broad smudge, but it answered their purpose very well. While Bevis was fretting and fuming over the lock – for he got white-hot with impatience, though he would and did do it – Mark had made a powder-horn by sawing off the pointed end of a cow's horn, and fitting a plug of wood into the mouth. For their shot they used a bag, and bought a mould for bullets.

The charger to measure the powder was a brass-drawn cartridge-case, two of which Mark had chanced to put in his pocket while they were at Jack's. It held more than a charge, so they scratched a line inside to show how far it was to be filled. At night the barrel was got out of the house, and taken up the meadows, three fields away, to a mound they had chosen as the best place. Mark brought a lantern, which they did not light till they arrived, and then put it behind the bushes, so that the light should not show at a distance.

The barrel was now charged with three measures of powder and two of shot rammed down firm, and then placed on the ground in front of a tree. From the touch-hole a train of powder was laid along the dry ground round the tree, so that the gun could be fired while the gunner was completely protected in case the breech blew out.

A piece of tar-cord was inserted in a long stick split at the end. Mark wished to fire the train, and having lit the tar-cord, which burned well, he stood back as far as he could and dropped the match on the powder. Puff – bang! They ran forward, and found the barrel was all right. The shot had scored a groove along the mound and lost itself in the earth; the barrel had kicked back to the tree, but it had not burst or bulged, so that they felt it would be safe to shoot with. Such a thickness of metal, indeed, would have withstood a much greater strain; and their barrel, rude as it was, was far safer than many flimsy guns.

The last thing to be made was the rest. For the staff they found a straight oak rod up in the lumber-room, which had once been used as a curtain-rod to an old-fashioned four-poster. Black with age, it was hard and rigid, and still strong; the very thing for their rest. The fork for the barrel to lie in was a difficulty, till Bevis hit on the plan of forming it of two pieces of thick iron wire. These were beaten flat at one end, a hole was bored in the top of the staff, and the two pieces of wire driven in side by side, when their flatness prevented them from moving. The wires were then drawn apart and hammered and bent into a half-circle on which the stock would rest.

The staff was high enough for them to shoot standing, but afterwards it was shortened, as they found it best to aim kneeling on one knee. When the barrel was fastened in the stock by twisting copper wire round, it really looked like a gun, and they jumped and danced about the bench-room till the floor shook. After handling it for some time they took it to pieces, and hid it till the cave should be ready, for so long a weapon could not be got out of the house very easily except in sections. Not such a great while previously they had felt that they must not on any account touch gunpowder, yet now they handled it and prepared to shoot without the least hesitation. The idea had grown up gradually. Had it come at all once it would have been rejected, but it had grown so imperceptibly that they had become accustomed to it, and never questioned themselves as to what they were doing.

By now the cave began to look like a cave, for every morning, sailing or rowing to New Formosa, they chopped for two or three hours at the hard sand. This cave was Mark's idea, but once started at work Bevis became as eager as he, and they toiled like miners. After the two headings had been driven in about five feet, they cut away the intervening wall, and there was a cavern five feet square, large enough for both to sit down in.

They had intended to dig in much deeper, but the work was hard, and, worse than that, slow, and now the matchlock was ready they were anxious to get on the island. So they decided that the cave was now large enough to be their store-room, while they lived in the hut, to be put up over the entrance. Bevis drew a sketch of the hut several times, trying to find out the easiest way of constructing it. The plan they selected was to insert long poles in the sand about three feet higher up than the top of the cave. These were to be placed a foot apart; and there were to be nine of them, all stuck in holes made for the purpose in a row, thus covering a space eight feet wide and eight high. From the cliff the rafters were to slope downwards till the lower and outward ends were six feet above the ground. That would give the roof a fall of two feet in case of rain.

Two stout posts were to be put up with a long beam across, on which the outer ends of the rafters were to rest. Two lesser posts in the middle were to mark the doorway. The roof was to be covered with brushwood to some thickness, and then thatched over that with sedges and reed-grass.

The walls they meant to make of hurdles stood on end, and fastened with tar-cord to upright stakes. Outside the hurdles they intended to pile up furze, brushwood, faggots, bundles of sedges – anything, in short. A piece of old carpeting was to close the doorway as a curtain. The store-room was five feet square, the hut would be eight, so that with the two they thought they should have plenty of space.

The semicircular fence of palisade of the hut, starting from the cliff on one side, and coming to it on the other, was to have a radius of ten yards, and so enclose a good piece of ground, where they could have their fire and cook their food secure from wild beasts or savages. A gateway in the fence was to be just wide enough to squeeze through, and to be closed by two boards nailed to a frame.

It took some time to settle all these details, for Bevis would not begin till he had got everything complete in his mind, but the actual work did not occupy nearly so long as the digging of the cave.

At last the hut was finished, and they could stand up, or walk about in it; but when the carpet-curtain was dropped, it was dark, for they had forgotten to make a window. But in the day time they would not want one, as the curtain could be thrown aside and the doorway would let in plenty of light, as it faced the south. At night they would have a lantern hung from the roof.

'It's splendid,' said Mark; 'we could live here for years.'

'Till we forgot what day it was, and whether it was Monday or Saturday,' said Bevis.

CHAPTER 5

Provisioning the Cave

NEXT day they took an iron bar with them, and pitched the stakes for the fence or stockade. Between the stakes they wove in willow rods and brushwood, so that thus bound together, it was much stronger than it looked, and no one could have got in without at least making a great noise. The two boards, nailed together for the gate, were fastened on one side to a stouter stake with small chains like rude hinges. On the other there was a staple and small padlock.

'It's finished,' said Mark, as he turned the key and locked them in.

'First,' said Bevis slowly, tracing out the proceedings in his imagination; 'first we must bring all our things – the gun and powder, and provisions, and great-coats, and the astrolabe, and spears, and leave them all here.'

'Pan ought to come,' said Mark, 'to watch the hut.'

Pan was Bevis's spaniel.

'So he did; he shall come, and besides, if we shoot a wild duck he can swim out and fetch it.'

'Now go on,' said Mark. 'First, we bring everything and Pan.'

'Tie him up,' said Bevis, 'and row home in the boat. Then the thing is, how are we to get to the island?'

'Swim,' said Mark.

'Too far.'

'But we needn't swim all up the New Sea. Couldn't we swim from where we landed that night after the battle?'

'Ever so much better. Let's go and look,' said Bevis.

Away they went to the shore on that side of the island, but

they saw in a moment that it was too far. It was two hundred yards to the sedges on the bank where they had landed that night. They could not trust themselves to swim more than fifty or sixty yards; there was, too, the risk of weeds, in which they might get entangled.

'I know!' said Bevis, 'I know! You stop on the island with Pan. I'll sail the *Pinta* into harbour, then I'll paddle back on the catamaran.'

'There!' said Mark, 'I knew you could do it if you thought hard. We could bring the catamaran up in the boat, and leave it in the sedges there ready.'

'I can leave half my clothes on the island,' said Bevis, 'and tie the rest on my back, and paddle here from the sedges in ten minutes. That will be just the savages do.'

'I shall come too,' said Mark. 'I shan't stop here. Let Pan be tied up, and I'll paddle as well.'

'The catamaran won't bear two.'

'Get another. There's lots of plans. I will come – it's much jollier paddling than sitting here and doing nothing.'

'Capital,' said Bevis. 'We'll have two catamarans, and paddle here together.'

'First-rate. Let's be quick and get the things on the island.'

'There will be such a lot,' said Bevis. 'The matchlock, and the powder, and the flour, and – '

'Ever so many cargoes,' said Mark.

'Come on. Sail home and begin.'

They launched the *Pinta*, and the spanking south-easterly breeze carried them swiftly into harbour. At home there was a small parcel, very neatly done up, addressed to 'Captain Bevis'.

'That's Frances's handwriting,' said Mark. Bevis cut the string and found a flag inside made from a broad red ribbon cut to a point.

'It's a pennant,' said Bevis. 'It will do capitally. How was it we never thought of a flag before?'

'We were so busy,' said Mark. 'Girls have nothing to do, and so they can remember these sort of stitched things.'

'She shall have a bird of paradise for her hat,' said Bevis. 'We shall be sure to shoot one on the island.'

'I shouldn't give it to her,' said Mark. 'I should sell it. Look at the money.'

In the evening they took a large box (which locked) up to the boat, carrying it through the courtyard with the lid open — ostentatiously open — and left it on board. Next morning they filled it with their tools. Bevis kept his list and pencil by him, and as they put in one thing it suggested another, which he immediately wrote down. There were files, gimlets, hammers, screw-drivers, planes, chisels, the portable vice, six or seven different sorts of nails, every tool indeed they had. The hatchet and saw were already on the island. Besides these there were coils of wire and cord, balls of string, and several boxes of safety and lucifer matches. This was enough for one cargo; they shut the lid, and began to loosen the sails ready for hoisting.

'You might take us once.'

'You never asked us.'

Tall Val and little Charlie had come along the bank unnoticed while they were busy.

'I wish you would go away,' said Mark, beginning to push the *Pinta* afloat. The ballast and cargo made her drag on the sand.

'Bevis,' said Val, 'let us have one sail.'

'All the times you've been sailing,' said Charlie, 'and all by yourselves, and never asked anybody.'

'And after we banged you in the battle,' said Val. 'If you did beat us, we hit you as hard as we could.'

'It was a capital battle,' said Bevis hesitatingly. He had the halyard in his hand, and paused with the mainsail half hoisted.

'Whopping and snopping,' said Charlie.

'Charging and whooping and holloaing,' said Val.

'Rare,' said Bevis. 'Yes; you fought very well.'

'But you never asked us to have a sail.'

'Not once – you didn't.'

'Well, it's not your ship. It's our ship,' said Mark, giving another push, till the *Pinta* was nearly afloat.

'Stop,' cried Charlie, running down to the water's edge. 'Bevis, do take us – '

'It's very selfish of you,' said Val, following.

'So it is,' said Bevis. 'I say, Mark – '

'Pooh!' said Mark, and with a violent shove he launched the boat, and leaped on board. He took a scull, and began to row her head round. The wind was north and light.

'I hate you,' said Charlie. 'I believe you're doing something. What's in that box?'

'Ballast, you donk,' said Mark.

'That it isn't. I saw it just before you shut the lid. It's not ballast.'

'Let's let them come,' said Bevis irresolutely.

'You awful stupe,' said Mark, under his breath. 'They'll spoil everything.'

'And why do you always sail one way?' said Val. 'We've seen you ever so many times.'

'I won't be watched,' said Bevis angrily: he unconsciously endeavoured to excuse his selfishness under rage.

'You can't help it.'

'I hate you,' pulling up the mainsail. Mark took the rope and fastened it; Bevis sat down to the tiller.

'You're a beast,' screamed little Charlie, as the sails drew and the boat began to move: the north wind was just aft.

'I never thought you were so selfish,' shouted Val. 'Go on – I won't ask you again.'

'Take that,' said Charlie, 'and that – and that.'

He threw three stones, one after the other, with all his might; the third, rising from the surface of the water, struck the *Pinta*'s side sharply.

'Aren't they just horrid?' he said to Val.

'I never saw anything like it,' said Val. 'But we'll pay them out, somehow.'

On the boat, Bevis looked back presently, and saw them still standing at the water's edge.

'It's a pity,' he said; 'Mark, I don't like it: shall we have them?'

'How can we? Of course they would spoil everything; they would tell everybody, and we could never do it; and, besides, the new island would not be a new island, if everybody was there.'

'No more it would.'

'We can take them afterwards – after we've done the island. That will be just as well.'

'So it will. They will watch us, though.'

'It's very nasty of them to watch us,' said Mark. 'Why should we take them for sails when they watch us?'

'I hate being watched,' said Bevis.

'They will just make everything as nasty for us as they can,' said Mark; 'and we shall have to be as cunning as ever we can be.'

'We will do it, though, somehow.'

'That we will.'

The light north wind wafted the *Pinta* gently up the New Sea: the red pennant, fluttering at the mast, pointed out the course before them. They disposed of their first cargo in the store-room, or cave, placing the tools in a sack – though the cave was as dry as a box – that there might not be the least chance of their rusting. The return voyage was slow, for they had to work against the wind, and it was too light for speed. They looked for Charlie and Val, but both were gone.

Another cargo was ready late in the afternoon. They carried the things up in the flag-basket, and, before filling the box, took care to look round and behind the shed where the sculls were kept, lest anyone should be spying. Hitherto they had worked freely, and without any doubt or suspicion: now they were constantly on the watch, and suspected every tree of concealing someone. Bevis chafed under this, and grew angry about it. In filling the box, too, they kept the lid towards the shore, and hoisted the mainsail to form a screen.

Mark took care that there should be some salt, and several bags of flour, and two of biscuits, which they got from a whole tinful in the house. He remembered some pepper too, but overlooked the mustard. They took several tins of condensed milk. From a side of bacon, up in the attic, they cut three streaky pieces, and bought some sherry at the inn; for they thought if they took one of the bottles in the house, it would be missed, and that the servants would be blamed. Some wine would be good to mix with the water; for though they meant to take a wooden bottle of ale, they knew it would not keep.

Then there was a pound of tea, perhaps more; for they took it from the chest, and shovelled it up like sand, both hands full at once. A bundle of old newspapers was tied up, to light the fire; for they had found, by experience, that it was not easy to do so with only dry grass. Bevis hunted about till he discovered the tin mug he had when he was a little boy, and two tin plates. Mark brought another mug. A few knives and forks would never be missed from the basketful in the kitchen; and, in choosing some spoons they were careful not to take silver, because the silver was counted every evening.

They asked if they could have a small zinc bucket for the boat; and when they got it, put the three pounds or more of knob sugar in it, loose; and covered it over with their Turkish bathing-towels, in which they had wrapped up a brush and comb. Just as they were about to start, they remembered soap and candles. To get these things together, and up to the *Pinta*, took them some hours, for they often had to wait awhile till people were out of the way before they could get at the cupboards. By the time they had landed, and stowed away this cargo, the sun was declining.

CHAPTER 6

More Cargoes — All Ready

NEXT morning the third cargo went; they had to row, for the New Sea was calm. It consisted of arms. Bevis's favourite bow, of course, was taken, and two sheaves of arrows; Mark's spears and harpoon; the crossbow, throw-sticks, the boomerang and darts; so that the armoury was almost denuded.

Besides these there were fish-hooks (which were put in the box), fishing-rods, and kettles; an old horn-lantern, the old telescope, the astrolabe, scissors and thread (which ship-wrecked people always have); a bag full of old coins, which were to be found in the sand on the shore, where a Spanish galleon had been wrecked (one of those the sunken galley had been conveying when the tornado overtook them); a small looking-glass, a piece of iron rod, six bottles of lemonade, a cribbage-board and pack of cards, and a bezique pack; a basket of apples, and a bag of potatoes. The afternoon cargo was clothes, for they thought they might want a change if it was wet; so they each took one suit, carefully selecting old things that were disused, and would not be missed.

Then there were the great-coats for the bed; these were very awkward to get up to the boat, and caused many journeys, for they could only take the one coat each at a time.

'What a lot of rubbish you are taking to your boat,' said mamma once. 'Mind you don't sink it: you will fill your boat with rubbish till you can't move about.'

'Rubbish!' said Bevis indignantly. 'Rubbish, indeed!'

They so often took the rugs that there was no need to conceal them. Mark hit on a good idea and rolled up the barrel of the matchlock in one of the rugs, and with it the ramrod. In the other they hid the stock and powder-horn, and so got them to the boat; chuckling over Mark's device, by which they removed the matchlock in broad daylight.

'If Val's watching,' said Bevis, as they came up the bank with the rugs, the last part of the load, 'he'll have to be smashed.'

'People who spy about ought to be killed,' said Mark. 'Everything ought to be done openly,' carefully depositing the concealed barrel in the stern-sheets. This was the most important thing of all. When they had got the matchlock safe in the cave, they felt that the greatest difficulty was surmounted.

John Young had brought their anvil, the 28-lb. weight, for them to the bank, and it was shipped. He bought a small pot for boiling, the smallest size made, for them in Latten, also a saucepan, a tin kettle, and teapot. One of the wooden bottles, like tiny barrels, used to send ale out to the men in the fields, was filled with strong ale.

They called at the cottage for the pot and the other things, which were in a sack ready for them. Loo fetched the sack, and Bevis threw it over his shoulder.

'I scoured them well,' said Loo. 'They be all clean.'

'Did you?' said Bevis. 'Here,' searching his pocket. 'Oh! I've only a fourpenny piece left.' He gave it to her.

'I can cook,' said Loo wistfully, 'and make tea.' This was a hint to them to take her with them; but away they strode unheeding. The tin kettle and teapot clashed in the sack.

'I believe I saw Val behind that tree,' said Bevis.

'He can't see through a sack though,' said Mark.

The wind was still very light, and all the morning was occupied in delivering this cargo. The cave or store-room was now crammed full, and they could not put any more without shelves.

'That's the last,' said Mark, dragging the heavy anvil in. 'Except Pan.'

'And my books,' said Bevis, 'and ink and paper. We must keep a journal of course.'

'So we must,' said Mark. 'I forgot that. It will make a book.'

'*Adventures in New Formosa*,' said Bevis. 'We'll write it every evening after we've done work, don't you see.'

When they got home he put his books together – the *Odyssey*, *Don Quixote*, the grey and battered volume of ballads, a tiny little book of Shakespeare's poems, of which he had lately become very fond, and Filmore's rhymed translation of *Faust*. He found two manuscript books for the journal; these and the pens and ink-bottle could all go together in the final cargo with Pan.

All the while these voyages were proceeding they had been thinking over how they should get away from home without being searched for, and had concluded that almost the only excuse they could make would be that they were going to spend a week or two with Jack. This they now began to spread about, and pretended to prepare for the visit. As they expected, it caused no comment. All that was said was that they were not to stop too long. Mamma insisted upon Bevis writing home. Bevis shrugged his shoulders, foreseeing that it would be difficult to do this as there was no post-office on New Formosa; but it was of no use, she said he should not go unless he promised to write.

'Very well,' said Bevis. 'Letters are the stupidest stupidity stupes ever invented.'

But now there arose a new difficulty, which seemed as if it could not be got over. How were they to tell while they were away on the island, and cut off from all communication with the mainland, what was going on at home; whether it was all right and they were supposed to be at Jack's, or whether they were missed? For though so intent on deceiving the home authorities, and so ingenious in devising the means, they stopped at this.

They did not like to think that perhaps Bevis's governor and mamma, who were so kind, would be miserable with anxiety on finding that they had disappeared. Mark, too, was anxious about his jolly Old Moke. With the usual contradiction of the mind they earnestly set about to deceive their friends, and were equally anxious not to give them any pain. After all their trouble, it really seemed as if this would prevent the realization of their plans. A whole day they walked about and wondered what they could do, and got quite angry with each other from simple irritation.

At last they settled that they must arrange with someone so as to know, for if there was any trouble about them they meant to return immediately. Both agreed that little Charlie was the best they could choose; he was as quick as lightning, and as true as steel.

Bevis thought and considered that Charlie must give them a signal – wave a handkerchief. Charlie must stand on some conspicious place visible from New Formosa; by the quarry would be the very place, at a certain fixed time every day, and wave a white handkerchief, and they could look through the telescope and see him. If anything was wrong, he could take his hat off and wave that instead. Mark thought it would do very well, and set out to find and arrange with Charlie.

Being very much offended because he had not been taken for a sail, Charlie was at first very off-hand, and not at all disposed to do anything. But when shrewd Mark let out as a great secret that he and Bevis were going to live in the wood at the end of the New Sea for a while like savages, Charlie began to relent, for all his sympathies went with the idea.

Mark promised him faithfully that when he and Bevis had done it first, he should come too if he would help them. Charlie gave in and agreed, but on condition that he should be taken for a sail first.

So it was settled – Charlie to have a sail and then every afternoon at four o'clock he was to stand just above the quarry and wave a white handkerchief if all was right. If Bevis and Mark were missed he was to take off his hat, and wave that. As he had no watch, Charlie was to judge the time by the calling of the cows to be milked — the milkers make a great hullabaloo and shouting, which can be heard a long distance off.

'I said we were going to live in the wood,' Mark told Bevis when he came back. 'Then he won't think we're on the island. If he plays us any trick he'll go and try and find us in the wood.'

While Mark was gone about the signal, Bevis, thinking everything over, remembered the letter he had promised to write home. To post the letter one or other of them must go on the mainland, and if by day someone would very likely see them and mention it, and then the question would arise why they came near without going home? Bevis went up to the cottage, and told Loo to listen every evening at ten o'clock out of her window, which looked over the field at the back, and if she heard anybody whistle three notes, 'Foo-tootle-too', to slip out, as it would be them.

'That I will,' said Loo, delighted. 'I'll come in a minute.'

Charlie had his sail next morning, but they took care not to go near the island. Knowing how sharp his eyes were, they tacked to and fro in Mozambique and Fir-Tree Gulf. Charlie learned to manage the foresail in five minutes, then the tiller, and to please him the more they let him act as captain for a while. He promised most faithfully to make the signal every day, and they knew he would do it.

In the afternoon they thought and thought to see if there was anything they had forgotten, and to try and call things to mind, wandered all over the house, but only recollected one thing — the gridiron. There were several in the kitchen. They took an old one, much burnt, which was not used. With this and Bevis's books they visited New Formosa, rowing up towards evening, and upon their return unshipped the mast, and took it and the sails home, else perhaps Val or someone would launch the *Pinta* and try to sail in their absence. They meant to padlock the boat with a chain, but if the sails were in her it would be a temptation to break the lock. There was now nothing to take but Pan, and they were so eager for the morning that it was past midnight before they could go to sleep.

The morning of 3 August – the very day Columbus sailed – the long-desired day, was beautifully fine, calm, and cloudless. They were in such haste to start they could hardly say 'Goodbye.'

They had got out into the meadow with Pan, when Bevis's mother came running after.

'Have you any money?' she asked, with her purse in her hand.

They laughed, for the thought instantly struck them that they could not spend any money on New Formosa, but they did not say they did not want any. She gave them five shillings each, and kissed them again. She watched them till they went through the gateway with Pan, and were hidden from sight.

Pan leaped on board after them, and they rowed to the island. It was so still, the surface was like glass. The spaniel ran about inside the stockade, and sniffed knowingly at the coats on the bedstead, but he did not wag his tail or look so happy when Bevis suddenly drew his collar three holes tighter and buckled it. Bevis knew very well if his collar was not as tight as possible Pan would work his head out. They fastened him securely to the post at the gateway in the palisade, and hastened away.

When Pan realized that they were really gone, and heard the sound of the oars, he went quite frantic. He tugged, he whined, he choked, he rolled over, he scratched, and bit, and shook, and whimpered; the tears ran down his eyes, his ears were pulled over his head by the collar, against which he strained. But he strained in vain. They heard his dismal howls almost down to the Mozambique.

'Poor Pan!' said Bevis. 'He shall have a feast the first thing we shoot.'

They had left their stockings on the island, and everything

else they could take off, so as not to have very large bundles on their backs while paddling, and took their pocket-knives out of their trousers' pockets and left them, knowing things are apt to drop out of the pockets. The *Pinta* was drawn up as far as she would come on the shore at the harbour, and then fastened with a chain (which they had ready) to a staple and padlocked. Mark had thought of this, so that no one could go rowing round, and he had a piece of string on the key with which he fastened it to the button-hole of his waistcoat so that it might not be lost.

This done, they got through the hedge, and retraced the way they had come home on the night of the battle, through the meadows, the cornfields, and lastly across the wild waste pasture or common. From there they scrambled through the hedges and the immense bramble thickets, and regained the shore opposite their island.

They went down the marshy level to the bank, and along it to the beds of sedges, where, on the verge of the sea, they had hidden the catamarans. There they undressed, and made their clothes and boots into bundles, and slung them over their shoulders with cord. Then they hauled their catamarans down to the water.

CHAPTER 7

New Formosa

SPLASH!

'Is it deep?'

'Not yet.'

Bevis had got his catamaran in and ran out with it some way, as the water was shallow, till it deepened, when he sat astride and paddled.

'Come on,' he shouted.

Splash!

'I'm coming.'

Mark ran in with his in the same manner, and sitting astride paddled about ten yards behind.

'Weeds,' said Bevis, feeling the long rough stalks like string dragging against his feet.

'Where? I can't see.'

'Under water. They will not hurt.'

'There goes a flapper' (a young wild duck). 'I hope we shan't see the magic wave.'

'Pooh!'

'My bundle is slipping.'

'Pull it up again.'

'It's all right now.'

'Holloa! Land,' said Bevis, suddenly standing up.

He reached a shallow where the water was no deeper than his knees.

A jack struck. 'There,' said Mark, as he too stood up, and drew his catamaran along with his hand.

Splash!

Bevis was off again paddling in deeper water. Mark was now close behind.

'There's a coot; he's gone into the sedges.'

'Parrots,' said Mark, as two wood-pigeons passed over.

'Which is the right channel?' said Bevis, pausing.

They had now reached the great mass of weeds which came to the surface, and through which it was impossible to move. There were two channels: one appeared to lead straight to the island, the other wound about to the right.

'Which did we come down in the *Pinta*, when we hid the catamarans?' said Mark.

'Stupe, that's just what I want to know.'

'Go straight on,' said Mark; 'that looks clearest.'

So it did, and Bevis went straight on; but when they had paddled fifty yards they both saw at once that they could not go much farther that way, for the channel curved sharply, and was blocked with weeds.

'We must go back,' said Mark.

'We can't turn round.'

'We can't paddle backwards. There, I'm in the weeds.'

'Turn round on the plank.'

'Perhaps I shall fall off.'

'Sit sideways first.'

'The plank tips.'

'Very well, I'll do it first,' said Bevis.

He turned sideways to try and get astride, looking the other way. The plank immediately tipped and pitched him into the water, bundle and all.

'Ah!' said Mark. 'Thought you could do it easy, didn't you?'

Bevis threw his right arm over the plank, and tried to get on it; but every time he attempted to lift his knee over, the catamaran gave way under him. His paddle floated away. The bundle of clothes on his back, soaked and heavy, kept him down.

Mark paddled towards him, and tried to lift him with one

hand, but nearly upset himself. Bevis struggled hard to get on, and so pushed the plank sideways to the edge of the weeds. He felt the rough strings again winding round his feet.

'You'll be in the weeds,' said Mark, growing alarmed. 'Come on my plank. Try. I'll throw my bundle off.' He began to take it from his back. 'Then it will just keep you up. Oh!'

Bevis put his hands up, and immediately sank under the surface, but he had done it purposely, to free himself from his bundle. The bundle floated, and the cord slipped over his head. Bringing his hands down Bevis as instantly rose to the surface, bumping his head against the catamaran.

'Now I can do it,' he said, blowing the water from his nostrils.

He seized the plank, and lay almost all along in the water, so as to press very lightly on it, his weight being supported by the water, then he got his knee over and sat up.

'Hurrah!'

The bundle was slowly settling down when Mark seized it.

'Never mind about the things being wet,' he said. 'Sit still; I'll fetch your paddle.'

Dragging the bundle in the water by the cord, Mark went after, and recovered Bevis's paddle. To come back he had to back water, and found it very awkward even for so short a distance. The catamaran would not go straight.

'Oh! what a stupe I was,' said Bevis. 'I've got on the same way again.'

In his hurry he had forgotten his object, and got astride facing the island as before.

'Well, I never,' said Mark. 'Stop – don't.'

Bevis slipped off his catamaran again, but this time not being encumbered with the bundle he was up on it again in half a minute, and faced the mainland.

'There,' said he. 'Now you can come close. That's it. Now give me your bundle.'

Mark did so. Afterwards Bevis took the cord of his own

bundle, which being in the water was not at all heavy. 'Now you can turn.'

Mark slipped off, but managed so that his chest was still on the plank. In that position he worked himself round and got astride the other way.

'Done very well,' said Bevis; 'ever so much better than I did. Here.'

Mark slung his bundle, and they paddled back to the shallow water, Bevis towing his soaked dress. They stood up in the shallow and rested a few minutes, and Bevis fastened his bundle to his plank just in front of where he sat.

'Come on.' Off he went again, following the other channel this time. It wound round a bank grown with sedges, and then led straight into a broader and open channel, the same they had come down in the boat. They recognized it directly, and paddled faster.

'Hark! there's Pan,' said Mark.

As they came near the island, Pan either scented them or heard a splashing, for he set up his bark again. He had choked himself silent before.

'Pan! Pan!' shouted Bevis, whistling.

Yow – wow – wow!

'Hurrah!'

'Hurrah!'

They ran up on the shore of New Formosa, and began to dance and caper, kicking up their heels.

Yow-wow – wow-wow!

'Pan! I'm coming,' said Bevis, and began to run, but stopped suddenly.

Thistles in the grass and trailing briers stayed him. He put on his wet boots, and then picking his way round, reached the hut. He let Pan loose. The spaniel crouched at his feet and whimpered, and followed him, crawling on the ground. Bevis patted him, but he could not leap up as usual, the desertion had quite broken his spirit for the time. Bevis went into the

237

hut, and just as he was, with nothing on but his boots, took his journal and wrote down 'Wednesday'.

'There,' said he to Mark, who had now come, more slowly, for he carried the two bundles, 'there, I've put down the day, else we shall lose our reckoning, don't you see.'

They were soon dressed. Bevis put on the change he had provided in the store-room, and spread his wet clothes out to dry in the sun. Pan crept from one to the other; he could not get enough patting, he wanted to be continually spoken to and stroked.

He would not go a yard from them.

'What's the time?' said Bevis, 'my watch has stopped.' The water had stopped it.

'Five minutes to twelve,' said Mark. 'You must write down, "We landed on the island at noon." '

'So I will tonight. My watch won't go; the water is in it.'

'Lucky mine did not get wet too.'

'Hang yours up in the hut, else perhaps it will get stopped somehow, then we shan't know the time.'

Mark hung his watch up in the hut, and caught sight of the wooden bottle.

'The first thing people do is to refresh themselves,' he said. 'Let's have a glass of ale: splendid thing when you're ship-wrecked – '

'Here's a mug,' said Mark, who had turned over a heap of things and found a tin cup. They each had a cupful.

'Matchlock,' said Bevis.

'Matchlock,' said Mark. For while they drank both had had their eyes on the gun-barrel.

'Pliers,' said Bevis, taking it up. 'Here's the wire; I want the pliers.'

It was not so easy to find the pliers under such a heap of things.

'Store-room's in a muddle,' said Mark.

'Put it right,' said the captain.

'I've got it.'

Bevis put the barrel in the stock, and began twisting the copper wire round to fasten it on. Mark searched for the powder-horn and shot-bag. Three strands were twisted neatly and firmly round the barrel and stock – one near the breech, one half-way up, the third near the muzzle. It was then secure.

'It looks like a real gun now,' said Mark.

'Put your finger on the touch-hole,' said Bevis. Mark did so, while he blew through the barrel.

'I can feel the air,' said Mark; 'the barrel is clear. Shall I measure the powder?'

'Yes.'

Bevis shut the pan, Mark poured out the charge from the horn and inserted a wad of paper, which Bevis rammed home with the brass ramrod.

Bow-wow – bow-yow!

Up jumped Pan, leaped on them, tore round the hut, stood at the doorway and barked, ran a little way out, and came back again to the door, where, with his head over his shoulder, as if beckoning to them to follow, he barked his loudest.

'It's the gun,' said Mark. Pan forgot his trouble at the sound of the ramrod.

Next the shot was put in, and then the priming at the pan. A piece of match or cord prepared to burn slowly, about a foot and a half long, was wound round the handle of the stock, and the end brought forward through the spiral of the hammer.

Mark went to the hut, fetched a handful of biscuits and two apples, and began to eat them.

'We must shoot something,' said Bevis. 'We can't eat much of that stuff.'

'Let's go round the island,' said Mark, 'and see if there's anything about. Parrots perhaps.'

'Pigeon-pie,' said Bevis.

'Parrot-pie; just the thing.'

'Hammer Pan, or he'll run on first and spoil everything.'

CHAPTER 8

First Day

BEVIS lit the match, and they went quietly into the wood. Pan had to be hammered now and then to restrain him from rushing into the brambles. They knew the way now very well, having often walked round while building the hut looking for poles, and had trampled out a rough path winding about the thorns. The shooting at the teak-tree and the noise of Pan's barking had alarmed all the parrots; and though they looked out over the water in several places, no wild-fowl were to be seen.

As they came round under the group of cedars to the other side of the island Mark remembered the great jack or pike which he had seen there, almost as big as a shark. They went very softly, and peering round a blue-gum bush, saw the jack basking in the sun, but a good way from shore, just at the edge of some weeds. The sunshine illumined the still water, and they could see him perfectly, his long cruel jaws, his greenish back and white belly, and powerful tail.

Drawing back behind the blue gum, Bevis prepared the matchlock, blew the match so that the fire might be ready on it, opened the pan, and pushed the priming up to the touch-hole, from which it had been shaken as he walked, and then advanced the staff or rest to the edge of the bush. He put the heavy barrel on it, and knelt down. The muzzle of the long matchlock protruded through the leafy boughs

He looked along, and got the gun straight for the fish, aiming at the broadest part of the side; then he remembered that a fish is really lower in the water than it appears, and depressed the muzzle till it pointed beneath the under-line of the jack.

When Bevis's finger first pressed the trigger of the matchlock he had the barrel of his gun accurately pointed. But while he pulled the match down to the pan an appreciable moment of time intervened; and his mind too – so swift is its operation – left the fish, his mark and object, and became expectant of the explosion. The match touched the priming. Puff!

Bang! the ball rushed forth, but not now in the course it would have taken had a hair-trigger and a spring instantly translated his original will into action. In these momentary divisions of time which had elapsed since he settled his aim, the long barrel, resting on the staff and moving easily on its pivot, had imperceptibly drooped a trifle at the breech and risen as much at the muzzle.

The ball flew high, hit the water six inches beyond the fish, and fired at so low an angle ricocheted, and went skipping along the surface, cutting out pieces of weed till the friction dragged it under, and it sank. The fish swished his tail like a scull at the stern of a boat or the screw of a steamer, but swift as was his spring forward, he would not have escaped had not the ball gone high. He left an undulation on the surface as he dived unhurt.

Bevis stamped his foot to think he had missed again.

'It was the water,' said Mark. 'The bullet went duck and drake; I saw it.'

'We must have a top-sight.'

'We won't use bullets again till we have a sight.'

'No, we won't. But I'm sure I had the gun straight.'

'So we had the rifle straight, but it did not hit.'

'No, no more did it. There's something peculiar in bullets – we will find out. I wanted that jack for supper.'

As they had not brought the powder-horn with them, they walked back to the hut.

'We ought to keep the gun loaded,' said Mark, as they reached the hut.

'Yes, but it ought to be slung up, and not put anywhere where it might be knocked over.'

'Let's make some slings for it.'

After loading the gun this time with a charge of shot, and ramming it home with the brass ramrod – Mark enjoyed using the ramrod too much to hurry over it – they set to work and drove two stout nails into the uprights on the opposite side to the bed. To one of these nails a loop of cord was fastened; to the other a similar piece was tied at one end, the other had a lesser loop, so as to take on or off the nail. When off it hung down, when on it made a loop like the other. The barrel of the gun was put through the first loop, and the stock then held up while the other piece of cord was hitched to its nail, when the long gun hung suspended.

'It looks like a hunter's hut now,' said Bevis, contemplating the matchlock. 'I'll put my bow in the corner.' He leaned his bow in the corner, and put a sheaf of arrows by it.

'My spear will go here,' said Mark.

'No,' said Bevis. 'Put the spear by the bed-head.'

'Ready for use in the night?'

'Yes; put a knob-stick too. That's it. Now look.'

'Doesn't it look nice?'

'Just doesn't it!'

'Real hunting.'

'Real as real.'

'If Val, and Cecil, and Ted could see!'

'And Charlie.'

'They would go wild.'

'The store-room *is* a muddle.'

'Shall we put it straight?'

'And get things shipshape?'

'Yes.'

They began to assort the heaped-up mass of things in the cave, putting tools on one side, provisions on the other, and odd things in the centre. After awhile Mark looked up at his watch.

'Why, it's past five! Tea-time at home.'

'I don't know,' said Bevis. 'I expect the time's different – it's longitude.'

'We are hours later, then?'

'While it's tea-time here, it's breakfast there.'

'When we got to bed, they get up. Here's the astrolabe. Take the observation.'

'So I will.'

The sun was lower now, just over the tops of the trees. Bevis hung the circle to the gate-post of the stockade and moved the tube till he could see the sun through it. It read 20° on the graduated disk.

'Twenty degrees north latitude,' he said. 'It's not on the Equator.'

'But it's in the tropics.'

'Oh, yes! – it's in Cancer, right enough. It's better than the Equator: they are obliged to lie still there all day long; and it's all swamps and steaming moisture and fevers and malaria.'

'Much nicer here.'

'Oh! Much nicer.'

'How lucky! This island is put just right.'

'The very spot!'

'There ought to be a ditch outside the palisade,' said Mark. 'Like they have outside tents to run the water away when it rains. I've seen them round tents.'

'So there ought. We'll dig it.'

They fetched the spades and shovelled away half an hour, but it was very warm, and they sat down presently inside the fence, which began to cast a shadow.

'Lemonade,' said Mark. Bevis nodded; and Mark fetched and opened a bottle, then another.

'There are only four left,' he said.

'A ship ought to come every year with these kind of things,' said Bevis.

'It ought to be wrecked, and then we could get the best things from the wreck. Shall we do some more shooting?'

'Practising. We ought to practise with ball; but we said we would not till we had a sight.'

'But it's loaded with shot, and it's my turn; and there's nothing for supper, or dinner tomorrow.'

'No more there is. One thing, though, if we practise shooting, we shall frighten all the birds away.'

'Ducks,' said Mark, 'flappers and coots, and moorhens, they're all about in the evening. The sun's going down: let's shoot one.'

'Very well.'

Mark got down the matchlock, and lit the match. He went first, and Bevis followed, two or three yards behind, with Pan. They walked as quietly as possible along the path they had made round the island, glancing out over the water at intervals. As they approached the other end of the island, where the ground was low and thick with reed-grass and sedges, they moved still more gently. They saw two young ducks, but they were too far; and, whether they heard or suspected something, swam in among a bed of rushes on a shoal. Mark stooped, and went down to the water's edge. Bevis stooped and followed, and there they set up the gun on the rest, hidden behind the fringe of sedges and reed-grass they had left when cutting them for the roof.

The muzzle almost, but not quite, protruded through the sedges, and they sat down to wait on some of the dry grasses they had reaped, but did not carry, not requiring all they had cut. The ground so near the edge was soft and yielding, and this dry hay of sedge and flag better to sit on. Bevis held Pan by the collar, and they waited a long time while the sun sank to the north-westwards, almost in front of them.

'No twilight in the tropics,' whispered Mark.

'But there's the moon,' said Bevis.

The moon being about half full, was already high in the sky, and her light continued the glow of the sunset. Restless as they were, they sat still, and took the greatest care in slightly changing their positions for ease not to rustle the dry sedges. Pan did not like it, but he reconciled himself after awhile. Presently Mark, who was nearest the standing sedges, leaned forward and moved the gun. Bevis glanced over his shoulder and saw a young wild duck among the weeds by the shoal.

'Too far,' he whispered. It looked a long way.

Mark did not answer; he was aiming. Puff – bang! Bow-wow! Pan was in the water, dashing through the smoke before they could tell whether the shot had taken effect or not. The next moment they saw the duck struggling and splashing, unable to dive.

'Lu – lu!'

'Go on, Pan!'

'Catch him!'

'Fetch him!'

'He's got him!'

'He's in the weeds!'

'Look – he can't get back – the duck drags in the weeds.'

'Pan! Pan! Here – here!'

'He can't do it.'

'He's caught.'

'He'll sink.'

'Not he.'

'But he will.'

'No.'

After striving his hardest to bring the duck back through the thick weeds, Pan suddenly turned and swam to the shoal where the rushes grew. There he landed and stood a moment with the duck's neck in his mouth: the bird flapped and struggled.

'Here – here!' shouted Bevis, running along to attract the spaniel to a place where the weeds looked thinner. Mark whistled: Pan plunged in again; and this time, having learned the strength of the weeds, he swam out round them and laid the bird at their feet.

'It's a beauty.'

'Look at his webbed feet!'

'But he's not very big.'

'But he's a young one.'

'Of course: the feathers are very pretty.'

'He kicks still.'

'Kill him. There; now we must pluck him this evening. Some of the feathers will do for Frances.'

'Oh! Frances! She's no use,' said Mark, carrying his bird by the legs.

The head hung down, and Pan licked it. Plucking they found a tedious business. Each tried in turn till he was tired, and still there seemed no end to the feathers.

'There are thousands of them,' said Bevis.

'Just as if they could not have a skin.'

'But the feathers are prettier.'

'Well, you try now.'

Bevis plucked awhile. Then Mark tried again. This was in the courtyard of the hut. The moonlight had now quite succeeded to the day. By the watch it was past nine. Out of doors it was light, but in the hut Bevis had to strike a match to see the time.

'It's supper-time,' he said.

'Now they are having breakfast at home, I suppose.'

'I dare say we're quite forgotten,' said Bevis. 'People always are. Seven thousand miles away they're sure to forget us.'

'Altogether,' said Mark. 'Of course they will. Then some day they'll see two strange men with long beards and bronzed faces.'

'Broad-brimmed Panama hats.'

'And odd digger-looking dresses.'

'And revolvers in their pockets out of sight, coming strolling up to the door and ask for –'

'Glasses of milk, as they're thirsty, and while they're sipping – as they don't really like such stuff – just ask quietly if the governor's alive and kicking –'

'And the jolly Old Moke asleep in his arm-chair –'

'And if mamma's put up the new red curtains.'

'Then they'll stare – and shriek – '

'Recognize and rumpus.'

'Huge jollification!'

'Everybody tipsy and happy.'

'John Young tumbling in the pond.'

'Bells ringing.'

'We forgot to have tea,' said Mark.

'So we did; and tea would be very nice. With dampers like the diggers,' said Bevis. 'Let's have tea now.'

'Finish the horrid duck tomorrow,' said Mark. 'I'll hang him up.'

'Fire's gone out,' said Bevis, looking from the gateway. 'Can't see any sparks.'

'Gone out long ago,' said Mark. 'Pot put it out.'

They had left the pot on the ashes.

'It would be a good plan to light a fire inside the stockade now,' said Bevis. 'It will do to make the tea, and keep things away in the night.'

'Lions and tigers,' said Mark. 'If they want to jump the fence they won't dare face the fire. But it's very warm; we must not make it by the hut.'

'Put it on one side,' said Bevis, 'in the corner under the cliff. Bring the sticks.'

They had plenty of wood in the stockade, piled up, from the chips and branches and ends of the poles with which they had made the roof and fence. The fire was soon lit. Bevis got out the iron rod to swing the kettle. Mark went down and dipped the zinc bucket full of water.

'Are there any things about over the New Sea?' he said when he came back. 'It's dark as you go through the wood, and the water looks all strange by moonlight.'

'Very curious things are about I dare say,' said Bevis, who had lit the lantern, and was shaking tea into the tin teapot in the hut. 'Curious magic things.'

'Floating round; all misty, and you can't see them.'

'But you know they're there.'

'Genii.'

'Ghouls.'

'Vampires. Look, there's a big bat – and another; they're coming back again.'

'But are there no monsters?' said Mark, stirring the fire.

CHAPTER 9

Morning in the Tropics

THE flames darted up, and mingling with the moonlight cast a reddish-yellow glare on the green-roofed hut, the yellowy cliff of sand, throwing their shadows on the fence, and illuming Pan, who sat at the door of the hut. The lantern, which Bevis had left on the floor, was just behind the spaniel. Outside the stockade the trees of the wood cast shadows towards them; the moon shone high in the sky. The weird calls of water-fowl came from a distance; the sticks crackled and hissed. Else all was silent, and the smoke rose straight into the still air.

'Green eyes glaring at you in the black wood,' said Bevis. 'Huge creatures, with prickles on their backs, and stings: the ground heaves underneath, and up they come; one claw first – you see it poking through a chink – and then hot poisonous breath – '

'Let's make a circle,' said Mark. 'Quick! Let's lock the gate.'

'Lock the gate!' Mark padlocked it. 'I'll mark the wizard's foot on it. There' – Bevis drew the five-angled mark with his pencil on the boards – 'there, now they're just done.'

'They can't come in.'

'No.'

'But we might see them?'

'Perhaps, yes.'

'Let's play cards, and not look round.'

'All right. But the kettle's boiling. I'll make the tea.' He took the kettle off and filled the teapot. 'We ought to have a damper,' he said.

'So we did: I'll make it.' Mark went into the hut and got

some flour, and set to work and made a paste: you see, if you are busy, you do not know about things that look like shadows, but are not shadows. He pounded away at the paste; and after some time produced a thick flat cake of dough, which they put in the ashes and covered over.

They put two boards for a table on the ground, in front of the hut door and away from the fire, and set the lantern at one end of the table. Bevis brought the teapot and the tin mugs, for they had forgotten cups and saucers, and made tea; while Mark buttered a heap of biscuits.

'Load the matchlock,' said Bevis. Mark loaded the gun, and leaned it by the door-post at their backs, but within reach. Bevis put his bow and two arrows close at his side, as he sat down, because he could shoot quicker with his bow (in case of a sudden surprise) than with the matchlock. The condensed milk took a few minutes to get ready, and then they began. The corner of the hut kept off the glow from the fire; they leaned their backs against the door-posts, one each side, and Pan came in between. He gobbled up the buttered biscuits, being perfectly civilized; now from one, now from the other, as fast as they liked to let him.

'This is the jolliest tea there ever was,' said Mark. 'Isn't it jolly to be seven thousand miles from anywhere?'

'No bothers,' said Bevis, waving his hand as if to keep people at a distance.

'Nothing but niceness.'

'And do as you please.'

The cards were dealt on the two rough boards, and they played, using the old coins they had brought with them as counters. Pan watched a little while, then he retired, finding there was nothing more to eat, and stretched himself a few yards away. The fire fell lower, flickered, blazed again.

'What's the time?'

'Nearly twelve.'

'I'm tired.'

'Make the bed.'

They began to make it, and recollected that one of the rugs was under the teak tree, where they had hoisted it up for an awning. Bevis took his bow and arrow; Mark his spear. They called Pan, and thus, well armed and ready for the monsters, marched across to the teak, glancing fearfully around, expectant of green blazing eyes and awful coiling shapes; quite fearless all the time, and aware that there was nothing. They had to pull up the poles to get the awning down. On returning to the stockade, the gate was padlocked and the bed finished. The lantern, in which a fresh candle had been placed, was hung to a cord from the ceiling, but they found it much in the way.

'If there's an alarm in the night,' said Mark, 'and anybody jumps up quick, he'll hit his head against the lantern. Let's put it on the box.'

'Chest' said Bevis; 'it's always chest.'

Mark dragged the chest to the bedside, and put the lantern on it, and a box of matches handy. The matchlock was hung up; the teapots and mugs and things put away, and the spear and bow and knob-stick arranged for instant use. Bevis let down the carpet at the doorway, and it shut out the moonlight like a curtain.

'Good night.'

'Good night.'

'Good night, Pan,' said Bevis putting out his hand and touching Pan's rough neck. Almost before he could bring his hand back again they were both firm asleep.

After a while Pan stretched himself, got up, and went out. He could not leap the fence, but looking round it found a place where it joined the cliff, not quite closed up. They knew this, but had forgotten all about it. Pan pushed his head under, struggled, and scratched, till his shoulders followed as he lay on his side, and the rest followed easily. Roaming round, he saw the pot in which the bacon had been boiled still on the grey ashes of the fire under the teak. The lid was off, thrown aside, and he ran to the pot, put his paws on the rim, and lapped up the greasy liquor with a relish.

Loo, the cottage girl, could she have seen, would have envied him, for she had but a dry crust for breakfast, and would have eagerly dipped it in. Pan roamed round again, and came back to the hut and waited. In an hour's time he went out once more, lapped again, and again returned to watch the sleepers.

By and by he went out the third time and stayed longer. Then he returned, thrust his head under the curtain and uttered a short bark of impatient questioning, 'Yap!'

'The genie,' said Mark, awaking. He had been dreaming.

'What's the time?' said Bevis, sitting up in an instant, as if he had never been asleep. Pan leaped on the bed and barked, delighted to see them moving.

'Three o'clock,' said Mark. 'No; why it's stopped!'

'It's late, I know,' said Bevis, who had gone to the doorway and lifted the curtain. 'The sun's high; it's eight or nine, or more.'

'I never wound it up,' said Mark, 'and – well, I never! I've left the key at home.'

'It was my key,' said Bevis. One did for both in fact.

'Now we shan't know what the time is,' said Mark. 'Awfully awkward when you're seven thousand miles from anywhere.'

'Awful! What a stupe you were; where did you leave the key?'

'On the dressing-table, I think; no, in the drawer. Let's see, in my other waistcoat: I saw it on the floor; now I remember, on the mantelpiece, or else on the washing-stand. I know, Bevis; make a sundial!'

'So I will. No, it's no use.'

'Why not?'

'I don't know when to begin.'

'When to begin?'

'Well, the sundial must have a start. You must begin your hours, don't you see?'

'I see; you don't know what hour to put to the shadow.'

'That's it.'

'But can't you find out? Isn't the sun always south at noon?'

'But which is quite south?'

'Just exactly proper south?'

'Yes, meridian is the name. I know, the north star!'

'Then we must wait till night to know the time today.'

'And then till the sun shines again – '

'Till tomorrow.'

'Yes.'

'I know!' said Mark; 'Charlie. You make the sundial, and he'll wave the handkerchief at four o'clock.'

'Capital,' said Bevis. 'Just the very thing – like Jupiter's satellites; you know, they hide behind, and the people know the time by seeing them. Charlie will set the clock for us. There's always a dodge for everything. Pan, Pan, you old rascal.'

Bevis rolled him over and over. Pan barked and leaped on them, and ran out into the sunshine.

'Breakfast,' said Mark; 'what's for breakfast?'

'Well, make some tea,' said Bevis, putting on his boots. 'That was best. And, I say, we forgot the damper.'

'So we did. It will do for breakfast.'

The damper was raked out of the ashes, and having been left to itself was found to be well done, but rather burned on one side. When the burnt part had been scraped off, and the ashes blow from it, it tasted very fair, but extremely dry.

'The butter won't last long,' said Mark presently, and they sat down to breakfast on the ground at their two boards. 'We ought to have another shipload.'

'Tables without legs are awkward,' said Bevis, whose face was heated from tending the fire they had lit and boiling the kettle. 'The difficulty is, where to put your knees.'

'Or else you must lie down. We could easily make some legs.'

'Drive short stakes into the ground, and put the boards on the top,' said Bevis. 'So we will presently. The table ought to be a little one side of the doorway, as we can't wheel it along out of the way.'

'Big stumps of logs would do for stools,' said Mark. 'Saw them off short, and stand them on end.'

'The sun's very warm,' said Bevis.

The morning sunshine looked down into their courtyard, so that they had not the least shade.

'The awning ought to be put up here over our table.'

'Let's put it up, then. I say, how rough your hair looks.'

'Well, you look as if you had not washed. Shall we go and have a swim?'

'Yes. Put the things away; here's the towels.'

They replaced their breakfast things anywhere, leaving the teapot on the bed, and went down to the water, choosing the shore opposite Serendib, because on that side there were no weeds.

As they came down to the strand, already tearing off their coats, they stopped to look at the New Sea, which was still, smooth, and sunlit.

The immense sycamores stood out against the sky, with the broad green curve of their tops drawn along the blue. Except for a shimmer of uncertain yellow at the distant shore they could not see the reflection of the quarry which was really there, for the line of vision from where they stood came nearly level with the surface of the water, so that they did not look into it but along it.

Beneath their feet they saw to the bottom of the New Sea, and slender shapes of fish hovering over interstices of stones, now here, now gone. There was nothing between them and the fish, any more than while looking at a tree. The mere surface was a film, transparent, and beneath there seemed nothing. Across on Serendib the boughs dipped to the boughs that came up under to meet them. A moorhen swam, and her image followed beneath, unbroken, so gently did she part the water that no ripple confused it. Farther, the woods of the jungle far away rose up, a mountain wall of still boughs, mingled by distance into one vast thicket.

All the light of summer fell on the water, from the glowing sky, from the clear air, from the sun. The island floated in light, they stood in light, light was in the shadow of the trees, and under the thick brambles; light was deep down in the water, light surrounded them as a mist might; they could see far up into the illumined sky as down into the water.

The leaves with light under them as well as above became films of transparent green, the delicate branches were delineated with finest camel's-hair point, all the grass blades heaped together were apart, and their edges apparent in the thick confusion; every atom of sand upon the shore was sought out by the beams, and given an individual existence amid the inconceivable multitude which the sibyl alone counted. Nothing was lost, not a grain of sand, not the least needle of fir. The light touched all things, and gave them to be.

The tip of the shimmering poplar had no more of it than the moss in the covert of the bulging roots. The swallows flew in light, the fish swam in light, the trees stood in light. Upon the shore they breathed light, and were silent till a white butterfly came fluttering over, and another white butterfly came under it in the water, when looking at it the particular released them from the power of the general.

'Magic,' said Bevis. 'It's magic.'

'Enchantment,' said Mark; 'who is it does it – the old magician?'

'I think the book says it's Circe,' said Bevis; 'in the Ulysses book, I mean. It's deep enough to dive here.'

In a minute he was ready, and darted into the water like an arrow, and was set up again as an arrow glances to the surface. Throwing himself on his side he shot along. 'Serendib!' he shouted, as Mark appeared after his dive under.

'Too far,' said Mark.

'Come on.'

Mark came on. The water did not seem to resist them that morning, it parted and let them through. With long scoops of their arms that were uppermost, swimming on the side, they slipped on still between the strokes, the impetus carrying them till the stroke came again. Between the strokes they glided buoyantly, lifted by the water as swallows glide on the plane of the air.

Presently turning on his chest for the breast-stoke Bevis struck his knee, and immediately stood up.

Fortunately there were no stones, or his knee would have been grazed; the bottom was sand. Hearing him call Mark turned on his chest and stood up too. They waded some way, and then found another deep place, swam across that more carefully, and again walked on a shallow which continued to the shore of Serendib, where they stood by the willow boughs.

'Pan!'

CHAPTER 10

Planning the Raft

PAN had sat on the strand watching them till they appeared about to land on the other side, then at the sound of his name he swam to them. Now you might see how superior he was, for the two human animals stood there afraid to enter the island lest a rough bough should abrade their skins, a thorn lacerate, or a thistle prick their feet, but Pan no sooner reached the land than he rushed in. His shaggy natural coat protected him.

In a minute out came a moorhen, then another, and a third, scuttling over the surface with their legs hanging down. Two minutes more and Pan drove a coot out, then a young duck rose and flew some distance, then a dab-chick rushed out and dived instantaneously, then still more moorhens, and coots.

'Why, there are hundreds!' said Mark. 'What a place for our shooting!'

'First-rate,' said Bevis. 'It's full of moorhens and all sorts.'

So it was. The island of Serendib was but a foot or so above the level of the water, and completely grown over with willow osiers (their blue gum), the spaces between the stoles being choked with sedges and reed-grass, vast wild parsnip stalks or 'gix', and rushes, in which mass of vegetation the water-fowl delighted. They had been undisturbed for a very long time, and they looked on Serendib as theirs; they would not move till Pan was in the midst of them.

'We must bring the matchlock,' said Mark. 'But we can't swim with it. Could we do it on the catamarans?'

'They're awkward if you've got anything to carry,' said Bevis, remembering his dip. 'I know – we'll make a raft.'

'Then we can go to all the islands,' said Mark, 'that will be

ever so much better; why we can shoot all round them everywhere.'

'And go up the river,' said Bevis, 'and go on the continent,
the mainland, you know, and see if it's China, or South
America – '

'Or Africa or Australia, and shoot elephants – '

'And rabbits and hares and peewits, and pick up the pearls
on Pearl Island, and see what there is at the other end of the
world up there,' pointing southwards.

'We've never been to the end yet,' said Mark. 'Let's go back
and make the raft directly.'

'The catamaran planks will do capital,' said Bevis, 'and some
beams, and I'll see how Ulysses made his, and make ours like
it – he had a sail somehow.'

'We could sail about at night,' said Mark, 'nobody would see
us.'

'No; Val or Charlie would be sure to see in the daytime; the
stars would guide us at night, and that would be just proper.'

'Just like they used to – '

'Yes, just like they used to when we lived three thousand
years ago.'

'Capital. Let's begin.'

'So we will.'

'Pan! Pan!'

Pan was so busy routing out the hitherto happy water-fowl
that he did not follow them until they had begun to swim,
having waded as far as they could. The shoals reduced the
actual distance they had to swim by quite half, so that they
reached New Formosa without any trouble, and dressed. They
went to the hut that Bevis might read how Ulysses constructed
his ship or raft, and while they were looking for the book saw
the duck which they had plucked the evening before.

This put them in mind of dinner, and that if they did cook it
it would not be ready for them as it used to be at home. They
were inclined to let dinner take its chance, but buttered bis-

cuits were rather wearisome, so they concluded to cook dinner first, and make the raft afterwards. It was now very hot in the stockade, so the fire was lit under the teak tree in the shade, the duck singed, and hung on a double string from a hazel rod stuck in the ground. By turning it round the double string would wind up, and when left to itself unwind like a roasting-jack.

The heat of the huge fire they made, added to that of the summer sun, was too great – they could not approach it, and therefore managed to turn the duck after a fashion with a long stick. After they had done this some time, working in their shirt-sleeves, they became impatient, and on the eve of quarrelling from mere restlessness.

'It's no use our both being here,' said Mark. 'One's enough to cook.'

'One's enough to be cooked,' said Bevis. 'Cooking is the most hateful thing I ever knew.'

'Most awful hateful. Suppose we say you shall do it today and I do it tomorrow, instead of being both stuck here by this fire?'

'Why shouldn't you do it today, and *I* do it tomorrow?'

'Toss up, then,' said Mark, producing a penny. 'Best two out of three.'

'Oh! no,' said Bevis. 'You know too many penny dodges. No, no; I know – get the cards, shuffle them and cut, and who cuts highest goes off and does as he likes – '

'Ace highest?'

'Ace.'

The pack was shuffled, and Mark cut a king. Bevis did not get a picture-card, so he was cook for that day.

'I shall take the matchlock,' said Mark.

'That you won't.'

'That I shall.'

'You won't, though.'

'Then I won't do anything,' said Mark, sulking. 'It's not fair; if you had cut king you would have had the gun.'

Bevis turned his duck poking it round with the stick, then he could not help admitting to himself that Mark was right. If he had cut a king he would have taken the gun, and it was not fair that Mark should not do so.

'Very well,' he said. 'Take it; mind it's my turn tomorrow.'

Mark went for the matchlock, and came out of the stockade with it. But before he had gone many yards he returned into the hut, and put it up on the slings. Then he picked out his fishing-rod from the store-room, and his perch-line and hooks.

Looking round the island for a place to fish, he came to a spot where a little headland projected on the Serendib side, but farther down than where they had bathed. At the end of the headland a willow trunk or blue gum hung over the water, and as he came near a kingfisher flew off the trunk, and away round Serendib. Mark thought this a likely spot, as the water looked deep, and the willow cast a shadow on one side, and fish might come for anything that fell from the boughs. He dropped his bait in, and sat down in the shade to watch his blue float, which was reflected in the still water.

He had not used his right to take the matchlock, because when he came out with it and saw Bevis, whose back was turned, he thought how selfish he was, for he knew Bevis liked shooting better than anything. So he put the gun back, and went fishing.

Against his own wishes Bevis acknowledged Mark's reason and right; against his own wishes Mark forbore to use his right that he might not be selfish.

Mark's float did not move: it stood exactly upright, it did not jerk, causing a tiny ripple, then come up, and then move along, then dive and disappear, going down aslant. It remained exactly upright, as the shot-weight on the line kept it. There was no wind, so the line out of the water did not blow aside and cause the float to rotate. Long since he had propped his rod on a forked stick, and weighted the butt with a flat stone, to save himself the trouble of holding it.

He sat down, and Pan sat by him: he stroked Pan and then teased him; Pan moved away and watched, out of arm's reach. By and by the spaniel extended himself and became drowsy. Mark's eyes wearied of the blue float, and he too stretched himself, lying on his side with his head on his arm, so that he could see the float, if he opened his eyes, without moving. A wagtail came and ran along the edge of the sand so near that with his rod he could have reached it. Jerking his tail the wagtail entered the still water up to the joints of his slender limbs, then came out, and ran along again.

Mark's head almost touched the water: his hair (for his hat was off, as usual) was reflected in it, and a great brown water-beetle passed through the reflection. A dove – his parakeet – came over and entered the wood; it was the same Bevis afterwards heard cooing. Mark half opened his eyes, and thought the wagtail's tiny legs were no thicker than one of Frances's hair-pins.

The moorhens and coots had now recovered from the fright Pan had given them. As he gazed through the chinks of his eyelids along the surface of the water, he could see them one by one returning towards Serendib, pausing on the way among the weeds, swimming again, with nodding heads, turning this side and that to pick up anything they saw; but still, gradually approaching the island opposite. They all came from one direction, and he remembered that when Pan hunted them out, they all scuttled the same way. So did the wild duck; so did the kingfisher. 'I believe they all go to the river,' Mark thought; 'the river that flows out through the weeds. Just wait till we have got our raft.'

Something swam out presently from the shore of New Formosa; something nearly flush with the water, and which left a wake of widening ripples behind it, by which Mark knew it was a rat: for water-fowl, though they can move rapidly, do not cause much undulation. The rat swam out a good way, then turned and came in again. This coasting voyage he repeated down the shore several times.

To look along the surface, as Mark did, was like kneeling and glancing over a very broad and well polished table, your eyes level with it. The slightest movement was visible a great way – a little black speck that crossed was seen at once. The little black speck was raised a very small degree above the surface, and there was something in the water not visible following it.

The water undulated, but less than behind the rat. Now the moorhens nod their heads to and fro, as you or I nod: but this black speck waved itself the other way, from side to side, as it kept steadily onwards. Mark recognized a snake, swimming swiftly, its head (black only from distance and contrast with the gleam of the crystal top of the polished table) just above the surface, and sinuous length trailing beneath the water. He did not see whence the snake started, but he saw it go across to the weeds at the extreme end of Serendib, and there lost it.

By now the shadows had moved, and his foot was in the sunshine: he could feel the heat through the leather, Two bubbles came up to the surface close to the shore: he saw the second one start from the sand and rise up quickly with a slight wobble, but the sand did not move, and he could not see anything in it.

His eyes closed, not that he slept, but the gleam of the water inclined them to retire into the shadow of the lids. After some time there was a shrill pipe. Mark started, and lifted his head, and saw the kingfisher, which had come back towards his perch on the willow trunk. He came within three yards before he saw Mark; then he shot aside, with a shrill whistle of alarm, rose up and went over the island.

In starting up, Mark moved his foot, and a butterfly floated away from it; the butterfly had settled in the sunshine on the heated leather. With three flutters, the butterfly floated with broad wings stretched out over the thin grass by the shore. It was no more effort to him to fly than it is to thistledown.

The same start woke Pan. Pan yawned, licked his paw, got up and wagged his tail, looked one way and then the other, and then went off back to Bevis. The blue float was still perfectly motionless. Mark sat up, took his rod and wound up the winch, and began to wander homewards too, idly along the shore. He had gone some way when he saw a jack basking by a willow bush aslant from him, so that the markings on his back were more visible than when seen sideways, for in this position the foreshortening crowded them together. They are like the water-mark on paper, seen best at a low angle, or the mark on silk, and somewhat remind you of the mackerel.

CHAPTER 11

Kangaroos

So soon as he was sure the jack had not noticed him, Mark drew softly back, and with some difficulty forced a way between the bramble thickets towards the stockade. He thus entered a part they had not before visited, for as the trees and bushes were not so thick by the water, their usual path followed the windings of the shore. Trampling over some and going round others, Mark managed to penetrate between the thickets, having taken his rod to pieces, as it constantly caught in the branches.

Next he came to a place where scarcely anything grew, everything having been strangled by those Thugs of the wood, the wild hops, except a few scattered ash-poles, up which they wound, indenting the bark in spirals. The ground was covered with them, for having slain their supports they were forced to creep, so that he walked on hops; and from under a bower of them, where they were smothering a bramble bush, a nightingale 'kurred' at him angrily.

He came near the nightingale's young brood, safely reared. 'Sweet Kur-r-r!' The bird did not like it. These wild hops are a favourite cover with nightingales. A damp furrow or natural ditch, now dry, but evidently a watercourse in rain, seemed to have stopped the march of this creeping, twining plant, for over it he entered among hazel bushes; and then, seeing daylight, fancied he was close to the stockade; but to his surprise, stepped out into an open glade with a green knoll on one side.

The knoll did not rise quite so high as the trees, and there was a quantity of fern about the lower part, then an open lawn of grass, a little meadow in the midst of the wood. He saw a white tail disappear among the fern – there were then rabbits here.

'Bevis!' said Mark aloud. In his surprise he called to Bevis, as he would have done had Bevis been present. He ran to the knoll, and as he ran, more white tails – the little ones – raced into the fern, where he saw burrows and sand-heaps thrown out.

On the top of the knoll there were numerous signs of rabbits – places worn bare, and 'runs', or footpaths, leading down across the grass. He looked round, but could see nothing but trees, which hid the New Sea and the cliff at home.

Eager to tell Bevis of the discovery, and especially of the rabbits, which would furnish them with food, and were, above all, something fresh to shoot at, he ran down the hill so fast that he could not stop himself, though he saw something white in the grass. He returned, and found it was mushrooms, and he gathered between twenty and thirty in a few minutes – 'buttons', full-grown mushrooms, and overgrown ketchup ones. How to carry them he did not know, having used his handkerchief already, and left his coat at home, till he thought of his waistcoat, and took it off and made a rough bundle of them in it. Then he heard Bevis's whistle, the well-known notes they always used to call each other, and shouted in reply, but the shout did not penetrate so far as the shrill sound had done.

'Where's the gun?' said Bevis, coming to meet him.

'I left it at home.'

'No, you had it.'

'I put it back as you were not coming.'

'I never saw it.'

'It's in the hut.'

'Didn't you really take it?'

'No – really. We'll both go with the gun –'

'So we will.' Bevis regretted now that he had made any difficulty. 'No, it's your turn; you shall have it.'

'I shan't,' said Mark. 'Look here' – showing the mushrooms – 'splendid for supper, and I've found some rabbits!'

'Rabbits!'

'And a little green hill, and a kingfisher, and a jack. Come and get the gun, and let's shoot him. Quick.'

Mark began to run for the matchlock, and they left the duck to itself. Bevis ran with him, and Mark told him all about it as they went.

Having got the gun, as they came back Mark said perhaps Pan would eat the duck. Bevis called him, but he did not need the call. Gluttonous epicure as he was, Pan, at a whistle from Bevis, would have left the most marrowy bone in the world; but Bevis with a gun! why, Polly with a broomstick could not have stopped him.

Before they got to the willow bush it had been settled that Mark should shoot at the jack, as the matchlock was loaded with shot, and Bevis wanted to shoot with ball, and reserved his turn for the time when he had made the new sight. Bevis held Pan while Mark went forward. The jack was there, but Mark could not get the rest in a position to take a steady aim, because the willow boughs interfered so.

So Bevis knelt down, still holding Pan, and Mark rested the long heavy barrel on his shoulder. The shot plunged into the water, and the jack floated, blown a yard away, dead on his back; his head shattered, but the long body untouched. Pan fetched him out, and they laughed at the spaniel, he looked so odd with the fish in his mouth. Bevis wanted to see the glade and the rabbits' burrows, but Mark said, if the duck was done, it would burn to a cinder, so they went home to their dinner. By the time they reached the teak tree, the duck was indeed burned one side.

It was dry and hard for lack of basting, when they cut it up, but not unsavoury; and what made it nicer was that every now and then they found shots – which their teeth had flattened – shots from their own gun. These they saved, and Mark put them in his purse; there were six altogether. Mark gloried in the number, as it was a long shot at the duck, and they showed that he had aimed straight. The ale in the wooden bottle was now stale, so they drank water, with a little sherry in it; and then started to see the discovery Mark had made. Pan went with them. The old spaniel had been there long before, for he found out the rabbits the first stroll he took after landing from the *Pinta,* but could not convey his knowledge to them.

Bevis marked out a tree, behind which they could wait in ambush to shoot at the rabbits, as it was within easy range of their burrows; and then, as they felt it was now afternoon, they returned to the stockade, got the telescope and went up on the cliff to watch for Charlie's signal. The shadow of the gnomon on the dial had moved a good way since Bevis set it up. They had not the least idea of the hour, but somehow they felt that it was afternoon.

The sandy summit of the cliff was very warm, and the bramble bushes were not high enough to give them any shade; so that, to escape the sun, they reclined on the ground in front of the young oak-tree, and between it and the edge. Bevis looked through the telescope, and could see the sandmartins going in and out of their holes in the distant quarry.

Charlie was not on the hill, or, if so, he was behind a sycamore and out of sight; but they knew he had not yet made the signal, because the herd of cows was down by the hollow oak, some standing in the water. They had not yet been called by the milkers. Sweeping the shore of Fir-Tree Gulf, and down the Mozambique to the projecting bluff which prevented farther view, he saw a crow on the sand, and another perched on a rail; another sign that there was no one about.

'Any savages?' said Mark.

'Not one.'

'How did the rabbits – I mean the kangaroos – get here?' said Bevis presently. 'I don't think they could swim so far.'

'Savages might bring them,' said Mark. 'But they don't very often carry pets with them: they eat everything so.'

'Nibbling men like goats nibbling hedges,' said Bevis. 'We must take care: but how did the kangaroos get on the island?'

'It is curious,' said Mark. 'Perhaps it wasn't always an island – joined to the mainland and the river cut a way through the isthmus.'

'Or a volcano blew it up,' said Bevis. 'We will see if we can find the volcano.'

'But it will be gone out now.'

'Oh! yes. All those sort of things happened when there was no one to see them.'

'Before we lived.'

'Or anybody else.'

A large green dragon-fly darted to and fro, now under their feet and between them and the water; now overhead, now up to the top of the oak, and now round the cliff and back again; weaving across and across a warp and weft in the air. As they sat still he came close, and they saw his wings revolving, and the sunlight reflected from the membrane. Every now and then there was a slight snap, as he seized a fly, and ate it as he flew: so eager was he that when a speck of wood-dust fell from the oak, though he was yards away, he rushed at it and intercepted it before it could reach the ground. It was rejected, and he had returned whence he started in a moment.

'The buffaloes are moving,' said Mark. 'They're going up the hill. Get ready. Here, put it on my shoulder.'

The herd had begun to ascend the green slope from the water's edge, doubtless in response to the milker's halloo, which they could not hear on the island. Bevis rested the telescope on Mark's shoulder, and watched. In point of fact it was not so far but that they could have seen anyone by the quarry without a glass, but the telescope was proper.

'There he is,' said Mark.

Bevis, looking through the telescope, saw Charlie come out

from behind a sycamore, where he had been lying in the shadow, and standing on the edge of the quarry, wave his white handkerchief three times, with an interval between.

'It's all right. White flag,' said Bevis. 'He's looking. He can't see us, can he?'

'No there are bushes behind us. If we stood up against the sky perhaps he might.'

'I'll crawl to the dial,' said Bevis, and he went on hands and knees to the sundial, where he could stand up without being seen, as there were brambles and the oak between him and the cliff. He drew a line with his pencil where the shadow of the gnomon fell on the circle; that was four o'clock. Mark came after, creeping too.

'We won't sit there again,' said Mark, 'when it's signal-time. He keeps staring. You can see his face through the telescope. We will keep behind the tree.'

They went down to the hut, and Bevis made the sight for the matchlock. The short spiral of copper wire answered perfectly, and he could now take accurate aim. But after he had put the powder in, and was just going to put a bullet, he recollected the kangaroos. If he shot off much at a target with bullets at that time in the afternoon it would alarm everything on the island, for the report would be heard all over it. Kangaroos and water-fowl are generally about more in the evening than the morning, so he put off the trial with ball and loaded with shot.

It was of no use going into ambush till the shadows length-ened, so he set about getting the tea while Mark sawed off two posts, and drove them into the ground at one side of the door-way of the hut. Each post had a cross-piece at the top, and the two boards were placed on these, forming a table. Bevis made four dampers, and at Mark's suggestion buried a number of potatoes in the embers of the fire, so as to have them baked for supper, and save more cooking.

The mushrooms were saved for breakfast, and the jack, which was about two pounds' weight, would do for dinner.

When he had finished the table, Mark went to the teak tree, and fetched the two poles that had been set up there for the awning. These he erected by the table, and stretched the rug from them over the table, fastening the other two edges to the posts of the hut.

They had found the nights so warm that more than one rug was unnecessary, and the other could be spared for a permanent awning under which to sit at table. Some tea was put aside to be drunk cold, and it was then time to go shooting. Mark was to have the gun, but he would not go by himself, Bevis must accompany him.

They had to go some distance round to get at the glade, and made so much noise pushing aside branches, and discussing as to whether they were going the right way, that when they reached it, if any kangaroos had been out feeding, they had all disappeared.

'I will bring the axe,' said Bevis, 'and blaze the trees, then we shall know the way in a minute.'

Fixing the rest so that he could command the burrows on that side of the knoll, Mark sat down under the ash tree they had previously selected, and leaned the heavy matchlock on the staff. They chose this tree because some brake fern grew in front of it and concealed them. Pan had now come to understand this manner of hunting, and he lay down at once, and needed no holding. Bevis extended himself at full length on his back just behind Mark, and looked up at the sky through the ash branches.

The flies would run over his face, though Mark handed him a frond of fern to swish them with, so he partly covered himself with his handkerchief. The handkerchief was stretched across his ear like the top of a drum, and while he was lying so quiet a fly ran across the handkerchief there, and he distinctly heard the sound of its feet. It was a slight rustle, as if its feet caught a little of the surface of the handkerchief. This happened several times.

The sun being now below the line of the tree-tops, the glade was in the shadow, except the top of the knoll, up which the shadow slowly rose like a tide as the sun declined. Now the edge of the shadow reached a sand-heap thrown out from a burrow; now a thicker bunch of grass; then a thistle; at last it slipped over the top in a second.

Mark could see three pairs of tiny, sharp-pointed ears in the grass. He knew these were young rabbits, or kangaroos, too small for eating. They were a difficulty, they were of no use, but pricked up and listened, if he made the least movement, and if they ran in would stop larger ones from coming out. There was something moving in the hazel stoles across the glade which he could not make out, and he could not ask Bevis to look and see because of these minute kangaroos.

Ten minutes afterwards a squirrel leaped out from the hazel, and began to dart hither and thither along the sward, drawing his red tail softly over the grass at each arching leap as lightly as Jack drew the tassel of his whip over his mare's shoulder when he wished to caress and soothe her. Another followed, and the two played along the turf, often hidden by bunches of grass.

Mark dared not touch Bevis or tell him, for he fancied a larger rabbit was sitting on his haunches at the mouth of a hole fringed with fern. Bevis under his handkerchief listened to Pan snapping his teeth at the flies, and looked up at the sky till four parrots (wood-pigeons) came over, and descended into an oak not far off. The oak was thick with ivy, and was their roost-tree, though they did not intend to retire yet.

Presently he saw a heron floating over at an immense height. His wings moved so slowly he seemed to fly without pressure on the air – as slowly as a lady fans herself when there is no one to coquet with. The heron did not mean to descend to the New Sea, he was bound on a voyage which he did not wish to complete till the dusk began; hence his deliberation. From his flight you might know that there was a mainland some-where in that direction.

Bang! Mark ran to the knoll, but Pan was there before him, and just in time to seize a wounded kangaroo by the hind-quarters as he was paddling into a hole by the fore paws. Mark had seen the rabbit behind the fringe of fern move, and so knew it really was one, and so gently had he got the matchlock into position, moving it the sixteenth of an inch at a time, that Bevis did not know he was aiming. By the new sight he brought the gun to bear on the spot where he thought the rabbit's shoulder must be, for he could not see it, but the rabbit had moved, and was struck in the haunch, and would have struggled out of reach had not Pan had him.

The squirrel had disappeared, and the four parrots had flown at the report.

'This island is full of things,' said Bevis, when Mark told him about the squirrel. 'You find something new every hour, and I don't know what we shan't find at last. But you have had all the shooting and killed everything.'

'Well, so I have,' said Mark. 'The duck, and the jack, and the kangaroo. You *must* shoot something next.'

CHAPTER 12

Bevis's Zodiac

THEY returned to the hut and prepared the kangaroo and the fish for boiling on the morrow; the fish was to be boiled up in the saucepan, and the kangaroo in the pot. Pan had the paunch, and with his great brown eyes glaring out of his head with gluttony, made off with it to his own private larder, where, after eating his fill, he buried the rest. Pan had his own private den behind a thicket of bramble, where he kept some bones of a duck, a bacon bone, and now added this to his store.

Next, Mark with one of the old axes they had used to excavate the store-room, cut a notch in the edge of the cave, where it opened on the hut, large enough to stand the lantern in, as the chest would be required for the raft. They raked the potatoes out of the ashes, and had them for supper, with a damper, the last fragment of a duck, and cold tea, like golddiggers.

Bevis now recollected the journal he had proposed to keep, and got out the book, in which there was as yet only one entry, and that a single word, 'Wednesday'. He set it on the table under the awning, with the lantern open before him. Outside the edge of the awning, the moon filled the courtyard with her light.

'Why, it's only Thursday now,' said Mark. 'We've only been here one full day, and it seems weeks.'

'Months,' said Bevis. 'Perhaps this means Wednesday last year.'

'Of course: this is the next year to that. How we must have altered! Our friends would not know us.'

'Not even our mothers,' said Bevis.

'Nor our jolly old mokes and governors.'

'Shot a kangaroo,' said Bevis, writing; 'shot a duck and a jack – No. Are they jacks? That's such a common name.'

'No; not jacks: jack-sharks.'

'No; sun-fish: they're always in the sun.'

'Yes; sun-fish.'

'Shot a sun-fish: saw two squirrels, and a heron, and four parrots – '

'And a kingfisher – '

'Halcyon,' said Bevis, writing it down – 'a beautiful halcyon; made a table and a sundial. I must go up presently and mark the meridian by the north star.'

'Saw one savage.'

'Who was that?'

'Why, Charlie.'

'Oh yes, one savage; believe there are five thousand in the jungle on the mainland.'

'Seven thousand miles from anywhere. Put it down,' said Mark.

'Twenty degrees north latitude; right. There, look; half a page already!'

'And write down all the fish.'

'And everything. The language of the natives will be a bother. I must make a new alphabet for it. Look! that will do for A' – he made a tiny circle; 'that's B, two dots.'

'They gurgle in their throats,' said Mark.

'That's a gurgle,' said Bevis, making a long stroke with a dot over and under it; 'and they click with their tongues against the roofs of their mouths. No: it's awkward to write clicks. I know: there, CK, that's for click and this curve under it means a tongue – the way you're to put it to make a click.'

'Click! Click!'

'Guggle!'

'Then there's the names of the idols,' said Mark. 'We'd better find some.'

'You can cut some,' said Bevis; 'cut them with your knife out of a stick, and say they're models, as they wouldn't let you take the real ones. The names; let's see – Jog.'

'Hick-kag.'

'Hick-kag; I've put it down. Jog and Hick-kag are always quarrelling, and when they hit one another, that's thunder. That's what they say.'

Kaak! kaak! A heron was descending. The unearthly noise made them look up.

'Are there any tidal waves?' said Mark.

'Sometimes – a hundred feet high. But the thing is how did they get here? How did anybody ever get anywhere?'

'It's very crooked,' said Mark, 'very crooked: you can't quite see it, can you? Suppose you go and do the sundial: I'm sleepy.'

'Well, go to bed; I can do it.'

'Good night!' said Mark. 'Lots of chopping to do tomorrow. We ought to have brought a grindstone for the axes. You have got the plan ready for the raft?'

'Quite ready.'

Mark went into the hut, placed the lantern in the niche, and threw himself on the bed. In half a minute, he was firm asleep. Bevis went out of the courtyard, round outside the fence, and up on the cliff to the sundial. The stars shone brighter than it is usually thought they do when there is no moon; but in fact it is not so much the moon as the state of the atmosphere. There was no haze in the dry air, and he could see the Pole Star distinctly.

He sat down – as the post on which the dial was supported was low – on the southern side, with it between him and the north. He still had to stoop till he had got the tip of the gnomon to cover the North Star. Closing one eye, as if aiming, he then put his pencil on the dial in the circle or groove scratched by the compass. The long pencil was held upright in the groove, and moved round till it intercepted his view of the

star. The tip of the gnomon, the pencil, and the Pole Star were
in a direct line, in a row one behind the other.

To make sure, he raised his head and looked over the
gnomon and pencil to the star, when he found that he had not
been holding the pencil upright; it leaned to the east, and made
an error to the west in his meridian. 'It ought to be a plumb-
line,' he thought. 'But I think it's straight now.'

He stooped again, and found the gnomon and pencil correct,
and pressing on the pencil hard, drew it towards him out of the
groove a little way. By the moonlight when he got up he could
see the mark he had left, and which showed the exact north.
Tomorrow he would have to draw a line from that mark
straight to the gnomon, and when the shadow fell on that line
it would be noon. With the fixed point of noon and the fixed
point of four o'clock, he thought he could make the divisions
for the rest of the hours.

The moonlight cast a shadow to the east of the noon-line, as
she had crossed the meridian. Looking up, he saw the irregular
circle of the moon high in the sky, so brilliant that the scored
relievo worked enchased upon her surface was obscured by the
bright light reflected from it.

Behind him numerous lights glittered in the still water: near
at hand they were sharp clean points; far away they were short
bands of light drawn towards him. Bevis went to the young oak
and sat down under it. Cassiopeia fronted him, and Capella;
the Northern Crown was faint and low; but westward great
Arcturus shone, though the moon had taken the redness from
him. The cross of Cygnus was lying on its side as it was carried
through the eastern sky; beneath it the Eagle's central star
hung over the Nile. Low in the south, over the unknown river,
Antares, too, had lost his redness.

Up through the branches of the oak he saw Lyra, the purest
star in the heavens, white as whitest and clearest light may be,
gleaming at the zenith of the pale blue dome. But just above
the horizon northwards there was a faint white light, the faint-

277

est aurora, as if another moon was rising there. By these he knew his position, and that he was looking the same way as if he had been gazing from the large northern window of the parlour at home, or if he had been lying on the green path by the strawberries, as he sometimes did in the summer evenings.

Then the North Star, minute but clear – so small, and yet chosen for the axle and focus of the sky, instead of sun-like Sirius – the North Star always shone just over the group of elms by the orchard. Summer and winter, spring and autumn, it was always there, always over the elms – whether they were reddening with the buds and flowers of February, whether they were dull green now in the heats of August, whether they were yellow in October.

Dick and his Team, whose wagon goes backwards, swung round it like a stone in a sling whirled about the shoulders. Sometimes the tail of the Bear, where Dick bestrides his second horse, hung down behind the elms into the vapour of the horizon. Sometimes the Pointers were nearly overhead. If they were hidden by a cloud, the Lesser Bear gave a point; or you could draw a line through Cassiopeia, and tell the North by her chair of stars.

The comets seemed to come within the circle of Boötes – Arcturus you always know is some way beyond the tail of the Bear. The comets come inside the circle of the stars that never set. The governor had seen three or four appear there in his time, just over the elms under the Pole.

Between these two groups of tall trees – so tall and thick that they were generally visible even on dark nights – the streamers of the Aurora Borealis shot up in winter, and between them in summer the faint reflection of the midnight sun, like the lunar dawn which precedes the rising of the moon always appeared. The real day-dawn – the white foot of Aurora – came through the sky-curtain a little to the right of the second group, and about over a young oak in the hedge across the road, opposite the garden wall.

When the few leaves left on this young oak were brown, and rustled in the frosty night, the massy shoulder of Orion came heaving up through it – first one bright star, then another; then the gleaming girdle, and the less definite scabbard; then the great constellation stretched across the east.

As the constellation rose, so presently new vigour too entered into the trees, the sap moved, the buds thrust forth, the new leaf came, and the nightingale travelling up from the south sang in the musical April nights. But this was when Orion was south, and Sirius flared like a night-sun over the great oak at the top of the Home Field.

Sirius rose through the young oak opposite the garden wall, passed through the third group of elms, by the rick-yard, gleaming through the branches – hung in the spring above the great oak at the top of the Home Field, and lowered by degrees westwards behind the ashes growing at that end of the New Sea by the harbour. After it Arcturus came, and lorded the midsummer zenith, where now lucent Lyra looked down upon him.

Up, too, through the little oak came Aldebaran, the red Bull's Eye, the bent rod of Aries, and the cluster of the Pleiades. The Pleiades he loved most, for they were the first constallation he learned to know. The flickering Pleiades, the star-dusted spot in Cancer, and Leo, came in succession.

Antares, the harvest-star, scarcely cleared the great oak southwards in summer. He got them all from a movable planisphere, the very best star-maps ever made, proceeding step by step, drawing imaginary lines from one to the other, as through the Pointers to the Pole, and so knew the designs on our northern dome.

He transferred them from the map to the trees. The north group of elms, the north-east group, the east oak, the south-east elms, the southern great oak, the westward ashes, the orchard itself north-west – through these like a zodiac the stars moved, all east to west, except the enchanted circle about

279

the Pole. For the Bear and the Lesser Bear sometimes seemed to move from west to east when they were returning, swinging under to what would have been their place of rising.

Fixing them thus by night, he knew where many were by day; the Pole Star was always over the north elms – when the starlings stayed and whistled there before they flew to the house-top, when the rooks called there, before the sun set, on their way home to the jungle, when the fieldfares in the gloomy winter noon perched up there. The Pole Star was always over the elms.

In the summer mornings the sun rose north of east, between the second group of elms and the little oak – so far to the north that he came up over the vale instead of the Downs. The morning beams then lit up the northern or outer side of the garden wall and fell aslant through the narrow kitchen window, under the beam of the ceiling. In the evening the sun set again north-wards of the orchard, between it and the north elms, having come round towards the place of rising, and shining again on the outside of the garden wall, so that there seemed but a few miles between. He did not sink, but only dipped, and the dawn that travelled above him indicated his place, moving between the north and north-east elms, and overcoming the night by the little oak. The sun did not rise and sink; he travelled round an immense circle.

In the winter mornings the sun rose between the young oak and the third group of elms, red and vapour-hung, and his beams presently shot through the window to the logs on the kitchen hearth. He sank then between the south-westerly ashes and the orchard, rising from the wall of the Downs, and sinking again behind it. At noon he was just over, only a little higher than the great southern oak. All day long the outer side of the garden wall was in shadow, and at night, the northern sky was black to the horizon. The travelling dawn was not visible: the sun rose and sank, and was only visible through half of the great circle. The cocks crowed at four in the after-noon, and the rooks hastened to the jungle.

But by and by, when the giant Orion shone with his full width grasping all the sky, then in the mornings the sun's rising began to shift backwards — first to the edge of the third group of elms, then straight up the road, then to the little oak. In the afternoon, the place of setting likewise shifted backwards to the north, and came behind the orchard. At noon he was twice as high as the southern oak, and every day at noontide the shadows gradually shortened. The nightingale sang in the musical April night, the cowslips opened, and the bees hummed over the meadows.

Last of all, the sweet turtle-doves cooed and wooed; beauteous June wearing her roses came, and the sun shone at the highest point of his great circle. Then you could not look at him unless up through the boughs of a tree. Round the zodiac of the elms, and the little oak, the great oak, the ashes, and the orchard, the sun revolved; and the house, and the garden path by the strawberries — the best place to see — were in the centre of his golden ring.

The sward on the path on which Bevis used to lie and gaze up in the summer evening was real and tangible; the earth under was real; and so too the elms, the oak, the ash trees, were real and tangible — things to be touched, and known to be. Now like these, the mind, stepping from the one to the other, knew and almost felt the stars to be real and not mere specks of light, but things that were there by day over the elms as well as by night, and not apparitions of the evening departing at the twittering of the swallows. They were real, and the touch of his mind felt to them.

He could not, as he reclined on the garden path by the strawberries, physically reach to and feel the oak; but he could feel the oak in his mind, and so from the oak, stepping beyond it, he felt the stars. They were always there by day as well as by night. The Bear did not sink, the sun in summer only dipped, and his reflection — the travelling dawn — shone above him, and so from these unravelling out the enlarging sky, he felt as well as knew that neither the stars nor the sun ever rose or set. The heavens were always around and with him. The strawberries and the sward of the garden path, he himself reclining there, were moving through, among, and between the stars; they were as much by him as the strawberry leaves.

By day the sun, as he sat down under the oak, was as much by him as the boughs of the great tree. It was by him like the swallows.

The heavens were as much a part of life as the elms, the oak, the house, the garden and orchard, the meadow and the brook. They were no more separated than the furniture of the parlour, than the old oak chair where he sat, and saw the new moon shine over the mulberry tree. They were neither above nor beneath, they were in the same place with him; just as when you walk in a wood the trees are all about you, on a plane with you, so he felt the constellations and the sun on a plane with him, and that he was moving among them as the earth rolled on, like them, with them, in the stream of space.

The day did not shut off the stars, the night did not shut off the sun; they were always there. Not that he always thought of them, but they were never dismissed. When he listened to the greenfinches sweetly calling in the hawthorn, or when he read his books, poring over the *Odyssey*, with the sunshine on the wall, they were always there; there was no severance. Bevis lived not only out to the finches and the swallows, to the faraway hills, but he lived out and felt out to the sky.

It was living, not thinking. He lived it, never thinking, as the finches live their sunny life in the happy days of June. There was magic in everything, blades of grass and stars, the sun and the stones upon the ground.

The green path by the strawberries was the centre of the world, and round about it by day *and* night the sun circled in a magical golden ring.

Under the oak on New Formosa that warm summer night, Bevis looked up as he reclined at the white pure light of Lyra,

and forgot everything but the consciousness of living, feeling up to and beyond it. The earth and the water, the oak, went away; he himself went away: his mind joined itself and was linked up through ethereal space to its beauty.

The moon moved, and with it the shadow of the cliff on the water beneath, a planet rose eastwards over their new Nile, water-fowl clucked as they flew over.

'Kaak! Kaak! Another heron called, and his discordant piercing yell sounded over the water, seeming to penetrate to the distant and shadowy shores. The noise awoke him, and he went down to the hut. Mark was firm asleep, the lantern burned in the niche; Pan had been curled up by the bedside, but lifted his head and wagged his tail, thumping the floor as he entered. Bevis let down the curtain closing the doorway, put out the lantern, and in three minutes was as firm as Mark. After some time, Pan rose quietly and went out, slipping under the curtain, which fell back into its place when he had passed.

CHAPTER 13

The Raft

THEY did not get up till the sun was high, and when Mark lifted the curtain a robin flew from the table just outside, where he had been picking up the crumbs, across to the gate-post in the stockade.

The gate had not been shut — Pan was lying by it under the fence, which cast a shadow in the morning and evening.

'Pan!' said Mark; the lazy spaniel wagged his tail, but did not come.

'I shall go and finish the sundial while you get the breakfast,' said Bevis. It was Mark's turn today, and as he went out at the gate he stooped and patted Pan, who looked up with speaking affection in his eyes, and stretched himself to his full length in utter lassitude.

'Pan's been thieving,' said Mark. 'There was half a damper on the table last night, and it was gone this morning, and two potatoes which we left, and I put the skin of the kangaroo on the fence, and that's gone — '

'He couldn't eat the skin, could he?' said Bevis. 'Pan come here, sir.'

'Look at him,' said Mark, 'he's stuffed so full he can hardly crawl — if he was hungry he would come quick.'

'So he would. Pan, you old rascal! What have you done with the kangaroo skin, sir?'

Pan wagged his tail and looked from one to the other; the sound of their voices was stern, but he detected the goodwill in it, and that they were not really angry.

'And the damper?'

'And the potatoes? And just as if you could eat leather and fur, sir!'

Pan put his fore paws on Bevis's knee, and looked up as if he had done something very clever.

'Pooh! Get away,' said Bevis, 'you're a false old rascal. Mark, cut him some of that piece of bacon presently.'

'So I will — and I'll put the things higher up,' said Mark. 'I'll drive some nails into the posts and make a shelf, then you'll be done, sir.'

Pan, finding there was nothing more for him to eat, walked slowly back to the fence and let himself fall down.

'Too lazy to lie down properly,' said Bevis.

After breakfast they put up the shelf, and placed the eatables on it out of Pan's reach, and then taking their towels started for their bath.

'It might have been a rat,' said Mark; 'that looks gnawn.' He kicked the jack's head, which being shattered with the shot, had been cut off, and thrown down outside the gate. 'But Pan's very full, else he would come,' for the spaniel did not follow as usual. So soon as they had gone the robin returned to the table, took what he liked, ventured into the hut for a minute, and then perched on the fence above Pan before returning to the wood.

Bevis and Mark swam and waded to Serendib again. There was a light ripple this morning from the south-east, and a gentle breeze which cooled the day. They said they would hasten to construct the raft, so as to be able to shoot the water-fowl, but Bevis wanted first to try the matchlock with ball now he had fitted it with a sight. He fired three times at the teak tree, to which Mark pinned a small piece of paper as a bull's-eye, and at thirty yards he hit the tree very well, but not the paper. The bullets were all below, the nearest about four inches from the bull's eye. Still, it was much better shooting.

He then loaded the gun with shot, and took it and a hatchet — the two were a good load — intending to look in the wood for suitable timber, and keep the gun by him for a possible shot at something. But just as he had got ready, and Pan shaking himself together began to drag his idle body after him, he thought Mark looked dull. It was Mark's turn to cook, and he had already got the fire alight under the teak.

'I won't go,' he said; 'I'll stop and help you. Things are stupid by yourself.'

'Fishing is very stupid by yourself,' said Mark.

'Let's make a rule,' said Bevis. 'Everybody helps everybody instead of going by themselves.'

'So we will,' said Mark, only too glad, and the new rule was agreed to, but as they could not both shoot at once, it was understood that in this the former contract was to stand, and each was to have the matchlock a day to himself. The pot and the saucepan, with the kangaroo and the jack, were soon on, and they found that boiling had one great advantage over roasting, they could pile on sticks and go away for some time, instead of having to watch and turn the roast.

They found a good many small trees and poles such as they wanted not far from home, and among the rest three dead larches which had been snapped by a tornado. These dry trees were lighter and would float better than green timber. For the larger beams, or foundation of the raft, they chose aspen and poplar, and for the cross-joists firs, and by dinner-time they had collected nearly enough.

It was half past one by the sundial when Mark began to prepare the table; Bevis had gone to haul the catamaran planks up to the place where the raft was to be built. Under one of the planks, as he turned it over, there was a little lizard; the creature at first remained still as if dead, then not being touched ran off quickly, grasping the grass sideways with its claws as a monkey grasps a branch. With the end of a plank under each arm Bevis hauled these across to the other materials.

This time they had a nicer meal than any they had prepared: fish and game; the kangaroo was white and juicy, almost as white as chicken. There was sufficient left for supper, and a bone or two for Pan. The chopping they had done made them idle, and they agreed not to work again till the evening; they lounged about like Pan till the time appointed to look for Charlie's signal.

When they went up on the cliff it was a quarter past three by the dial, so they sat down in the shade of the oak where the brambles behind would prevent their being seen against the skyline. After awhile Mark crept on all fours to the sundial, and said it was half past three, and suddenly exclaimed that the time was going backwards.

The shadow of the gnomon slipped the wrong way; he looked up and saw a light cloud passing over the sun. Bevis had often seen the same thing in March, sitting by the southern window, when the shadow ran back from his pencil-line on the window-frame as the clouds began to cover up the blue roof. Charlie was rather late today, but he gave the signal according to promise: they saw him look a long while and then move away.

Directly after tea they began to work again at the preparations for the raft, cutting some more poles and sawing up those they had already into the proper lengths. They laboured on into the moonlight, which grew brighter every night as the moon increased, and did not cease till all the materials were ready.

They did not recognize how tired they were till they started for the hut; their backs, so long bent over the sawing, had stiffened in that position, and pained them as they straightened the sinews to stand upright; their fingers were crooked from continually grasping the handles; they staggered about as they walked, for their stiff limbs were not certain of foothold, and jerked them where the ground was uneven.

Mark sat down to light the fire in the courtyard, for they wanted some more tea; Bevis sat by him. They were dog-tired. Looking in the larder to lay out the supper, Mark saw the mushrooms, which had been forgotten; he hunted out the gridiron, and put two handfuls of them on. Now the sight of these savoury mushrooms raised their fainting spirits more than most solid food, and they began to talk again. While these were doing, Bevis cut Pan a slice of the cooked bacon on the shelf; it was rather fat, and pampered Pan, after mumbling it over his chops, carried it just outside the fence, and came back trying to look as if he had eaten it.

With the mushrooms they made a capital supper, but they were still very tired. Bevis got out his journal, but he only wrote down 'Friday', and then put it away, remarking that he must soon write a letter home.

Pan curled round by the bedside for about an hour, then he got up and slipped out under the curtain into the moonlight.

In the morning when they went to bathe there was a mist over the water, which curled along and gathered thicker in places, once quite hiding Serendib, and then clearing away and drawing towards the unknown river. The water was very warm.

They then began to nail the raft together. On the long thick beams they placed short cross-pieces of fir close together and touching; over these, long poles of fir lengthways, also touching; lastly, short planks across making the deck. There were thus four layers, for they knew that rafts sink a good deal and float deep, especially when the wood is green, as you may see a bough, or a tree trunk in the brook quite half immersed as it goes by on the current. It was built on rollers, because Bevis, consulting his book, read how Ulysses rigged his vessel:

> 'And roll'd on levers, launch'd her in the deep.'

And, reflecting, he foresaw that the raft being so heavy, would be otherwise difficult to move.

By noon the raft was ready – for they had decided to complete the rigging, bulwarks, and fittings when she was afloat – and with levers they began to heave her down.

She moved slowly, rumbling and crushing the rollers into the sward. By degrees with a 'Yeo! Heave-ho!' at which Pan set up a barking, the raft approached the water, and the forward part entered it. The weight of the rest prevented the front from floating, forcing it straight under the surface till the water rose a third of the way along the deck.

'Yeo! Heave-ho!'

Yow-wow-wow! Pan, who had been idle all the morning lying on the ground, jumped round, and joined the chorus.

'Now! Heave-ho! She's going! Now!'

'Stop!'

'Why?'

'She'll slip away – right out!'

'So she will.'

'Run for a rope.'

'All right.'

Mark ran for a piece of cord from the hut. The raft as it were hung on the edge, more than half in and heaving up as the water began to float her, and they saw that if they gave another push she would go out and the impetus of her weight would carry her away from the shore out of reach. Mark soon returned with the cord, which was fastened to two stout nails.

'Ready?'

'Go!'

One strong heave with the levers and the raft slid off the last roller, rose to the surface, the water slipping off the deck each side, and floated. Seizing the cord as it ran out, they brought her to, and Mark instantly jumped on board. He danced and kicked up his heels – Pan followed him and ran round the edge of the raft, sniffing over at the water. The raft floated first-rate, and the deck, owing to the three layers under it, was high above the water. These layers, too, gave the advantage that they could walk to the very verge without depressing it to the water. Mark got off and held the cord while Bevis got on, then they both shouted, 'Serendib!'

They pushed off with long poles, like punting. Pan swam out as soon as they had started, and was hauled on board. A short way from shore the channel was so deep the poles would not reach the bottom, but the raft had way on her and continued to move, and paddling with the poles they kept up the slow movement till they reached the shallows. Thence to Serendib they poled along, one each side. The end of the raft crashed in among the willow boughs, and the jerk as it grounded almost threw them down. Pan leaped off directly, and they followed, fastening the raft by the cord or painter to the willows.

Crashing through the new bamboos they at last reached the southern extremity of the island, where the shallow sea was covered with the floating leaves of weeds, over which blue dragon-flies flew to and fro.

'Everything's gone to the river again,' said Mark; 'and where's Pan? He's gone too, I dare say.'

A short bark in that direction in a few minutes made them look at an islet round which reed-mace rose in a tall fringe, and there was Pan creeping up out of the weeds, dragging his body after him on to the firm ground. He set up a great yelping on the islet.

'Something's been there,' said Bevis. 'Pan! Pan!' – whistling. Pan would not come: he was too excited. 'We must come here in the evening,' said Bevis, 'and make an ambush. There's heaps of moorhens.'

As there was nothing else to see on Serendib they worked a way between the blue gums back to the raft, and re-embarked for New Formosa. Just before they landed Pan dashed into the water from Serendib and swam to them. He did not seem quite himself, he looked as if he had done something out of the common and could not tell them.

'Was it a crocodile?' said Mark, stroking him. Pan whined, as much as to say, 'I wish I could tell you,' and then to give vent to his excitement he rushed into the wood.

CHAPTER 14

No Hope of Returning

AFTER fastening the raft they returned towards the hut, for they were hungry now, and knew it was late, when Pan set up such a tremendous barking that they first listened, and then went to see. The noise led them to the green knoll where the rabbit burrows were, and they saw Pan running round under the great oak thickly grown with ivy, in which Bevis had seen the wood-pigeons alight.

They went to the oak; it was very large and old, the branches partly dead and hung with ivy; they walked round and examined the ground, but could see no trace of anything. Mark hurled a fragment of a dead bough up into the ivy; it broke and came rustling down again, but nothing flew out. There did not seem to be anything in the tree.

'The squirrels,' said Bevis, suddenly remembering.

'Why, of course,' said Mark. 'How stupid of us! Pan, you're a donk.'

They left the oak and again went homewards: now Pan had been quite quiet while they were looking on the ground and up into the tree, but directly he understood that they had given up the search he set up barking again and would not follow. At the hut Bevis went in to cut some rashers from the bacon which had not been cooked and Mark ran up on the cliff to see the time.

It was already two o'clock – the work on the raft and the voyage to Serendib had taken up the morning. Bevis showed Mark where some mice had gnawn the edge of the uncooked bacon which had been lying in the store-room on the top of a number of things. Mark said once he found a tomtit on the shelf pecking at the food they had left there, just like a tomtit's impudence!

'Rashers are very good,' said Bevis, 'if you haven't got to cook them.' It was his turn, and he was broiling himself as well as the bacon.

Mark looked outside the gate – there was the slice of the cooked bacon Bevis had cut for the spaniel lying on the ground. Pan had not even taken the trouble to put it in his larder. But something else had gnawn at it.

'A rat's been here,' said Mark. 'Don't you remember the jack's head?'

'And mice in the cave,' said Bevis.

'And a tomtit on the shelf.'

'And a robin on the table.'

'And a wagtail was in the court yesterday.'

'A wren comes on the stockade.'

'Spiders up there,' said Mark, pointing to the corner of the hut where there was a web.

'Tarantulas,' said Bevis, 'and mosquitoes in the evening.'

'Everything comes to try and eat us up,' said Mark.

In the afternoon they did nothing but wait for Charlie's signal, which he faithfully gave, and then they idled about till tea. Pan did not come back till tea, and then he wagged his tail and looked very mysterious.

'What have you been doing, sir?' said Bevis. Pan wagged and wagged and gobbled up all the buttered damper they gave him.

'Now, just see,' said Mark. He got up and cut a slice of the cold half-cooked bacon from the shelf. Pan took it, rolled his great brown eyes, showed the whites at the corners, wagged his tail very short like the pendulum of a small clock, and walked outside the gate with it. Then he came back and begged for more buttered damper.

After tea they worked again at the raft, putting in the bulwarks, and carried the chest down to it for the locker. For a sail they meant to use the rug which was now hung up for an awning, and to put up a roof thatched with sedges in its place. The sun sank before they had finished, and they then got the matchlock – it was Mark's day – and went into ambush by the glade to see if they could shoot another rabbit. Pan had to be tied and hit once or twice; he wanted to race after the squirrels.

They sat quiet in ambush till they were weary and the moon was shining brightly, but the rabbits did not venture out. The noise Pan had made barking after the squirrels had evidently alarmed them, and they could not forget it.

Soon afterwards they drew down the curtain and went to sleep. As usual, Pan waited till they were firm asleep, and then slipped out into the moonlight. He was lounging in the court-yard when they got up. By the sundial it was eight, and having had breakfast, and left the fire banked up under ashes – wood embers keep alight a long time like that – they went down to bathe.

'How quiet it is!' said Mark. 'I believe it's quieter.'

'It does seem so,' said Bevis.

The still water glittered under the sun as the light south-east air drew over it, and they could hear a single lark singing on the mainland, somewhere out of sight.

'Somehow we can swim ever so much better here than we used to at home,' said Mark, as they were dressing again.

'Ever so much,' said Bevis; 'twice as far.' This was a fact, whether from the continuous outdoor life, or from greater confidence now they were entirely alone.

'How I should like to punch somebody!' said Mark, hitting out his fist.

'My muscles are like iron,' said Bevis, holding out his arm.

'Well, they are hard,' said Mark, feeling Bevis's arm. So were his own.

'It's living on an island,' said Bevis. 'There's no bother, and nobody says you're not to do anything.'

'Only there's the potatoes to clean. What a nuisance they are!'

They began to dimly perceive that, perhaps, after all, women might be of some use on the earth. They had to go back to the hut to get the dinner ready.

'The rats have been at the potatoes,' said Bevis. 'Just look!'

Mark came, and saw where something had gnawn the potatoes.

'And lots are gone,' he said. 'I'm sure there's a lot gone since yesterday.'

'Pan, why don't you kill the rats?' cried Bevis. Pan looked up, as much as to say, 'Teach me my business, indeed.'

'Bother!' said Mark.

'Bother!' said Bevis.

'Hateful!'

'Yah!' They flung down knives and potatoes.

'Let the cooking stop.'

'Come on.'

Away they ran to the raft, and pushed off, making Pan come with them, that he should not disturb the rabbits again. The spaniel was so lazy, he would not follow them till he was compelled. He sat gravely on the raft by the chest, or locker, while they poled along the shore, for it was too deep to pole in the middle of the channel. But at the southern end of New Formosa the water shoaled, and they could leave the shore. One standing one side, and one the other, they thrust the raft along out among the islets, till they reached Pearl Island, easily distinguished by the glittering mussel shells.

A kingfisher went by, straight for New Formosa. The marks of moorhens' feet were numerous on the shore and just under water, showing how calm it had been lately, for waves would have washed up the bottom and covered them. The islet was very small, merely the ridge of a bank, so they pushed off again. Passing the bamboos, they paused and looked at them – the tall stalks rose up around as if they were really in a thicket of bamboo.

'Hark!'

They spoke together. It was the stern and solemn note of a bell tolling. It startled them in the silence of the New Sea. The sound came from the hills, and they knew at once it was the bell at the church Big Jack went to. The chimes, thin perhaps and weak, had been lost in the hills, but the continuous toll of the five-minutes bell penetrated through miles of air.

'Ship's bell,' said Bevis presently, as they listened. 'In these latitudes the air is so clear you hear ships' bells a hundred miles.'

'Pirates?'

'No; pirates would not make a noise.'

'Frigate?'

'Most likely.'

'Any chance of our being taken off and rescued?'

'Not the least,' said Bevis. 'These islands are not down on any chart. She'll be two hundred miles away by tea-time. Bound for Kerguelen, perhaps.'

'We shall never be found,' said Mark. 'No hope for us.'

'No hope at all,' said Bevis. They poled towards Serendib, intending to circumnavigate that island. By the time they had gone half-way, the bell ceased.

'Now listen,' said Mark. 'Isn't it still?'

They had lifted their poles from the water, and there was not a sound (the lark had long finished), nothing but the drip, drip of the drops from the poles, and the slight rustle as the heavy raft dragged over a weed. They could almost hear the silence, as in the quiet night sometimes, if listening intently, you may hear a faint rushing, the sound of your own blood reverberating in the hollow of the ear; in the day it needs a shell to collect it.

'It is very curious,' said Bevis. 'But we have not heard a sound of anybody till that bell.'

'No more we have.'

'We are a long way from home – really,' said Bevis.

'Awful long way.'

'But really?'

'Of course – really. It feels farther today.'

They could touch the bottom with their poles all the way round Serendib, but as before, in crossing to New Formosa, had to give a stronger push on the edge of the deep channel to carry them over the shallower water. Directly they got near the hut. Pan rushed inside the fence and began barking. When they reached the place he was sniffing round, and every now and then giving a sharp, short bark, as if he knew there was something, but could not make it out.

'Rats,' said Mark, 'And they've taken the bacon bits Pan left outside the gate.'

Pan did not trouble any more when they came in. After preparing the rashers, and looking at the sundial, by which it was noon, Bevis went to look for mushrooms on the knoll, while Mark managed the dinner. Bevis had to go round to get to the knoll, and not wishing to disturb the rabbits more than necessary, made Pan keep close to his heels.

But when he reached the open glade, Pan broke away, and rushed towards the ivy-clad oak, set up a barking. Bevis angrily called him, but Pan would not come, so he picked up a stick, but instead of returning to heel, Pan dashed into the underwood, and Bevis could hear him barking a long way across the island. He thought it was the squirrels, and looked about for mushrooms. There were plenty, and he soon filled his handkerchief. As he approached the hut, Mark came to meet him, and said that happening to look to the shelf he had missed the piece of cooked bacon left there – had Bevis moved it?

CHAPTER 15

Something Has Been to the Hut

'No,' said Bevis. 'I left it there last night; don't you remember I cut a piece for Pan, and he would not eat it?'

'Yes; well, it's gone. Come and see.'

'They went to the shelf – the cooked bacon was certainly gone; nor was it on the ground or in any other part of the hut or cave.

'Pan must have dragged it down,' said Bevis; 'and yet it's too high, and besides, he didn't care for it.'

'He could not jump so high,' said Mark. 'Besides, he has been with us all the time.'

'So he has.' They had kept Pan close by them, ever since he disturbed the kangaroos so much. 'Then, it could not have been Pan.'

'And I don't see how rats could climb up, either,' said Mark. 'The posts' (to which the shelf was fixed) 'are upright – '

'Mice can run up the leg of a chair,' said Bevis.

'That's only a short way; this is – let me see – why, it's higher than your shoulder.'

'If it was not Pan, nor rats, what could it be?' said Bevis.

'Something's been here,' said Mark; 'Pan could smell it when he came in.'

'Something was in the oak,' said Bevis, 'And now he's gone racing right to the other end of the island.'

'Something took the bit of bacon on the ground.'

'And gnawed the jack's head.'

'And had the piece of damper.'

'And took the potatoes.'

298

'Took the potatoes twice – the cooked ones and the raw ones.'

'It's very curious.'

'I don't believe Pan could have jumped up – he would have shaken the other things off the shelf too, if he had got his great paws on.'

'It must have been something,' said Bevis; 'things could not go off by themselves.'

'There's something in the island we don't know,' said Mark, nodding his head up and down, as was his way at times when upset or full of an idea.

'Lions!' said Bevis. 'Lions could get up.'

'We should have heard them roar.'

'Tigers?'

'They would have killed Pan.'

'But you think there's one in the reeds.'

'Yes, but he did not come here.'

'Boas?'

'No.'

'Panthers?'

'No.'

'Something out of the curious wave you saw?'

'Perhaps. Well, it *is* curious now, isn't it?' said Mark. 'Just think; first, Pan could not have had it, and then rats could not have had it, but it's gone.'

'Pan, Pan,' shouted Bevis sternly, as the spaniel came in at the gateway hesitatingly; 'come here.' The spaniel crouched, knowing that he should have a thrashing.

'See if anything's bitten him,' said Mark. 'What have you been after, sir?'

He examined Pan carefully; there were no signs of a fight on him – nothing but cleavers or the seeds of goose-grass clinging to his coat. Bang – thump – thump! yow! Pan had his thrashing, and crept after them to and fro, not even daring to curl himself up in a corner, but dragging himself along on the ground behind them.

'Think,' said Mark, as he turned the mushrooms on the gridiron; 'now, what was it?'

'Not a fox?' said Bevis.

'No; foxes could not swim out here; there are plenty of rabbits for them in the jungle on the mainland.'

'Nor eagles?'

'No.'

'Might be a cat.'

'But there are no cats on the island, and, besides, cats would not take bacon when there were the two moorhens on the shelf.'

'No; Pan would have had the moorhens too, if it had been him.'

'So would anything, and that's why it's so curious.'

'Nobody could have come here, could they?' said Bevis. 'The punt's at the bottom, and the *Pinta*'s chained up – '

'And we must have seen them if they swam off.'

'Nobody can swim,' said Bevis, 'except you and me and the governor.'

'No,' said Mark, 'no more they can – not even Big Jack.'

'Nobody in all the place but us. It could not have been the governor, because if he found the hut he would have stopped to see who lived in it.'

'Of course he would. And besides, he could not have come without our knowing it; we are always about.'

'Always about,' said Bevis, 'and we should have seen footmarks.'

'Or heard a splashing.'

'And Pan would not bark at him,' said Bevis. 'No, it could not have been anyone; it must have been something.'

'Something,' repeated Mark.

They had dinner, and then, as usual, went up to the cliff for Charlie's signal.

'There's Charlie. There are two — three,' said Mark, snatching up the telescope. 'It's Val and Cecil. Charlie's waving his handkerchief.'

'There, it's all right,' said Bevis.

'They are pointing this way,' said Mark. 'They're talking about us. Can they see us?'

'No, the brambles would not let them.'

'I dare say they're as cross as cross,' said Mark.

'They want to come. I don't know,' said Bevis, as if considering.

'Know what?' said Mark sharply.

'That it's altogether nice of us.'

'Rubbish — as if they would have let *us* come.'

'Still, we are not them, and we might if they would not.'

'Now, don't you be stupid,' said Mark appealing. 'Don't *you* go stupid.'

'No,' said Bevis, laughing; 'but they must come after we have done.'

'Oh, yes, of course. See, they're going towards the firs: there, they're going to cross the Nile. I know, don't you see, they're going round the New Sea, like we did to try and find us —'

'Are they?' said Bevis. 'They shan't find us,' resentfully. The moment he thought the rest were going to try and force themselves on his plans, his mind changed. 'We won't go on the raft this afternoon.'

'No,' said Mark; 'nor too near the edge of the island.'

'We'll keep out of sight. Is there anything they could see?'

'The raft.'

'Ah! No; you think, when they get opposite so as to be where they could see the raft, then Serendib is between.'

'So it is. No, there's nothing they can see; only we will not go too near the shore.'

'No.'

'What shall we do this afternoon?' said Mark, as they went

down to the hut. Pan was idly lying in the narrow shade of the fence.

'We mustn't shoot,' said Bevis, 'and we can't go on the raft, because the savages are prowling round, and we mustn't play cards, nor do some chopping; let's go round the island and explore the interior.'

'First-rate,' said Mark; 'just the very thing; you take your bow and arrows – you need not shoot, but just in case of savages – and I'll take my spear in case of the tiger in the reeds, or the something that comes out of the wave.'

'And a hatchet,' said Bevis, 'to blaze our way. That would not be chopping.'

'No, not proper chopping. Make Pan keep close. Perhaps we shall find some footmarks of the Something – spoor, you know.'

'Come on. Down, sir.' Pan accordingly walked behind.

First they went and looked at the raft, which was moored to an alder, taking care not to expose themselves on the shore, but looking at it from behind the boughs. They said they would finish fitting it up tomorrow morning, and then tried to think of a name for it. Bevis said there was no name in the *Odyssey* for Ulysses' raft, but as Calypso gave him the tools to make it, and wove the sail for him with her loom, they agreed to call the raft the *Calypso*. Then they tried to find a shorter way in to the knoll, which they called Kangaroo Hill, but were stopped by the impenetrable blackthorns.

'What was that?'

'Hark!'

'Hark!'

Mark seized his spear; Bevis his bow.

'Listen!'

There was a whir above like wheels in the air, and a creaking sound with it. Suddenly something white appeared above the trees, which had concealed its approach, and a swan passed over descending. It was the noise of its wings and their creaking which sounded like wheels. The great bird descended aslant quite a quarter of a mile into the water to the south of them, and there floated among the glittering ripples.

'I thought it was the roc,' said Mark.

'Or a genie,' said Bevis. 'What a creaking and whirring it made!' Rooks' wings often creak as they go over like stiff leather, but the noise of a swan's flight is audible a mile or more.

It was not a wild swan, but one whose feathers had not been clipped. The wind rose a little, and sighed dreamily through the tops of the tall firs as they walked under them. They returned along the shore where the weeds came to the island, and had gone some way, when Mark suddenly caught hold of Bevis and drew him behind a bush.

CHAPTER 16

The Matchlock

'WHAT is it?' said Bevis.

'I saw a savage.'

'Where?'

'In the sedges on the shore there,' pointing across the weeds. 'I saw his head – he had no hat on.'

'Quite sure?' Bevis looked, but could not see anything.

'Almost very nearly quite sure.'

They watched the sedges a long time, but saw nothing.

'Was it Charlie, or Val, or Cecil?'

'No, I don't think so,' said Mark.

'They could not get round either,' said Bevis. 'If they crossed the Nile like we did, they could not get round.'

'No.'

'It could not have been anybody.'

'I thought it was; but perhaps it was a crow flew up – it looked black.'

'Sure to have been a crow. The sedges do not move.'

'No, it was a mistake – they couldn't get here.'

They went on again and found a wild bullace.

'This is the most wonderful island there ever was,' said Bevis; 'there's always something new on or about it. The swan – I shall shoot the swan. No, most likely it's sacred, and the king of the country would have us hunted down if we killed it.'

'And tied to a stake and tortured.'

'Melted lead poured into our mouths, because we shot the sacred swan with leaden bullets.'

'Awful. No, don't shoot it. There are currant-trees on the

island too – I've seen them, and there's a gooseberry bush up in the top of an old willow that I saw,' said Mark. 'Of course there are bananas; are there any breadfruit-trees here?'

'Certain to be some somewhere.'

'Melons and oranges.'

'Of course, and grapes – those are grapes,' pointing to bryony-berries, 'and pomegranates and olives.'

'Yams and everything.'

'Everything. I wonder if Pan will bark this time – I wonder if anything is gone,' said Bevis as they reached the stockade. Pan did not bark, and there was nothing missing.

They set to work now to make some tea and roast the moor-hens, having determined to have tea and supper together. The tea was ready long before the moorhens, and by the time they had finished the moon was shining brightly, though there were some flecks of cloud. They could not of course play cards, so Bevis got out his journal; and having put down about the honey-bird, and the swan, and the discoveries they had made, went on to make a list of the trees and plants on the island, and the birds that came to it. They had seen a small flock of seven or eight missel-thrushes pass in the afternoon, and Mark said that all the birds came from the unknown river, and flew on towards the north-north-west. This was the direction of the waste, or wild pasture.

'Then there must be mainland that way,' said Bevis; 'and I expect it is inhabited and ploughed, and sown with corn, for that's what the birds like at this time of the year.'

'And the other way – where they come from – must be a pathless jungle,' said Mark. 'And they rest here for a moment as they cross the ocean. It is too far for one fly.'

'I shall get up early tomorrow morning,' Bevis said, 'I'll load the matchlock tonight, I want to shoot a heron.'

He loaded the matchlock with ball, and soon afterwards they let the curtain down at the door, and went to bed, Bevis repeating 'Three o'clock, three o'clock, three o'clock,' at first aloud and then to himself, so as to set the clock of his mind to wake him at that hour. Not long after they were asleep, Pan as usual went out for his ramble.

Bevis's clock duly woke him about three, and lifting his head he could see the light through the chinks of the curtain, but he was half inclined to go to sleep again, and stayed another quarter of an hour. Then he resolutely bent himself to conquer sleep, slipped off the bed, and put on his boots quietly, not to wake Mark. Taking the matchlock, he went out and found that it was light, the light of the moon mingling with the dawn, but it was misty. A dry vapour, which left no dew, filled the wood so that at a short distance the path seemed to go into and lose itself in the mist.

Bevis went all round the island, following the path they had made. On the Serendib side he neither saw nor heard anything, but as he came back up the other shore, a lark began to sing far away on the mainland, and afterwards he heard the querulous cry of a pewit. He walked very cautiously, for this was the most likely side to find a heron, but whether they heard his approach or saw him – for they can see almost as far as a man when standing, by lifting their long necks – he did not find any. When he reached the spot where the 'blaze' began that led to Kangaroo Hill, he fancied he saw something move in the water a long way off through the mist.

He stopped behind a bush and watched, and in a minute he was sure it was something, perhaps a duck. He set up the rest, blew the match, opened the lid of the pan, knelt down and looked along the barrel till he had got it in a line with the object. If the gun had been loaded with shot he would have fired at once, for though indistinct through the vapour he thought it was within range, but as he had ball, he wanted to see if it would come nearer, as he knew he could not depend on a bullet over thirty yards. Intent on the object, which seemed to be swimming, he began to be curious to know what it was, for it had now come a little closer, and he could see it was not a duck, for it had no neck; it was too big for a rat: it must be the creature that visited the island and took their food – the idea of shooting this animal and surprising Mark with it delighted him.

He aimed along the barrel, and got the sight exactly on the creature, then he thought he would let it get a few yards closer, then he depressed the muzzle just a trifle, remembering that it was coming towards him, and if he did not aim somewhat in front the ball would go over.

Now it was near enough he was sure – he aimed steadily, and his finger began to draw the match down when he caught sight of the creature's eye. It was Pan.

'Pan!' said Bevis. He got up, and the spaniel swam steadily towards him.

'Where have you been, sir?' he said sternly. Pan crouched at his feet, not even shaking himself first. 'You rascal – where have you been?'

Bevis was inclined to thrash him, he was so angry at the mistake he had almost made, angry with the dog because he had almost shot him. But Pan crouched so close to the ground under his very feet that he did not strike him.

'It was you who frightened the herons,' he said. Pan instantly recognized the change in the tone of his voice, and sprang up, jumped round, barked, and then shook the water from his shaggy coat. It was no use evidently now to think of shooting a heron; the spaniel had alarmed them, and Bevis returned to the hut. He woke Mark, and told him.

'That's why he's so lazy in the morning,' said Mark. 'Don't you recollect? He sleeps all the morning.'

'And won't eat anything.'

'I believe he's been home,' said Mark. 'Very like Polly throws the bones out still by his house.'

'That's it: you old glutton!' said Bevis.

Pan jumped on the bed, licked Mark, then jumped on Bevis's knees, leaving the marks of his wet paws, to which the sand

had adhered; then he barked and wagged his tail as much as to
say, 'Am I not clever?'

'Oh! yes,' said Mark, 'you're very knowing, but you won't do
that again.'

'No, that you won't, sir,' said Bevis. 'You'll be tied up tonight.'

'Tight as tight,' said Mark.

'Just think,' said Bevis. 'He must have swum all down the
channel we came up on the catamaran. Why, it's a hundred and
fifty yards –'

'Or two hundred – only some of it is shallow. Perhaps he
could bottom some part –'

'But not very far – and then run all the way home, and then
all the way back, and then swim off again.'

'A regular voyage – and every night too.'

'You false old greedy Pan!'

'To leave us when we thought you were watching while we
slept.'

'To desert your post, you faithless sentinel.'

Pan looked from one to the other, as if he understood every
word; he rolled up the whites of his eyes and looked so pious,
they burst into fits of laughter.

They thought it of no use to go to sleep again now, so they
lit the fire, and prepared the breakfast. By the time it was ready
the mist had begun to clear; the sky became blue overhead,
and while they were sitting at table under the awning, the first
beams shot along over Serendib to their knees. Bevis said after
breakfast he should practise with the matchlock, till he could
hit something with the bullets. Mark wanted to explore the
unknown river, and this they agreed to do; but the difficulty, as
usual, was the dinner. There was nothing in their larder but
bacon for rashers, and that was almost gone. Rashers become
wearisome, ten times more wearisome when you have to cook
them too.

Bevis said he must write his letter home – he was afraid he

might have delayed too long – and take it to Loo to post that night; then he would write out a list of things, and Loo could buy them in the town, potted meats, and tongues, and soups, that would save cooking, only it was not quite proper. But Mark got over that difficulty by supposing that they fetched them from the wreck before it went to pieces.

Bevis wrote the letter, dating it from Jack's house up in the hills. It was very short. He said they were very well, and jolly, and should not come back for a little while yet – but would not be very long – this was in case anyone should go up to see them. But when he came to read it through for mistakes, the deceit he was practising on dear mamma stood out before him like the black ink on the page.

'I don't like it,' he said. 'It's not nice.'

'No; it's not nice,' said Mark, who was sitting by him. 'But still – '

'But still,' repeated Bevis, and so the letter was put in an envelope and addressed.

In the evening, as the sun sank, Mark tried for bait and succeeded in catching some; these were for the trimmers. Then they laid out the night-line for eels far down the island where the edge looked more muddy. To fill up the time till it was quite moonlight, they worked at a mast for the raft, and also cut some sedges and flags for the roof of the open shed, which was to be put up in place of the awning.

They supposed it to be about half past nine when they pushed off on the raft, taking with them the letter, a list of things to be got from the town to save the labour of cooking, and the flag-basket. The trimmers were dropped in as they went. Mark was going to wait by the raft till Bevis returned under the original plan, but they agreed that it would be much more pleasant to go together, the raft would be perfectly safe. They found the channel without difficulty, the raft grounded among the sedges, and they stepped out, the first time they had landed on the mainland.

As they walked they saw a fern-owl floating along the hedge by the stubble. The beetles hummed by and came so heedlessly over the hedge as to become entangled in the leaves. They walked close to the hedge because they knew that the very brightest moonlight is not like the day. By moonlight an object standing apart can be seen a long distance, but anything with a background of a hedge cannot be distinguished for certain across one wide field. That something is moving there may be ascertained, but its exact character cannot be determined.

As they had to travel beside the hedges and so to make frequent detours, it occupied some time to reach the cottage, which they approached over the field at the back. When they were near enough, Bevis whistled – the same notes with which he and Mark called and signalled to each other. In an instant they saw Loo come through the window, so quickly that she must have been sleeping with her dress on; she slipped down a lean-to or little shed under it, scrambled through a gap in the thin hedge, and ran to them.

She had sat and watched and listened for that whistle night after night in vain. At last she drew her cot (in which her little brother also slept) across under the window, and left the window open. Her mind so long expecting a whistle responded in a moment to the sound when it reached her dreaming ear. She took the letter (with a penny for the stamp) and the list and basket, and promised to have the things ready for them on the following evening.

'And remember,' said Bevis, 'remember you don't say anything. There will be a shilling for you if you don't tell – '

'I shouldn't tell if there wurdn't no shilling,' said Loo.

'You mind you do not say a word,' added Mark. 'Nobody is to know that you have seen us.'

'Good night,' said Bevis, and away they went. Loo watched them till they were lost against the dark background of the hedge, and then returned to her cot, scrambling up the roof of the shed and in at the window.

They got back to the island without any difficulty, and felt quite certain that no one had seen them. Stirring up the embers of the fire, they made some tea, but only had half a cold damper to eat with it. This day they had fared worse than any day since they arrived on New Formosa. They were too tired to make a fresh damper (besides the time it would take) having got up so early that morning, and Bevis only entered two words in his journal – 'Monday – Loo'.

Then they fastened Pan to the door-post, allowing him enough cord to move a few yards, but taking care to make his collar too tight for him to slip his head.

CHAPTER 17

The Mainland

In the morning, after the bath, Mark examined the night-line, but it was untouched; nor was there a kangaroo in the wires they had set up in their runs. Poling the raft out to the trimmers they found a jack of about two pounds on one, and the bait on another had been carried off, the third had not been visited. Bevis wanted to explore the Waste, and especially to look at the great grey boulder, and so they went on and landed among the sedges.

Making Pan keep close at their heels, they cautiously crept through the bramble thickets – Pan tried two or three times to break away, for the scent of game was strong in these thickets – and entered the wild pasture, across which they could not see. The ground undulated, and besides the large ant-hills, the scattered hawthorn bushes and the thickets round the boulders intercepted the view. If any savages appeared they intended to stoop and so would be invisible; they could even creep on hands and knees half across the common without being seen. Pan was restless – not weary this morning – the scent he crossed was almost too much for his obedience.

They reached the boulder unseen – indeed there was no one to see them – pushed through the bushes, and stood by it. The ponderous stone was smooth, as if it had been ground with emery, and there was little circular basins or cups drilled in it. With a stick Bevis felt all round and came to a place where the stick could be pushed in two or three feet under the stone, between it and the grass.

'It's hollow here,' he said; 'you try.'

'So it is,' said Mark. 'This is where the treasure is.'

314

'And the serpent, and the magic lamp that has been burning ages and ages.'

'If we could lift the stone up.'

'There's a spell on it; you couldn't lift it up, not with levers or anything.'

Pan sniffed at the narrow crevice between the edge of the boulder and the ground – concealed by the grass till Bevis found it – but showed no interest. There was no rabbit there. Such great boulders often have crevices beneath, but whether this was a natural hollow, or whether the boulder was the capstone of a dolmen was not known.

Whir-r-r!

A covey of partridges flew over only just above the stone, and within a few inches of their heads, which were concealed by it. They counted fourteen – the covey went straight out across the New Sea, eastwards towards the Nile. From the boulder they wandered on among the ant-hills and tall thistles, disturbing a hare, which went off at a tremendous pace, bringing his hind legs right under his body up to his shoulders in his eagerness to take kangaroo bounds.

Presently they came to the thick hedge which divided the Waste from the cornfields. Gathering a few blackberries along this, they came to a gate, which alarmed them, thinking someone might see, but a careful reconnaissance showed that the reapers had finished and left that field. The top bar of the gate was pecked, little chips out of the wood, where the crows had been.

'It's very nice here,' said Mark. 'You can go on without coming to the Other Side so soon.'

After their life on the island, where they could never walk far without coming in sight of the water, they appreciated the liberty of the mainland. Pan had to have several kicks and bangs with the stick; he was so tempted to rush into the hedge, but they did not want him to bark, in case anyone should hear.

'Lots of kangaroos here,' said Bevis, 'and big kangaroos too –

hares you know; I say, I shall come here with the matchlock some night.'

'So we will.'

There was a gap in the corner, and as they came idling along they got up into the double mound, when Bevis, who was first, suddenly dropped on his knees and seized Pan's shaggy neck. Mark crouched instantly behind him.

'What is it?' he whispered.

'Someone's been here.'

'How do you know?'

'Sniff.'

Mark sniffed. There was the strong pungent smell of crushed nettles. He understood in a moment — someone had recently gone through and trampled on them. They remained in this position for five minutes, hardly breathing, and afraid to move.

'I can't hear anyone,' whispered Mark.

'No.'

'Must have gone on.'

Bevis crept forward, still holding Pan with one hand; Mark followed, and they crossed the mound, when the signs of someone having recently been there became visible in the trampled nettles, and in one spot there was the imprint of a heel-plate.

'Savages,' said Bevis. 'Ah! Look.'

Mark looked through the branches, and a long way out in the stubble, moving among the shocks of wheat, he saw Bevis's governor. They watched him silently. The governor walked straight away; they scarcely breathed till he had disappeared in the next field.

'Very nearly done,' said Mark.

'We won't land again in daylight,' said Bevis.

'No — it's not safe; he must have been close.'

'He must have got up into the mound and looked through,' said Bevis. 'Perhaps while we were by the gate.'

'Most likely. He came across the stubble; why, he was that side while we were this.'

'Awfully nearly done; why, it must have been the governor who startled the partridges!'

'Stupes we were, not to know someone was about.'

'Awful stupes.'

They walked back to the raft, keeping close to the hedge, and crept on all fours among the ant-hills so as to pass the gateway without the possibility of being seen, though they knew the governor was now too far to observe them.

Later on, as they were going through the stubble to meet Loo, they saw something move, and keeping quite still by the hedge, it came towards them, when they knew it was a fox. He came down the furrow between the lands, and several times went nosing round the shocks of wheat, for he looks on a plump mouse as others do on a kidney for breakfast. He did not seem to scent them, for when they stepped out he was startled and raced away full speed. At the whistle Loo brought the flag-basket, heavy with the tinned tongues and potted meats they had ordered. She was frequently sent in to the town on errands from the house, so that there was no difficulty at the shop. Bevis inquired how all were at home; all were well, and then wished her good night after exacting another promise of secrecy. Loo watched them out of sight.

That evening they had a splendid supper on New Formosa, and sat up playing cards.

They fastened Pan up as before at the door-post before going to bed, and gave him several slices of rolled tongue. They slept the instant they put their heads on the hard doubled-up great-coats which formed their pillows.

CHAPTER 18

Something Comes Again

ABOUT the middle of the night Pan moved, sat up, gave a low growl, then rushed outside to the full length of his cord, and set up a barking.

'Pan! Pan!' said Bevis, awakened.

'What is it?' said Mark.

Hearing their voices and feeling himself supported, Pan increased his uproar. Bevis ran outside with Mark and looked round the stockade. The moon was low behind the trees. The stars shone white and without scintillating. They could distinctly see every corner of the courtyard; there was nothing in it.

'It's the something,' said Mark. Together they ran across to the gateway in the stockade, though they had no boots on. They looked outside; there was nothing. Everything was perfectly still, as if the very trees slept.

'We left the gate open,' said Bevis.

'I don't believe it's ever been locked but once,' said Mark.

They locked it now, and returned to the hut. Pan wagged his tail, but continued to give short barks as much as to say, that *he* was not satisfied, though they had seen nothing.

'What can it be?' said Mark. 'If Pan used to swim off every night, he could not have had all the things.'

'No. We'll look in the morning and see if there are any marks on the ground.'

They sat up a little while talking about it, and then reclined; in three minutes they were firm asleep again. Pan curled up, but outside the hut now; once or twice he growled inwardly.

In the morning they remembered the incident the moment

they woke, and before letting Pan loose, carefully examined every foot of the ground inside the stockade. There was not the slightest spoor. Nor was there outside the gate; but it was possible that an animal might pass there without leaving much sign in the thin grass. When Pan was let free he ran eagerly to the gate, but then stopped, looked about him, and came back seeming to take no further interest. The scent was gone.

Watching for Charlie in the afternoon, they reclined on the cliff under the oak, resting, and talking but little. The light of the sun was often intercepted by thin white clouds slowly drifting over, which, like branches, held back so much of the rays that the sun could occasionally be looked at. There was enough ripple to prevent them from seeing any basking fish, but the shifting, uncertain air was not enough to be called a breeze.

Lying at full length inside the shadow of the oak, Bevis gazed up at the clouds, which were at an immense height, and drifted so slowly as to scarcely seem to move, only he saw that they did because he had a fixed point in the edge of the oak boughs. So thin and delicate was the texture of the white sky-lace above him that the threads scarcely hid the blue which the eye knew was behind and above it. It was warm without the pressure of heat, soft, luxurious; the summer, like them, reclined, resting in the fullness of the time.

The summer rested before it went on to autumn. Already the tips of the reeds were brown, the leaves of the birch were specked, and some of the willows dropped yellow ovals on the water; the acorns were bulging in their cups, the haws showed among the hawthorn as their green turned red; there was a gloss on the blue sloes among the 'wait-a-bit' blackthorns, red threads appeared in the moss of the canker-roses on the briers. A sense of rest, the rest not of weariness, but of full growth, was in the atmosphere; tree, plant, and grassy things had reached their fullness and strength.

They remained idle under the oak for some time after Charlie had made the usual signal; but when the shadow of the wood came out over the brambles towards the fence Mark reloaded the matchlock, and they went into ambush by Kangaroo Hill among the hazel bushes, this time on the opposite side. The hazel bushes seemed quite vacant; only one bird passed while they were there, and that was a robin, come to see what they were doing, and if there was anything for him.

Mark had a shot at last at a kangaroo, but though Pan raced his hardest it escaped into the bury. It was of no use to wait any longer, so they walked very slowly round the island, waiting behind every bush, and looking out over the water. There was nothing till, as they returned the other side, they saw the parrots approach and descend into the ivy-grown oak. Bevis held Pan while Mark crept forward from tree-trunk to tree-trunk till he was near enough, when he put the heavy barrel against a tree, in the same way Bevis had done. His aim was true, and the parrot fell.

It had been agreed that Bevis should have the gun at night, for he wished to go on the mainland and see if he could shoot anything in the Waste, but, still unsatisfied, Mark wanted yet another shot. The thirst of the chase was on him; he could not desist. Since there was nothing else he fired at and killed a thrush they found perched on the top of the stockade. Mark put down the gun with a sigh that his shooting was over.

Bevis waited till it was full moonlight, putting down a few things in his journal, while Mark skinned three of his finest perch, which he meant to have for supper. To be obliged to cook was one thing, to cook just for the pleasure of the taste was a different thing. He skinned them because he knew the extreme difficulty of scraping the thick-set hard scales. Presently Bevis loaded the gun; he was going to do so with ball, when Mark pointed out that he could not be certain of a perfectly accurate aim by moonlight. This was true, so he reluctantly put shot. Mark's one desire was to fetch down his game; Bevis wished to kill with the precision of a single bullet.

They poled the raft ashore, and both landed, but Mark stayed among the bramble thickets holding Pan, while Bevis went out into the Waste. He did not mean to stay in ambush long anywhere, but to try to get a shot from behind the bushes. Crouching in the brambles, Mark soon lost sight of him, so soon that he seemed to have vanished; the ant-hills, the tall thistles, and the hawthorns concealed him.

Bevis stepped noiselessly round the green ant-hills, some-times startling a lark, till, when he looked back, he scarcely knew which way he had come. In a meadow or a cornfield the smooth surface lets the glance travel at once to the opposite hedge, and the shape of the enclosure or one at least of its boundaries is seen, so that the position is understood. But here the ant-hills and the rush-bunches, the thickets of thistles and brambles, gave the ground an uneven surface, and the haw-thorn trees hid the outline.

There was no outline; it was a dim uncertain expanse with shadows, and a grey mist rising here and there, and slight rust-lings as pads pressed the sward, or wings rose from roost. Once he fancied he saw a light upon the ground not so far off; he moved that way, but the thistles or bushes hid it. A silent owl startled him as it slipped past; he stamped his foot with anger that he should have been startled. Twice he caught a glimpse of white tails, but he could not shoot running with the matchlock.

Incessantly winding round and round the ant-hills, he did not know which way he was going, except that he tried to keep the moon a little on his left hand, thinking he could shoot better with the light like that. After some time he reached a boulder – another, not so large as that they had examined together; this was about as high as his chest.

He leaned against it and looked over; there was a green waggon track the other side, which wound out from the bushes, and again disappeared among them. Though he knew that Mark could not be far, and that a whistle would bring him, he felt utterly alone. It was wilder than the island – the desolate thistles, the waste of rushes, the thorns, the untouched land which the ants possessed and not man, the cold grey boulder, the dots of mist here and there, and the pale light of the moon.

Suddenly something came round the corner of the smooth green waggon track, and he knew in an instant by the peculiar amble that it was a hare. The long barrel of the matchlock was cautiously placed on the stone, and he aimed as well as he could, for when looked at along a barrel objects have a singular way of disappearing at night. Then he paused, for the hare still came on. Hares seem to see little in front; their eyes sweep each side, but straight ahead they are blind till the air brings them the scent they dread.

All at once the hare sat up – he had sniffed Bevis, and the same minute the flash rushed from the muzzle. Bevis ran directly and found the hare struggling; almost as soon as he had lifted him up Pan was there. Then Mark came leaping from ant-hill to ant-hill, and crushing through the thistles in his haste. As Mark had come direct from the shore he knew the general direction, and they hurried back to the raft, fearing some of the savages might come to see who was shooting on the mainland. Once on the island, as the perch were cooking, the game was spread out on the table – three moorhens, a coot, a dabchick, a wood-pigeon, a hare, and the jack Mark had caught.

Of all the hare, or rather leveret, for it was a young one, was the finest. His black-tipped ears, his clean pads, his fur – every separate hair with three shades of colour – it was a pleasure to smooth his fur down with the hand.

'This is the jolliest day we've had,' said Mark. 'Real hunting – real island – and no work and no cooking, except just what we like. It's splendid.'

'If only Val and Cecil could see,' said Bevis, handling the ears of his hare for the twentieth time. 'Won't they go on when we tell them?'

As they were fastening up Pan at the doorway before lying down they recollected the visit of the unknown creature on the previous night, and went out and padlocked the gate. The matchlock was loaded with shot, which did not require so accurate an aim, and was therefore best for shooting in a hurry, and instead of being hung up it was leaned against the wall as more accessible, and the priming seen to. A long candle was put in the lantern on the niche and left burning, so that if awakened they could see to get the gun at once. The creature went off so quickly that not a moment must be lost in shooting if it came again, and they said to each other (to set the clock of their minds) that they would not stop to listen, but jump up the second they awoke if Pan barked. This time they thought they should be sure to see the animal at least, if not shoot it.

CHAPTER 19

The Tiger from the Reeds

PAN did bark. It seemed to them that they had scarcely closed their eyes; in reality they had slept hours, and the candle had burned short. The clock of their minds being set, they were off the bed in an instant. Bevis, before his eyes were hardly open, was lighting the match of the gun; Mark had darted to the curtain at the door.

There was a thick mist and he could see nothing; in a second he snatched out his pocket-knife (for they slept in their clothes), and cut the cord with which Pan was fastened up just as Bevis came with the gun. Pan raced for the aperture in the fence at the corner by the cliff – he perfectly howled with frantic rage as he ran and crushed himself through. They were now under the open shed outside the hut, and heard Pan scamper without; suddenly his howl of rage stopped, there was a second of silence, then the dog yelled with pain. The next moment he crept back through the fence, and before he was through something hurled itself against the stockade behind him with such force that the fence shook.

'Shoot – shoot there,' shouted Mark, as the dog crept whining towards them. Bevis lifted the gun, but paused.

'If the thing jumps over the fence,' he said. He had but one shot; he could not load quickly. Mark understood.

'No – no, don't shoot. Here – here's the bow.'

Bevis took it and sent an arrow at the fence in the corner with such force that it penetrated the willow-work up to the feather. Then they both ran to the gate and looked over. All this scarcely occupied a minute.

But there was nothing to see. The thick white mist concealed everything but the edge of the brambles near the stockade and the tops of the trees farther away.

'Nothing,' said Mark. 'What was it?'

'Shall we go out?' said Bevis.

'No – not till we have seen it.'

'It would be better not – we can't tell.'

'You can shoot as it jumps the fence,' said Mark. 'if it comes; it will stop a minute on the top.'

Unless they can clear a fence, animals pause a moment on the top before they leap down. They went back to the open shed with a feeling that it would be best to be some way inside the fence, and so have a view of the creature before it sprang. Mark picked up an axe, for he had no weapon but a second arrow which he had in his hand; the axe was the most effective weapon there was after the gun. They stood under the shed, watching the top of the stockade and waiting.

Till now they had looked upon the unknown as a stealthy

thief only, but when Pan recoiled they knew it must be something more.

'It might jump down from the cliff,' said Bevis.

While they watched the semi-circular fence in front the
creature might steal round to the cliff and leap down on the
roof of the hut. Mark stepped out and looked along the verge of
the sand cliff. He could see up through the runners of the
brambles which hung over the edge, and there was nothing
there. Looking up like this he could see the pale stars above the
mist. It was not a deep mist – it was like a layer on the ground,
impenetrable to the eye longitudinally, but partially transparent vertically. Returning inside, Mark stooped and examined
Pan, who had crept at their heels. There were no scratches on
him.

'He's not hurt,' said Mark. 'No teeth or claws.'

'But he had a pat, didn't he?'

'I thought so – how he yelled! But you look, there's
no blood. Perhaps the thing hit without putting its claws
out.'

'They slip out when they strike,' said Bevis, meaning that as
wild beasts strike their claws involuntarily extend from the
sheaths. He looked. Pan was not hurt; Mark felt his ribs too,
and said that none was broken. There were no fragments of fur
or hair about his mouth, no remnants of a struggle.

'I don't believe he fought at all,' said Bevis. 'He stopped – he
never went near.'

'Very likely. Now I remember – he stopped barking all at
once; he was afraid!'

'That was it; but he yelled –'

'It must have been fright,' said Mark. 'Nothing touched him.
Pan, what was it?'

Pan wagged his tail once, once only; he still crouched and
kept close to them. Though patted and reassured, his spirit had
been too much broken to recover rapidly. The spaniel was
thoroughly cowed.

'It came very near,' said Bevis. 'It hit the fence while he was getting through.'

'It must have missed him – perhaps it was a long jump. Did you hear anything rush off?'

'No.'

'No more did I.'

'Soft pads,' said Bevis, 'they make no noise like hoofs.'

'No, that was it, and it's sandy too.'

'Let's go and look again.'

'So we will.'

They went to the gate – Pan, they noticed, did not follow – and looked over again, this time longer and more searchingly. They could see the ground for a few yards, and then the mist obscured it like fleece among brambles.

'Pan's afraid to come,' said Mark, as they went back to the shed.

'The fire ought to be lit,' said Bevis. 'They are afraid of fire.'

'You watch,' said Mark. 'and I'll light it.'

He drew on his boots, and put on his coat – for they ran out in waistcoat and trousers – then he held the gun while Bevis did the same; then Bevis took it, and Mark hastily gathered some sticks together and lit them, often glancing over his shoulder at the fence behind, and with the axe always ready to his hand. When the flames began to rise they felt more at ease; they knew that wild beasts dislike fire, and somehow fire warms the spirit as well as the body. The morning was warm enough: they did not need a fire; but the sight of the twisted tongues as they curled spirally and broke away was restorative as the heat is to actual bodily chill. Bevis went near. Even the spaniel felt it; he shook himself and seemed more cheerful.

'The thing was very near when we first went out,' said Bevis. 'I wish we had run to the gate directly without waiting for the gun.'

'But we did not know what it was.'

'No.'

'And I cut Pan loose directly.'

'It had only to run ten yards to be out of sight in the mist.'

'And it seems so dark when you first run out.'

'It's lighter now.'

'There's no dew.'

'Dry mist – it's clearing a little.'

As they stood by the fire the verge of the cliff above the roof of the hut came out clear of vapour, then they saw the trees outside the stockade rise as it were higher as the vapour shrunk through them; the stars were very faint.

'Lu – lu!' said Mark, pointing to the crevice between the fence and the cliff, and urging Pan to go out again. The spaniel went a few yards towards it, then turned and came back. He could not be induced to venture alone.

'Lions *do* get loose sometimes,' said Bevis thoughtfully. He had been running over every wild beast in his mind that could by any possibility approach them. Cases do occur every now and then of vans being overturned, and lions and tigers escaping.

'So they do, but we have not heard any roar.'

'No, and we must have come on it if it stops on the island,' said Bevis. 'We have been all round so many times. Or does it go to and fro – do lions swim?'

'He would have no need to,' said Mark – 'I mean not after he had swum over here. He wouldn't go away for us – he could lie in the bushes.'

'Perhaps we have gone close by it without knowing,' said Bevis. 'There's the "wait-a-bit" thorns.'

They had never been through the thicket of blackthorn.

'Pan never barked though. He's been all round the island with us.'

'Perhaps he was afraid – like he was just now.'

'Ah, yes, very likely.'

'And we hit him, too, to keep him quiet, not to startle the kangaroos.'

'Or the water-fowl. So we did; we may have gone close by it without knowing.'

'In the "wait-a-bits" or the hazel.'

'Or the sedges, where it's drier.'

'Foxes lie in withy beds – why should not this?'

'Of course; but I say – only think, we may have gone within reach of its paw ten times.'

'While we were lying down too,' said Bevis, 'in ambush. It might have been in the ferns close behind.'

'All the times we walked about and never took the gun,' said Mark, 'or the bow and arrow, or the axe, or anything – and just think! Why, we came back from the raft without even a stick in our hands.'

'Yes – it was silly; and we came quietly, too, to try and see it.'

'Well, we just were stupid!' said Mark. 'Only we never thought it could be anything big.'

'But It must be.'

'Of course It is: we won't go out again without the gun, and the axe – '

'And my bow to shoot again, because you can't load a matchlock quick.'

'That's the worst of it; tigers get loose too sometimes, don't they? And panthers more often, because there are more of them.'

'Yes, one is as dangerous as the other. Panthers are worse than lions.'

'More creepy.'

'Cattish. They slink on you; they don't roar first.'

'Then perhaps it's a panther.'

'Perhaps. This is a very likely place, if anything has got loose; there's the jungle on the mainland, and all the other woods, and the Chase up by Jack's.'

'Yes, plenty of cover – almost like forest.'

Besides the great wood in which they had wandered there were several others in the neighbourhood, and a Chase on the hills by Jack's, so that in case of a beast escaping from a caravan it would find extensive cover to hide in.

'Only think,' said Bevis, 'when we bathed!'

'Ah!' Mark shuddered. While they bathed naked and unarmed, had It darted from the reeds they would have fallen instant victims without the possibility of a struggle even.

'It *is* horrible,' said Bevis.

'There are reeds and sedges everywhere,' said Mark. 'It may be anywhere.'

'It's not safe to move.'

'Especially as Pan's afraid and won't warn us. *If* the thing had seen us bathing; It could not, or else – ah!'

'They tear so,' said Bevis. 'It's not the wound so much as the tearing.'

'Like bramble hooks,' said Mark. The curved hooks of brambles and briers inflict lacerated hurts worse than the spikes of thorns. Flesh that is torn cannot heal like that which is incised. 'Oh! stop! panthers get in trees, don't they? It may have been up in that oak that day!'

'In the ivy: we looked!'

'But the ivy is thick, and we might not have seen! It might have jumped down on us.'

'So it might any minute in the wood.'

'Then we can't go in the wood.'

'Nor among the sedges round the shore.'

'Nor the brambles, nor fern, nor hazel.'

'Nowhere – except on the raft.'

'Then we must take care how we come back.'

'How shall we sleep!'

'Ah – think, it might have come any night!'

'We left the gate open.'

'Oh! how stupid we have been.'

'It could kill Pan with one stroke.'

'And Pan was not here; he used to swim off.'

'Directly he was tied up, you recollect, the very first night he barked – no, the second.'

'It may have come *every* night before.'

'Right inside the stockade – under the awning.'

'Into the hut while we were away – the bacon was on the shelf.'

'If It could jump up like that, it could jump the fence.'

'Of course; and it shows it was a cat-like creature, because it could take one thing without disturbing another. Dogs knock things down, cats don't.'

'No, panthers are a sort of big cat.'

'That's what gnawed the jack's head.'

'And why there was no mark on the ground – their pads are so soft, and don't cut holes like hoofs.'

'The kangaroos too, you remember: very often they wouldn't come out. Something was about.'

'Of course. How could we have been so stupid as not to see this before!'

'Why, we never suspected.'

'But we ought to have suspected. You thought you saw something move in the sedges on Sunday.'

'So I did – it was this thing; it must have been.'

'Then it swims off and comes back.'

'Then if we hunt all over the island and don't find It – we're no safer, because It may come off to us any time.'

'Any time.'

'What *shall* we do?'

'Can't go home,' said Bevis.

'Can't go home,' repeated Mark.

They could not desert their island: it would have been so like running away too, and they had so often talked of Africa and shooting big game. Then to run away when in its presence would have lowered them in their own estimation.

'Can't,' said Bevis again.

'Can't,' again repeated Mark. They *could* not go – they must face It, whatever it was.

'We shall have to look before every step,' said Bevis. 'Up in the trees – through the bushes – and the reeds.'

'We must not go in the reeds much; you can't tell there – '

'No, not much. We must watch at night. First one, and then the other.'

'And keep the fire burning. There ought to be a fence along the top of the cliff.'

'Yes – that's very awkward: you can't put stakes in hard sand like that.'

'We must drive in some – and cut them sharp at the top.'

'What a pity the stockade is not sharp at the top! Nails, that's it: we must drive in long nails and file the tops off!'

'And put some stakes with nails along the cliff – the thing could not get in quite so quick.'

'The gate is not very strong: we must barricade it.'

'Wish we could lock the door!'

'I should think so!'

Now they realized what is forgotten in the routine of civilized life – the security of doors and bolts. Their curtain was no defence.

'Barricade the door.'

'Yes, but not too close, else we can't shoot – we should be trapped.'

'I see! Put the barricade round a little way in front. Why not have two fires, one each side?'

'Capital. We will fortify the place! Loop-holes. The weak spot will be the edge of the cliff up there. If we put a fire there people may see it – savages – and find us.'

'That won't do.'

'No: we must fortify the edge somehow, stakes with nails for one thing. Perhaps a train of gunpowder!'

'Ah, yes. Lucky we've got plenty to eat. It won't be nice not
to have the gun loaded. I mean while loading the thing might
come.'

'We've got plenty to eat.'

'And I wanted a lot of shooting today,' said Mark.

'All that's spoiled.'

'Quite spoiled.'

Yesterday they had become intoxicated with the savage joy
of killing; they had planned slaughter for today. Today they
were themselves environed with deadly peril. This is the opposite side of wild life: the forest takes its revenge by filling the
mind with ceaseless anxiety.

'The sun!' said Bevis with pleasure, as the rays fell aslant
into the open shed. The sun had been above the horizon some
little while, but had been concealed by the clouds and thick
vapour. Now that the full bright light of day was come there
seemed no need of such intense watchfulness! It was hardly
likely that they would be attacked in their stockade in broad
daylight; the boldest beasts of prey would not do that unless
driven hard by hunger.

But when they began to prepare the breakfast, there was no
water to fill the kettle: Mark generally went down to the shore
for water every morning. Although they had no formal ar-
rangement, in practice it had gradually come about that one
did one thing and one another: Mark got the water, Bevis cut
up wood for the fire. Mark had usually gone with the zinc
bucket, whistling down to the strand merry enough. Now he
took up the bucket, but hesitated.

'I'll come,' said Bevis. 'One can't go alone anywhere now.'

'The other must always have the matchlock ready.'

'Always,' said Bevis, 'and keep a sharp look-out all round
while one does the things. Why, the gun is only loaded with
shot, now I remember!'

'No, more it is: how lucky It did not jump over! Shot would
have been of no use.'

'I'll shoot it off,' said Bevis — 'our ramrod won't draw a charge — and load again.'

'Yes, do.'

Bevis fired the charge in the air, and they heard the pellets presently falling like hail among the trees outside. Then he loaded again with ball, blew the match, and looked to the priming; Mark took the axe in one hand and the bucket in the other, and they unlocked the gate.

'We ought to be able to lock it behind us,' he said.

'We'll put in another staple presently,' said Bevis. 'Step carefully to see if there are any marks on the ground.'

They examined the surface attentively, but could distinguish no footprints: then they went to the fence where the creature had sprung against it. The arrow projected, and near it, on close investigation, they saw that a piece of the bark of the interwoven willow had been torn off as if by a claw. But look as intently as they would they could not trace it further on such ground; the thin grass and sand would not take an imprint.

'Pads,' said Bevis, 'else there would have been spoor.'

'Tiger, or panther then: we must take care,' said Mark. 'Pan's all right now, look.'

Pan trotted on before them along the well-known path to the shore, swinging his tail and unconcerned. As they walked they kept a watch in every direction, up in the trees, behind the bushes, where the surface was hollow, and avoided the fern. When Mark had dipped, they returned in the same manner, walking slowly and constantly on the alert.

CHAPTER 20

The Fortification

ENTERING the stockade, they locked the gate behind them, a thing they had never done before in daylight, that they might not be surprised. After breakfast Bevis began to file off the heads of the nails, which was slow work, and when he had done five or six, he thought it would be handier to drive them into the posts first, and file them off afterwards, as they could both work then instead of only one. They had but one vice to hold the nail, and only one could use it at a time. So the nails, the longest and largest they had, were driven into the stakes of the stockade about a foot apart – as near as the stakes stood to each other – and thus, not without much weariness of wrist, for filing is tedious, they cut off the heads and sharpened them.

Next they got together materials for barricading the door of the hut, or rather the open shed in front of it. To cut these they had to go outside, and Mark watched with the matchlock while Bevis chopped.

Poles were nailed across the open sides from upright to upright, not more than six inches asunder right up to the beam on two sides. They allowed plenty of space to shoot through, but nothing of any size could spring in. On the third, the poles were nailed across up to three feet high, and the rest prepared and left ready to be lashed in position with cords the last thing at night.

When these were put up there would be a complete cage, from within which they could fire or shoot arrows, and be safe from the spring of the beast. Lastly, they went up on the cliff to see what could be done there. The sand was very hard, so that to drive in stakes the whole length of the cliff edge would have taken a day, if not two days.

They decided to put up some just above the hut, so as to prevent the creature leaping on to the roof, and perhaps tearing a way through it. Bevis held the matchlock this time and watched while Mark hewed out the stakes, taking the labour and the watching in turn. With much trouble, these were driven home and sharpened nails put at the top, so that the beast approaching from behind would have to leap over these before descending the perpendicular cliff on to the hut. The fortifications was now complete, and they sat down to think if there was anything else.

'One thing,' said Mark: 'we will take care and fill the kettle and the bucket with water this evening before we go to sleep. Suppose the thing came and stopped just outside and wouldn't go away?'

'Besieged us – yes, that would be awkward; we will fill all the pots and things with water, and get in plenty of wood for the fires. How uncomfortable it is without our bath!'

'I feel horrid.'

'I *must* have a bath,' said Bevis. 'I *will* have a swim.'

'We can watch in turn, but if the panther sees anyone stripped it's more likely to try and seize him.'

'Yes, that's true: I know! Suppose we go out on the raft!'

'Right away.'

'Out to Pearly Island and swim there: there are no sedges there.'

'Hurrah! If he comes we should see him a long way first.'

'Of course, and keep the gun ready.'

'Come on.'

'First drive in the staple to lock the gate outside.'

This was done, and then they went down to the raft, moving cautiously and examining every likely place for the beast to lie in ambush before passing. The raft was poled round and out to Pearl Island, on which no sedges grew, nor were there any within seventy or eighty yards. Nothing could approach without being seen.

Yet, when they stood on the brim ready to go into the water the sense of defencelessness was almost overpowering. The gun was at hand and the match burning, the axe could be snatched up in a moment, the bow was strung and the sharp arrows by it.

But without their clothes they felt defenceless. The human skin offers no resistance to thorn or claw or tusk. There is nothing between us and the enemy, no armour of hide; his tusk can go straight to our lives at once. Standing on the brink they felt the heat of the sun on the skin: if it could not bear even the sunbeams, how could so sensitive and delicate a covering endure the tiger's claw?

'It won't do,' said Mark.

'No.'

'Suppose you watch while I swim, and then you swim and I watch?'

'That will be better.'

Bevis stepped on board the raft, threw his coat loosely round his shoulders – for the sun, if he kept still, would otherwise redden and blister, and cause the skin to peel – and then took up the matchlock. So soon as Mark saw he had the gun ready, he ran in, for it was too shallow to plunge, and then swam round the raft, keeping close to it. When he had had his bath, he threw the towel round his shoulders to protect himself from the heat, as Bevis had with his coat, and took the gun. Bevis had his swim, and then they dressed.

Poling the raft back to the island, they observed the same precautions in going through the trees to the hut. Once Mark fancied there was something in the fern, but Pan innocently ran there before they could call to him, and as nothing moved they went to the spot, and found that two fronds had turned yellow and looked at a distance a little like the tawny coat of an animal. Except under excitement and not in a state of terrorism they would have recognized the yellow fern in an instant.

They reached the hut without anything happening, and as they could not now wander about the island in the careless way they had hitherto done, and had nothing else to do, they cooked two of the moorhens. The gate in the stockade was locked, and the gun kept constantly at hand. A good deal of match was consumed, as it had to be always burning, else they could not shoot quickly. Soon the sense of confinement became irksome: they could not go outside without arming to the teeth, and to walk up and down so circumscribed a space was monotonous – indeed, they could not do it after such a freedom.

'Can't move,' said Mark.

'Chained up like dogs.'

'I hate it.'

'Hate it! I should think so!'

'But we can't go out.'

'No.'

They had to endure it; they could not even go up to see the time by the dial without one accompanying the other with the gun as guard. It was late when they had finished dinner, and went up to watch for the signal. On the cliff they felt more secure, as nothing could approach in front, and behind the slope was partly open; still, one had always to keep watch even there. Mark sat facing the slope with the gun: Bevis faced the New Sea with the telescope. The sky had clouded over, and there was more wind, in puffs, from the south-east. Charlie soon came, waved the handkerchief, and went away.

'I wish he was here,' said Bevis.

'So do I now,' said Mark, 'And Val and Cecil – '

'And Ted.'

'Yes. But how could we know that there was a panther here?'

'But it serves us right for not asking them,' said Bevis. 'It was selfish of us.'

'Suppose we go ashore and send Loo to tell Charlie and Val – '

'Last night,' said Bevis, interrupting , 'why – while I was out in the wilderness and you were in the thicket the thing might have had either of us.'

'No one watching.'

'If one was attacked, no one near to help.'

'No.'

'But we could both go together, and tell Loo, and get Charlie and Val and Cecil and Ted. If we all had guns now!'

'Five or six of us!'

'Perhaps if we told the people at home, the governor would let me have one of his: then we could load and shoot quick!'

'And the Jolly Old Moke would let me have his! and if Val could get another and Ted, we could hunt the island and shoot the creature.'

Mark was as eager now for company as he had been before that no one should enjoy the island with them.

'We could bring them all off on the raft,' said Bevis. 'It would carry four, I think.'

'Twice would do it then. Let's tell them! Let's see Loo, and send her! Wouldn't they come as quick as lightning!'

'They would be wild to help shoot it.'

'Just to have the chance.'

'Yes; but I say! what stupes we should be,' said Bevis.

'Why? How?'

'After we have had all the danger and trouble, to let them come in and have the shooting and the hunt and the skin.'

'Triumph and spoils!'

'It's *our* tiger,' said Bevis.

'We'll have him!'

'Kill him!'

'Yow – yow!'

Pan caught their altered mood and leaped on them, barking joyously. They went down into the stockade and considered if there was anything they could do to add to their defences, and at the same time increase the chances of shooting the tiger.

'Perhaps he won't spring over,' said Mark; 'suppose we leave the gate open? else we shan't get a shot at him.'

'I want a shot at him while he's on the fence,' said Bevis – 'balanced on the top, you know, like Pan sometimes at home.' In leaping a fence or gate too high for him they had often laughed at the spaniel swaying on the edge and not able to get his balance to leap down without falling headlong. 'I know what we will do,' he continued, 'we'll put out some meat to tempt him.'

'Bait.'

'Hang up the other birds – and my hare – no – shall I? He's such a beauty. Yes, I will. I'll put the hare out too. Hares are game; he's sure to jump over for the hare.'

'Drive in a stake half-way,' said Mark, meaning half-way between the cage and the stockade. 'Let's do it now.'

There were several pieces of poles lying about, and the stake was soon up. The birds and the hare were to be strung to it to tempt the beast to leap into the enclosure. The next point was at what part should they aim? At the head, the shoulders, or where? as the most fatal.

They sat down inside the cage and imagined the position the beast would be in when it approached them. Mark was to load the matchlock for the second shot in any case, while Bevis sent arrow after arrow into the creature. Pan was to be tied up with a short cord, else perhaps the tiger or panther would insert a paw and kill him with a single pat.

'But it's so long to wait,' said Mark. 'He won't come till the middle of the night.'

'He's been in the day when we were out,' said Bevis. 'Suppose we go up on the cliff, leave the gate open, and if he comes shoot down at him?'

'Come on.'

They went up on the cliff, just behind the spiked stakes,

taking with them the gun, the axe, and bow and arrows. If the beast entered the enclosure they could get a capital shot down at him, nor could he leap up; he would have to go some distance round to get at them, and meantime the gun could be reloaded. They waited; nothing entered the stockade but a robin.

'This is very slow,' said Mark.

'Very,' said Bevis. 'What's the use of waiting? Suppose we go and hunt him up.'

'In the wood?'

'Everywhere – sedges and fern – everywhere.'

'Hurrah!'

Up they jumped full of delight at the thought of freedom again. It was so great a relief to move about that they ignored the danger. Anything was better than being forced to stay still.

'If he's on the island we'll find him.'

'Leave the gate open, that we may run in quick.'

'Perhaps he'll go in while we're away, then we can just slip up on the cliff and fire down – '

'Jolly!'

'Look very sharp.'

'Blow the match.'

They entered among the trees, following the path which led round the island. Bevis carried the matchlock, Mark the bow and arrows and axe, and it was arranged that the moment Bevis had fired he was to pass the gun to Mark, and take his bow. While he shot arrows, Mark was to load and shoot as quick as he could. The axe was to be thrown down on the ground, so that either could snatch it up if necessary. All they regretted was that they had not got proper hunting-knives.

First they went down to the raft moored on the alder bough as usual, then on to the projecting point where Mark once fished; on again to where the willow tree lay overthrown in the water, and up to the firs under which they had reclined. Then they went to the shore at the uttermost southern extremity, and sent Pan into the sedges. He drove out a moorhen, but they did not shoot at it now, not daring to do so lest the beast should attack them before they could load again.

Coming up the western side of the island, they once thought they saw something in the bushes, but found it to be the trunk of a fallen tree. In going inland to Kangaroo Hill they moved more slowly as the wood was thicker, and intent on the slightest indication; the sudden motion of a squirrel climbing a beech startled them. From the top of the green knoll they looked all round, and thus examined the glade. There was not the slightest sign. The feathers of a wood-pigeon were scattered in the grass in one place, where a hawk had struck it down. This had happened since they were last at the glade. It was probably one of the pigeons that roosted in the ivy-grown oak.

Crossing to the oak, they flung sticks up into the ivy; there was no roar in response. While here they remembered the wires, and looked at them, but there was nothing caught, which they considered a proof that the rabbits were afraid to venture far from their burrows while the tiger, or whatever beast it was, was prowling about at night.

Returning to the shore, they recollected a large bed of sedges and reed-grass a little way back, and going there Bevis shot an arrow into it. The arrow slipped through the reed-grass with a slight rustle till it was lost. The spaniel ran in, and they heard him plunging about. There was nothing in the reed-grass.

Lastly they went to the thicket of 'wait-a-bit' blackthorn. Pan did go in, and that was as much; he soon came out, he did not like the blackthorn. But by throwing stones and fragments of dead branches up in the air so that they should descend into the midst of the thicket they satisfied themselves that there was nothing in it.

The circuit of the island was completed, and they now crept up quietly to the very verge of the cliff behind the spiked stakes. The stockade was exactly as they had left it; Pan looked over the edge of the cliff into it, and did not even sniff. They went down and rested a few minutes.

There never was greater temerity than this searching the island for the tiger. Neither the bullet nor their arrows would have stayed the advance of that terrible beast for a moment. Inside their stockade and cage they might withstand him; in the open he would have swept them down just as a lady's sleeve might sweep down the chessmen on the board.

'He can't be on the island,' said Mark.

'It's curious we did not see any sign,' said Bevis. 'There are no marks or footprints anywhere.'

'If there was some clay now – wet clay,' said Mark, 'but it's all sandy; his claws would show in clay like Pan's.'

'Like a crab.' Pan's footprint in moist clay was somewhat crab-shaped.

'Is there no place where he would leave a mark?'

'Just at the edge of the water the moorhens leave footprints.'

'That would be the place, only we can't look very close to the edge everywhere.'

'There's the raft; we could on the raft.'

'Shall we go on the raft?'

'Suppose we go all round the island?' said Bevis, 'on the raft.'

'We never have been,' said Mark. 'Not close to the shore.'

'No; let us pole round close to the shore – all round, and see if we can find any spoor in the shallows.'

They went to the raft and embarked. As they started a crimson glow shot along under the clouds; the sun was sinking, and the sky beamed. The wind had risen and the wavelets came splash, splash, against the edge of the raft. Some of the yellow leaves of the willows floated along and fell on the deck. They poled slowly, and constantly grounded or struck the shore, so that it occupied some time to get round, especially as at the southern extremity it was so shallow they were obliged to go a long way out.

In about an hour they reached the thick bed of reed-grass into which Bevis had shot his arrow, and as the raft slowly glided by Mark suddenly exclaimed, 'There it is!'

There it was – a path through the reed-grass down to the water's edge – the trail of some creature. Bevis stuck his pole into the ground to check the onward movement of the raft. The impetus of the heavy vessel was so great, though moving slowly, that it required all his strength to stay it. Mark came with his pole, and together they pushed the raft back, and it ran right up into the reed-grass and grounded. Pan instantly leapt off into the path and ran along it wagging his tail; he had the scent, though it seemed faint, as he did not give tongue. They stood at the bulwark of the raft and looked at the trail.

CHAPTER 21

The Trail

AT the water's edge some flags were bent, and then the tall grass, as high as their chests, was thrust aside, forming a path which had evidently been frequently trodden. There was now no longer the least doubt that the creature, whatever it was, was of large size, and as the trail was so distinct the thought occurred to them both at once that perhaps it had been used by more than one. From the raft they could see along it five or six yards, then it turned to avoid an alder. While they stood looking Pan came back; he had run right through and returned, so that there was nothing in the reed-bed at present.

Bevis stepped over the bulwark into the trail with the matchlock; Mark picked up the axe and followed. As they walked their elbows touched the grass each side, which showed that the creature was rather high than broad, lean like the whole feline tribe, long, lean, and stealthy. The reed-grass had flowered, and would soon begin to stiffen and rustle dry under the winds. By the alder a bryony vine that had grown there was broken and withered; it had been snapped long since by the creature pushing through.

The trail turned to the right, then to the left round a willow stole, and just there Pan, who trotted before Bevis, picked up a bone. He had picked it up before and dropped it; he took it again from habit, though he knew it was sapless and of no use to him. Bevis took it from his mouth, and they knew it at once as a duck's drumstick. It was polished and smooth, as if the creature had licked it, or what was more probable, carried it some distance, and then left it as useless. They had no doubt it was a drumstick of the wild duck Mark shot.

The trail went straight through sedges next. These were trampled flat; then as the sedges grew wider apart they gradually lost it in the thin, short grass. This was why they had not seen it from the land. There the path began by degrees; at the water's edge, where the grasses were thick and high, it was seen at once. Try how they would, they could not follow the trail inland; they thought they knew how to read 'sign', but found themselves at fault. On the dry, hard ground the creature's pads left no trail that they could trace. Mark cut off a stick with the axe and struck it up in the ground, so that they could find the spot where the path faded when walking on shore, and they returned to the raft. On the way they caught sight of Bevis's arrow sticking in the trunk of the alder, and withdrew it.

At the water's edge they looked to see if there was any spoor. In passing through the reed-grass the creature had trampled it down, and so walked on a carpet of vegetation which prevented any footprints being left on the ground, though it was moist there. At the water's edge perhaps they might have found some, but in pushing the raft up the beams had rubbed over the mud and obliterated everything. When they got on the raft they looked over the other bulwark, and a few yards from the shore noticed that the surface of the weeds growing there appeared disturbed.

The raft was moved out, and they found that the weeds had been trampled; the water was very shallow, so that the creature in approaching the shore had probably plunged up and down as the spaniel did in shallow water. Like the reed-grass the trampled weeds had prevented any footprints in the ooze. They traced the course the creature had come out for full thirty yards, and the track pointed straight to the shore of the mainland, so that it seemed as if it started at no great distance from where they used to land.

But when they had thrust the raft as far as this, not without great difficulty – for it dragged heavily on the weeds and some-

times on the ground – the marks changed and trended southwards. The water was a little deeper and the signs became less
and less obvious, but still there they were, and they now
pointed directly south. They lost them at the edge of the
weeds; the water was still shallow, but the character of the
bottom had changed from ooze to hard, rock-like sand. Here
they met the waves driven before the southerly wind, and
coming from that part of the New Sea they had not yet explored. The wind was strong enough to make it hard work to
pole the raft against it, and the spray dashed against the willow
bulwark.

These waves prevented them from clearly distinguishing the
bottom, though the water was very shallow; but then they
thought if it had been calm the creature's pads would have left
no marks on such hard sand. It was now more than an hour
after sunset, and the louring clouds rendered it more dusky
than usual so soon. The creature had evidently come from the
jungle southwards, but it was not possible to go there that
night in the face of the rising gale. The search must be suspended till morning.

Hastening home they found the stockade just as it had been
left, and lost not a moment in lighting the fires, one on each
side of the hut, the wood for which had already been collected.
The gate was padlocked, the kettle put on, and they sat down
to rest. A good supper and strong tea restored their strength.
They sat inside the cage at the table, and needed no lantern, for
the light of the two fires lit up the interior of the stockade.

As it became later the hare and the birds were fastened to
the stake for a bait, more wood was heaped on the fires, and
last of all the remaining poles were lashed to the uprights of
the shed, forming a complete cage with horizontal bars. The
matchlock was placed handy, the bow and arrows laid ready,
and both axes, so that if the beast inserted his paw they could
strike it.

Cards were then drawn to see who should go to sleep first,

and as Bevis cut highest, he went into the hut to lie down. But after he had been there about a quarter of an hour he jumped up, quite unable to go to sleep. Mark said he did not feel the least sleepy either, so they agreed that both should sit up. Till now they had been in the outer shed or cage, but Mark thought that perhaps the creature would not come if it saw them, so they went inside the hut, and made Pan come too. The curtain was partly let down and looped aside, so that they had a view of the stockade, and the lantern lit and set in the niche.

They could hear the wind rushing over the trees outside, and every now and then a puff entered and made the lantern flicker. The fires still burned brightly, and as nothing came the time passed slowly. Bevis did not care to write up his journal, so at last they fell back on their cards and played bezique on the bed. After a time this too wearied. The tea and supper had refreshed them; but both had worked very hard that day – a long day too, as they had been up so early – and their interest began to flag. The cards were put down, and they stood up to recover their wakefulness, and then went out into the cage.

The fires still flickered, though the piles of wood were burnt through, and the sticks had fallen off, half one side, half the other. The wind had risen and howled along, carrying with it a few leaves which blew against the bars. It was perfectly dark, for the thick clouds hid the moon, and drops of rain were borne on the gale. They would have liked to replenish the fires, but could not get out without unlashing several of the bars, and, as Mark said, the creature would be more likely to come as the fires burned low. Weary and yawning they went back into the hut and sat down once more.

'One thing,' said Mark: 'suppose he were to stay just outside the stockade – I mean if he comes and we shoot and hit him till he is savage, and don't kill him; well, then, if he can't get in to us, don't you see, when it is day he'll go outside the stockade and lie down.'

'So that we can't go out.'

'And there he'll stay, and wait, and wait.'

'And stay till we are starved.'

'We could not shoot him through the stockade.'

'No. Or he could go up on the cliff and watch there and never let us out. Our provisions would not last for ever.'

'The water would go first.'

'Suppose he does that, what shall we do then?' said Mark.

'I don't know,' said Bevis languidly.

'But, now, you think.'

'Bore a tunnel through the cliff to the sea,' said Bevis, yawning. 'I am so sleepy – and one get out and swim round and fetch the raft.'

'Tunnel from the cave right through?'

'Straight right through.'

'We shall beat him anyway,' said Mark.

'Of course we shall. Wish he'd come! Oh!' – yawning – 'Let us go to sleep: Pan will bark.

'Not both,' said Mark.

'Both.'

'No.'

Mark would not agree to this. In the end they cut cards again, and Mark won. He stretched himself out on the bed, and asked Bevis what he was going to do. Bevis took one of the great-coats (his pillow), placed it on the floor by the other wall of the hut, sat down, and leaned back against the wall. In this position, with the curtain looped up, he could see straight out across to the gateway of the stockade, which was visible whenever the embers of the fires sent up a flash of light. Pan was close by curled up comfortably. He put the matchlock by his side so that he could snatch it up in a moment. 'Good night,' he said; Mark was already firm asleep.

Bevis put out his hand and stroked Pan; the spaniel recognized the touch in his sleep, and never moved. Now that it was so still, and there was no talking, Bevis could hear the sound of the wind much plainer, and once the cry of a heron rising harsh above the roar. Sometimes the interior of the stockade seemed calm, the wind blew over from the tops of the trees to the top of the cliff, and left the hollow below in perfect stillness. Suddenly, like a genie, the wind descended, and the flames leapt up on each side from the embers. In a moment the flames fell and the enclosure without was in darkness.

All was still again except the distant roar in the wood. A fly kept awake by the lantern crawled along under the roof, became entangled in a spider's web and buzzed. The buzz seemed quite loud in the silent hut. Pan sighed in his slumber. Bevis stretched his legs and fell asleep, but a gnat alighted on his face and tickled him. He awoke, shook himself, and reproached himself for neglecting his duty. The match of the matchlock had now burned almost away; he drew the last two inches up farther in the spiral of the hammer, and thought that he would get up in a minute and put some more match in. Ten seconds later and he was asleep; this time firmly.

The last two inches of the match smouldered away, leaving the gun useless till another was lit and inserted. Down came the genie of the wind, whirling up the grey ashes of the fires and waking a feebler response. The candle in the lantern guttered and went out. As the dawn drew on above them the clouds became visible, and they were now travelling from the north-north-west, the wind having veered during the night.

A grey light came into the hut. The strong gusts of the gale ceased, and instead a light steady breeze blew. The clouds broke and the sky showed. A crow came and perched on the stockade, then flew down and picked up several fragments; it was the crow that had pecked the jack's head. He meditated an attack on the hare and the birds strung to the stake, when Pan woke, yawned and stretched himself. Instantly the crow flew off.

Sunbeams fell aslant through the horizontal bars on to the table. Pan got up and went as far as the short cord allowed him; there was a crust under the table; he had disdained it last night at supper, when there was meat to be had, now he ate it. He gave a kind of yawning whine, as much as to say, 'Do wake up'; but they were sleeping far too sound to hear him.

Mark woke first and sat up. Bevis had slept a long time with his back to the wall, but had afterwards gently sunk down, and was now lying with his head on the bare ground of the floor. Mark laughed, Pan wagged his tail and looked at Bevis as if he understood it. Mark touched Bevis, and he instantly sat up, and felt for the gun as if it was dark.

'Why!'

'It's morning.'

'He hasn't been?'

'No.'

They unlashed the bars, let Pan loose, and went out into the courtyard. It was a beautiful fresh morning. There were no signs whatever of the creature having visited the place, neither outside nor in. They were much disappointed that it had not come, but supposed the wind and the roughness of the waves had deterred it from venturing across.

After breakfast, on looking at the sundial, they were surprised to find it ten o'clock. Then taking the matchlock, bow, and axe, as before, they started for the bed of reed-grass, thinking that the creature might possibly have come to the island without approaching the stockade. The danger had now grown familiar, and they did not care in the least; they walked straight to the place without delay or reconnoitring. The trail had not apparently been used during the night, a small branch of ash had been snapped off and blown on to it, and the waves and wind had smoothed away the disturbed appearance of the weeds.

As the wind was favourable and not rough, they at once resolved to sail to the south and examine the shore there, and if they could hit upon the trail to follow it up. But first they must have their bath at Pearl Island. They returned to the hut, put the hare and birds that had been hung on the stake inside the hut, and lashed up the bars, determined that the creature at all events should not have the game in their absence.

Then locking the gate of the stockade, they went to the raft, and bathed at Pearl Island. The mast was then stepped, the stays fastened, and the sail set. Bevis took the rudder and put it in the water over the starboard quarter – it was like a long, broad oar – the sail filled, and the heavy craft began to drive before the wind.

CHAPTER 22

Voyage in the *Calypso*

SURGING along the *Calypso* sought the south, travelling but little faster than the waves, but smoothing a broad wake as she drove over them. Bevis held the oar-rudder under his right arm, with his hand on the handle, and felt the vibration of the million bubbles rising from the edge of the rudder to the surface. Piloting the vessel, Mark sometimes directed him to steer to the right, and sometimes to the left.

It was afternoon when they moored the *Calypso* in the usual place. They were hungry and hastened to the hut, intending to begin the pit directly after dinner, when as they came near, Pan ran on first and barked by the gate.

'Ah!'

'He's been!'

They ran, forgetting even to look at the match of the gun. There was nothing in the enclosure; but Pan sniffed outside, and gave two short 'yaps' as much as to say, 'I know.'

'Reeds,' said Bevis. 'He's in the reeds.'

'He heard us coming and slipped off – he's hiding.'

'We shall have him! Now!'

'Now directly!'

'This minute!'

With incredible temerity they ran as fast as they could go to the bed of reed-grass in which they had discovered the trail. Pan barked at the edge; Bevis blew the match.

'Lu – lu – lu! go in!'

'Fetch him out.'

'Hes – ess – go in!'

'Now! Have him!'

Pan stopped at the edge and yapped in the air, wagging his tail and hesitating.

'He's there!' said Bevis.

'As sure as sure,' said Mark. Their faces were lit up with the wild joy of the combat; as if like hounds they could scent the quarry.

'Go in,' shouted Bevis to the spaniel angrily. Pan crouched, but would not go. Mark kicked him, but he would not move.

'Hold it,' said Bevis, handing the matchlock to Mark. He seized the spaniel by his shaggy neck, lifted and hurled him by main force a few yards crash among the sedges. Pan came out in an instant.

'Go in, I tell you!' shouted Bevis, beside himself with anger; the spaniel shivered at his feet. Again Bevis lifted him, swung him, and hurled him as far this time as the reed-grass. The next instant Pan was at his feet again. Encouragement, persuasion, threats, blows, all failed; it was like trying to make him climb a tree. The dog could not force his nature. Mark threw dead sticks into the reed-grass; Bevis flung some stones.

'You hateful wretch!' Bevis stamped his foot. 'Get away.' Pan ran back. 'Give me the gun – I'll go in.'

If the dog would not, he would hunt the creature from its lair himself.

'Oh, stop!' said Mark, catching hold of his arm, 'don't – don't go in, – you don't know!'

'Let me go.'

'I won't.'

'I will go.'

They struggled with each other.

'Shoot first,' said Mark, finding he could not hold him. 'Shoot an arrow – two arrows. Here – here's the bow.'

Bevis seized the bow and fitted the arrow.

'Shoot where the path is,' said Mark. 'There – it's there' – pointing. Bevis raised the bow. 'Now shoot!'

'Oh!' cried a voice in the reeds, 'don't shoot!'

Bevis instantly lowered the bow.

'What?' he said.

'Who's there?' said Mark.

'It's me – don't shoot me!'

'Who are you?'

'Me.'

They rushed in and found Loo crouching behind the alder in the reed-grass; in her hand was a thick stick which she dropped.

'How dare you!' said Bevis.

'How did you get here?' said Mark.

'Don't you be angry!' said Loo.

'But how dare you!'

'On our island!'

'Don't you – don't you!' repeated Loo.

'You!'

'You!' One word but such intense wrath.

'Oh!' cried Loo, beginning to sob.

'You!'

'You!'

'Oh! Don't! He were so hungry.' Sob, sob.

'Pooh!'

'Yah!'

'Yow – wow!' barked Pan.

'He – he,' sobbed Loo. 'He – he –'

'He – what?'

'He were so hungry.' Sob, sob.

'Who?'

'Samson.'

'Who's Samson?'

'My – y – lit – tle – brother.'

'Then you took our things?' said Mark.

'He – he – kept on crying.'

'You had the damper –'

'And the potatoes –'

'And the bacon – '

'You didn't – didn't care for it,' sobbed Loo.

'Did you take the rabbit-skin?' said Mark.

'Yes – es.'

'But Samson didn't eat that; did he?'

'I – I – sold it.'

'What for?'

'Ha'-penny of jumbles for Samson.' Jumbles are sweets.

'How did you get here?'

'I come.'

'How?'

'I come.'

'It's disgusting,' said Bevis, turning to Mark; 'spoiling our island.'

'Not a tiger,' said Mark. 'Only a girl.'

'It's not proper,' said Bevis in a towering rage. 'Tigers are proper, girls are not proper.'

'No; that they're not.'

'It's not the stealing.'

'No; it's the coming – '

'Where you're not wanted – '

'Horrible!'

'Hateful!'

'What shall we do?'

'Can't kill her.'

'Nor torture her.'

'Nor scalp her.'

'Yow – wow!'

'Tie her up.'

'If we were savages we'd cook you!'

'Limb at a time.'

'What *can* we do with her?'

'Let me stop,' said Loo pleadingly.

'Let *you* stop! You!'

'I can cook and make tea and wash things.'

'Stop a minute,' said Mark. 'Perhaps she's a native.'

'Ah!' This was more proper.

'Are you a savage?'

'If you says so,' said Loo penitently.

'Are you very sorry?'

'You're sure you're a savage?'

'Will she do?'

'You're our slave.'

'Ar-right', said Loo, her brown eyes beginning to sparkle through her tears. 'I'll be what you wants.'

'Mind you're a slave.'

'So I be.'

'You'll be thrashed.'

'Don't care. Let I bide here.'

'I suppose we must have her.'

'You're a great nuisance.'

'Ar-right.'

'Slave! Carry that.' Mark gave her the axe.

'And that.' Bevis gave her the bow. Loo took them proudly.

'You're to keep behind. Pan's to go before you.'

'Dogs first, slaves next.'

'Make her fetch the water.'

'Chop the wood.'

'Turn the spit.'

'Capital; we wanted a slave!'

'Just the thing.'

'Hurrah!'

'But it's not so nice as a tiger.'

'Oh! No!'

'Nothing like.'

They marched out of the reed-grass, Pan and the slave behind.

'But how did you get here?' said Bevis, stopping suddenly.

'I come, I told you.'

'Can you swim?'

'No.'

'There's no boat.'

'Did you have a catamaran?'

'What be that?'

'Why don't you tell us how you got here?'

'I come – a-foot.'

'Waded? You couldn't.'

'I walked drough't' – i.e. through it.

They would not believe her at first, but she pointed out to them the way she had come by the shoals and sedge-grown banks; the course she had taken curved like half a horse-shoe. First it went straight a little way, then the route or ford led to the south and gradually turned back to the west, reaching the mainland within sixty or seventy yards of the place where they always disembarked from the raft. It took some time for Loo to explain how she had done it, and how she came to know of it, but it was like this:

Once now and then in dry seasons the waters receded very much, and they were further lowered by the drawing of hatches that the cattle might get water low down the valley, miles away. As the waters of the New Sea receded the shallower upper, or southern end, became partly dry. Then a broad low bank of sand appeared stretching out in the shape of half a horse-shoe, the extremity of which being much higher was never submerged, but formed the island of New Formosa. At such times anyone could walk from the mainland out to New Formosa dryshod for weeks together.

This was how the island became stocked with squirrels and kangaroos; and it was the existence of the rabbits in the burrows at the knoll that had originally led to Loo's knowledge of the place. Her father went there once when the water was low to ferret them, and she was sent with his luncheon to and fro. That was some time since, but she had never forgotten, and often playing about the shore, had no difficulty in finding the shoal. The route or ford was, moreover, marked to anyone who knew of its existence by the tops of sandbanks, and sedge-grown islets, which were in fact nothing but high parts of the same long, curved bank.

There was not more than a foot deep of water anywhere the whole distance, and often not six inches. This was in August; in winter there would be much more. Tucking up her dress she had waded through easily, feeling the bottom with a thick stick to guide her steps. The worst place was close to the island, by the reed-grass, where she sunk a little in the ooze, but it was only for a few yards.

At the hut the weapons were laid aside, and the slave put out the dinner for them. Bevis and Mark sat, one each side of the table, on their stools of solid blocks, Pan sat beside Bevis on his haunches expectant; the slave knelt at the table.

She was bare-headed. Her black hair having escaped, fell to her waist, and her neck was tawny from the harvest sunshine. The torn brown frock loosely clung about her. Her white teeth gleamed; her naked feet were sandy like Pan's paws. Her brown eyes watched their every movement; she was intent on them. They were full of their plans of the island; she was intent on them.

She ate ravenously, more eagerly than the spaniel. Seeing this, Bevis kept cutting the preserved tongue for her, and asked if Samson was so very hungry. Loo said they were all hungry, but Samson was most hungry. He cried almost all day and all night, and woke himself up crying in the morning. Very often she left him, and went a long way down the hedge because she did not like to hear him.

'But,' objected Bevis, 'my governor pays your father money, and I'm sure my mamma sends you things.'

So she did, but Loo said they never got any of them; she twisted up her mouth very peculiarly to intimate that they were intercepted by the ale-barrel. Bevis became much agitated; he said he would tell the governor, he would tell dear mamma, Samson should not cry any more. Loo should take home one of the tins of preserved tongue, and the potatoes, and all the game there was – all except the hare.

Now Bevis had always been in contact almost with these folk, but yet he had never seen. His face became quite white; he was thoroughly upset. It was his first glance at the hard roadside of life. He said he would do all sorts of things; Loo listened pleased but dimly doubtful, she could not have explained herself, but she, nevertheless, knew that it was beyond Bevis's power to alter these circumstances. Not that she hinted at a doubt; it was happiness enough to kneel there and listen.

Then they made her tell them how many times she had been to the island, and all about it, and as she proceeded, recognized one by one, little trifles that had previously had no meaning till now they were connected and formed a continuous strand. Put into order it was like this.

CHAPTER 23

The Captive

THEY arrived on Wednesday; Wednesday night Pan stayed in the hut with them, and nothing happened. Thursday night, Pan swam off to the mainland, and while he was away Loo made her first visit to the island, coming right to the hut door or curtain. Till she reached the permanent plank table under the awning and saw the remnants of the supper carelessly left on it, she had had no thought of taking anything.

The desire to share, if ever so secretly, in what they were doing alone led her there. So intense was that desire that it overcame her fear of offending them; she must at least see what they were doing. From the sedges she had watched them go to the island in the *Pinta* so many times that she was certain that was the place where they were. In wading off to the island by moonlight she caught a glimpse of the sinking fire inside the stockade, the glow thrown up on the cliff, and so easily found her way to the hut. Had Pan been there he would have barked, but he was away; so that she came under the awning and saw all their works – the stockade, the hut, and everything, increasing her eagerness.

After she had examined the place and wondered how they could build it, she saw the remnants of the supper on the table, and remembering Samson, took them for him. The rabbit's skin was hung on the fence, and she took it also, knowing that it would fetch a trifle; in winter it would have been worth more. She thought that these things were nothing to them, that they did not care about them, and threw them aside like refuse.

The second time she came was on Saturday morning, while they were exploring Serendib. When they were on Serendib she could cross to New Formosa in broad daylight unseen, because New Formosa lay between and the woods on it concealed anyone approaching from the western side. Her mother and elder sisters were reaping in the cornfields beyond the Waste, and she was supposed to be minding the younger children, instead of which she was in the sedges watching New Formosa, and directly she saw Bevis and Mark pole the raft across to Serendib she waded over.

She visited the hut, took a few potatoes from the store in the cave, and spent some time wondering at everything they had there. As she was leaving they landed from the raft, and Pan sniffing her in the wood ran barking after her. He knew her very well and made no attempt to bite, still he barked as if it was his duty to tell them someone was on the island. Thinking they would run to see what it was, she climbed up into the ivy-grown oak, and they actually came underneath and looked up and did not see her.

They soon went away fancying it must be a squirrel, but Pan stopped till she descended, and then made friends and followed her to the reed-grass, whence so soon as she thought it safe she waded across to the mainland. Busy at the hut they had no idea that anything of the kind was going on, for they could not see the water from the stockade. On Sunday morning she came again, for the third time, crossing over while they were at Bamboo Island, and after satiating her curiosity and indulging in the pleasure of handling their weapons and the things in the hut, she took the cold half-cooked bacon from the shelf, and the two slices that had been thrown to Pan, and which he had left uneaten.

When they returned Pan knew she had been; he barked and first ran to the ivy-grown oak, but finding she was not there he went on and discovered her in the reed-grass. He was satisfied with having discovered her, and only licked her hand. So soon as everything was quiet she slipped across to the mainland, but in the afternoon, being so much interested and eager to see what they were doing, she tried to come over again, when Mark saw her head in the sedges, Loo crouched and kept still so long they concluded there was no one there.

It was the same afternoon that they looked at the oak for marks of claws, but her naked feet had left no trace. She would very probably have attempted it again on Monday night, but that evening they came with the letter and list of provisions, and having seen them and spoken to them, and having something to do for them, her restless eagerness was temporarily allayed. That night was the first Pan was tied up, but nothing disturbed him.

But Tuesday night, after they had been for the flag basket, the inclination to follow them became too strong, and towards the middle of the night, when, as she supposed, Pan was on shore (for she had seen him swim off other nights), she approached the hut. To her surprise Pan, who was tied up, began to bark. Hastening away, in her hurry she crossed the spot where Pan hid his treasures, and picked up the duck's drumstick, but finding it was so polished as to be useless, dropped it among the reed-grass.

Wednesday night she ventured once more, but found the gate in the stockade locked; she tried to look over, when Pan set up his bark. She ran back a few yards to the bramble bushes and crouched there, trusting in the thick mist to hide her, as in fact it did. In half a minute, Mark having cut the cord, Pan rushed out in fury, as if he would fly at her throat, but coming near and seeing who it was, he dropped his howl of rage, and during the silence they supposed he was engaged in a deadly struggle.

Whether she really feared that he would spring at her, he came with such a bounce, or whether she thought Bevis and Mark would follow him and find her, she hit at Pan with a thick stick she carried. Now Pan was but just touched, for he swerved, but the big stick and the thump it made on the ground frightened him and he yelped as if with pain and ran back. As he ran she threw a stone after him; the stone hit the fence and shook it, and knocked off the piece of bark from the willow which they afterwards supposed to have been torn by the claw of the tiger.

Hearing them talking, and dreading every moment that they would come out, she remained crouched in the brambles for a long time, and at last crept away, but stayed in the reed-grass till the sun shone, and then crossed to the mainland. Thursday she did not come, nor Thursday night, thinking it best to wait awhile and let a day and night elapse. But on Friday morning, having seen them sail to the south in the *Calypso* while they were exploring the swamp, she waded over, and once more looked at the wonderful hut and the curious cage they had constructed about the open shed.

She was so lost in admiring these things and trying to imagine what it could be for, that they had returned very near the island before she started to go. She got as far as the reed-grass and saw them come up poling the raft.

On the raft while facing the island they could not have helped seeing her, so she waited, intending to cross when they entered the stockade and were busy there. But Pan recognized that she had been to the stockade. They ran at once to the reed-grass, as they now knew of the trail there, and discovered her. The reason Pan would not enter the reeds, even when hurled among them, was his fear of the thick stick.

'Stupes we were!' said Bevis.

'Most awful stupes!'

'But it's not proper,' said Bevis. 'I wish it had been a tiger.'

'It would have been so capital. But we've got a slave.'

'Where's she to sleep tonight?'

'Anywhere in the wood.'

'Slave, you're to cook the hare for supper.'

'And mind you don't make a noise when we're out hunting and frighten the kangaroos.'

Loo said she would be as quiet as a mouse.

'We shall want some tea presently. I say!' said Mark, 'we've forgotten Charlie!'

He ran up on the cliff, but it was too late; Charlie had been and waved his cap three times, in token that all was not quite right at home. Still, as Loo told them she was certain everyone was quite well at home, they did not trouble about having missed Charlie. Mark wished to go shooting again round Serendib, and they started, leaving the slave in charge of the hut to cook their supper.

Mark had the matchlock, and Bevis poled the raft gently round Serendib, but the water-fowl seemed to have become more cautious, as they did not see any. Bevis poled along till they came to a little inlet, where they stopped, with blue gum branches concealing them on either hand. Mark knelt where he could see both ways along the shore; Bevis sat back under the willows with Pan beside him.

They were so quiet that presently a black-headed reed-bunting came and looked down at them from a willow bough. Moths fluttered among the tops of the branches, the wind was so light that they flew whither they listed, instead of being borne out over the water. The brown tips of a few tall reeds moved slightly as the air came softly; they did not bow nor bend; they did just sway, yielding assent.

Every now and then there was a rush overhead as five or six starlings passed swiftly, straight as arrows, for the firs at the head of Fir-Tree Gulf. These parties succeeding each other were perhaps separate families gathering together into a tribe at the roosting-trees. Over the distant firs a thin cloud like a black bar in the sky spread itself out, and then descended funnel-shaped into the firs. The cloud was formed of starlings, thousands of them, rising up from the trees and settling again. One bird as a mere speck would have been invisible; these legions darkened the air there like smoke.

But just beyond the raft the swallows glided, dipping their breasts and sipping as they dipped; the touch and friction of

the water perceptibly checked their flight. They wheeled round
and several times approached the surface, till having at last the
exact balance and the exact angle they skimmed the water,
leaving no more marks than a midge.

Over the distant firs a heron came drifting like a cloud at his
accustomed hour; from over the New Nile the call of a par-
tridge, 'caer-wit – caer-wit', sounded along the surface of the
water. There was a slight movement and Bevis saw the match
descending, an inverted cone of smoke darted up from the
priming, and almost before the report Pan leaped overboard.
Mark had watched till two moorhens were near enough
together; one he shot outright and Pan caught the other.

At the report the heron staggered in the air as if a bullet had
struck him – it was his sudden effort to check his course – and
then recovering himself he wheeled and flew towards the
woods on the mainland. Bevis said he must have a heron's
plume. To please Mark he poled the raft to Bamboo Island,
and then across to the sedgy banks at the southern extremity
of New Formosa, but Mark did not get another shot. They then
landed and crept quietly to Kangaroo Hill. The rabbits had
grown suspicious, and they did not see one, but Pan suddenly
raced across the glade – to their great annoyance – and
stopped on the verge of the wood.

There he picked up a rabbit in his mouth, and they recollected the wires they had set. The rabbit had been in a wire
since the morning. 'It will do for Samson,' said Bevis.

When they returned to the hut the full moon – full but low
down – had begun to fill the courts of the sky with her light,
which permitted no pause of dusk between it and the sunset.
The slave's cheeks were red and scorched from the heat of the
fire, which she had tended on her knees, and her chin and
tawny neck were streaked with black marks. Handling the
charred sticks with her fingers, the fingers had transferred
the charcoal to her chin. The hare was well cooked considering
the means, or rather the want of means, at her command;

perhaps it was not the first she had helped to prepare. Searching in the store-room she found a little butter with which she basted it after a manner; they had thought the butter was all gone, they were too hasty – impatient – to look thoroughly. There was no jelly, and it was dry, but they enjoyed it very much sitting at the plank table under the shed.

They had removed the poles on one side of the shed as there was nothing now to dread, but on the other two sides the bars remained, and the flames of the expiring fire every now and then cast black bars of shadow across the table. The slave would have been only too glad to have stayed on the island all night – if they had lent her a great-coat or rug to roll up in she would have slept anywhere in the courtyard – but she said Samson would be so wretched without her, he would be frightened and miserable. She must go; she would come back in the morning about ten.

They filled the flag-basket for her with the moorhens, the rabbit, the dabchick and thrush, and a tin of preserved tongue. There were still some fragments of biscuit; she said Samson would like these best of all. Thus laden, she would have waded to the mainland, but they would not let her – they took the raft and ferried her over, and promised to fetch her in the morning if she would whistle. She could whistle like a boy. To Loo that voyage on the raft, short as it was, was something beyond compare. She had to pass the prickly stubble field with her bare feet – stubble to the naked foot is as if the broad earth were a porcupine's back. But long practice had taught her how to wind round at the edge where there was a narrow and thistly band of grass – for thistles she did not care.

'Good night, slave.'

They poled back to the island, and having fastened Pan up, were going to bed, when Bevis said he wanted the matchlock loaded with ball, as he meant to rise early to try for a heron. Mark fired it off, and in the stillness they heard the descending shot rattle among the trees. The matchlock was loaded with ball, and Bevis set the clock of his mind to wake at three. It was still early in the evening, but they had had little or no rest lately, and fell asleep in an instant; they were asleep long before the slave had crept in at her window and quieted Samson with broken biscuits.

The alarum of his mind awoke Bevis about the time he wished. He did not wake Mark, and wishing to go even more quietly than usual left Pan fastened up; the spaniel gave a half-whine, but crouched as Bevis spoke and he recognized the potential anger in the tones of his voice. From the stockade Bevis went along that side of the island where the weeds were, and passed the *Calypso*, which they had left on that side the previous evening. He went by the 'blazed' trees leading to Kangaroo Hill, then past the reed-grass where they had captured the slave, but saw nothing. Thence he moved noiselessly up through the wood to the more elevated spot under the spruce firs, where he thought he could see over that end of the island without being seen or heard.

There was nothing; the overthrown willow trunk lay still in the water, flush with the surface, and close to it there was a little ripple coming out from under a bush, which he supposed was caused by a water-rat moving there. Till now he had been absorbed in what he was doing, but just then, remembering the cones which hung at the tops of the tall firs, he looked up and became conscious of the beauty of the morning, for it was more open there, and he could see a breadth of the sky.

Upon the willow trunk prone in the water, he saw a brown creature larger than any animal commonly seen, but chiefly in length, with sharp-pointed, triangular ears set close to its head. In his excitement he did not recognize it as he aimed. Behind the fir trunks he was hidden, and he was on high ground – animals seldom look up – the creature's head too was farthest from him. He steadied the long, heavy barrel against a fir trunk, heedless of a streak of viscous turpentine sap which his hand pressed.

The trigger was partly drawn – his arm shook, he sighed – he checked himself, held his breath tight, and fired. The ball plunged and the creature was jerked up rebounding, and fell in the water. He dashed down, leaped in – as it happened the water was very shallow – and seized it as it splashed a little from mere muscular contraction. Aimed at the head, the ball had passed clean through between the shoulders and buried itself in the willow trunk. The animal was dead before he touched it. He tore home and threw it on the bed: 'Mark!'

'Oh!' said Mark. 'An otter!'

Their surprise was great, for they had never suspected an otter. No one had ever seen one there that they had heard of, no one had even supposed it possible. These waters were far from a river, they were fed by rivulets supporting nothing beyond a kingfisher. To get there the otter must have ascended the brook from the river, a bold and adventurous journey, passing hatches and farm-houses set like forts by the water's edge, passing mills astride the steam.

The hare had been admired, but it was nothing to the otter, which was as rare there as a black fox. They looked at its broad flat head, the sharp, triangular ears set close to the head, the webbed feet, the fur, the long tail decreasing to a blunt point. It must be preserved; they could skin it, but could not stuff it; still it must be done. The governor must see it, mamma, the Jolly Old Moke, Frances, Val, Cecil, Charlie, Ted, Big Jack – all.

While they breakfasted, while they bathed, this was the talk. Presently they heard the slave's whistle and fetched her on the raft. Now Loo, cunning hussy, waited till she was safely landed on the island, and then told them that dear mamma and Frances were going that day up to Jack's to see them. Loo had been sent for to go to the town on an errand, and she had heard it mentioned. Instead of going on the errand she ran to play slave.

Charlie had had some knowledge of this yesterday, and

waved his cap instead of the white handkerchief as a warning, but they did not see it. If mamma and Frances drove up to Jack's to see them, of course it would be at once discovered that they were not at Jack's, and then what a noise there would be!

'Hateful,' said Mark. 'It seems to me we're getting near the hateful "Other Side".'

CHAPTER 24

The Black Sail

Now, at the Other Side, i.e. at home, things had gone smoothly for them till the day before, in a measure owing to the harvest, and for the rest to the slow ways of old-fashioned country people. Busy with the harvest, there was no visiting, no one came down from Jack's, and so the two slipped for a moment out of the life of the hamlet. Presently Bevis's short but affectionate letter arrived, and prevented any suspicion arising, for no one noticed the postmark. Mamma wrote by return, and when her letter addressed to Bevis was delivered at Jack's you would have supposed the secret would have come out. So it would in town life – a letter would have been written saying that Bevis was not there, and asking where to forward it.

But not so at the old house in the hills. Jack's mother put it on the shelf, remarking that no doubt Bevis was coming, and would be there tomorrow or next day. As for Jack, he was too busy to think about it, and if he had not been he would have taken little notice, knowing from former experience that Bevis might turn up at any moment. The letter remained on the shelf.

On the Saturday the carrier left a parcel for Bevis – at any other time a messenger would have been sent, and then their absence would have been discovered – but no one could be spared from the field. The parcel contained clean collars, cuffs, and similar things which they never thought of taking with them, but which mamma did not forget. Like the letter, the parcel was put aside for Bevis when he did come; the parcel indeed was accepted as proof positive that he was coming.

371

Everyone being so much in the fields, mamma was left alone, and wearying of it, asked Frances to come up frequently to her; Frances was willing enough to do so, especially as she could talk unreservedly of Big Jack, so that it was a pleasure to her to come. At last, on the Friday, as Bevis did not write again, his mother proposed that they should drive up to Jack's and see how the boys were on the morrow. Frances was discreetly delighted: Jack could not come down to see her just now, and with Bevis's mother she could go up and see him with propriety. So it was agreed that the dogcart should be ready early on Saturday afternoon. Charlie learned something of this – he played in and out the place, and waved his cap thrice as a warning.

Frances came, and the dogcart was at the door when Loo (who had been sent on an errand to the town – a common thing on Saturdays) rushed up to the door, thrust a letter into mamma's hand, and darted away.

'Why!' said she. 'It's Bevis – why!' she read aloud, Frances looking over her shoulder: 'Dear Mamma, Please come up to the place where the boats are kept directly you get this and mind you come this very minute' (twice dashed). 'We are coming home from New Formosa in our ship the *Calypso*, and want you to be there to see the things we have brought you, and to hear all about it. Mind and be sure and come this very minute, please.'

Wondering and excited with curiosity, the two ladies ran as fast as they could up the meadow footpath, and along the bank of the New Sea, till they came to a clear space where the trees did not interfere with the view. Then, a long way up, they saw a singular-looking boat with a black sail.

'There they are!'

'They're coming!'

'What *can* they have been doing?'

'That is not the *Pinta*!'

'This has a black sail!'

The sail was black because it was the rug, an old-fashioned one, black one side and grey the other. After long discussion Bevis and Mark had decided that the time had come when they must return from the island, for if Bevis's mother went to Jack's and found they were not there, her anxiety would be terrible, and they could not think of it. So Bevis wrote a letter and sent Loo back with it at once, and she was to watch and see if his mother did as she was asked. If she started for the shore Loo was to raise a signal, a handkerchief they lent her for the purpose.

Loo displayed the signal. The sail was then hoisted and they bore down right before the wind. With dark sail booming out the *Calypso* surged ahead; the mariners saw the two ladies on the shore, and waved their hands and shouted. Bevis steered her into port, and she grounded beside the *Pinta*. The first caress and astonishment over: 'Where are your hats?' said Frances.

'Where are your collars?' said his mother. 'And gracious, child! just look at his neck!'

As for hats and collars they had almost forgotten their existence, and having passed most of the time in shirt sleeves like gold-miners with necks and chests exposed, they were as brown as if they had been in the tropics. Mark especially was tanned. Bevis was too fair to brown well. The sun and the wind had purified his skin almost to transparency with a rosy olive behind the whiteness.

Frances placed her hand on her brother's shoulder, but did not kiss or speak to him as once she had done. Something told her that this was not the boy she ordered to and fro.

They could not believe that the two had really spent all the time on an island. This was the eleventh morn since they had left – it could not be: yet there was the raft in evidence.

'Let us row them up in the *Pinta*,' said Mark.

'In a minute,' said Bevis. 'Get her ready; I'll be back in a minute – half a second.' He ran along the bank to a spot whence

373

he knew he could see the old house at home through the boughs. He wanted just to look at it – there is no house so beautiful as the one you were born in – and then he ran back.

There was a little water in the boat, but not much; they hauled out some of the ballast, the ladies got in and were rowed direct to New Formosa. The stockade – so well defended, the cage before the door, the hut, the cave, their interest knew no bounds.

'But you did not really sleep on this,' said Bevis's mother in a tone of horror, finding the bed was nothing but fir branches; she could not be reconciled to the idea.

The matchlock, the niche for the lantern, the marks where their fires had been, the sundial, there was no detail they did not examine: and lastly they went all round the island by the well-worn path. This occupied a considerable time; it was now too late to drive up to Jack's and the object was removed, but Bevis's mother, ever anxious for others' happiness, whispered to Frances that she would write and send a messenger, and ask Jack to come down tomorrow – surely he could spare Sunday – to bring back the parcel, and see the wonderful island.

When at last they landed the ladies, there was Charlie on the bank, and Cecil and Val, who had somehow got wind of it – they were wild with curiosity not unmingled with resentment. These had to be rowed to New Formosa, and they stayed longer even than the ladies, and insisted on a shot each with the matchlock. So it was a most exciting afternoon for these returned shipwrecked folks. In the evening they had the dogcart, and drove in to Latten with the otter to have it preserved.

They did not see much or think much of the governor till towards supper-time – Mark had snatched half an hour to visit his Jolly Old Moke and returned like the wind. The governor was calmly incredulous: he professed to disbelieve that they had done it all themselves, there must have been a man or two to help them. And if it was true, how did they suppose they were going to pay for all the damage they had done to the trees on the island?

This was a difficult question, they did not know that the governor could cut the trees if he chose, indeed they had never thought about it. But having faced so many dangers they were not going to tremble at this. They could not quite make the governor out, whether he was chafing them, or whether he really disbelieved, or whether it was cover to his anger. In truth, he hardly knew himself, but he could not help admiring the ingenuity with which they had effected all this.

He was a shrewd man, the governor, and he saw that Bevis and Mark had the ladies on their side. Besides, when faced with gleaming eyes, sun-burned skin, ringing voices and shouts of laughter, how could he help but waver and finally melt and become as curious as the rest? In the end they actually promised, as a favour, to row him up to their island tomorrow.

The governor, having been rowed to the island, examined the fortifications, read the journal, and looked at the iron-pipe gun, and afterwards, reflecting upon these things, came to the conclusion that it would be safer and better in every way to let Bevis have the use of a good breech-loader. He evidently must shoot, and if so he had better shoot with a proper gun. When this decision was known, Mark's governor could do nothing less, and so they both had good guns put into their hands.

CHAPTER 25

The Antarctic Expedition

AUTUMN passed, and the winter remained mild till early in January when the first green leaves had appeared on the woodbine. One evening Polly announced that it was going to freeze, for the cat as he sat on the hearthrug had put his paw over his ear. If he sat with his back to the fire, that was sign of rain. If he put his paw over his ear that indicated frost.

It did freeze, and hard. The wind being still, the New Sea was soon frozen over except in two places. There was a breathing-hole in Fir-Tree Gulf about fifty or sixty yards from the mouth of the Nile. The channel between New Formosa and Serendib did not 'catch', perhaps the current from Sweet River Falls was the cause, and though they could skate up within twenty yards, they could not land on the island. Jack and Frances came to skate day after day; Bevis and Mark, with Ted, Cecil, and the rest fought hockey battles for hours together.

One afternoon, being a little tired, Bevis sat on the ice, and presently lay down for a moment at full length, when looking along the ice – as he looked along his gun – he found he could see sticks or stones or anything that chanced to be on it a great distance off. Trying it again, he could see the skates of some people very nearly half a mile distant – though his eyes were close to the surface – even if he placed the side of his head actually on the ice. The skates gleamed in the sun, and he could see them distinctly; sticks lying on the ice were not clearly seen so far as that, but a long way, so that the ice seemed perfectly level.

As the sun sank the ice became rosy, reflecting the light in the sky; the distant Downs too were tinted the same colour.

After it was dark Bevis got a lantern, which Mark took five or six hundred yards up the ice, and then set it down on the surface. Bevis put his face on the ice as he had done in the afternoon and looked along. His idea was to try and see for how far the lantern would be visible. As the sticks and skates had been visible a good way, he supposed the light would be apparent very much farther.

Instead of which, when he had got into position and looked along the ice with his face touching it, the lantern had quite disappeared, yet it was not so far off as he had seen the skates – skates are only an inch or so high, and the candle in the lantern was four or five. He skated two hundred yards nearer and then tried. At this distance, with his eyes as close to the ice as he could get them, he could not see the light itself, but there was a glow diffused in the air where he knew it was.

This explained why the light disappeared. There was a faint and invisible mist above the ice – the ice-blink – which at a long distance concealed the lantern. If he lifted his head about eighteen inches he could see the light so that the stratum of mist, or ice-blink, appeared to be about eighteen inches in thickness. When he skated another hundred yards closer he could just see the light with his face on the ice as he had done the skates by day. So that after sunset it was evident this mist formed in the air just above the ice. Mark tried the same experiment with the same result, and then they skated slowly homewards, for as it was not moonlight they might get a fall by coming against a piece of twig half-sunk in and frozen firmly.

Suddenly there was a sound like the boom of a cannon, and a crack shot across the broad water from shore to shore. The 'who-hoo-whoop' of the noise echoed back from the wood on the hill, and then they heard it again in the coombes and valleys, rolling along. As the ice was four or five inches thick it parted with a hollow roar: the crack sometimes forked, and a second running report followed the first. Sometimes the crack seemed to happen simultaneously all across the water. Occasionally they could hear it coming, and with a distinct interval of time before it reached them.

Up through these cracks or splits a little water oozed, and freezing on the surface formed barriers of rough ice from shore to shore, which jarred the skates as they passed over. These splits in no degree impaired the strength of the ice. Later on as they retired they opened the window and heard the boom again, weird and strange in the silence of the night.

One day a rabbit was started from a bunch of frozen rushes by the shore, and they chased it on the ice, overtaking it with ease. They could have knocked it down with their hockey sticks, but forebore to do so.

Till now the air had been still, but presently the wind blew from the south almost a gale; this was straight down the water, so, keeping their skates together and spreading out their coats for sails, they drove before the wind at a tremendous pace, flying past the trees and accumulating such velocity and their ankles ached from the vibration of the skates. Nor could they stop by any other means than describing a wide circle, and so gradually facing the wind. Bevis began to make an ice-raft to slide on runners and go before the wind with a sail like the ice-yachts on the American lakes.

But by the time the frame was put together, and the blacksmith had finished the runners, a thaw set in.

The wind rushing over the ice no longer firm and rigid quickly broke up the surface, and there was a tremendous grinding and splintering, and chafing of the fragments. For the first few days these were carried down the New Sea, but presently the wind changed. The black north swooped on the earth and swept across the waters. Fields, trees, woods, hills, the very houses looked dark and hard, the water grey, the sky cold and dusky. The broken ice drifted before it and was all swept up to the other end of the New Sea and jammed between and about the island. They could now get at the Pinta, and resolved to have a sail.

'An arctic expedition!'

'Antarctic – it is south!'

'All right.'

'Let us go to New Formosa.'

'So we will. But the ice is jammed there.'

'Cut through it.'

'Make an ice-bow.'

'Be quick.'

Up in the workship they quickly nailed two short boards together like a V. This was lashed to the stem of the *Pinta* to protect her when they crashed into the ice. They took a reef in the mainsail, for though the wind does not seem to travel any swifter, yet in winter it somehow feels more hard and compact and has a greater power on what it presses against. Just before they cast loose, Frances appeared on the bank above, she had called at the house, and hearing what they were about, hastened up to join the expedition. So soon as she had got a comfortable seat, well wrapped up in sealskin and muff, they pushed off, and the *Pinta* began to run before the wind. It was very strong, much stronger than it had seemed ashore, pushing against the sail as if it were a solid thing. The waves followed, and the grey cold water lapped at the stern.

Beyond the battle-field as they entered the broadest and most open part the black north roared and rushed at them, as if the pressure of the sky descending forced a furious blast between it and the surface. Angry and repellent waves hissed as their crests blew off in cold foam and spray, stinging their cheeks. Ahead the red sun was sinking over New Formosa, they raced towards the disk, the sail straining as if it would split. As the boat drew near they saw the ice jammed in the channel between the two islands.

It was thin and all in fragments; some under water, some piled by the waves above the rest, some almost perpendicular, like a sheet of glass standing upright and reflecting the red sunset. Against the cliff the waves breaking threw fragments of ice smashed into pieces; ice and spray rushed up the steep sand and slid down again. But it was between the islands that the waves wreaked their fury. The edge of the ice was torn into jagged bits which dashed against each other, their white saw-like points now appearing, now forced under by a larger block.

Farther in the ice heaved as the waves rolled under: its surface was formed of plates placed like a row of books fallen aside. As the ice heaved these plates slid on each other, while others underneath striving to rise to the surface struck and cracked them. Down came the black north as a man might bring a sledgehammer on the anvil, the waves hissed, and turned darker, a white sea-gull (which had come inland) rose to a higher level with easy strokes of its wings.

Splinter — splanter! Crash! grind, roar; a noise like thousands of gnashing teeth.

Bevis had his hand on the tiller; Mark his on the halyard of the mainsail; neither spoke, it looked doubtful. The next instant the *Pinta* struck the ice midway between the islands, and the impetus with which she came drove her six or seven feet clear into the splintering fragments. They were jerked forwards, and in an instant the following wave broke over the stern, and then another, flooding the bottom of the boat. Mark had the mainsail down, for it would have torn the mast out.

With a splintering, grinding, crashing, roaring; a horrible and inexpressible noise of chaos — an orderless, rhythmless noise of chaos — the mass gave way and swept slowly through the channel. The impact of the boat acted like a battering-ram and started the jam. Fortunate it was for them that it did so, or the boat might have been swamped by the following waves. Bevis got out a scull, so did Mark, and their exertions kept her straight; had she turned broadside it would have been awkward even as it was. They swept through the channel, the ice at its edges barking willow branches and planting the shore; large plates were forced up high and dry.

'Hurrah!' shouted Mark.

'Hurrah!'

At the noise of their shouting thousands of starlings rose from the osiers on Serendib with a loud rush of wings, blackening the air like a cloud. They were soon through the channel, the ice spread in the open water, and they worked the boat under shelter of New Formosa, and landed.

'You are wet,' said Bevis as he helped Frances out.

'But it's jolly!' said Frances, laughing. 'Only think what a fright *he* would have been in if he had known!'

Having made the boat safe – there was a lot of water in her – they walked along the old path, now covered with dead leaves damp from the thaw, to the stockade. The place was strewn with small branches whirled from the trees by the gales, and in the hut and further corner of the cave were heaps of brown oak leaves which had drifted in. Nothing else had changed; so well had they built it that the roof had neither broken down nor been destroyed by the winds.

During the frost a blackbird had roosted in a corner of the hut under the rafters; sparrows too had sought its shelter, and wrens and blue-tits had crept into the crevices of the eaves. Next they went up on the cliff; the sundial stood as they had left it, but the sun was now down.

From the height, where they could hardly stand against the wind, they saw a figure afar on the green hill by the sycamores, which they knew must be Big Jack waiting for them to return. Walking back to the *Pinta* they passed under the now leafless teak tree marked and scored by the bullets they had fired at it.

Before embarking they baled out the water in the boat, and then inclined her, first one side and then the other, to see if she had sprung a leak, but she had not. The ice-bow was then hoisted on board, as it would no longer be required, and would impede their sailing. Frances stepped in, and Bevis and Mark settled themselves to row out of the channel. With such a wind it was impossible to tack in the narrow strait between the islands. They had to pull their very hardest to get through. So soon as they had got an offing the sculls were shipped, and the sails hoisted, but before they could get them to work they were blown back within thirty yards of the cliff. Then the sails drew, and they forged ahead.

It was the roughest voyage they had ever had. The wind was dead against them, and no matter on which tack every wave sent its spray, and sometimes the whole of its crest, over the bows. The shock sometimes seemed to hold the *Pinta* in mid-career, and her timbers trembled. Then she leaped forward and cut through, showering the spray aside. Frances laughed and sang, though the words were inaudible in the hiss and roar and the rush of the gale through the rigging, and the sharp, whip-like cracks of the fluttering pennant.

The velocity of their course carried them to and fro the darkening waters in a few minutes, but the dusk fell quickly, and by the time they had reach Fir-Tree Gulf, where they could get a still longer 'leg' or tack, the evening gloom had settled down. Big Jack stood on the shore, and beckoned them to come in: they could easily have landed Frances under the lee of the hill, but she said she should go all the way now. So they tacked through, the waves getting less in size as they approached the northern shore, till they glided into the harbour. Jack had walked round and met them. He held out his hand, and Frances sprang ashore. 'How *could* you?' he said, in a tone of indignant relief. To him it had looked a terrible risk.

'Why, it was splendid!' said Frances, and they went on together towards Longcot. Bevis and Mark stayed to furl sails, and leave the *Pinta* shipshape. By the time they had finished it was already dark: the night had come.

On their way home they paused a moment under the great oak at the top of the Home Field, and looked back. The whole south burned with stars. There was a roar in the oak like the thunder of the sea. The sky was black, black as velvet, the black north had come down, and the stars shone and burned as if the wind reached and fanned them into flame.

Large Sirius flashed; vast Orion strode the sky, lording the heavens with his sword. A scintillation rushed across from the zenith to the southern horizon. The black north held down the buds, but there was a force in them already that must push out in leaf as Arcturus rose in the East. Listening to the loud roar of the oak as the strength of the north wind filled them —

'I should like to go straight to the real great sea like the wind,' said Mark.

'We *must* go to the great sea,' said Bevis. 'Look at Orion!'

The wind went seawards, and the stars are always over the ocean.